TWISTED TALES

OF THE

TWENTIETH

CENTURY

—◦⦕⦆◦—

Dear Dean,

J.A. BIERMAN

Thank You
for the love & support!
-J.

A special note of gratitude to my wonderful wife, family, and friends who pushed me to complete these stories even when times were tough, and writer's block walled me off from progress.

I also wish to thank You, the reader, for your interest in this collection of beauty, madness, and tragedy.

With love,

J.A. Bierman

1900-1949 Collection

1. Anything for a Dream
2. A Puzzle Play
3. Maplewood Seven
4. A Beautiful Day in Budapest
5. The Shape of Grace

Anything

for a

Dream

The Dream

Crisp mountain air and the refreshing scent of subalpine fir filled Charles Attwood with fervor. He stood upon a prominent ridge that commanded a panorama of the Paradise and Nisqually River valleys. While admiring the evergreen forest below, his ears absorbed the faint blare of a train at Brown's Junction; its echo ferried up the lowest canyon by a west wind. His eyes soon lifted to the Tatoosh Mountains, whose saw-blade summits cut the near horizon, granting an impressive view of two silvery peaks that ascended like twin titans over the rugged range that sequestered them. After soaking in the scenery, Charles turned toward the towering alp above. "Ah! Mount Rainier, Great Tahoma, mother of Washington waters. You are proof that nature outranks humanity. Truly, an attestation of the sublime forces that created this world."

"You praise the mountain as if it possesses deific qualities," Felix chuckled while rounding a small snow-capped boss to catch up with his friend.

"Come now, Dr. Beauchamp. Surely, there are cryptic facets to our fair planet that humans cannot comprehend. Even when we do, we either inadvertently destroy it amidst feeding our cupidity or sabotage it to impede that of an adversary."

"Your words ring true, Dr. Attwood, but humans will never prove capable of destroying a volcano, neither with dynamite nor machines."

Charles grinned. "Destruction finds all things, my friend. It just takes grit or time. After a while, materials unravel, tensions form, and, eventually, an earthquake rips the world in two."

Felix rolled his eyes. "An earthquake, no matter its size, could never quarter the world like a cracker. For a paleontologist, you sure have a terrible perception of natural sciences."

"For a geologist, you sure have a terrible sense of natural humor," Charles parried.

The trekkers bypassed a rocky bend on their unmarked path, then slowed their pace when they set foot upon the bank of an ice flow. "If you're impressed by the glacier under our feet," Felix commented through his strong but steady breath, "take a look at the icy crown of our fair mountain queen." He pointed at the noble peak above. "Those are monstrous glaciers up there, Charles, monstrous! When people imagine volcanoes, all that comes to mind are explosions, billowing pyroclastic flows, and rivers of vibrant lava. Many are reminded of the destruction of Pompeii or Krakatoa. Yet common folk quickly forget about the fantastic nature of these living mountains. Their activity has vehemently forged our world for countless eons. Equally so, their dormancy humbly nurtures entire ecosystems. Did you know that many ancient civilizations worshiped volcanoes as gods?"

"Yes, Felix, I know about Vulcan and Hephaestus. I have studied enough human history. Do you think that there is any chance of an eruption today?"

"Highly unlikely. However, until we improve our technology and research methods, we cannot accurately predict seismic activity, the prime indicator of eruptions. We remain dependent on disciplined observation, but I have great hope for the future of science."

Charles chuckled. "So glad I invited the eminent Felix Beauchamp on my journey up Rainier. Who better to accompany me than a famous Canadian mountaineer?"

"Other than Muir, Tyndall, Whymper, and Mummery, there are no famous mountaineers, not yet, at least."

"Whatever you say, my friend. I pray our expedition is worth the trouble. I do relish a good ramble, although this is reminiscent of a fairytale quest. To unearth prehistoric fossils on a volcano, the uncanniest of places, would surely boost my reputation and increase my chance of gaining a position at an institution of international reverence. Neither would I mind a glint of fame if fate should have it."

"And who better to accompany you than a famous Canadian mountaineer," Felix laughed.

"A geologist specializing in volcanoes is necessary when ascending one," Charles playfully remarked. "You are, more precisely, a volcanologist. That makes you unique. And I'm certain that your commentaries on all we observe will prove of paramount importance to the development of modern science. In this sense, we are pioneers."

Felix felt the urge to jokingly whoop when he suddenly broke through a soft spot in the glacier and swiftly plunged down a chute made of smooth ice and rock. He screamed, digging his fingers into the walls as if to stop a giant from swallowing him, but to no avail. He slid into the deep, then *thump*.

"I am alive," Felix whispered, his bottom throbbing from the hard and abrupt landing. He sat momentarily and breathed deeply to collect himself and regain his senses. When he finally came to it, darkness confronted him. He remembered the many caves he had surveyed over the years, considering their pertinence to geology, yet none chilled him to the bone as this one. He rubbed the flanks of his sore thighs until his vision adjusted. Reaching for his pickaxe, he found that it had escaped its holster. He groaned and gained his feet gradually to avoid inflaming any muscles that might soon ail him. Once upright, he found that he stood at the center of a circular beam of light deplaned from the opening above. Beyond arm's reach loomed nothing but an abyss. Felix wheeled about and looked up at Charles, whose distant face, framed by black rock and a scrim of blue sky, reminded him of a silhouette portrait one might notice on a bedroom wall.

"Are you all right?" Charles shouted.

"Yes, yes, I'm fine. Fetch a branch and toss it down, will you? I wish to see where I am." Felix bent his eyes back to the darkness and muttered, "A cave beneath a river of ice is surely some kind of phenomenon. How intriguing." Charles soon reappeared and dropped an arm-sized branch of subalpine fir down the chute. Felix withdrew a long scarf, a matchstick, and a small, corked bottle of kerosene from his backpack. He clothed the end of the branch with the scarf and doused it with petroleum, then struck the match and ignited the makeshift torch.

The firelight not only exposed the whereabouts of his pickaxe, which he snatched up and held close to his chest, but also the chamber's ample capacity, enough to house a dozen horses at the very least. The walls and floor shimmered softly, revealing dampness typical of island hollows or inland limestone caverns. The observation prompted Felix to conclude that this cave served as drainage for glacial melt, which filtered out through fissures and conduits in the mountain's outer, less compact layers, eventually forming springs near the base. Such a discovery on the breast of Mt. Rainier, the unlikeliest of places, filled him with zeal.

"Do you need help?" Charles asked, his voice strained with concern.

Felix wanted more time. "I will soon. Best you prepare to utilize the rope in your pack."

"Aren't you glad I brought it? Some complain that twine is unnecessary in the realm of science. Well, I say-"

"Yes, yes, Charles. It was a good idea. Would you please affix it to a rock and let me know when it's tight?"

While Charles headed toward the glacier's edge to find a firm roping anchor, Felix allowed his curiosity to blossom. With each step more prudent than the last, he slowly wandered away from the ring of daylight. As darkness strove to envelop him, so too did the quiet of the mountain. The only sounds to caress his ears were the ebb and flow of his breath, the creak of his boot heels against smooth stone, and a *drip-drip* that echoed from the deep toward which he carefully walked.

After a few minutes, he approached what he believed to be the source of the drip. Caution slipped from his mind for merely a moment, and he tripped into a puddle of warm water, nearly losing his grip on the torch. "A hot spring must be near," he muttered, trying to rationalize the temperature and abrupt rise in humidity.

Felix stood and hoisted the torch over his head. It shed brilliance upon the cavern wall, where he noticed a hued layer of andesite at eye level, a bizarre anomaly that further stroked his curiosity. Yearning to steal a sample, he chipped the volcanic material with his pickaxe. The stone cracked like hard sand, doling a little chunk into his palm.

However, he quickly became distracted by a tiny, almost inaudible song of cracking and creaking. He glanced up to find the entire wall starting to fissure like the onset of a cacophonous hailstorm. As the noise rapidly amplified, saucers of rock began to plummet. Felix panicked with curses under his breath and darted away as a mass of andesite the size of an elephant collapsed upon the cavern floor with a thunderous boom. A cloud of dust seized the air, nearly extinguishing the torch and choking Felix.

The haze began to disperse. Felix returned the pickax to its holster after a long bout of coughing. While wiping his glasses on the sleeve of his jacket, his distorted vision caught sight of a strange glow by his boots. He pressed his glasses to his face and crouched low. Waving the surviving torchlight over the ground, he realized he stood upon a scattered treasure trove of crystals. "What a strange place this is!" He picked one up of the larger gems, which fit snugly in his hand, and rotated it under the firelight. "Dear God," he whispered, immediately mesmerized by its uniqueness. Its raw, contorted facets refracted kaleidoscopic shapes in every direction like some accidental product of ancient alchemy.

Amidst staring in wonder at the geometric colors, something in his peripheral vision lured his attention, an anomaly in the wall that beetled like the hidden answer in an optical illusion. Realizing what he saw, he dropped the crystal and rushed back to the chute, where Charles had just lowered the rope. "What in God's name happened, Felix? I heard an explosion of sorts. Are you hurt?"

"Get down here, Charles. There is something you must see. Hurry, hurry!"

The scientists hustled to the inner hollow, where the disseminated crystals on the ground quickly bewitched Charles. He picked up one and palmed it to the fire, amazed by its natural color and clarity.

"Forget the crystals," insisted Felix. "Allow me to shed light on something *extraordinary*." He lifted the torch to the new cavern wall. Embossed in the volcanic rock was a humongous skeleton, perfectly fossilized in the final movement of its life. "This...this, my friend, surpasses human comprehension."

Charles stepped closer. His jaw dropped enough to welcome a bird into his mouth. "It is magnificent. Look at that head, the horned brows, spiked crest, dagger-like teeth, elongated snout, the bones black as obsidian. Its body is beyond breathtaking. Each bone appears completely intact, unmarred by its geological cage. Look at the curvature of those spectacular wings, arched in preparation for escape or frozen in the thick of flight. And the length of that serpentine tail. If alive during the Mesozoic Era, it might have struck down any dinosaur with a single blow. My God, Felix, do you realize what you've unearthed?"

"A dragon."

"My esteemed friend, this is an incredible discovery!"

"Indeed, it is," Felix assented while adjusting his glasses. "Arguably the greatest discovery in human history. Still, I cannot help but wonder why here, why under the skin of Rainier? If we possessed more information about its eruption history, at the very least, I could formulate a rudimentary explanation. Unfortunately, we only know that this volcano formed in the last two million years, mostly within the Pleistocene Epoch, far short of the dinosaur eras. However, that would place the dragon's life in a timeline shared by our human ancestors of the great ice age."

He clapped with a laugh and "eureka" as if he had struck a vein of gold. "Good God, Charles, do you realize what this means? Humans have talked about dragons for millennia, installing them as prominent characters in folklore and mythology, spanning hundreds of cultures across the globe. Scientists and philosophers of the modern age have tried to prove the existence of dragons but failed to uncover authentic knowledge. Yet before our very eyes is evidence of it all! Our predecessors would weep with astonishment and envy at our treasure."

"We are pioneers," Charles cried, reveling in a stew of excitement. "We must inform the press, universities, historical societies, museums, President Roosevelt; all must hear and see. Scientists worldwide will abdicate an arm and leg just to look at this ancient creature. Long have I dreamed of such a discovery. It will take me, no, take *us*, right to the top. Come, Felix, we need to muster an army of diggers to excavate this wondrous beauty."

"Hold on," countered Felix, assuaging his adrenaline. "The dragon is not flying anywhere, and nobody else knows, so we do not need to rush and leave room for error. Anything can go awry with such a precarious project. We must start with the basics and build from there while considering possible ramifications."

"What do you have in mind?" Charles folded his arms.

"Gathering strong laborers for this job will be painless, but we need them to stay silent upon completion. We require local communities to remain deaf to our discovery until you and I formally unveil it. The jabbering mouth of a single worker could precipitate robbery or worse. Therefore, it would behoove us to lavish our employees with extra earnings for their performance and discretion. The crystals in this cave are quite valuable, unlike anything I have ever seen, probably formed due to the dragon's entombment. A man can trade a sack of these for a decent life. I believe they are more than ample to compensate anyone we enlist."

"As for further study and exposure," Felix continued, "we need to find a destination for the skeleton before we arrange transport out of the mountains. The University of Washington would be perfect as it is not too far from here and already has facilities to house and study such a discovery. One of us would need to go there and convince the faculty to permit us entry and prepare space. Once approved and placement is promised, we could then arrange transport from Ashford to Seattle."

"Ensuring our complete success," Charles concluded. "Brilliant, Felix, brilliant!" He ogled the dragon one last time before starting toward the outer chamber. "Come now, my fellow pioneer. We must hasten down the mountain and begin our work at once. Dreams don't build themselves."

"Before we depart, Charles, we need a sample. No one at the university will believe us without physical evidence. Quick, help me up on this rock. I want to extract three teeth."

THE EXCAVATION

After spending the night in Longmire at the base of the mountain, the eager scientists hurried to the nearby village of Ashford, where they divided responsibilities. Although Charles had earned the title of paleontologist after years of hands-on experience excavating prehistoric fossils, Felix bore the reputation of a young John Muir. While often modest as a monk, he had long demonstrated himself as an expert mountain climber and earned international recognition for his proficiency in extracting volcanic material. Furthermore, his native country of Canada celebrated him as a champion of geoscience, notably for his work in the Coast Mountains of British Columbia and the Mackenzie Mountains of the Yukon Territory. All that considered, it fell upon Felix to purchase the tools, hire laborers, climb Rainier, dig out the dragon, and safely transport each bone back to Ashford.

Charles fancied himself a modern-day Cicero - highly sociable, well-versed in oration and Western philosophy, respected among his peers, and always willing to lend a voice to those in need of political justice. He also prided himself as a scientific salesman, having repeatedly persuaded many Darwin-haters to become Darwin-lovers without ever showing them the good book of biological science -- *On the Origin of Species*. According to Charles, these attributes made him the perfect candidate to travel to Seattle and speak with the academic community at the University of Washington. The goal was to entice them with notions of scientific fantasy coming to fruition, granting the dragon an interim place in their facility for further study and eventual public exploitation.

"I am certain that the administrative board will be thrilled and pose no opposition," Charles boasted, as if failure had never bullied him before. The scientists felt optimistic about their endeavor and embraced before parting ways.

While Charles set off to Brown's Junction to catch a train bound for Puget Sound, Felix commenced his portion of the project with the haste of a young Nikola Tesla. He visited the local supply store and spoke to the owner about business connections with industrial companies in the port town of Tacoma. He struck a deal within minutes, guaranteeing the arrival of sturdy supplies in eight to ten days. While awaiting these goods, Felix decided to acquaint himself with a few

Nisqually natives, who agreed to work for him, pending they received handsome wages and fair treatment. Felix then paid the provincial postal carriers to ride out as far as Eatonville to put up posters along their routes and advertise his employment offer. After a week, about two dozen men showed up on Felix's cabin doorstep. Some came from lumberyards, two from the railroad, and the rest were coal miners who had hurried down from Wilkeson, Carbonado, and Fairfax.

Once Felix assembled his team and received the supplies he had ordered – brought to him from Brown's Junction by carriage and horseback – he departed Ashford for Longmire, where he received the unfortunate news that lumbering and mining were banned in the newly established Mount Rainier National Park. Worried that people might confuse his excavation party for a group of hungry industrialists, Felix felt the need to expedite his trek and began the ascent of Rainier the following morning.

While barely a month of autumn had passed, the snowpack was already beginning to accumulate, and the nastier storms of winter would soon batter the region. Felix worried that if the dig persisted into November or beyond, not only would he fail to complete his job for lack of warmth and food, but the heaviest snow and ice would seal the cave until another lucky fool fell through the glacier. By then, Felix and his team would be slow-deteriorating corpses, mistaken as hunters from the ice age, and the world might never learn that dragons once roamed the Earth.

Marching a platoon of workers and a mule-drawn wagon up a snow-coated volcano proved more difficult than Felix had foreseen. All the past mountain expeditions he had led or accompanied required significantly fewer supplies and capable hands than this one. The wagon proved clumsy, the mule stubborn, and the laborers skeptical. It took the strength of everyone to keep it all balanced and moving forward.

Felix feared they would suffer the same fate as the Donner Party should they get lost or remain too long on the mountain. Luckily, he recalled the location of the small, unnamed glacier under which the cave resided. It was on the south side of the mountain between the glaciers of Paradise and Nisqually, just above the timberline, roughly seven thousand feet, near a rocky ledge that granted a panoramic view of the Tatoosh Range, Mount Adams, and Mount Saint Helens.

As the team approached the glacier, Felix scanned the area for a marker - a stake with a small red flag that Charles had placed by the chute entrance. "Where could it be?" he wondered aloud.

The team combed, scraped, picked, and shoveled in the snow for the marker or chute. Chewing his lips in frustration, Felix assumed the marker was lost, either buried in the snow or blown away by violent winds. Unfortunately, without the flag to indicate the point of entry, searching for the chute proved as painful as looking for a pebble in a mud pit. Felix felt foolish for failing to consider the unpredictability of the weather. After all, it was far from his first extraction or high-elevation study. Perhaps the dragon had gotten the best of him. Either way, the hunt consumed more hours than he wished, and discouragement rippled across the faces of his team.

Vexation further struck Felix and his men when a nasty squall descended from the higher slopes, forcing them to retreat to John L. Reese's Camp of the Clouds in the upper Paradise Valley. There they posed as a large research group from the US Geological Survey and tented alongside the season's lingering hikers, who had never seen such unusual and miserable scientists.

That night, the reaper of frost chewed lips, nipped at the skin, and burrowed into chests, narrowly repelled once the men gathered around their fires to eat canned beans and drink coffee or whiskey. A dark-skinned miner from Fairfax named Hershel lightened up the mood with his harmonica, never stopping to recoil at the countless racial slurs hurled his way. Ignoring the needless incivility, Felix found the evening to be quite pleasant.

With the morning came renewed determination. Felix pressed up the mountain again, yet frustration seized him like violent illness when he stepped upon the familiar glacier. The snowfield had replenished itself overnight and looked as pristine as a moonbeam on a Yukon winter night.

"Not a single hole remains from yesterday's search," Felix grumbled, unsure about his next move. He refused to force the men back to Camp of the Clouds and spend another day trudging up the mountainside only to shovel the same spots repeatedly. Worse, if he failed to find the cave, the miscarried promise of a handsome reward would likely sway these men to mutiny. The last thing he wanted was to become a frozen corpse beneath a snow bed.

The men seemed irritated by Felix's sudden lack of confidence. Yet, just as they began to fuss, a Nisqually named John, who had hardly done any work the day before, walked across the glacier and drove his shovel into a soft spot wherein the snowpack slowly began to concave. When Felix noticed the man shoveling with all his might, he shouted for the whole team to assist. Within minutes, they uncovered the entrance to the barrel-wide chute into which Felix had fallen nearly three weeks earlier.

Felix laughed and patted the Nisqually on the shoulder. "How did you find this so easily? Have you been here before?"

John shook his head. "No. Through the wind, Tahoma whispers of the way. For what purpose, I do not know, although it is certainly not without warning. You must understand, Dr. Beauchamp, that the spirit of the mountain would rather us depart or perish in the cold than reveal its greatest secrets to those who cannot keep them."

Felix replied with a casual nod, pretending to shrug off the stark words. Nevertheless, they sunk deep, reminding him that, although he fancied himself a scientist, he had always struggled internally to debunk supernatural elements, especially any originating from pre-Christian cultures and religions. He had witnessed many strange, esoteric occurrences while working in the Coast Mountains of British Columbia. He remembered a local healer whose caution to foreigners held a similar meaning to John's words.

Still, although Felix found it necessary to consider the native's advice, like the ambitious captains who led the golden age of exploration, he would not forgo the excavation, not for any amount of money or divine threats. The dragon was worth it all. However, to compensate for his insecurities respecting superstition, Felix decided to promote John as his assistant. He hoped the man's wisdom, like the healer he once met, would protect him from whatever consequences might spring from this enterprise.

Without wasting more time, Felix commanded his laborers to chip away the glacier and expose the rocky terrain beneath. At precisely two o'clock, three hefty sticks of Nobel dynamite blasted the water-formed chute with a boom that resounded like thunder up and down the slopes of Rainier, frightening every bird and marmot on the south side, not to mention Felix, who did not realize the noise would carry so intensely.

He imagined the troubled rangers scratching their heads or readying to march up the mountain and arrest the excavators. Felix remembered then that, for scientific purposes, he could have obtained a permit of sorts. 'Blasted,' he thought, knowing that he shouldn't have been so hasty in this endeavor and considered the idea sooner. He had always been savvy about legalities. Yet, gazing upon the now walk-in entrance to the dragon den reminded him why it had slipped his mind.

Once the workers cleared the debris, the men shoveled out a full path to avoid slipping on the smooth rock that made up the base of the destroyed chute. The first chamber required little artificial illumination, considering daylight now beamed through its new yawning mouth. While the men jumped at the chance to claim their dry sleeping spots and unravel bedrolls throughout the cave like a troop of weary soldiers, Felix and John visited the main cavern to set up lanterns.

John noticed the crystal shards scattered across the floor like broken glass. "What do you plan to do with these," he asked.

"First and foremost," Felix answered, pushing his spectacles up his nose, "you and I shall collect every shard and place it in these." He pulled two burlap sacks from his backpack and handed one to the Nisqually. "The gems are compensation for the laborers. You will divvy their shares per my instruction. Of course, as my assistant, I'd like you to reserve a little extra for yourself."

John's silent disapproval emanated through his stern scowl. Yet, with the reservedness of a monastic, he started gathering the crystals. Before bending down to do his share of the picking, Felix held his brightest lantern toward the dragon. As if laying eyes on it for the first time, he stood in awe, too engrossed by jet-black bones to look away.

John lifted his eyes to the fossilized creature and stumbled backward. "Dr. Beauchamp, no! Sir, we cannot dig that out. It belongs to the mountain, to the Spirit of Tahoma."

"Why did you think I hired you, John?"

"To dig up a dinosaur or something related."

"This is a dragon. It is of the sort, not a spirit, but a flying beast of a bygone world. And I intend to extract it from the volcano immediately."

"With respect, Dr. Beauchamp, I must tell you that bad luck will haunt those who remove it from its home."

"How can you be so sure?"

John's lips quivered as if words suddenly piled up behind his teeth. However, he remained silent, likely hoping his final statement proved convincing enough.

"Do you wish to get paid?" Felix snubbed, determined that his discovery and the dream it promised trumped all threats.

The native nodded, reluctance steaming from his sigh.

Felix scratched his beard and approached his assistant. "How about this? Since your shovel led me back to this cave, you will do no more digging. You will only supervise the others. That way, you can rest easy knowing that your hands did not contribute to the physical removal of this dragon. But if you choose this, I must rescind my offer to pay you extra. I'll dock your compensation by one quarter, considering you'll not be performing any labor."

"I accept the demotion," John answered in all seriousness. "Despite that my needs may be great, I will not slight the spirits for any amount of wealth."

Felix felt likewise but neither voiced nor acted upon it. Abandoning such a monumental discovery, not to mention international fame and fortune, out of fear for the supernatural would not sit well with Charles Attwood or any member of the science community. He had to stand his ground and persist without revealing his teetering stance. After all, he was the one who discovered the only genuine proof of dragons.

Felix composed himself and decided to summon the men. As they entered, he watched their reactions to the dragon, each expression stirring excitement in his stomach. Some slouched with gaping mouths or simply stared, while others crossed their hearts and uttered prayers to their chosen deities. Either way, they looked as if their imaginations were running wild. Now seemed as good a time as any for Felix to reiterate his rule of discretion while John quietly distributed half of the team's compensation, the rest of which would be administered once the bones found safe transport down the mountain to Ashford.

"And trust me when I say," Felix added, "you shall find no difficulty buttoning your mouths with the incredible earnings you are and shall later receive. Furthermore, I must impart that performing this task with excruciating fastidiousness is imperative. We must work in harmony. Be aware of your fellow diggers and mind your manners."

"Also, be kind to the dragon. Chisel the rock with delicate precision to avoid chipping fossils. Upon removal, give each bone directly to me. I will carry it to the cave entrance and remove the excess material, then wrap the bone in a dampened cloth, jacket it with burlap strips of wet plaster, wait for it to dry, and place it gently in the wagon outside. Gentlemen, this procedure must run smoothly. I require everyone's complete focus and cooperation. If a single bone goes missing, regardless of its condition, I will hold everyone here accountable, and each of your purses shall be reduced by half. As you might have realized by now, the reward is substantial. I know you will not disappoint me. Got it? Now, let's dig out a dragon!"

The men commenced without whining or weeping over the task, removing the sediment surrounding the skeleton. Felix wasn't the least surprised to find that the miners performed with the highest accuracy, able to bring their chisels close enough to the bones without inflicting damage, almost as if trained to do so at university. The others, chiefly the former lumbermen and railroaders, proved less confident in their work, striking their tools more outwardly to avoid fracturing the fossils or their neighbor's fingers.

After three miners extracted the first piece from the andesite wall, a claw, Felix carried it to the portal, where he carefully scraped off the remaining clods of earth. The task felt more arduous than anticipated, but his determination pushed him through any waves of doubt. While jacketing the piece in plaster, he laughed at his scant familiarity with the process, which he felt he executed with the same accuracy as the miners. He had once attended the excavation of a Brontosaurus in northern Montana, watching the paleontologists labor, noting their errors and complaints. It seemed that the experience, and a few others like it, proved worthwhile, for he felt he knew what to expect and avert while handling this dragon.

After three days of grueling work, two severed fingers, five bloodied hands, four whiskey-induced brawls, and more insults than Felix dared recount, the team excavated everything but the head and wings. It seemed that all was going according to plan, if not better, and at a rate that Felix did not expect. However, he quickly found himself lagging on his portion of the work. It took him much longer to properly shell one fossil than three men to dig one out of the mountain. After a bout of frustration and self-deprecating utterances, Felix noticed that Hershel had been booted from the digging crew and sat barefoot in a pool of warm water.

"Everything all right with you?" Felix asked him.

"Nothing I ain't used to, Dr. Beauchamp."

"That's most unfortunate. A wise man once said that the burden of many is an opportunity for one. And I sense you'd be of great help to me. Care to assist with the jacketing?"

Hershel chuckled. "Gladly, Doc. Just show me what to do."

Felix had commenced the excavation on a cold, cloudy Wednesday afternoon. By Sunday morning, those clouds had darkened and grown bitter to the point that tiny flakes began to drift down from the heavens. Within a few hours, the snowfall increased tenfold. The temperature in the entry cave plummeted dramatically. While pulling the mule inside, a few employees approached Felix and asked if they could move camp to the inner hollow where the air felt warm, even make do with the damp floor if it meant avoiding the cold. Felix shifted his eyes to the ground before shaking his head and rerouting his vision to the petitioners.

"I'm terribly sorry," he answered. "I'm concerned that inhabiting the dragon chamber would compromise the operation. Our success depends on the conditions we create. Therefore, remain where you are, please."

Some men sighed or groaned at his response, clearly used to rejection in their primary occupation. However, a few voiced their growing animosity under their breath. Felix heard the curses and insults and wondered if he was being too harsh. He had always led teams experienced in geological digs, never as impromptu and rugged as this. And, to his displeasure, the laborers were not the only problem.

While the wagon remained outside, well-anchored by ropes and stones to the artificial, recessed island of mountain skin within the nameless glacier, the harsh elements severely threatened the integrity of the fossils, regardless of their plaster jackets. Felix needed to protect his treasure at all costs. The dragon held far more value than any crystals, any number of men, his own life included. The product of this excavation would prove vital to understanding a piece of history long fantasized by adults and children alike. In essence, it was mythology meeting reality. Even if every member of his team perished on Rainier, as long as the fossils made it to the civilized world, humanity would learn that dragons existed. And if Felix happened to die as well, at least he would be remembered as the one who discovered the evidence.

Or so he hoped.

The operation continued. John supervised the workers while Felix and Hershel combated a frigid north wind that swept down from the high peak. They spent fifty strenuous minutes erecting an improvised wagon cover using hemp rope and Felix's tent sheet. They hurried inside as soon as they finished but occasionally popped their heads out to ensure the shelter had not blown away. It worked well throughout the afternoon, but a vicious gale rode upon the chariot of night.

While jacketing the first wing fossil, Felix heard a *zip* sound from beyond the mouth of the cave. He ignored it. *Zip*. Without further thought, he dropped the bone and bolted outside. The wind clawed violently at the makeshift cover, throttling it this way and that, fraying the ends. Felix cursed and jumped at the sheet, hoping to batten it before it was too late.

Mother Tahoma suddenly expelled a second blast just as Felix touched the cloth. *Shoo*. The sheet split apart and whisked into the darkness. Felix panicked and hurried back into the cave, knifed open his sleep sack, and laid it over the cart. Luckily, he realized quickly enough that the bedroll would not suffice, even with rocks to anchor it. Kicking himself, he called Hershel out to help him haul the fossils inside and lay them beyond the reach of snow and water.

While a quarter of the cave remained susceptible to outside weather, half of the unexposed area rapidly filled with dragon fossils of all sizes, leaving little comfort space for the laborers. A handful of them had already groaned about sleeping near the mule. Now, they boldly detested moving their sleeping bags around the cave to make room for a pile of bones. By the time Felix and Hershel finished unloading the cart, all the men had migrated into the excavation chamber, bearing silent scowls of resentment.

"You need to return to the cave entrance," Felix complained after following the men into the inner room. "We cannot compromise anything."

His demands were met with gritted teeth and mutinous growls. Someone may even have thumbed the hammer of a pistol. Felix understood their irritation, having to sleep and work on a cold mountainside, but wasn't the wage worth the trouble? He dared not ask. Another refusal from his lips would have earned him a beating and a toss over the cliff. These men were feral at heart like eighteenth-century pirates, yoked by their insatiable hunger for riches and a hot meal.

Felix had been consumed by the dream of scientific glory when preparing for the project, never thinking it might behoove him to purchase a gun in Ashford. He had no wish to blast the life out of someone; it was simply a matter of safety for him and the dragon. He regretted this as he returned to the entry chamber, feeling defeated and praying that the scrappy lot he had hired would resist the temptation to unite against him.

Felix didn't think the evening could get any worse. Then, the miners, who had proudly served as the excavation team's core, exhausted their supply of whiskey. Fearing robbery, the men of other trades stashed away their flasks. A pock-faced, barrel-chested miner named Willie, who had been babbling since Longmire about his ability to outdrink anyone, suddenly began shouting about the whiskey shortage, prodding his fellow sots into a rabble.

"No whiskey, no work!" they cried.

"It's that Dr. Beauchamp." Willie egged them on. "First, he tried to make us sleep in the cold. Now we find out he didn't bring enough whiskey to keep us warm. I bet he didn't pack enough food either."

"No whiskey, no work!" the others continued.

Felix reveled in a glass of fine whiskey, especially bourbon, but he did not lust for it. He preferred to drink to success, usually at the end of a long project or a wedding. He currently carried a flask in his backpack, which he had hoped to save for his return to Ashford, where he would drink to either triumph or defeat. Unfortunately, he had left his pack near the entry of the excavation chamber. And he only remembered that because he heard Willie announce, "Look, look, Dr. Beauchamp is hiding whiskey from us! He's got a nice silvery canteen sticking out of a pocket in his sack. I haven't seen him take one swig since we started. It must be full, and it's all for us!"

28

Felix rushed into the inner cavern and routed to his backpack. "Everyone, please, relax!" he urged as sweat began to bead over his brows. "This is not necessary."

"If you want us to finish the job, give us your flask!" Willie barked.

"You don't need it," John exclaimed, pushing the crowd back with his presence. "You're already drunk of spirit. Come now, friend, have some dignity."

"I don't give a damn," Willie snarled. "For all we've done, we deserve an entire barrel of liquor. Now it's freezing outside, and the boss refuses to share his ration. He thinks he's better than us and wants it all for himself. Well, I say to hell with him."

"*Assez, Assez,*" Felix shouted, his voice reverberating through each fissure of the cavern. "Gentlemen, the excavation is near completion. If we work as diligently as we have and remove the skull by tomorrow, I promise we'll be off the mountain in two days. I swear there will be plenty of whiskey and tobacco, or whatever you want, once we're back in Ashford. You can sell your crystals for an exceedingly high price and buy your way to happiness. You need only work in this cave one more day. So, please, let's be civil."

"Burn in hell, Beauchamp!" Willie howled, spit flying from a gap between his teeth.

"Burn in hell, Beauchamp!" echoed the others.

The workforce stood against Felix with furrowed brows, flared nostrils, and grimaces that could frighten even the haughtiest dogs. John proved the only exception, trying to bridle Willie and those who followed his lead. Felix had never dealt with such unruly men. They looked like impoverished marmots, cold and filthy, weary of the altitude and unable to tolerate another minute on the mountain. Who could blame them? The lack of whiskey just happened to be the match in the powder keg. Felix recognized this and attempted once again to appease and calm his employees, reiterating their rewards upon achieving his goal.

However, amid Felix's concluding proclamation, "We can do this, all for one and one for all," Willie drew a revolver from his back as if someone had secretly slipped it into his hand. He shoved John aside, stepped away from the men, and raised the barrel. Felix tossed the metal flask at Willie's feet, hoping the miner would take the bait, but he kept coming. John shouted while two tosspots dove for the free drink. The rest of the men just stood like statues and stared. Felix felt his spine press into a jagged spur of rock in the cavern wall. "John," he yelled. "John, anyone, please, stop him! Do something!"

Willie levered the pistol hammer with his thumb and laughed as he lurched forward. Felix closed his eyes, shielded his face with his arms, and cried out one last time. The gunshot screamed like dynamite, deafening every ear in the cavern.

Felix found that he still breathed. He was alive,

standing and thinking, though if anyone was speaking or moving, he heard none of it. He lowered his arms and opened his eyes to find Willie face down on the wet floor, dark blood pooling around his head, the gun on the ground at Felix's feet. He glanced about the cavern, spotting confusion and pain on everyone's face, their heads filled with the same shrill ring that plagued him. Then he noticed Hershel in the corner, who gave a curt nod and returned to the entry chamber.

After a few minutes, Felix felt his hearing slowly return. He picked up Willie's gun and shoved it into his backpack. "Take the body outside," he told John. The Nisqually's lips trembled as if he wished to speak, but Felix added a second command, louder this time, his quivering voice directed at everyone in the room. "The night is over. Get some rest. We finish tomorrow and leave the following day. No arguments, no excuses."

Felix passed the grumbling men and went into the entry cave, where the resonation of music overcame his heated ears. The mule lay against the far wall, still rattled from the gunshot but doing his best to relax and listen to the slow rhythm of Hershel's harmonica tune. Felix rounded the piles of jacketed fossils and sat beside the miner. He warmed his hands over a flame that struggled to survive on minimal kindling.

"Wonderful music, Hershel, and most welcome," Felix remarked, slowing his breath to quell his trembling muscles. He craned half a Hershey Bar from his coat pocket, hoping the sweet treat would steal his thoughts from the swelling anger and frustration inside him. "I owe you my life. Thank you. I had no idea you were armed and quite the sharpshooter. I should have suspected something like this would happen. I'm such a fool. I should have been more prepared. Goddamn animals think one little flask between them will satisfy their thirst. Not a chance. That ugly bastard, Willie, nearly blew my brains out over that stupid little flask. The nerve! Seems John's the only one of them who has any sense. And you, of course, you were fantastic."

Hershel pulled the harmonica from his lips. "You're most welcome, Doc. You're a good man and Willie was a mean soul. He's the one who got the others to rally against me. I could have killed him then, but, well, it doesn't matter now. He got what was coming to him. But hey, listen, I'd call all those men crazy if that didn't make me a hypocrite."

"What do you mean? It's not like you were among them."

Hershel leaned closer. "If we were fighting over a beautiful woman, you can rest assured that I would have been the one pulling a gun on you. Everyone has a vice. It's just that many folks happen to hide it well, while an unfortunate number of people have dug themselves too deep to care about public opinion. I prefer the warmth of a different woman every night.

Hard lust, they call it. Though, to me, it's more like a change of scenery. My perversion is almost casual, but it's a vice, nonetheless. 'Course, it costs me, which is why I'm here with you. Also, I got kin in Chicago that I'd like to help."

Felix nodded and unwrapped the partially devoured Hershey Bar, thinking that his love for chocolate might not have been lechery but was undoubtedly a habit that did not benefit his teeth. He wondered whether the dragon would become his next obsession if it wasn't already. As the voices in the other chamber calmed, he looked to the wide opening where an earthen wall once stood and, above it, a hole through which he had accidentally fallen. Silence overcame him when John and another miner carried Willie outside into the frigid darkness. He heard the thump of the body hit the snow and lowered his eyes as the men returned inside.

"Do you believe in destiny?" Felix asked once he and Hershel were alone again.

"I believe in God. And if God presents me with a promising path, I'd say that's my destiny."

"Simple. I like it. You know, Hershel, you talk as though you received a proper education. Is that so?"

"My mother, Ruth, was a cook for a wealthy family in Mississippi whose cotton fields were maintained by my father, Sam, and his crew. Ruth learned to read recipes at a young age, which eventually carried her toward books, usually borrowed from the plantation house library. She educated my brother and me through writers like Alexander Dumas and Jules Verne. Sadly, I rarely get the opportunity to read these days. The train of life has steered me to this soggy, green corner of the world. But what about you, Doc? What's your take on destiny?"

"Growing up Catholic," Felix mumbled, still chewing his last bite of chocolate. He crumpled the wrapper and tossed it into the fire. "Growing up Catholic, my parents taught me that only Jesus could enlighten one's life. As a science student at university, I learned the contrary, that only nature, philosophy, poetry, and chemistry can enlighten. Many of my friends are atheists, while a sizable number more are about as religious as the Pope. I'd say I've been in the middle of the road for at least fifteen years. Destiny never played a role in my life, though I suppose I really never thought about it until now. Yet, looking back on how I found the dragon, I can't help but believe that some form of universal providence is responsible. If God is real, it was Him who brought me here. If there is no God, then I must be the luckiest man in the world."

"Everybody gets lucky sometimes," Hershel chuckled.

Felix laughed. "Still, things have gone a bit awry here. The weather is horrible. A crazed drunk nearly killed me. And the men are probably a hair's width from uniting to throw me over a cliff. Worse, I'm terrified that we might lose a few bones before we get back to Ashford, if we get back."

"Don't fret, Doc," Hershel advised, rubbing the top of his harmonica with his index finger. "You'll get your dragon bones off the mountain. I have faith in you."

"Faith." Felix considered the word and remembered John's warning about the spirit of Tahoma. "Let me ask you something else, Hershel. What do you want out of this life?"

The miner shrugged. "I suppose I want what every human secretly wants. Peace, love, and prosperity." He pocketed the mouth harp. "Peace of mind for my heart and a woman bold enough to wrangle me into submission."

"How far would you go to achieve your peace, love, and prosperity?" Felix laughed and shook his head. "And a woman bold enough to wrangle you into submission?"

The glow of the fire reflected like sunlight in Hershel's eyes. "Anything for a dream, Doc."

Felix concurred with a slow nod. "Anything for a dream."

Despite the rough night, the following day proved fruitful. The once disgruntled employees finished the job, excavating the entire skull in under six hours. Felix, utterly impressed, chose not to ask but guessed that Willie's death may have struck fear in them. Luck, too, might have worked its magic. That or the whim of the big boss upstairs. "Who could say?" Felix mumbled as he and Hershel jacketed the dragon's lower jaw. "Anything for a dream." He took comfort in the miner's presence like a long-lost brother of sorts. Felix even considered hiring Hershel as his assistant once the dragon business concluded, if ever such an end existed, given the gravity of the discovery.

When his pocket watch ticked across a quarter to four, Felix grinned at the inner cavern wall, a jagged rock face devoid of dragon bones. To prove his satisfaction and please the men, he ordered John to divvy another portion of their compensation, which they vigorously stuffed into their rucksacks. Meanwhile, Felix stepped out of the cave, finding that the harsh weather, which had troubled the excavation for days, had vanished.

He smiled at the sky and playfully imagined his removal of the dragon compared to the extraction of a decayed tooth. The Spirit of Tahoma must have felt relieved enough to dismiss the storm that once shielded her head, or so Felix hoped. Still, the recent weather had bequeathed an astounding volume of snow upon the slopes of Rainier, as if the mountain had bathed in sticky sugar.

In the early hours of the following morning, Felix, John, and Hershel broke the wagon from its icy chains and generously greased the axles. Whooping with anticipation of departure, the men eagerly assisted Felix in transferring the jacketed fossils from the cave to the cart's bed. The dragon weighed heavily upon the wooden frame, making the mule's task painfully onerous. Therefore, tackling Rainier's steep, rugged slopes would prove a grueling endeavor, not to mention the responsibility of safeguarding the bones and every member of the excavation party, including the poor mule. Concern nipped at Felix, but John and Hershel assured him they would encourage the men to work together.

As promised, everyone unitedly struggled alongside the mule, utilizing every muscle and ounce of willpower to shovel out a path and keep the wagon rolling at a steady but secure speed. Unfortunately, the route that had guided Felix up the mountain now hid beneath a sea of snowdrifts. This change in the landscape rendered all options of descent perplexing and problematic, endangering the entire team regardless of what they decided.

To make matters worse, and against Felix's wishes, while inching their way down a natural rampart protruding from the body of a steep escarpment, one of the leading miners' frustrations bested him to the point that he carelessly steered the mule over a patch of ice. The weary, stubborn animal groaned and clicked its teeth, quickly choosing to stand its ground. Amid calls to quiet his exasperations and leave the mule alone, the hot-headed miner tugged on the reins until the irritated creature finally jerked forward, then abruptly recoiled and threw its head askance. Without a moment for anyone to think or act, the miner lost footing and tumbled over the face of the precipice like a ragdoll in a watery torrent. Felix cringed when he saw the man's body slam into a serrated pinnacle of rock jutting from the side of a drift.

Similarly, a second, icy incident nearly flung the wagon over a ridge into Paradise Valley. 'Too close,' Felix thought. A few more obstacles hindered them, but Felix pushed his party to their limits, constantly reminding them of the whiskey and wealth awaiting them in Ashford. Eventually, after suffering the mountain's many rigorous tests, he and his crew entered Longmire at twilight, hid the wagon in the nearby woods, and enjoyed a well-deserved slumber.

In the morning, Felix exchanged his weary-eyed mule and a sack of crystals for four sinewy horses to pull the wagon for the remaining journey. Before leaving, he implored the stableman to treat the mule respectfully and feed him well, motivating the lad with an extra handful of small crystal shards. While Felix and Hershel hitched the horses to the wagon, the now-former excavators approached him unitedly. Their eyes shone brightly, having slept well, and filled their bellies with hot food and strong drink at his expense.

However, the scowls they bore hinted at their impatience to head out and receive the last quarter of compensation. As promised, Felix happily paid off what he owed his laborers upon arriving in Ashford. None spared even a morsel of gratitude before exiting the town wealthier than Felix would ever know.

As everyone dispersed, Felix kindly asked John and Hershel to linger for a few more days to help arrange and assess the fossils. John declined without hesitation, his voice just loud enough to break through the stonework of his face. "I want nothing more to do with this dragon. It belongs to the Spirit of Tahoma. Abducted from its bed of rock, it will bring misery to those who deny it peace."

John the Nisqually accepted his final compensation with an expression as cold as the mountain. However, as he turned to leave, Hershel shook his head and spat at the native's feet. "You're a hypocrite, John, you know that. You're like a cowardly soldier who refuses to kill an enemy, then waits for the battle to end so that you can loot the dead."

John held his tongue and left Ashford as Hershel turned to Felix, extended a hand, and smiled. "I'm all yours, Doc, until you've got no use for me."

Felix nodded and shook the man's hand. "No longer interested in mining, eh?"

"Underground is the last place I want to be when you release a dragon upon the world."

Together, Felix and Hershel rented a cabin near the edge of town, where they laid out the hundreds of fossils in preparation to clean each one. As night came on, a fusion of crackling firewood and harmonica melodies sedated Felix with comfort and achievement. He leaned back in a rocker and thought of the great skull resting securely in the cart outside the window.

He wondered how the marvelous creature had perished, its age at death, and the duration of its entombment. He imagined it alive, eyes like brilliant garnets and scales as tough and sharp as steel, its appendages moving with the grace of an eagle. Perhaps it roared like a lion, hissed like a snake, or spoke like a human. Mythology tells of numerous dragons across many cultures, all unique, molded by ancient minds to fit the world in which they lived, or so Felix had learned from books.

He further wondered, if the dragon suddenly and miraculously burst to life, would it be of like mind to the dinosaurs and wish to devour him, or would it have intelligence and impart its opinion on the great follies of humankind? Felix chuckled and sipped from a flask he had purchased in Longmire, chasing it with a freshly rolled cigarette. Despite all the troubles on the mountain, he had returned to Ashford utterly triumphant.

With a satisfying hum, he wondered when Charles would return and what news he would bring from Seattle. A flash of concern crossed his mind, a scant thought that the dream would never come true and that the world would never learn the truth about dragons. "Impossible," he mumbled. "Now that it's out of the mountain and in my hands, how could the dream fail?" He looked at Hershel, feeling reassured and relaxed, allowing his joy to brim again. He laughed and announced, "We possess evidence that dragons once existed. We're going to be famous the world over."

"We all get lucky sometimes, Doc," Hershel concurred with a grin.

THE PERSUASION

Charles Attwood gazed upon the Port of Seattle with a curious grin. Having grown up in Sacramento, the golden heart of California, he had always loved cities of burgeoning power. They felt ripe with intrigue and learned people to whom he believed were of like mind to him and equally aspiring. As one of the newer hubs of urban life in America, and considering its distance from New York and San Francisco, Charles concluded that Seattle would be the best place to reveal the most significant discovery of humankind. 'Where better to deliver illumination than the gray world of the northwest,' he thought with hands rubbing.

More importantly, he needed to convince the scientific ears at the University of Washington of this incredible finding. The hard evidence rested in his leather satchel, three dragon teeth, each one larger than the other and still sharp as a set of finely honed knives. They ignited his ardor, cueing visions of success coupled with endless possibilities. He and Felix would become heroes to people of every social rank and class. They would be pioneers. He bathed in these heavenly thoughts as the train pulled into the newly opened King Street Station.

Charles floated through the city with his head on a cloud and his mind in a dreamy haze. He eventually found himself seated at the edge of a bed in a hotel room, staring through the window at Elliot Bay. While delicately stroking the largest dragon tooth like a purring kitten, he muttered, "I will be the most famous scientist in the world. Forget Einstein, Tesla, Planck, Hall, Marconi. Forget them all. Charles Attwood will rise to the top of the list, utterly glorified. I may not be an inventor or mathematical genius, but I will stand triumphant as the man who turned mythology into reality. It is not some serpent beast of Hades, Midgard, or the Arthurian tales, but the bones of a legitimate dragon." He cuddled the tooth to his beating heart, tumescent with the vision of power.

An hour later, Charles stepped out of a buggy with a tight tie and puffed chest, prepared to enter Denny Hall, the administrative office at the University of Washington. He briefly examined his attire, reassuring himself that he embodied academia. Before arriving in Seattle, Charles had spent eleven days in the port town of Tacoma, seeking the finest tailors and clothing stores. Eventually, he settled on an old shopkeeper who seemed oddly ecstatic to trade a complete gentlemen's suit – frock coat and leather shoes included – for Charles's dirty mountaineering clothes. As Charles exited the store, he pilfered a well-crafted poplar cane resting in a bin of parasols by the front door. 'The poor old fool,' he had thought with a snicker, feeling as affluent as he now appeared.

Charles Attwood drew a silver watch from his coat pocket as a slump-backed horse towed the buggy from the university campus. "Nearly eleven o'clock," he announced as if he had been asked the time. While strutting toward the administrative building, he shook his satchel to ensure he did not forget the fossilized teeth in the hotel room. Their weight helped cloak Charles in confidence.

Before entering the collegiate edifice, he turned southeast, where one could take in Mount Rainier's majesty on a sunny day. Through the gray clouds resembling wet clay, he imagined the *dragon* as he had seen it, a marvelous skeletal system black as onyx and more precious than oil. He felt his joy rising and chuckled, yet a flicker of worry speared him to the ground when he considered Felix's progress or lack thereof.

It would be a long and arduous day for Charles, striving to convince the university's science professionals to meet with him suddenly and all at once. He began speaking to faculty members of various statuses, evading the term dragon as he pitched the purpose of his presence to avoid immediate discrediting. Instead, he stated that he needed an audience to whom he could present substantial evidence of an extraordinary discovery that would shake the world.

Charles had imagined that natural curiosity would prompt these scientists to grant him the time of day. To his discontent, most shut their office doors in his face. Others reluctantly consented to hear him out, just not during school hours. Neither were they willing to stick around for an evening conference. One professor, Dr. Kalvin Wicks, even scolded him like a child. "Unless you're willing to reveal what you discovered here and now, I say, how dare you enter this prestigious place peddling ambiguity."

Charles retreated to his hotel, wrecked by defeat. However, staring at the dragon's teeth reignited his visions, inspiring him to return with a more convincing pitch the following day. Using words like *fossil* and *excavation* proved enough to convince some professors to meet with him on Saturday morning. A few narrowly escaped his persuasion, so to best nudge concession, he offered to buy them all breakfast pastries once his presentation concluded.

At nine o'clock on Saturday morning, a dozen scientists and a few administrators filed into a classroom that Charles had reserved the day before. Whispers of doubt and regret clouded the air, raining discouragement on Charles, who stood at the podium awaiting any lagging participants. He occasionally flashed his eyes to the satchel resting on a rectangular oaken table in front of the chalkboard. Anxious to begin, he eavesdropped on a handful of adverse conversations, which further chipped away at the confidence he had built before arriving. While studying the dubious expressions of those who mocked his initial pitch, the final attendees arrived.

Charles quietly sipped from a cup of water, then panned over the eyes of his audience. They seemed to stare with blended expressions of apprehension and curiosity, hoping the presentation was worth the time they could have been spending with family or tending to personal work.

"Ladies and gentlemen," Charles announced before clearing his throat. "I would like to commence this presentation with a small but gracious address of appreciation. My gratitude for your attendance holds no bounds. I swear by all books of religion and tomes of science that your time will not be wasted. Please trust that I will make it worth your while. Thank you."

"Now, having opened my heart to you fine people, please allow me to formally introduce myself. My name is Dr. Charles Attwood. Some of you may have heard of me through my published theories on dinosaur extinction, or my academic essays on the history of California marine life, or even my paleontological studies with the University of

California and Colorado State University. I have twenty-two years of paleontological experience. I have been the first to unearth and document two distinct, small species of dinosaur, ten prehistoric marine creatures, and several dozen specimens of extinct vegetation." He brought his hands together. "You might be asking yourself or your neighbor why I just listed my achievements. It is to eschew all skepticism upon unveiling my latest discovery. I am neither an amateur nor a common lunatic. Like you, I am an established professor of contemporary science."

Charles grinned and opened his satchel. "As humans, we are naturally conversant with the folklore and mythologies of our ancestors. However, when most of us in today's society consider these tales of beasts, heroes, and deities, we classify them as fantasy or, at the very least, highly exaggerated representations of real events and figures. Even the Bible is vulnerable to scrutinization and is increasingly regarded as a document of imaginative history."

"My friends, we are now living in the Golden Age of Science. We must reexamine everything we've ever learned and believed to uncover old, obstructed truths. We require hypotheses and experimentation, observation, and recordation. Authenticity is of paramount importance. It is what we wish to see and smell. We yearn to touch it with our fingers and hear it if possible. Ladies and gentlemen, I possess a piece of fantasy that you may examine with all your senses.

It is evidence of a creature that humans have long dreamed of understanding, confirming that upon our beloved Earth, there once existed monsters we call *dragons*."

The audience shuffled in their seats, stabbing the air with scoffs and doubtful chuckles. One individual even proclaimed their skepticism through an unnecessarily loud cough, while another simply stood and exited.

"Please, please, esteemed peers, do not impugn me. You must consider the possibility. The Sumerians, Chinese, Norsemen, Romans, Greeks, Persians, Celts, Egyptians, Bantu, Mayans, Aztecs, every culture we have ever studied has tales and artifacts that portray great dragons. If you open any book of mythology and folklore, you will inevitably encounter this beast. And if not by the term *dragon*, they are wyrms, wyverns, serpents, cockatrices, and basilisks. Regardless of title, they are all relative to one another and have stood as powerful symbols throughout human history, even today. Now, I ask you, why would numerous cultures across the globe, many of whom never communicated with one another, share this unique organism? Doubtless, they existed in some form, a time and place. We can begin to examine that point in history right now. Look! Feast your eyes on these incredible samples."

Charles removed the three bulbous teeth from his satchel and delicately undressed the cloth that enveloped them. When he placed the fossils on the table, one of the professors shouted, "Those are dinosaur bones."

"No, sir," Charles parried, hardly hiding the bulk of his disgust behind quivering lips. "I assure you they are not. My associate, Professor Felix Beauchamp from the University of Montreal, is excavating the dragon at this very instant. He and I came upon this marvelous finding while ascending the slopes of Mount Rainier. These teeth were extracted from a wall of andesite by our own hands. And I traveled a great distance to deliver this undeniable proof to you, the premier minds of academia."

"Did you say Professor Felix Beauchamp?" remarked Dr. Edward Rhys, a Welshman of prestigious reputation. Charles had once witnessed him standing beside John Muir at a Sierra Club conference in San Francisco. "You should have mentioned his name from the start. I am well acquainted with Dr. Beauchamp. He and I met in Vancouver many years ago while aiding the Geological Survey of Canada. The man is renowned for his reports on the volcanic regions of the Yukon Territory and British Colombia. Such a figure of esteemed qualifications ought to stand before us and deliver this presentation, not to diminish any status you carry, Dr. Attwood. I mean to say, shouldn't a paleontologist like yourself be on-site with this supposed dragon?"

"Dr. Rhys, I recognize that my claim sounds

farfetched. And I understand that it is highly unusual for a geologist to perform the duties of a paleontologist. However, Dr. Beauchamp is famous for his sediment extraction techniques, which are tremendously necessary for our excavation, considering its unique location within a volcanic cavern. If you had seen the placement with your own eyes, you would undoubtedly concur with our decision. Now, please just... well, here, see for yourself."

Charles loaned the teeth to his audience until the objects circulated enough to rouse a fuss. "If you have a healthy appreciation of prehistoric life and have analyzed as many fossils as I have in my experience, your conclusion ought to be absolute. These teeth cannot possibly belong to a dinosaur or any known nonmammalian aquatic species. We can adjudge this through deduction. These choppers are finely serrated, a trait quite common in sharks, yet no fish on this earth has dentition of this size or dramatic shape."

"Ergo, we turn to reptiles and try to compare my dragon to crocodiles. Yet, I feel you will find it painfully indisputable that these teeth, given their enormity, could never belong to any species of crocodilia. A deeper correlation: Dr. Edward Cope and his associates revealed an Allosaurus that possessed denticulation with a ziphodont display. Akin to my dragon? I think not! For, you see, all disentombed theropod teeth are dull. Even the best preserved are only as rough as glass-paper. Dare to touch the tip of my dragon teeth, and you might very well bleed. They are sharp as a dagger fresh from the smithy, even after eons of encasement in the volcanic makeup of Rainier."

"What do you take us for?" Professor Kalvin Wicks barked, springing to his feet. "My field of science may not be paleontology, but logic and probability cannot rule out that *all* dinosaur teeth taper off during the fossilization process. For all I know, you just discovered the first of such a gem. Or perhaps you just sharpened a dull one yourself."

"Sir, I must protest," Charles retaliated as the audience groaned and grumbled. "I pride myself as a master of bones and a man of honor. And while you have the freedom to challenge the incisiveness of these teeth, as is the nature of good science, please consider their pigment. No fossilized teeth, with or without the aforementioned traits, are black *and* glossy as obsidian." The room hummed with deliberation.

"Do you honestly expect us to believe you?" goaded Professor Wicks. "That could be paint or dye or a mutation of sorts. Darwin once said "

Charles sliced into the retort. "I assure you that these teeth are not painted. They are authentic as our living flesh, here and now. The truest of true. Darwin would agree."

Dr. Wicks shook his head and laughed. "You know what, Dr. Attwood? You strike me as a wanton postulant, a charlatan hoping to beguile imperative minds to amass investments only to evaporate into the world of commoners. I believe this is a ploy. You should have dug the whole skeleton out before coming here. So, unless you can produce more substantial proof of this... this *dragon*, I highly suggest you abandon Seattle with your ridiculous fantasies and nail them to paper. I'm confident that dream readers and literary folk, at least, would find familiarity with the subject you're peddling. As an esteemed member of the scientific community at the University of Washington, I reject your findings and take my leave of this ruse. And you can keep your breakfast pastries, likely as stale as your prospect."

Dr. Wicks stepped out with his chin held high and chest puffed. Other board members hastily followed without explanation, each one mimicking others' shrugs of disappointment. As their feet shuffled toward the door, Charles clasped his hands and begged them to wait. Just as his hopes were ready to collapse, Dr. Edward Rhys approached him alongside a gentleman of refined taste in garb.

"Dr. Attwood, I would like to introduce you to my friend, Mr. John Charles Olmsted of the Olmsted Brothers Company, a landscape architectural firm out of Massachusetts. He recently completed a major fair in Portland, the Lewis and Clark Centennial Exposition, and is now planning an exposition right here at the University of Washington."

Charles nearly burst into laughter as his blood spiked with sweet optimism. He gleefully shook hands with Mr. Olmsted. "Bravo! Believe it or not, I attended your exposition in Portland and found it perfectly enticing. The sophisticated ambiance left me helplessly curious. I could not refrain from swooning over the vibrant oriental exhibits."

"Thank you, Dr. Attwood," John Olmsted retorted with a tilt of his head, a hint of Swiss German on his speaking palate. "You're too kind. As you can imagine, I am a man engrossed in business, so my time is precious. Dr. Rhys and I were conversing with the headmaster yesterday when one of the local professors mentioned your little conference. Both of us felt compelled to reserve time for the morning. Hence, here we are, quite taken by your speech and specimens despite the community's hasty abandonment."

"Do you truly believe you found a fossilized dragon?" Dr. Rhys inquired with a glimmer of zeal in his eyes.

Charles nodded. "I swear on the graves of my forefathers, I speak with the utmost candor."

John Olmsted tugged on his lapels. "Where is the dragon now?"

"As I explained earlier, my business partner, Dr. Felix Beauchamp, is currently excavating the specimen in a cave on the heights of Mount Rainier, after which we are to rendezvous in Ashford. Despite our lack of communication since parting ways a few weeks ago, I'm quite confident that his share in our onerous endeavor proved fruitful. He is a man of devotion and knows, as do I, the magnitude of this finding."

Dr. Rhys grinned wide enough to reveal his tea-stained teeth. "If you indeed unearthed a dragon, it would be the most extraordinary discovery in human history. As a child in Wales, I was very fond of Arthurian legends and dragon myths. I once believed in their existence, hoping to one day admire one. Considering my love for medieval lore and my deep respect for Dr. Beauchamp, if you are not opposed, I would like to accompany you back to Ashford to view this treasure. If I find your claim to be true, I will speak to the heads of the university on your behalf. For an authentic dragon, they would weep with joy and surely compensate you just to jump at the chance to study such a creature in their facilities."

"I, too, would like to accompany you," Olmstead added. "If all goes well and Dr. Rhys confirms your case, I will personally ensure that your dragon is the premier exhibit at the Alaska-Yukon-Pacific Exposition, right here at the University of Washington. Henceforth, the world will eat from your palm. You, Dr. Attwood, shall become the Dragon Man, finder of legends and myths. You will be known to history as the one who proved all folklore correct."

"Me, the Dragon Man? I could hardly "

"Do not perturb, Dr. Attwood," Olmsted challenged

cheerfully. "I'm glad to aid in boosting your notoriety. You strike me as a man whose skills the world ought to recognize."

Dr. Rhys concurred. "And I will further that exposure by contacting my friends at the Smithsonian Institution in Washington D.C. and the Museum of Natural History in New York. I'm sure every scientist, historian, and government will be stupefied by your impressive find. But enough promises. Come now, Dr. Attwood, let us travel to Ashford and examine your dragon."

~

As soon as Charles took his seat on the train bound for Tacoma, he fantasized about the prospect of fame and fortune. He grinned whenever he considered himself the *Dragon Man*, sole appropriator of the most glorified and legendary creature in human lore. He envisioned a swell of money, harems of women, trains of pleasure, and a world relishing the arrival of his revered presence.

Perhaps President Roosevelt would commend Charles's laurels by creating an American order of knights and bestowing upon him the highest honor. He felt like a grand hero already. But what of Felix Beauchamp? Charles wondered if his Canadian counterpart would impede his shot at immortality. He frowned at the taxing possibility and silently prayed that he could lose Felix somewhere along the road to celebrity.

Charles spent much of the train ride jesting and discussing prospects with John Olmsted. He ballooned with delight at the fortunes that awaited him. In the meantime, Edward Rhys remained solemn with his nose buried in a book of poems. Despite his desire to win everyone's favor, Charles felt confident that should any form of competition arise between him and Felix, Dr. Rhys would undoubtedly side with the latter. Therefore, he decided not to pay mind to the Welshman and, instead, bent his ears and persuasive tongue to John Olmsted, who appeared more than ecstatic to associate with one man over two. For a landscape designer, he certainly harbored a high number of influential contacts he was willing to divulge for the sake of coupling his name to the dragon. 'Who wouldn't?' Charles thought with his ears perked like a fox.

THE SPIRIT
OF TAHOMA

Felix and Hershel sat on the edge of the wagon bed, laughing and smoking cigars after a hard day's work in an abandoned lumberyard just outside Ashford. It was the culmination of a project that Felix once imagined would take the strength and skill of ten men. Yet, between them, it proved a smooth and fulfilling endeavor, merely taking up more time than if they had more hands.

After a few days of stripping fossils, Felix and Hershel carefully cleaned and rejacketed each piece, girding them for transportation. However, once complete, Felix felt it necessary to reconstruct the dragon on a flat surface, assured that the elements would not permeate the hardened plaster. So, when he discovered the old lumberyard while strolling in the woods near the Nisqually River, he felt it would be the perfect place to recreate history.

Restoring the dragon to its proper structure seemed quite puzzling at first. Since the dragon had been extracted from its natural, upright form, where nearly half the skeleton lay completely buried in andesite, Felix and Hershel needed to imagine how the beast would appear from a flattened, even broken point of view.

Then, considering they could not erect a standing model, fossils representing one side of the creature had to be mirrored in a second, lesser display. On top of it, they had only memory to serve as their true blueprint. Following a long week of light snow and drudgery, they managed to reassemble the sleeping monster, wrapping up with the placement of its large, cumbersome skull. Staring at the dragon with its body laid out like two lizards, all bones intact and inventoried, they clasped each other's shoulders and laughed.

"Truly, I couldn't have done it without you," Felix happily confessed.

While halfway through their celebratory cigars, a local boy whom Felix had hired as a watchman approached and alerted him that Charles Attwood had arrived in Ashford. Felix snuffed out his victory smoke, charged Hershel with the lot, and hurried to the center of town. He felt dusty and disheveled like a miner fresh from the hole, primarily upon greeting his business partner, who wrapped himself in deluxe attire as if returning from an urbane vacation.

Salutations filled the air, trailed by light titters and feigned smiles, ending with an introductory handshake between Felix and John Olmsted, whose stiff disposition conveyed his apathy toward their meeting. Inversely, Dr. Edward Rhys embraced Felix with jubilant laughter. Several years had passed since their last encounter, but they spoke as if their days of chumming had never ended. Felix regarded Dr. Rhys as one of the most versatile scientists in Western erudition and felt unquestionably grateful for his advent to witness the greatest discovery in human history.

Felix and Dr. Rhys began to prattle when Charles intervened, "Excuse me, Felix, but where is the dragon? I've done nothing but assume all went well. Is it here in its entirety?"

"Why don't you see for yourself, Charles." Felix gestured toward the southern woods. "Gentlemen, please, right this way." While leading the visitors through the sleepy mountain town, Felix's anxiousness got the best of him, though he managed a hushed tone. "Charles, what fortune awaits us? Will our dragon be placed in a national museum or the Smithsonian or a university? Will we have access to laboratories?"

"I'm still chipping at those slabs, though John

Olmsted has vowed that his contacts will prove extremely receptive. But, please, don't concern yourself with him. He's a bit unrelenting and annoyingly economical. When it comes to him, let me do the talking. As for Dr. Rhys, he appears to find comfort in your presence, so it will fall upon you to grind his wheel. From what I've heard, he poses many fantastic offers, even more than Olmsted."

The group soon encountered Hershel at the edge of the lumber yard, where a grove of old cedars and young firs separated Ashford from the evergreen forest that covered the river valley. While Charles and John Olmsted hardly masked their chagrin toward the former miner's presence, Dr. Rhys introduced himself politely and stepped forward without prejudice. Before Charles found an opportunity to trouble Felix about his dark-skinned assistant, Rhys and Olmsted froze in their shoes, jaws dropped toward the earth in awe. A curious crow drew near but whisked in fright when a joyous clamor shattered the quiet woodland air.

"This is magnificent," Dr. Rhys cried with the gleeful eyes of a child. "My skin is crawling with horripilation."

"This is something out of a fairytale," Olmsted commented with a grin twisting into his cheeks. "I must have this for the Alaska-Pacific-Yukon Exposition. The fair serves to publicize the development of the American Northwest, but this dragon would make such an addition that any compliment I voice falls short of justice. If anyone should dare argue, which I now doubt with every fiber of my being, we will harangue them, for this majestic creature is of Washington earth, carved from the flesh of Mount Rainier."

"Ah, I can see it now. The press will eat it up. Dr. Attwood, your discovery is beyond breathtaking. We must transport it to Seattle at once. Doubtless, our good Welshman, Edward, will concur when I state that every scientist and professor at the university will shiver with ecstasy and then regret walking out on your presentation. They will plead forgiveness before begging for possession of this unrivaled gem."

"Indeed, indeed," Dr. Rhys giggled, stepping to Felix's side. "Truly, my friend, there are no words that can accurately illustrate the severe magnitude of this treasure. It is a miracle."

"It is extraordinary," appended Olmsted, moving to stand abreast with Charles.

"Mr. Olmsted," Charles said in a softer voice, his tone glazed with hubris. "I believe acquiring secure transportation will prove to be a simple task. Trustworthy railroad companies are very accessible these days. However, the fees for such an encumbrance are enormous. To ferry the dragon without impairment, we need a sturdy, secure railcar."

"Oh, you need not worry about finances, Dr. Attwood," Olmsted remarked, the tips of his smile still raised upon pillars of ambition. "My firm will contribute beyond necessity to bear affiliation with you and your dragon. And I guarantee that Mr. William Moore, the mayor of Seattle, will devote just as much funding, if not more, to designate your dragon as a permanent attraction in one of his city's outstanding institutions."

He painted the air with his hand. "Can you envision it, Dr. Attwood? Newspaper headlines across the globe will scream your name through bold print. The press will photograph you beside the dragon as if you were the knight that slew it. And I shall stand beside you, the Olmsted Brothers Company, your number one sponsor."

"I like the sound of that, Mr. Olmsted."

"Please, call me John. We are friends. Allies. Compatriots. Just remember, Charles, once we return to Seattle, public hype will skyrocket. Yet, you and I will elegantly waltz across the dance hall of society with the Blue Danube as our theme. Grandiose! Furthermore, Seattle is indebted to me, so I guarantee that the University of Washington will bequeath upon you a thousand honors. Of course, we must first compose a formal pact, a contract. Loose ends are profoundly pesky, don't you concur? Once we have arrived at King Street Station, I will expedite a directive to a local business associate who will swiftly produce a fair document."

"We have an accord, John. With my dragon, we will

set the world on fire."

"That's the spirit, Charles. Now, let's hasten this legendary creature to Seattle."

Dr. Rhys had been speaking playfully to Felix about the dragon in his modest, scientific manner, but the geologist heard none of it. His ears had homed in on Charles and John Olmsted, utterly disturbed. Each word that dropped from their tongues blackened his heart like venom. A torrent of ire might have inundated him without his strong equanimity. Even Edward Rhys, who entertained Felix with happy compliments and attainable prestige, did not detect the burgeoning animosity in his friend.

"Now, wouldn't that be lovely, Felix?" Dr. Rhys concluded as if all were heard. "Even merry old England will fall to her knees before you."

The older gentleman's words tumbled to the wayside as Felix whitened his knuckles into fists. "*Oui*, yes, Edward, I couldn't agree more. Will you please excuse me for one moment? I deeply apologize."

Felix stepped to Charles and pulled him aside where none harkened but Hershel, allowing Olmsted and Rhys to rejoin and bask in the glory of the dragon.

"What are you doing?" Felix hissed.

"Discussing business with John Olmsted. What do you think I'm doing?"

"I think you're acting roguishly, conducting private transactions without my involvement."

"Did you eavesdrop on my conversation?"

"How could I not with how loud you appear to be conspiring against me? Not once did my name arise in your elaborate plans with Olmsted, who, parenthetically, appears to have ignored my involvement in this discovery."

"Pshaw! Felix, that is nonsense."

"Sense, Charles, complete sense! If I had not fallen into that cave, the existence of dragons would persist as a myth."

"You would never have fallen into that cave if not for my generous invitation to climb and explore Mount Rainier."

"Oh, you believe the recognition is exclusively yours simply because it was your idea to climb a volcano, a stunt you wouldn't have dared endeavor without my accompaniment. Go to hell, Charles. You know very well that without my cooperation, that dragon would still sleep behind a slate of andesite, not to mention that it was me who orchestrated our plans and oversaw the entire excavation with all concomitant labors."

"Felix, you goddamn fool "

"Gentlemen," Dr. Rhys interjected. "Is there a problem?"

"No, no problems here." Charles's voice pitched too high. "Isn't that right, Dr. Beauchamp?"

Felix bit his lip, shielding his embarrassment. "No trouble at all, Edward."

Hershel guarded the dragon while Olmsted treated Charles, Felix, and Dr. Rhys to a hot meal at one of

Ashford's charming little inns. Naturally, the high-profile architect quickly complained about the savorless food, condemning the aloofness of the village in a buoyant manner.

While Olmstead and Charles discussed prospects, Dr. Rhys gloated about his latest project at the local university. Although Felix appeared intrigued by his friend's exploits, his attention remained on the deceitful agreements resounding from the other end of the table. Each of Olmsted's little promises felt like a snub and a stab at Felix's dream. And in no time at all, Charles seemed to fatten with exultation. His head looked like a hot-air balloon fueled by fantasy gas. Felix did all he could to avoid striking across his dinner plate and gouging the man's eyes.

"The Alaska-Pacific-Yukon Exposition will be quite extravagant," Dr. Rhys exclaimed. "John's employee, James Frederick Dawson, is the principal architect for the fair. I believe his contribution, as well as that of Howard and Galloway, will prove successful. John will return to Massachusetts soon, but not before unveiling the dragon to Seattle's elite. It will be a marvelous spectacle. But it won't end there, Felix. In the waning days of the exposition, I will contact some friends at Yale and the Smithsonian."

Felix turned to him. "Yale? The Smithsonian?"

"Again, only after Mr. Olmsted and his collaborators exhibit your dragon. The exposition will last for a few months. Afterward, we should be able to transfer the fossils by train to the East Coast, although I cannot guarantee anything just yet."

"No, but he can." Felix discreetly nudged his head toward the landscape designer.

"Don't fret about him, old friend. He's just a businessman, a mind of economics ever in flux. The rest of us, however, are rock-solid scientists. And scientists must stick together."

Felix sipped his coffee and shot a glance at Charles. "Not all adhesives endure, Edward." He slowly rose from his chair. "Gentlemen, please excuse me for one moment. I need to step outside."

Felix felt refreshed by the crisp mountain air. However, it did not alleviate the plight that bedeviled him. Was his partner's actions a genius marketing scheme, or was Charles truly deliberating secret benefits with Olmsted? Over their eight-year friendship, Felix had observed that Charles Attwood maintained an aura of perplexity with the hope of appearing so clever or intelligent that it rendered him mysterious.

Contrarily, Charles consistently failed to conceal his ambitions for global recognition, but neither had he previously shown symptoms of disloyalty. Rather than suffer ridicule before publication like Marcelino Sanz de Sautuola with his finding of the cave at Altamira, Charles yearned to stake his claim as the Hernán Cortés of paleontology. He yearned to discover the unbelievable and exploit it to the highest degree for the greatest rewards. Anything for a dream.

On the other hand, Felix felt like Nikola Tesla when he began to butt heads with Thomas Edison. After all, he's the one who found the dragon, then labored with a rough cohort of miners and lumberjacks on the mountain, one of whom nearly killed him. It was he whose blood boiled with frustration and dubiety throughout the entire excavation project. And for what, to have his quasi-embellished partner sweep him aside and stamp his name on the discovery?

"I will not ebb to his shadow," Felix growled to the wind before returning to the table and polishing off his plate with a straight face. Charles and John Olmsted had wrapped up their privy exchange and now gaily discussed American paleontology with Dr. Rhys. As dinner concluded, a plan came to fruition. In the morning, Olmsted and Rhys would ride to Brown's Junction to secure a railcar while Felix, Charles, and Hershel would load the fossils into the wagon. Once the group reunited, they would transport the dragon to the railroad depot, set out for Tacoma, then transfer trains to Seattle. No one disagreed, especially Felix Beauchamp.

In the night, while everyone slept, Felix remembered the last words of John the Nisqually. *It belongs to the Spirit of Tahoma. Abducted from its bed of rock, it will bring misery to those who deny it peace.* Were these supernatural forces now arbitrating the situation, ruining Felix's dream? Or was Charles capriciously deceiving him without a morsel of respect? Perhaps these possibilities were working concurrently or were simply the same thing from a different perspective.

Felix brooded until a satisfying solution crept into his mind and prodded his gut. "Dreams change," he whispered to the cool air of his cabin bedroom, justifying his idea. "Sages of all cultures and eras claim that one may discover fame and fortune yet never unearth contentment in themselves. Without peace, wealth is worth no more than dust. And I, for one, would prefer a lifetime of peace over the evanescence of pleasure. But for peace, at this point, I must... hmm. Indeed, yes." He drew up his fur blanket and gazed at the ceiling. "I must become like Siegfried the warrior, who sought the golden treasure guarded by the dragon Fafnir."

~

Felix awoke, feeling calm and collected. He washed his face, dressed appropriately, swished some whiskey in his mouth, and roused Hershel from his slumber in the adjacent room. Within the hour following breakfast, per the established accord, Mr. Olmsted and Dr. Rhys rented horses and rode to Brown's Junction to acquire a railcar. In the meantime, Felix and Hershel labored in the dirt lot, bundling dragon bones together with twine and carefully placing them into bulky crates on the wagon. Charles stood nearby and watched, curious as to why his associate abstained from making conversation.

"Something the matter, Felix?"

"Nothing at all, Charles."

"Hershel, what's wrong with Dr. Beauchamp?"

"Nothing to my knowledge, Mr. Attwood."

"*Doctor* Attwood," Charles sternly corrected.

"Nothing to my knowledge, *Doctor* Attwood."

Charles sighed. "Felix, I've been talking with John Olmsted."

"I'm quite aware."

"Listen, friend. Mr. Olmsted understands and respects the business partnership you and I have formed. We share equal ownership of the dragon, fifty-fifty. In this sense, we are, by default, one enterprise.

Considering that, though not to stomp on toes, Olmsted and his architectural firm do not wish to associate with various representatives of a single organization or group. He prefers one delegate. Over the past two days, John has passionately voiced his endorsement of my business ethics and desires to continue affiliation with our partnership through me. Solely me."

Felix felt his cheeks redden. "All is clear as a crystal lake, Charles. Olmsted wants you to relinquish my allotted right to the dragon. He seeks to cut me out of the picture."

"Good gracious, no! You've misconstrued my context. You are still very much in the picture. In every ordeal regarding the dragon, *our* names will boldly stand abreast. Neither of us will gain recognition without the other. We are a team. I only mean to relay that John Olmstead, as a representative of his own company, wishes to consort with one person, which happens to be me."

"He bears no antipathy toward you, Felix. Trust me on this. Plus, your part of this project proved far more exhausting than mine. You labored so diligently on the mountain, inspiring me to undergo an equal level of exertion. Fifty-fifty."

"That is why you do not need to attend any business meetings or press conferences. I will tend to all matters. Your name will shine like the sun without effort on your part. You can even return to the University of Montreal with the knowledge that, in a few weeks, your name will stamp the front page of every newspaper from Seattle to Shanghai."

Felix remembered the Spirit of Tahoma and resisted exploding like a volcano. "You know what, Charles? You're right. I hear my curtain call. I do miss Montreal and should return to my primary profession. I will leave it to you to see this endeavor through. I trust you will advocate on my behalf with sheer gumption. You will not disappoint me."

"I am honored by your words, Felix, and revel in your gracious endorsement. Your faith in my championing warms my heart. Mr. Olmsted and Dr. Rhys have promised too much for their own good, but you can rest assured that I will demand outright fulfillment. Please, do not worry."

"I've no care in the world," Felix replied soberly.

Charles flashed a grin and headed back into Ashford.

Hershel suddenly broke his labor rhythm. "I must say, Dr. Beauchamp, that man is one conniving, narcissistic, son of a bitch. His plan to deceive you is plain as a rain cloud in the sky. I'm honestly shocked you let him talk to you like that. I would've broken his jaw if it were me. That bony white snake in the grass needs a good whooping, anything to remind him of his place in the world."

"Soon enough, Hershel, that bony white snake in the grass will receive a good whooping and remember his place. I guarantee it."

~

John Olmsted and Dr. Rhys returned from Brown's Junction around dusk. Olmsted had purchased a secure freight car that would attach to a small passenger train scheduled to arrive the following afternoon.

While Charles and Felix received this information, Hershel parked the wagon behind the inn, then cloaked it with thick cloth tarps weighed down by rope and stones. The scientists reconvened with him shortly afterward with some blankets and whiskey.

"These should suffice, Hershel," Felix said.

"Do you feel comfortable guarding the dragon all night?" Charles asked, worry and mistrust saturating his words.

Hershel laughed. "In this town, yes. I don't think anyone will come near me."

"Good, good," Charles exclaimed as he lifted his hat in farewell.

"Well, I'm off to get some shuteye," Felix causally relayed. "I'm exhausted. Don't hesitate to call me if you need assistance, Hershel."

Charles shifted to the lodge's veranda, watching Felix stroll across the main road into his cabin and shut the door. Charles then hurried to meet Olmsted and Rhys for supper at the biggest table the inn's proprietor offered. The meal lacked flavor, compensated by a handsome abundance of alcohol. Once his esteemed peers retired for the evening, Charles ventured outside to ensure Hershel remained on duty.

While rounding the perimeter of the inn, he glanced at Felix's cabin, its windows black and aura silent. His foot readied another step when his peripherals caught sight of a figure behind the logged residence. At first, the shadow crept lithely like a lone robber. Then, it bolted across the darkened village square. Suspicion incited Charles to pursue it in haste.

"Curse you, Felix, for your attempt at trickery," he muttered.

Charles maintained the trail for a few minutes, monitoring how the shadow propelled from wall to tree, tree to post, and so on. He sloppily mimicked its maneuvers until... nothing. He listened for anything abnormal but could only hear the acoustics of a typical woodland night. Frustration forced his lips to scrunch. Were paranoia and alcohol consumption unitedly potent enough to breed a single, hominid hallucination?

Feeling duped by his mind, Charles shook off his disgruntlement and retreated to the inn. Before climbing the steps of the veranda, his attention bent to a foggy store window from which streamed the glow of firelight. He slithered to the framed glass and gingerly rubbed away a circle of moisture. A burly gentleman with a long brown beard sat comfortably beside a table, pouring black powder into a small rust-colored cylinder. Charles felt relieved that it was not Felix, albeit he wondered why this man labored at such a late hour.

"Mr. Attwood," resounded a familiar, baritone voice.

Charles jumped backward and reached for the invisible gun in his belt, then realized it was Hershel who had scared him.

"Why are you out here past midnight, Mr. Attwood? It's mighty cold."

"It's *Doctor* Attwood! And never mind me. What are you doing? Aren't you supposed to be guarding the wagon?"

"I am guarding the wagon. It's right there." Hershel pointed to the inn.

Charles quickly discerned the buckboard in the bright blue moonlight, resting right where he had last seen it, still tightly sheathed.

"I'm so sorry, Dr. Attwood. I thought you were a stray drunk wandering in the night looking for a warm place to shelter. Once I recognized you, I came over to make sure you were in decent shape. You never know what or who might be lurking in the night."

Charles glanced at the wagon a second time. "Is Felix awake?"

"I doubt it, Sir. Far as I know, he's been in his cabin since we parted earlier. He did polish off his flask, so I reckon his head's still on the pillow."

"Very well," Charles conceded, inhaling deeply. "Back to your post, Hershel."

"Walking back right now, Mr. Attwood."

Charles gritted his teeth at that last remark, then returned to the lodge, yet felt troubled by a stream of bubbles pressing on his stomach lining. Accompanying this sensation was a strange suspicion that Hershel was concealing something. He wondered if the man plotted mischief, scheming to purloin a few fossils or conspiring to steal the whole dragon and reap all the rewards.

Charles sipped water from the cup on his bedside table before resting his head on the feather-stuffed pillow. He thought of Felix then, perceiving that the esteemed geologist had feigned his support and reluctantly agreed to Olmsted's contact preferences.

"Nevertheless," Charles whispered to his pillow, "Beauchamp is an honorable man, loyal as a soldier. It's Hershel I cannot trust."

~

In the morning, about an hour before their scheduled departure, Felix privately met with Charles, politely admitting his abhorrence toward John Olmsted. "I figured if we are to endure as business partners, I best come clean and divulge my feelings. So, there it is. Now you're aware."

Charles glowed with joy. "Believe me when I say there is no harm in your distaste for Mr. Olmsted. That is why I will be the one to tolerate and work with him. Oh Felix, my dear friend, I'm extremely grateful that you confessed your burden to me." He paused to scratch his chin. "Speaking of amicable integrity, I must inform you of something that troubles me. I believe Hershel is hatching a scheme. I caught him slacking on the job last night, wandering around town as if searching for someone or something."

"Worry no more, Charles. Hershel was only following my orders. I allowed him to recess if it pleased him, provided the wagon remained in view. A watchman acting fainéant on duty promotes confidence in bandits, enabling them to proceed incognizant of the prearranged snare."

"The only possible bandit in this far-flung neck of the woods is your henchman. How can you be sure he harbors no yearning to heist our dragon?"

75

Felix folded his arms. "Trust me, Charles, when I confidently say that Hershel will not loot the dragon. Neither will he betray our friendship. I've compensated him with enough crystals for a life of passivity and great luxury. Rest easy, friend."

Charles sighed acceptance with a lingering hint of skepticism, then clasped his associate's shoulder. "You're one of the good ones, Felix. Now, let's move that dragon to Seattle and become pioneers!"

An eight-mile dirt road connected Ashford to Brown's Junction, and although the surrounding forest did not obstruct the route, the wagon's weight slowed the driving horses.

Felix didn't mind the hour-and-a-half journey. This was a lovely little part of America. And although a white autumnal blanket covered the region, it was a beautiful sunny day. Hershel sat beside his employer in the driver's box while Charles, Mr. Olmsted, and Dr. Rhys perched comfortably in their saddles.

Felix tried to follow the Welshman's example and soak in the landscape through quiet observation but felt continuously bothered by Olmsted, who hardly quit tooting his honors and accomplishments. Naturally, Charles basked in the Swiss man's words as if he were John Muir or Theodore Roosevelt. Considering Olmsted's barrel of promises, Felix couldn't blame his knavish associate for acting like an enraptured lover. Regardless of any minor form of pity, Felix sustained his loathing of both men.

They soon arrived at Brown's Junction, a lumber village with a railroad depot at its heart. The train rested at the station platform with two coaches and three cattle cars, the last of which belonged to Mr. Olmsted. The depot manager approached the wagon as it pulled up beside the platform. "Carriage cars need to be loaded from the ramp on the other side," he demanded. "In the meantime, Mr. Olmsted, you and your guests may enter the second passenger car, number 102. I reserved it just like you asked."

"Thank you, Mr. Hammond." Olmsted handed the stationmaster a few coins. "Dr. Rhys, Dr. Attwood, please follow me aboard while Dr. Beauchamp and his friend load up our glorious prize."

Charles cleared his throat. "Let us be diplomatic, John. Dr. Beauchamp ought to board with us, wouldn't you agree? He is, after all, a shareholder in this grand endeavor."

"I concur," Dr. Rhys added.

Olmstead rolled his eyes toward Felix, who, standing beside Hershel and the wagon, stared at the freight carrier with a happy smirk. The landscape designer curtly nodded. "If that is your request, Charles, I will oblige you." He sighed. "Dr. Beauchamp, will you please join us? Mr. Hammond's laborers can help your man load the goods."

Felix shrugged in consideration. "I'm grateful for your kindness, but I feel it would behoove us all if I assisted in this process rather than people unfamiliar with the fragility of our cargo."

"Nonsense," Charles rebutted. "Let Hershel do his duty and take charge. That is why you paid him, correct?"

"Don't worry, Doc," Hershel whispered. "I can take care of this. Trust me. You'll get your peace."

"Are you sure? Some of these crates are too dangerous for one man to carry, especially the big one containing the skull."

"I've worked with danger since the day I followed you up that mountain, Dr. Beauchamp."

"All right." Felix slowly nodded and shook Hershel's hand. "Anything for a dream, right?"

"Anything for a dream, Doc."

While Hershel drove the wagon to the loading flank of the cattle car, Felix accompanied the others aboard the coach, wearing an impish half-grin.

"I don't trust your man," Charles whispered through his teeth as they filed down the aisle.

Felix stopped and turned to face him. "Then why didn't you let me help him?"

Charles hesitated. "The depot staff was paid well to ensure our cargo is completely secured."

"You paid them to watch Hershel? You really believe he would steal fossils?"

"These are the most valuable fossils ever discovered. Nothing can go wrong, do you understand, Felix? That is also why I need you here now."

"You don't trust me either."

Charles laughed under his breath. "You have me all wrong, Felix. It's just that you and I, we are scientists, and scientists must stick together."

"Not all adhesives endure, Charles."

Felix plopped his bottom upon a rear-facing bench, brought his ankle to a knee, and stroked his beard. Charles selected the adjacent window seat and leered at his partner while Dr. Rhys and Mr. Olmsted sat inversely. The four gentlemen remained mute until a passenger attendant stepped onto the coach and promptly offered to retrieve some spirits and smokes. Olmsted ordered cigars and wine for everyone. However, just as the attendant turned a heel, Felix raised his hand. "*Excusez-moi monsieur*, please abstain from bringing me wine. I will take a glass of your finest bourbon, neat."

"Dr. Beauchamp," Olmsted hissed as the server walked away, "you insult me. I ordered wine to celebrate our astounding business arrangement and the incredible discovery that made it possible. Wine is supposed to be a symbol of our impending fruition. Why would you impoverish my poetic gesture?"

"Now, now, John," Dr. Rhys remarked, hoping to calm the landscape designer.

"No, Edward, I have a right to know why he disgraces my generosity. His mind possesses alternative ambitions."

"Perhaps," Felix answered with a smile.

Charles frowned, his eyes abruptly alive with

suspicion.

"*Je plaisante!* I'm joking." Felix laughed. "Please, Mr. Olmstead, you misjudge my motive. Whiskey is my victory drink. And bourbon, well, bourbon is my favorite."

Olmsted leaned forward in his seat. "You can drink whiskey after you partake in our toast with wine, Dr. Beauchamp. Ultimately, we are *all* victorious today and must share in the glory as equals."

"I'll keep to my bourbon, monsieur. I'm celebrating a personal victory."

Olmsted's mouth twitched while Charles's face tightened. Dr. Rhys, on the other hand, remained speechless, his eyes on the stagnant scenery beyond the window. Yet when the train blew its whistle a minute later to begin its journey to Tacoma, he turned to Felix with his brows bent curiously. "Is your friend not joining us?"

"Unfortunately, no. Hershel served his purpose with unrelenting honor. But he has a life to live elsewhere, a good life. Although, I am certain our paths will cross again."

Charles squinted out the window as the train rounded its first bend. "I see him now. He's waving at us from the driver-box of your wagon."

Felix tapped his chest with his right hand. "It's his now."

"He has a bulbous sack beside him and a brown satchel in his hand."

"Compensation," Felix replied with mirth in his voice. "Healthy compensation."

An instant later, the passenger attendant entered the room from the leading coach. A box of cigars, four glasses, a bottle of wine, and a small flask of bourbon lay on his tray. He cut the cigars and passed them around before pouring each man a glass of wine. Of course, Felix denied his offer and said, "I believe the bourbon is for me."

The server exited the coach, leaving the four gentlemen alone. As cigar smoke clouded the ceiling and with his eyes on Charles, John Olmsted lifted his glass into the air. The others did likewise. "To the dragon," he announced, "The greatest discovery in history."

"To the dragon," echoed the others.

A terrible and explosive thunder suddenly rocked the train. Debris blasted like meteorites through windows and into the surrounding forest. Mr. Olmsted and Dr. Rhys tossed their wine glasses aside, dropped to the floor, and covered their heads, shouting for God to protect them. Charles pressed a cheek to the cracked window as the train braked with a scream.

"No," he cried. "Not my dragon. Not my dragon! Now I'll never be famous. I'll never get to prove to the world that they truly existed."

Still seated as if immune to the tumult and bearing a soft smile of contentment, Felix adjusted his spectacles, puffed his cigar, and hoisted his glass of bourbon into the air. "*À la santé et à la paix!* Anything for a dream."

A
PUZZLE
PLAY

Dear Lyov,

I am sorry I do not write as often as I should. It's hard to get letters across the border these days. Every mail car is thoroughly inspected. Many are uncoupled from their prescribed trains and sent to Leningrad or Moscow. I pray this letter and all others I've sent over the years have reached your hands.

Whether you've chosen to stop writing to me or the patrols confiscated them, I do not know. Even if state security has robbed and read our letters, they have yet to reveal any hostility. And should Joseph Stalin ever decide that my life offends him, he and his henchmen are more than welcome to visit me. Let them learn the truths I endure. Nevertheless, Lyov, I pray you have not forgotten your mother, how much I care for you, how much I love you. You are still my treasured son, my one and only star.

Speaking of truths, I never told you what happened to your father. Long have I kept it secret, fearing how you might react and carry it in your heart. No longer can I bottle this up, especially with how frightening things have become here. It makes me sad. Yet, a part of me thanks God every day for giving you to my Finnish cousins before the coming of what I now believe to be the worst of times in Russia. Anyway, this letter, this story, which I form from old journal entries and input from memories, might shed light on any questions or doubts you harbor. I hope it unburdens you as I pray it unburdens me.

Before I turn back the clock, let me give you my perspective on your father, Yakov Brevsky, and some details on his past, which I do not believe we discussed while you were young. Your father was my sun and moon, circling and illuminating my heart, day and night. He was a provider, a joker, a craftsman, and a fine father to you. He had the necessary qualities to render him what some might call a good and honest man. Of course, we are all flawed in some respects.

Your father fiercely believed that a man should work to support the household over which he presides as owner or ruler. I'm unsure why he followed this old mentality since his mother spent just as much time in the field as his father. Nevertheless, because of this conviction, Yakov never found his way around the kitchen. Even chicken noodle soup proved a challenge for the ages.

His spelling chopped words into pieces, forcing him to seek help whenever he wished to scribe a letter to his brother in Minsk. He was lucky I enjoyed writing. Another imperfection was that he did not know how to fold or wash clothes. And above all, he did not take kindly to losing games. Neither did he appreciate my aptitude for solving puzzles. I suppose I would be a liar if I claimed our marriage seemed perfect, but I still believe it was beautiful, despite the madness before the end.

In 1908, when Yakov was twenty-four years old, his parents booted him off their farm for becoming too lazy, so he went to Petrograd to find work and prove them wrong. On this same day, a frightened horse broke from its carriage and charged through the city streets like a bull. Your father had just exited a barber shop when the horse came rushing toward him. My father, Arvo, shoved him out of the way, saving his life. I happened to be with my father that day, so upon thanking him, Yakov noticed me, smiled, and asked if he could court me.

"Got a job?" my father asked. "No? Well, it takes dirty hands and strong wood to build a house. No working life, no loving wife."

Yakov asked for our address, which my father gave with a nod, apparently recognizing the young man's determination. Certain as the sky is blue, Yakov showed up on our doorstep in the country the following afternoon, stating that he had found work. Arvo and Polina turned to me and asked what I thought of him. The rest is history.

The factory in Petrograd, now Leningrad, where your father spent most of his days, produced tools for the military and upcoming automotive plants. He neither hated nor loved his employer. And although they did not tolerate improvisation within the system, Yakov occasionally boasted of minor achievements while in uniform. I took his word for it since he neither invited me to visit the facility nor introduced me to any of his peers. I presumed his career, while often dreary and tedious, filled any voids beyond our family's scope. As you might recall, we did not necessarily need the money, but he felt his job kept us all happy and healthy.

Yakov held to his daily routine with the precision of a Swiss watch, never chancing to diminish his reputation as a man of punctuality. He awoke around four o'clock to wash his face and dress, usually tiptoeing about so as not to disrupt my slumber. Once in uniform, he slunk to the kitchen for tea and bread with butter, cheese, and a piece of dried meat, sometimes an apple or handful of berries if in season.

He would then smoke a cigarette on the porch before driving out of the country and into the city. He typically returned around a quarter-to-three in the afternoon with greasy brows and oil-stained clothes, although he reassured me more than often that he at least washed his hands before leaving the factory. Stepping through the doorway, Yakov would smile at your grandmother, then pat your head, if you recall, and kiss my cheek before pouring himself a small glass of vodka, which accompanied him to the bathtub.

Once clean and dressed for the evening, and I hope you remember this better than anything in your childhood, your father would spend time with you, usually outside for play or teaching you survival skills or making a game out of shooting the birds that lingered in our miserable little garden. You two often refused to return inside when the weather was warm, forcing me to stomp onto the porch and nag about your cooling supper.

Once his belly bulged with satisfaction, Yakov typically found his way to the storage room to tinker with clocks and strange devices, slowly honing his dream craft as an inventor. When projects on the workbench proved too frustrating, he relaxed by the hearth and read books or rolled cigarettes. Depending on the weather, he drove to the closest village twice weekly to drink with friends. That was Yakov's life. It worked for him, and it worked for me.

On a frosty day in late October 1916... wait, no, scratch that. I cannot start the story just yet. I should also give you some history of myself and my side of the family. Although I'm sure, by now, you have conjured up a bank of devilish images about me. However, those may be based on fading memories, old emotions, and new opinions. Therefore, I feel it might help you to understand my way of thinking, at least how I used to think.

As you may recall, unlike your father, I spent my days at home. I felt complacent, never troubled by the urge to adventure beyond my known world, and for good reason. The house in which we lived, the same beneath whose degrading roof I now write, had been constructed by my father, Arvo, where he and your grandmother, Polina, raised me to the best of their abilities.

Arvo Laukkanen lived an enterprising but righteous existence, the runt of an affluent family that owned enormous swaths of land and several reindeer farms near Lappeenranta in Finland. Rather than wear their wealth bombastically like their peers, the Laukkanen family humbly revealed it through exceptional generosity.

While my father loved his family very much, he yearned to create a life devoid of their golden strings, ever striving to prove himself the strongest among his five brothers. He began his divergence in 1884 by leaving his Finnish fiancé for Polina, a Russian nurse he met in Kotka. Although his ambition hastily moved him to her home village across the border, his heart still forced a hand to keep ritual contact with his family in Finland.

He never minded their letters, but often scoffed or cursed whenever they sent us gifts, which always seemed abnormally handsome. When they imported a new Wolseley-Siddeley from England and made us the proud owners of an automobile, Arvo burst with such anger that he loaded up his best rifle and shot the tires to ensure that no one could drive it.

After a fever took Arvo's life in the summer of 1910, my Laukkanen cousins began delivering us monthly rations of food and chopped wood, occasionally throwing in clothing or foreign trinkets. Unlike my father, Yakov and I gratefully embraced their hospitality. They supplied us so amply that, after a year, we realized we no longer needed Russian goods. We received everything at no cost from Finland.

Following your birth, a few months after my father's passing, I advocated moving to Finland to live closer to my cousins. My mother argued that my father had built our house to perpetuate his legacy of prideful separation through my children and me. Yakov agreed. Therefore, we stayed in the hinterland of the Karelian Isthmus, about thirty-five kilometers north of Petrograd.

Even though we had an abundance of quality necessities, and I mentioned this earlier, your father opted to uphold his position at the factory. I should have protested, but his happiness supplied my contentment. Besides wanting to live near my Finnish relatives, I harbored little adoration for change. In fact, I might just say that I dreaded change and prayed daily for the continuation of a peaceful life. Unfortunately, change is an essential part of nature that no human can genuinely challenge, even when it enters our homes, especially when we fear it.

Now, Lyov, I will begin the story.

~

On a frosty day in late October 1916, Yakov came home a tad later than usual. He greeted us as he normally would, ate a small lunch, bathed, and spent time with you in the yard. While he seemed his ordinary self, I detected a spark of apprehension in him. I stared at him from across the table during supper, hoping he would consider my abnormal lull. He eventually offered me a familiar smile to convey a sense of delight, yet his eyes housed a tale I yearned to understand.

"Yakov, did something happen at work today?"

"Something always happens at work," he jested.

"No, I mean, did anything out of the ordinary occur?"

"Yes, but I have faith that a remedy is underway." A momentary grin pushed his cheeks up and shrunk his eyes. "Please, don't worry about it, Sinikka, my sweet golden-haired angel. Trust that nothing will change for us here. I love you."

"I love you, too." I sighed in relief and returned to my meal.

Yakov did not go out that evening, which I thought odd, considering he drove to the village every Tuesday and Friday to drink and play cards with a few comrades. Neither did he tinker in the storage room. Instead, he sat by the hearth with a glass of milky vodka and rolled cigarettes. I presumed it to be a simple coping method to alleviate the stress he endured at the factory that day. I thought, who doesn't occasionally take on a monotonous task to numb their mind?

The following week, everything seemed better than usual. Your father glowed with such jubilance that I felt he might surprise me with a handsome gift. And he did, a bouquet, which he gave me on Wednesday. Then, he tried to fold clothes with me on Thursday and help me cook dinner on Friday. What a week! I felt nothing short of joy.

Yet this wave of bliss began to crash on a snowy afternoon in early November when he stepped into the house with a frown slashed into his round face. Before I could ask about his mood, he suppressed the emotion with a laugh and kiss, then went about his daily routine as if nothing pestered him. Not that I was his mother, but my maternal instincts told me something was amiss. Maybe there had been trouble with a colleague, or his employer had chosen to spit nasty words his way. Then again, he hardly divulged anything that happened at work besides small feats and pleasant irregularities.

As I mentioned earlier, I understood little of the world beyond my four walls in those days. I knew of evil kings and empires and a terrible war raging across Europe, although Yakov made it sound like all of it was far away and beyond our concern. Still, I could not help but wonder if the growing international war milled his emotions and, therefore, his mood. I brushed the notion aside, feeling that Yakov would have, at the very least, prepared us to leave if such dangers approached.

After supper, Yakov left to drink with his comrades. He ordinarily spent two or three hours out and about, but I fell asleep waiting for him that night. I don't remember what time he got home. My lids cracked to the soft sounds of him sliding into bed. He assumed I was asleep since I didn't move when he spooned his body to mine. I wondered what had kept him out for so long. My imagination ran through several scenarios, each more distressing than the last. However, I had never been one to give in to disappointment, especially in my relationship with Yakov. Without profound justification, I denied the surfacing of such an emotion. Therefore, with exertion, I cast aside all negative thoughts.

Yakov left the house right on schedule despite his nearly sleepless night. Shoving away my increased worries again, I went about my day, which began with a visit from my two favorite Finnish cousins. Unable to resist showcasing their young, gentlemanly charm, Elias and Taavi Laukkanen greeted me with smiles, kisses, and "*Moi, kaunis serkku, Sinikka!*" How nice it is to be called beautiful while receiving a box of pastries. Taavi claimed that his wife produced the most exquisite sweets in Finland. With the delectable flavor of wild raspberry and French vanilla in my mouth, I could not argue no matter how much I prided myself as a skillful baker.

While Elias and Taavi unloaded crates of food and supplies from their truck, they informed me of some crop shortages in Finland and that their reindeer were not fattening properly. I sympathized but didn't think much of it. Fortunately, despite the war, their wealth allowed them to import goods from Scandinavia, Britain, Holland, France, and America. I felt like a worldly woman, having gained the opportunity to taste the foods of foreign nations. Then again, I could not remember the last time I had eaten something produced in Russia other than the onions, carrots, and beets from our garden, not to mention the bread I baked every few days.

Once my cousins had emptied their truck and brought everything inside the house, they hugged me, proclaimed "*Nähdään pian, Sinikka*," and returned to Finland. Not sure if you recall, Lyov, but you and I sifted through several crates with my mother, shelving as much as we could before your father came home.

Halfway done, I remember breaking open a tin of Earl Grey and inhaling the refreshing, citrusy scent of black tea with bergamot oil. I nearly melted to the floor. When Yakov stepped through the front door that afternoon, I pranced toward him with a steaming cup. "Look what Elias and Taavi brought this time, Earl Grey from England! And there are other fantastic goods from across the Baltic."

"That's nice, Sinikka," he huffed. "I will pass on the tea. I want to eat. I'm hungry."

I should have questioned him, yet I let it slide like water over rocks. I shrugged and drank the tea while he ate his lunch in silence. He drove out again that evening, but instead of heading east to the village, he veered south toward the main road that led to the city. I had been lying in bed for a few hours when he finally returned home. I thought he would speak. Instead, he kissed my neck softly, placed his head on the pillow, and shut his eyes. I wanted to rouse him and ask why he went away for two consecutive nights. Unfortunately, I could not bring myself to interrogate him, especially once he spent the next night at home.

However, he hopped in the Wolseley the following evening. He did the same on Sunday, Monday, Tuesday, and Wednesday. He stayed home and tinkered into the small hours on Thursday, although I could not make out the usual clinking sounds. On Friday, he didn't come back from work. I remember you asking me repeatedly, "When's Papa going to be home?" I felt the dark flower of fear beginning to burgeon in my stomach. How could I answer you when I knew nothing?

Yakov eventually snuck in around midnight, opening the bedroom door to find me sitting up with the lamp ablaze. "Where were you?" I hissed, unable to endure another night without an answer. "I've been worried sick."

"I was working, Sinikka," he answered casually while slowly stripping away his thick winter clothes. "Working very hard."

"You work five to two, Yakov. Less of a shift than most laborers these days."

"Darling, there's been many issues at the factory."

"Like what?"

He chewed on air for a moment. "A few employees recently decided to take some time off, so I've been covering for them. Nothing I cannot handle, my love."

He looked me straight in the eyes. "You do not need to worry. Just stay here and take care of Lyov as you always have. Be strong and happy."

I considered his sharp gaze and chaperoning words. A surge of gall rushed to the tip of my tongue, but the loyalty in my heart restrained any wild thoughts from escaping. I loved your father to the point of agony, and I knew that he loved me just as much. In all our years together up to that point, Yakov never lied to me.

Therefore, I let my insecurities tumble to the wayside and smiled at him. Finding a small form of acceptance, I pressed my palms to his clean-shaven cheek with my fingertips and bent my neck back to expose some skin. I felt his mood shift, a weary but triumphant laugh in his breath. He leaned in to kiss me. Without disrupting his passion, I turned off the lamp.

November raced by, and December followed hot on its heels. Yakov worked his regular day shift and returned home to begin his afternoon routine, only to drive back to the city four nights out of the week, usually climbing into bed around eleven o'clock. We were blessed with a beautiful Christmas, although I thought with all the extra hours your father had endured, he would have earned more money for more gifts.

You and I received only a handful of things compared to the prior year, some new utensils for the kitchen and a pair of winter hats woven by locals in

Novgorod. It's not that I needed presents from Yakov, considering we received plenty of goods from my cousins. Instead, his inexpensive purchases caused me to consider what he did with his excess wages and where he stored them, especially since he was not fond of banks. Before my imagination caught on, I swallowed my prejudice with the shortsighted presumption that he kept everything in a safe in the storage room.

The first few days of 1917 seemed quiet and pleasant despite the frightening news of war that Yakov carried home tucked under his arm. He continued his newer routine complacently. Mama felt more ill than usual, but the British tea and imported food helped heighten her awareness. You, Lyov, had grown a *ladon* since I last measured you in September, a pinch over 7.5 centimeters by today's standards. I reminded you each morning that you would become a strong, working man with keen intelligence like your father and grandfather.

Yet, as your mother, I could never forgive myself if I allowed you to go through life without learning housekeeping skills. My grandmother once told my father Arvo that husbands, at any cost of social status or wallet girth, should know how to support a household just as a wife should be familiar with carpentry or factory labor. Unlike Yakov, unable to cook or write without help, I wished to mold you to impress. Women like a man who strives to provide for them. They also relish a partner who knows his way around the kitchen or garden, how to work a broom, and, of course, take care of children. With grooming you properly as one of my new goals, I felt that 1917 would be a wonderful year.

At the start of the second week of January, I became aware of an anomaly in Yakov's new schedule. Whenever he returned from his five-to-two shift, he wore his blue uniform stained with oil, yet he left for his second shift, the one to cover missing employees, garbed much more casually. I observed him over the coming days to confirm my suspicion that this was not a one-time occurrence. Black trousers, a shirt, a coat, and boots every evening, but no uniform. I felt not only alarmed but stupid for not having noticed it before.

Upon further consideration, I remembered Yakov once explaining that anyone who came to work without their designated suit would face severe penalties. I reminded my brooding self that I knew very little about his job, let alone his life beyond our house, except what he divulged to me. Perhaps I contemplated too intensely, for a wave of anxiety soon rolled over my mind, and I suddenly felt lost.

I didn't know what to think of my husband. The emotion felt alien, and I hated it. Never had I suffered the urge to challenge the integrity of a family member, especially the love of my life. And yet, I said nothing. I knew that I needed to be more inquisitive and confront Yakov directly. I really should have. It would have saved me a lot of grief. Then I remembered the tragedy of Mariya Galkin.

Barely a month before, I had been sweeping the porch when I saw a funeral carriage pass along the nearby road. Not much occurred in our part of the country, so concern drove me to see who had died. Turned out that Mariya Galkin, an old friend who I had not seen in years despite that she lived just down the road, had drunk herself to death. I was told that her husband, Boris, had been sleeping with two women and that when Mariya asked him about the red marks on his neck, he beat her bloody, took their two little girls, and never returned. I did not question whether this story was true, but it wasn't the first time I had heard of such an incident, so I believed it.

Mariya's death had instilled such fear in me that my gut twisted and hardened into a wall that denied me a voice. Like many peasant women in those days, I felt scared to lose anything. A man could beat his wife or leave and take what he wanted since he was considered the head of the household and the legal owner of all possessions, including children. Long had women been fighting for more rights, especially in the cities. Yet, in the rural country, little had changed. And although I knew my husband and loved him, too many stories like Mariya's had stricken me with a deep, unparalleled terror.

I did my best to feign normality over the coming days. I must have appeared proficient as a thespian, for Yakov neither questioned me nor showed any signs of doubt. Then again, he did not linger in the house long enough to notice whether I maintained old habits. By the middle of January, he visited the city every night of the week with lengthened hours. Notwithstanding a constant and severe lack of sleep, he frequently rushed out of the house as early as four o'clock and returned as late as one or two in the morning. My dreams, once serene, slowly mutated into nightmares, each one more harrowing than the last. I started to consider their meanings. Maybe the events that haunted my sleep alluded to what my husband did behind my back.

A moment of impulse seized me one morning in late January. After asking you to help your grandmother clean the kitchen and organize our canned foods, I grabbed a lantern from the closet and snuck into the storage room. I first noticed that the floor needed sweeping and that crates of failed projects lined the dark perimeters. Metal scraps, wood shavings, tools, toys, candles, papers, and dust-bound books lay scattered across two work benches like the remains of a miniature city recently ravaged. Cobwebs clung to corners. The musky scents of dust and rat feces stung my nostrils.

I felt certain that the proof I needed to convince myself to accost Yakov hid in this cluttered tinkerer nest. I scoured the room, sifting through boxes and bins. I peeled open decaying tomes and pried out cubbies. I lifted and overturned objects hoping to find a secret compartment. I dug through newspaper piles and tubs filled with your old baby clothes. Although I sensed the lunacy of my actions nibbling at my brain, I knew I could not give up, no matter how badly I wanted to weep. A scream lodged in my throat. My hands began to tremble. Then, a sigh of relief. I found it.

My eye caught a faint gleam peeking from behind a wooden tool chest on the floor. I put the lantern down and moved the trunk. An iron safe sat upon a throne of timber planks, its steel handle well-polished and gears greased. A padlock clung to two parallel metal loops holding the door tightly to its frame. I wondered, how did he get this in here without my knowing? The question dissolved when I noticed the hoop of a small key inserted into the base of the lock. I turned it with prudence, removed the fastening, and lifted the handle. My muscles tensed as the safe slowly opened. And there it sat, *nothing*.

I found it extremely difficult to believe my eyes. Knowing that your father loathed banks, if he had been working more than his usual shift, his excess wages would have been right there in the safe. Considering that my cousins generously supplied our house with imports, we had little need for domestic goods. Therefore, with next to nothing for Yakov to purchase, I assumed all his money would be saved. But if that was truly the case, where did he keep it? I knew every nook and cranny in our house. He could never hide anything from me except, of course, in the storage room, where I rarely ventured. I felt certain I would uncover his money and prove the legitimacy of his overtime hours. Yet there I stood, shaking my head.

"Nothing," I whispered as if it were a curse. "Yakov has nothing. He lied to me. But what does this mean?"

As the day rolled on, I rummaged through a few scenarios on how to go about asking Yakov why he lied. If I blurted accusations, he would probably deny them, fabricate an excuse, and lecture me about my ignorance. If I admitted that I raked through his stuff without proof of purpose, he might grow angry and leave the house or worse.

I thought of Mariya Galkin. Predictions would be effortless if I felt confident in his honesty, as always. Unfortunately, this was not the case. I remained the stymied detective, nervous but desperate for clues to solve this puzzle. Having enjoyed reading mystery tales when I was young, I knew I needed at least two evidence samples to lend weight to my argument. But where to begin?

I drew myself a bath. My father used to tell me that sitting in hot soapy water clears the mind of distress. I prayed it was true. I needed a new canvas to draft fresh thoughts and maneuvers to yield results. As I relaxed in the water, smoking a cigarette, I inadvertently glanced at the heater.

The contraption, a Ruud Instantaneous Automatic

Water Heater, looked like a miniature steam engine standing on one end. Taavi had imported five of them from America after one of his trips out west - one for himself, one for Elias, another for their parents, one for cousin Orvokki, and one for me. With a little help from his comrade, Sergei, your father removed the old iron furnace, a relic that often froze in winter, and installed the American automated device. They rigged it to the house's piping structure, which my father had pieced while constructing the frame with my mother's father and brother. The system drew water from the clear creek just beyond our garden. Without such an incredible setup, and if not for my father's ingenuity and Taavi's immense generosity, I would still avoid baths during winter.

"Thank you, Papa," I whispered to the steamy air. "Thank you, Taavi." I suddenly felt a spark in the back of my brain. Taavi. Yes, yes. Taavi, Elias, and a hint of patience. I now knew how to solve the puzzle that was my husband's mischief. No longer would I remain soaked in the wintry waters of unawareness. The piping-hot truth drew near.

Two days later, my cousins arrived around ten o'clock with news, good and bad. The good news: I received a small box of Norwegian chocolate bars called Freia. The unwelcome news: the European continental markets closed due to the extremity of what was now called the Great War. Therefore, the only goods Elias and Taavi could secure and deliver originated in the Nordic countries. Although the supplies appeared less extravagant than average, yet still decent quality, my cousins assured me it would only last until the end of February. They had hoped that the chocolate surprise would ease any apprehension. It did.

Once all the wooden crates of usual goods were inside the house, Elias and Taavi bid farewell and started toward their truck. I followed them beyond the snow-coated porch and stopped them before they could open their doors.

"I need a favor," I exclaimed in Finnish.

Taavi sighed. "Sinikka, we love you very much, but we are already doing you a favor by driving a good distance once a month with a truck full of food and supplies. It's getting a little dangerous. This winter is harsh, and the war is spreading quickly."

"Please, just do this one thing for me."

Elias shook his head. "Sinikka, we do not have the time to-"

"Yakov is living a double life," I cried, my eyes welling. "At least, I think so."

They glanced at each other with their mouths agape until Elias lifted a brow in my direction. "A double life, you say? For how long?"

"Months."

Taavi drummed his fingers on the truck and stepped forward. "Do you have any idea of what he might be doing? Do you have any proof?"

"I'm seeking the answer to both questions, though my heart tells me I'm right."

Taavi kicked a tuft snow. "What do you need from us?"

"Yakov drives the only automobile we own, but you have a truck."

Elias scratched his chin. "It sounds like you want us to follow him."

"*Kyllä*. That's exactly right. I need you to observe where he goes and who he sees."

After a moment of silent consideration, the brothers agreed.

While waiting for Yakov to return from his primary work shift, my cousins occupied the day with Polina, you, and me. They would later thank me for keeping them around as they thoroughly enjoyed spending time with us, drinking tea, eating chocolate, and sharing humorous stories. I loved my family so much that my eyes watered every time we burst into laughter at once. I had dozens of cousins in Finland who I had not seen since before my father's passing, but even the two that regularly visited so rarely lingered to socialize.

Oh, how I wished to leave Russia and live close to them! Life would have been more comfortable and refreshing. How could it not be? Elias and Taavi affably occupied my attention to the point that I needed to remind myself of the present puzzle. Yakov never really appreciated my problem-solving skills.

Every time we played games, he became a sore loser.

About an hour past noon, I advised Elias and Taavi to drive their truck to the trees on the hill just west of the property. Growing up on a vast reindeer farm, they knew how to watch for wolves from a good vantage point and hunt in hazardous weather conditions.

Therefore, they patiently awaited Yakov's arrival and second departure. As expected, your father came home, ate, bathed, spent time with you, and went out again around five o'clock. I peered through the window just as the lights of the Wolseley veered south. My cousins raced past the house a minute later, holding their distance with the knowledge that so few people drove motorized vehicles, at least in those days. I prayed that Yakov remained blind to the pursuit and genuine toward me.

As the night persisted, my mind swelled with sour thoughts and immoral possibilities. I sat with my mother after tucking you into bed. "I think I have gout," she muttered unexpectedly. "My father, your *dedushka*, had gout by the time he turned fifty-four. And his mother suffered from gout at a younger age. I don't know if it's coincidence or natural."

Barely managing to poke a hole in my stormy thoughts, I smiled at my mother. "I'm sorry, Mama. Maybe your side of the family overeats fish and sweets or drinks too much alcohol."

"Alcohol, certainly! If I were younger, I'd abandon drinking or at least calm down, but I'm old, and life is too short to forgo simple pleasures."

"Well, before Elias and Taavi bring us supplies again, I'll have them speak to a physician and get some medicine for you."

"There's no good medicine in our cold cut of the world, dear." She bobbed her head and lent me a soft grin that stretched the wrinkles of her long laugh lines. "You know, it's days like today that a tiny part of me wishes we had moved to Finland. I never told you this, but Arvo often mentioned returning to Lappeenranta or Kotka. Your cousins own vast estates, you know. I'm sorry I pushed you and Yakov into staying here. It's just that Russia is my home and your home, and your father built "

"Not right now, Mama, please."

"I'm just glad that my beautiful daughter won such a loyal and respectable husband. He reminds me a lot of your father, you know."

I held my breath and marched straight into the kitchen to fix a glass of vodka, then hastened to my room and shut the door. I don't remember the rest of that night. I don't recall Yakov coming home or even falling asleep. However, I do remember waking up as he prepared himself for work. My mouth spewed a few sentences, but they came out all bedraggled. He responded gently and kissed me before leaving. I must have conked out again, for I soon opened my eyes to your handsome face and little hands shaking my shoulder. "Mama, mama, it's time to get up. I'm hungry." Feeling sluggish, I put my feet on the floor and briefly massaged my face. My head throbbed a bit, though not enough that I couldn't dress and cook breakfast for you, my darling innocent.

After breakfast, you and I went outside to shovel snow off the garden. We had planted four handfuls of tiny seeds back in autumn, hoping to yield at least fifty onions and beets. We had taken an hour out of each day ever since to check on the slow-growing crops. We nearly finished the task when my cousins pulled up in their truck. A wave of dread washed over me as they walked toward the garden with long, wan faces. I knew the answer before the words became real. Elias took you to play by the frozen creek while Taavi and I stood like scarecrows among the struggling onion and beet sprouts.

"We followed Yakov into Petrograd," he began while pocketing his gloved hands. "He wove through several dim-lit streets before entering the industrial district. He parked beside a huge factory and hurried inside. We posted between lamp poles to remain out of sight. He didn't show his face for some time, so we figured he was working and would stay there for a while."

"Just as we decided to leave, he appeared, exiting the building with two gentlemen in fur coats and woolen caps. After shaking their hands, he cranked the Wolseley's engine and took off. We immediately cranked our truck up and pursued him to a housing complex somewhere outside the Vyborgsky District. He parked on the street next to a buggy and two other vehicles, then stepped out more cautiously than a man trying to outmaneuver a pack of wolves." Taavi paused to glance at you chasing Elias by the creek.

"Where did he go, Taavi? You must tell me."

"He walked to the front door of the complex and knocked. Even from a distance, he looked nervous and shaky, as if he knew he was doing something wrong. About a minute later, a red-haired woman opened the door. She smiled at Yakov, touched his forearm, and kissed him."

"Where did she kiss him?" I demanded.

"On the lips."

"For how long?"

Taavi cleared his throat. "Not long, a second, maybe two. Then she pulled him inside and closed the door. Elias and I were shocked and disappointed, and we both felt we should have gone after him." Taavi sighed, his weariness plain. "We decided to stay put, hoping he would leave as quickly as he arrived. Unfortunately, the hours passed, and we tried to stay alert, but our eyelids became heavy. I apologize, dear cousin. We fell asleep. By the time we awoke, the Wolseley had gone. We came straight here, didn't even stop for tea. Sinikka, I'm so sorry. I know you prayed for good news. Elias and I did too."

A tempest of emotions compounded and flooded me. Disorientation. Sorrow. Hatred. Hurt. I felt sick and thought of Mariya Galkin again and wondered what had roused her suspicions toward her husband, Boris. I did not know Boris well, but I had met him enough to learn that he possessed a cold heart, always cursing and yelling at his family, even in front of guests. Yakov, on the other hand, had always been warm, jovial, and caring.

One might think that an abusive spouse is more likely to sleep around, but cruelty is not attractive, especially not to lonely women. They crave affection, laughter, and the loving smile of a man who can make their heart bubble with joy. Yakov was such a man. And working in the city, he must have encountered eager women charmed by his wits and sparkling eyes. But would he have recognized such opportunities and acted upon them?

I had undoubtedly endured dreams of his treachery. However, my daytime mind could not imagine my husband beneath a sheet with another woman. Yet, my cousins had witnessed the truth. Yakov had betrayed me for a woman in the city, a devil woman with flaming hair. I felt like a complete and utter fool. Ten years of love and bliss reverted to hot ashes blowing in the wind. He betrayed me, betrayed you, our son. How could he have forsaken us? Weeping in Taavi's arms, I wondered about the duration of this atrocity. When and where did they first meet? Did he love her? Were there others before her or, worse, simultaneously?

"Dear cousin," Taavi whispered while stroking my hair. "For all we know, there is more to this than we witnessed."

"Highly unlikely," Elias commented as he and you returned to the garden.

"Mama, what's wrong?" you asked me in your finest Finnish.

I wept harder.

"Good job, Elias. Dolt! Now, look at what you did. I was trying to calm her."

"What's wrong with my Mama?" you whined, tugging at my coat while eying our cousins.

"Your mother is having a rough day."

"No, Taavi," Elias argued. "Do not hide what we saw. It was painfully obvious! Yakov is committing adultery, the gravest of sins. I'm sorry, Sinikka. Like you, we had prayed he would stay at the factory."

"What's adultery, Mama?" you asked, concern straining your sweet voice. "Did Papa do something bad?"

My heart shattered.

"We will explain that later," Elias answered sharply.

Taavi released me from his arms. "Is Yakov at work right now?"

"Yes," I blubbered.

Taavi lifted my chin. "Maybe it would be best if *we* talk to him."

"No, no, no, no, no," I protested, unable to form clear thoughts. "Please, just... just go to your wives and children. Go home. Thank you for all your help. I love you both very much. Please, go and be happy, and I will see you in a month, okay?"

"Sinikka." Elias touched my arm. "I think we ought to stay here for a few hours and keep you company."

"No," I said. "No, nothing can appear out of the ordinary. No one in Russia can learn of this. Not a single person can know that you were here today, not even my mother. You went back to Finland yesterday, as far as she's concerned. Lyov shouldn't even know." I looked at you, your blazing blue eyes staring up at me, shimmering with bewilderment.

"All right, all right," Taavi concurred. "We will leave, Sinikka, but you must be extremely careful. If we don't receive a letter from you within a few weeks, we'll be coming out here earlier than usual. At worst, we'll pack your bags and move you to Finland. We will protect you and Lyov. I promise."

I inhaled deeply and nodded. You did not understand, and I didn't have the wherewithal to word it correctly to you, so I merely said, "Someday." Taavi and Elias soon bid us farewell, climbed into their truck, and headed back to Finland. As they vanished around the forested hill to the west, I knelt in the snow and softly pressed my hands to your cheeks. I searched your eyes, vivid and welcoming like my father's, concealing wisdom in your shyness. I grinned and told you to go inside. "Give your *babushka* a big hug." You smiled at me and walked back to the house in silence.

After hearing the door shut, I broke down upon the cold earth, neither caring about the frosty bite nor the rumble in my stomach. I felt completely cloven, my son's purity polluted. If the world had swallowed me in that moment, I would have accepted with a fervent laugh.

~

Yakov joked with you and Polina at the dinner table. He included me in his merriment, to which I feigned smirks to keep his curiosity at bay, although I felt my lack of care proved all too plain at that point. I thought you might tell your father about what happened in the garden or at least Taavi and Elias's extended visit the day before. However, you instinctively acted the fool. Such a bright child. Even when Yakov asked about the origin of the goods my cousins delivered, you shrugged and looked to me for answers. It was then that your father decided to inquire about my passive attitude.

"I have a headache," I muttered, my tone as flat as my expression. "I should rest." Without finishing supper, I tossed my napkin on the table. "I'll clean up later."

I paced into the bedroom and collapsed upon the layers of blankets. My emotions surged to the surface, pressuring an explosion. "No," I told myself. "Crying is not an option." If Yakov saw me like that, he would feel obligated to interrogate me. I felt neither the wit nor strength to fight. I could only pray that he would stay home for the evening and keep to himself. Of course, luck did not favor me. He went out again.

The following week felt blurry as a blizzard in deep winter, a glass of violent thoughts and vodka. Yakov certainly noticed my indelicacy. On Thursday afternoon, he asked if I had been drinking more than usual. I sneered and threw myself into his leather lounge chair, sucking down half a cigarette as he turned his cheek and left. The clear river of love in which I once blithely swam now ran black as coal. I felt myself drowning.

Each time he stepped out that door, I wondered if it would be the last, whether he would finally run away with the red-haired woman or come home to find me sitting in a chair with my head cocked back and vodka pooled in my throat. I began to consider my husband's death, imagining various methods to kill him—smother him in his sleep, shoot him with his rifle, pour a flammable liquid over the car engine, poison his food and drink—to name a few.

I suddenly remembered the time my papa overheard me plotting to hurt my Russian cousin, Nadiya. She had always been jealous of my golden hair, so much so that she once shoved me into a mud puddle and said that my parents would have to shave my head to get the gunk out. Although that was not true, Nadiya's hatred had cut me low. Papa opened the door to my room that evening and sat on the floor beside me, where I had been drawing hideous pictures of my plan.

He shook his head and spoke to me in Finnish. "Sinikka, I know you're upset, but Nadiya is your cousin. Family and friends often mock each other, almost always pushing limits. My brothers used to dump buckets of reindeer piss on my head in front of pretty girls. That was their way of teasing. I hated it, as you might expect, but rivalry is natural among relatives. Just because Nadiya embarrassed you doesn't mean you need to return the favor. Revenge is like an ointment. It can soothe the pain but cannot heal the wound."

My hands trembled at the memory. My heart would remain torn even if I went the distance and killed Yakov. I would have to live on knowing that I murdered my husband. Guilt kicks the heels of those trying to escape their misdeeds, or so goes another proverb by Arvo. I felt hot tears trailing down my cheeks. The cup in hand touched my lips. The burn of vodka came and went. Empty. Polina entered the kitchen to tell me that you had fallen asleep. I poured another glass and continued until my world spun and crashed into a pillow.

As they intended, Taavi and Elias arrived one morning in early February to check on me since I never wrote to them about any changes or my condition. They brought an assortment of treats, from Freia chocolates and British tea to Finnish candy and Swedish vodka. As they unloaded the goods, they asked about my health and the state of my marriage. My answer made them grimace. They embraced me with apologies, showering me with compliments. I denied their attempt at bolstering my self-esteem. I felt like a depressed, haggard fool. My mouth then spat a sentence that even I did not expect. "I need to see him."

"You need to see who?" Elias's gaze sharpened.

"I need to see Yakov walk into that building. I must witness him with the red-haired woman."

Taavi shook his head and fanned the air as if to stop something. "Sinikka, I do not think that is wise."

I felt a ball in my throat, yet I broke through it. "For the love you bear me, cousins, please drive me there tonight. I must end the madness that plagues me like a goddamn disease. My heart is broken. My mind is in turmoil. God only knows what Lyov and Polina think of me. It's time I confront Yakov and rebuild myself. And if I am to face my fears and challenge him, I cannot prove he is having an affair by merely claiming that I heard of it from another's mouth. I need to tell him I saw it with my own two eyes. Do you understand?"

"We do," Taavi answered, looking at his brother, who offered a shallow nod. "We will do it, but you will ask no more of us. And I beg you, *we* beg you, do not mention our names to him. There must be no evidence of our involvement."

"You have my word," I promised.

"Good. And when this is all over, Sinikka, you're coming to Finland. No more of this. Between your family troubles and the war getting closer, we can no longer deliver aid, not for a good while. So please, once you have resolved your issues with Yakov, if you can do that, we will bring two trucks to move your family to safety. Okay?"

"*Kyllä*," I answered with a small sense of relief. "Yes, when all has ended, I will go with you to Finland, with or without Yakov."

Although the sky shimmered with stars and snow had not fallen for many days, it was the coldest evening to hit the Karelian Isthmus since the winter of 1910. I dressed three layers thick with a fur cap that nearly blocked my sight. Such a mission as I had chosen required sharp observation, so I drank a few cups of strong tea before leaving the house.

However, I found it strange that, while following Yakov toward the city in Taavi's truck, my mind lay not on my husband but on you, my son. Loss of innocence is inevitable in all children as they grow, but I felt yours would fade sooner than expected because of my emotions and the actions they created. This terrified me. I felt like a monster. You had already asked about adultery and what misdeeds your father might have done. I could not begin to imagine your reaction when you would finally learn the reality of the situation and what I endured to discover it. I was about to ask Taavi to turn around when Petrograd speared into view.

I will admit that I always found the capital as interesting and colorful as any fantasy city of fiction. Of course, I had not visited for nearly ten years, so my memory of it felt dreamy. Whenever Papa needed goods unavailable in the countryside, he went to the city with me as his companion, eager to enjoy the markets and music and the Tsar's palace, which looked like a magical fortress.

In those days, the city held the name Saint Petersburg. Following the outbreak of the war with Germany and its allies, the Russian government changed the name to Petrograd, expunging the German words *sankt* and *burg*. Its name made no difference to me, especially when I now viewed it as nothing less than an immense grid of human power. Full streets and narrow alleys sewed marketplaces, apartments, offices, factories, mills, and colorful onion-domed churches into a grandiose blanket of urbanization. It was madness.

Even in the dead of winter, electric trams scuttled along their snow-plowed tracks, moving abreast of slow buggies and pedestrians. Black smoke billowed from factory chimneys, and white smoke from housing complexes. Trains and ships blew their whistles to call upon workers and tradespeople. Imperial soldiers stood noticeably, their eyes trailing civilians as if searching for someone. I did not gain the opportunity to see the Winter Palace, but I remember that it stood somewhere along the Neva River near the city center, beating proudly as the heart of a vast nation. Living in the countryside for so long, I had forgotten what a real city looked like and how it felt.

My attention returned to our pursuit when we dodged a man bolting across the street and sharply turned into the industrial Kalininsky District. Here, Yakov parked in front of an enormous factory. Just as my cousins previously observed, he stepped inside for a long time and, later, exited alongside two gentlemen with whom he shook hands before taking off in the Wolseley again. He then drove westward, turning here and there, weaving through the city with the ease of an unsuspecting mind. As the Wolseley began to slow down, Taavi slipped the truck into a dark spot on the left side of the road and let the engine rest. Yakov circled back at the end of the block, parking between two automobiles on the other side of the street.

"This is the place," Elias whispered.

"Strange," Taavi added. "Last time, he got out of the car as soon as he stopped. I wonder if he's waiting for someone."

I searched the area until I noticed a pair of imperial officers walking toward the street corner adjacent to Yakov. He lowered his black woolen cap and stared at them. The guards glanced in his direction but paid no mind and walked behind a building. Yakov quickly burst from the car and hurried to the housing complex door in a receded brick archway.

The guards returned not a moment too soon,

vigilant as a pair of wild cats on the prowl. They drew up their bayonet-tipped rifles and stepped onto the open street corner, twisting their heads this way and that. Despite the darkness protecting my cousins and me, we instinctively ducked behind the truck's dashboard. Nevertheless, curiosity lifted my head to find Yakov slinking low with his spine pressed to the door of the building. After a heart-pumping minute, the guards ceased their concerns and marched away. Yakov put a hand over his chest and peeked beyond the archway to ensure his safety.

"What was that about?" Taavi whispered.

"He hid from the officers," Elias remarked. "Strange considering other people are in the area tonight, and no one else is acting funny."

I, too, should have questioned my husband's movements, but I was too busy grinding my teeth through a fit of anxiety. Yakov had lied to me for months, lied to both of us. He had kept us in the dark about his double life for so long that I felt crazy, so crazy that I had forced my cousins to pursue him down a snow-laden road in the heart of winter, all the way to the busiest city in Russia with the hope of catching him in the act. I was ready to see the red-haired harlot, eager to lay eyes on the face and body that had hooked my husband and reeled him away from my trust.

Then it happened.

Yakov composed himself and knocked on the door. I had hoped with all my heart that my cousins were sorely wrong, but I should have known better than to second-guess them. They had always told the truth, unlike my husband. A woman with hair as bright as freshly peeled carrots appeared. My blood began to boil, and I wondered what this woman possessed that drew Yakov like a moth to a flame.

I squinted to focus better, hungering to glimpse this tramp. She looked like a mannequin, perfectly framed with an asymmetrical face, rosy cheeks, red lips, curvy waist, and bold hips. *Saastainen huora*! She kissed Yakov on the lips. I growled another curse. She pulled him into the house and quickly shut the door.

"Let me out. I'm going to kill him."

"Sinikka, no," Elias commanded, grabbing my arm.

"You're not leaving this truck," Taavi confirmed.

"Did you see how that filthy whore touched my Yakov? I refuse to let her get away with it. Give me one reason why I shouldn't kick that door down."

Taavi shook his head while crushing his lower lip with his incisors. "I had a feeling this was a bad idea. We're leaving right now."

"No, don't," I cried from behind Elias's firm grip while Taavi jumped out of the car to wind the engine into high gear. As we sped out of Petrograd, I shouted and beat the seat like a spoiled child. Taavi growled at me to act maturely and assuage my emotions. However, rage roiled over my senses, shut my ears, and threw my hands upon the steering wheel.

For a moment, I fought my cousin for control and

nearly drove us into an icy ditch, but Elias reeled me back and into his arms, shushing me like a baby. I struggled, shook, and groaned until I finally gave up, then pressed my cheek to his coat and wept into his sleeve. He patted me on the back, whispering words of comfort all the way home.

~

The house knew only silence that night. Mama sat on the sofa, her neck bent and mouth agape, snoring up a storm. You lay across the cushion with your head on her lap, lids twitching to the dream within your head. I wanted to smile at the preciousness but could not find a fleck of joy to let loose. I dragged myself into bed with tears searing my reddened cheeks. I crawled under the sheets and blankets, not even bothering to slip on a nightgown or remove my shoes. My head thumped into the pillow. I stared at the dark wall.

My mind raced across a hundred images and words, yet it always returned to "Yakov is having an affair" with the memory of that fire-scalped witch kissing my husband. Eventually, I came to another imposing thought—what next? I admit that splitting up would have been the hardest but best choice. I never believed in love after betrayal, so our marriage was certainly kaput. Did I even need to confront him at this point? Was I to pack up my belongings and take my son and mother to Finland without him knowing? Or was it worth the trouble to hash everything out in an argument, potentially ending up like Mariya

Galkin?

"Perhaps I should smother him in his sleep," I carved into a page in my diary. "Maybe I ought to bash his head with a hammer."

In the end, I dared to defy my greatest fears. When Yakov entered the bedroom around one in the morning, I hit him with all I had. "You are a disgusting maggot," I snarled. "*Pala koiranpaskaa.*"

"Sinikka." He stepped back and hit his shoulder against the frame of the door. "What's wrong? Why are you angry?"

"You are what's wrong, Yakov. You are why I am angry. *Jumalauta valehtelija.*"

"Stop cursing in Finnish. I... I don't understand."

"That carrot-headed harlot in Vyborgsky. You've been paying her nightly visits for nearly half a year. Sleeping with another woman, Yakov, I never thought you to be the type. Do you realize we have been married for ten years? Ten years! That's one-third of my life, an enormous chunk of my existence wasted by your sleazy, disloyal actions. Filthy pig! If my father was here "

"Darling, darling, what are you talking about? What carrot-headed harlot?"

"Are your ears clogged with her sweat?"

"Sinikka, nothing of what you speak has happened. I've been working every night, laboring diligently to benefit our family."

"Shame on you, Yakov. Where do you get the gall to

lie to your bride? I thought I was your lady and, you... you, my noble prince. I've been telling my family for years that you're the most honest man in the world and that I'm... and that I'm lucky to be yours. Even my father, who loved you as a son, now rolls over in his grave, utterly abashed. He would suffer a second death if he knew of your promiscuity, that you happily bent over that... that filthy mannequin in Petrograd."

"How dare you accuse me of such a thing!" he roared before stepping back and lassoing his frustration. "Dear wife, I am still your honest husband. I swear to God, I've done nothing wrong."

"Nothing wrong? Are you mad?" I couldn't stop myself. "You thought yourself so sly, so confident that no clues tumbled to the wayside. Come on, Yakov. Of all people, you know that I love puzzles. Classic jigsaw pieces, board games, word problems, mysteries. You know I can't help myself when one appears before me, and you know I'm good at it. But I haven't touched a real puzzle since you became one. And I must say, you are the worst puzzle I've ever had to solve, the only puzzle I never wished to solve but had to for the sake of our family. Disgraceful."

"You say you *labored* all those extra nights, and for what? You brought no spare money to the table. You saved nothing. And I ought to know. I searched through the storage room. I looked in the safe. I felt like a maniac, unable to fathom what you did beyond these walls. But then I saw it with my own two eyes. I saw you, Yakov. I saw that red-haired woman kiss you. I saw her pull you into the building with a loving smile. I was there."

"How did you "

"I have relatives, you idiot. You know they would do anything to help me."

"Elias and Taavi?"

"Do not speak their names. They are no longer your family. This marriage is over, Yakov. We are done, finished. You can beat me if you like and walk out the door right now, but you will never take Lyov from me. I will not end up like Mariya Galkin."

"Mariya Galkin? Your old friend who drank herself to death because Boris..." His words trailed as he plopped on the edge of the bed. I thought he would finally confess the truth, but he merely laughed. "Sinikka, you have it all wrong. Never in my life would I think to compromise our marriage, let alone beat you and take our son from you. I know it's not unheard of around here for a man to commit such terrible acts, like Boris, but that's not me. I've loved you since the day I met you, when your father rescued me from that irate horse in the city. I know you remember. You know I adore you to the ends of the Earth. Sleeping with another woman is a sin not within my nature. Lying, too. You know this."

"Yet you did both." I paced the room like a caged lion, my eyes red with tears.

"No, Sinikka, I did not. Please, hear me out."

"I hope your defense is worth the breath."

"I won't defend something that doesn't exist. Listen, there are things that, well..." He released a lengthy exhale and closed his eyes for a moment. "Do you remember that terrible incident in 1905 when the Tsar left the palace, and his imperial soldiers shot Father Gapon's peaceful procession in the street?"

"What the hell, Yakov? That has nothing to do with—"

"Please, just answer the question, Sinikka. Do you remember that event?"

"Yes, I believe it was a few weeks after my sixteenth birthday. My uncle made a big stink about it. So what? Who cares!"

Yakov ignored me and continued. "Since that bloody Sunday, even before, our home, our great Mother Russia, has been spiraling into disarray. Nikolai Romanov, the dastardly Tsar, is poison to our country. Our nation deeply suffers from his every word and deed. You would never know because you get everything from your wealthy Finnish cousins, who apparently failed to inform you that Russia owns Finland and has for a long time."

He shook his head at me. "Sinikka, you do not go into the city every day like me. You do not see what is really happening. There are food shortages and economic deficits. Innocent people are dying. This winter, especially, has proven brutal to our people. Worse, even while the tsar and his puppets are at war with Germany, his administrative substitutes do nothing to combat the horrific events at home. They purposely ignore the lament of the Russian people."

"Yakov, what does this political nonsense have to do with you sleeping with that woman?"

"It has everything to do with it. That red-haired woman is not my mistress. She is Yuliya, the wife of Dimitri Pasternak, a former coworker and good comrade of mine. She is only a doorkeeper made to appear as a lover or an accepting spouse to those who enter. What you saw is what needs to be seen by the public. Do not think I would ever hurt you. Yuliya is an associate of mine, nothing more."

"Associate... associate of what?"

"Sinikka, I know you are not often aware of what transpires beyond this house. Let me tell you that a radical event is about to occur. Change is coming to Russia, and we must stand on the right side when it happens. Strikes and marches are on the way."

"Associate of what, Yakov?" I barked.

"The Bolsheviks."

"Bolsheviks?"

"Our party, under the mastermind, Vladimir Lenin, is plotting. We are readying ourselves for the revolution. All is coming to a head."

"Our, we? I am not a Bolshevik. I am no turncoat, Yakov. My parents were tsarists, despite imperial politics, because it was under Romanov rule that they could live well in this house. Therefore, I, too, am a tsarist. The Romanovs have ruled Russia for three hundred years. They raised it to rival the great powers of Europe. They *are* Mother Russia."

"I know you're angry with me, Sinikka, but what you say is fallible. The Romanovs are traitors and murderers. You cannot be a tsarist. My wife will not praise the imperial government, not while the Romanovs, a string of Hapsburg whelps, are ruining this country. The same country that birthed you and made you who you are today."

"Remember that I am half Finnish and very proud of it."

"Arvo was Finnish, sure, and you can speak that language, but you only do so with your cousins and our son occasionally or when you curse. But you were born in *this* house on *this* side of the border from a mother whose Slavic blood runs deeper than that of any Romanov. You are just as Russian as me."

My hands clenched and trembled. "This is not important to me right now, Yakov."

"Well, it is to me!" he shouted. "It means everything to me as it should to you."

I gritted my teeth, my ears so hot that I might have been blowing steam. "Do you know what my father said about the incident in 1905? He said that although he and my mother sided with Father Gapon and the factory workers, their protest only brought chaos. Instead of a massive crowd, a small group of representatives should have made an appointment and met with the tsar. They could have acted diplomatically and avoided all that trouble and blood."

"You are ignorant of the truth if you honestly think that way, Sinikka. Please, do not be so blind. Far more occurred in 1905 than what you know, what preceded the incident, the strikes that followed. And it's only worsened over the past decade. Our country is begging for true reform. And your precious Finland, they're in the same fiery boat as us."

I laughed in his face. "So, this is it? This is what you've been doing all these months behind my back. All this time, I thought you were lying to me for the sake of sleeping with another woman. Yet, I suffered a storm of worry, anger, and madness because of political conferences? That's it? In the most twisted of ways, it's almost worse. You lied about going to meetings, stupid meetings. Why?"

He paused, likely to consider his words. "I admit that I lied. Yes, fine, and it was foolish, but I only did so because I feared your reaction. The same way you feared mine. You are far more fragile than you would ever admit, Sinikka. You are afraid of change. You are like a thin piece of glass, and I did not want to crack you. But clearly, that was unavoidable. Either way, I didn't deceive our marriage. Neither was I so dishonest. In my eyes, attending these meetings is a form of work. And it is challenging work at that."

"Dear wife, I concealed it to keep you safe. Also, they are not political conferences but gatherings of concerned citizens. You must understand what the Social Democratic Labor Party represents and what we are trying to accomplish. Grigori Rasputin may be dead, but there is still corruption in the Winter Palace. And we yearn to help those suffering under the continued oppression of the tsar. To be a Bolshevik is to fight tyranny. What we strive to achieve is for the good of the common people, the good of the working class, the good of Mother Russia."

"I cannot believe you, Yakov. Your words slay me. You say that you did not deceive our marriage, yet what is a lie but falsehood, a form of betrayal. You are a liar, a traitor to your wife, and, apparently, to your monarch as well. You are a Judas."

He grabbed my wrist. "I am no Judas. I am a loyalist, fully dedicated to our family and this great nation, not to Nikolai Romanov and his greedy family. The quality of a country should never be second to its sovereign's personal gains and pleasures. You must recognize that. Please, Sinikka, come to a gathering. Come so that you can understand why I commit so much time to this matter. I beg of you."

I felt crazy that politics turned out to be my husband's mistress. "I will not listen to you anymore, Yakov. Not about the tsar, not about your long nights in the city, and certainly not about my joining your mutinous cause. I will sleep in my mother's room from now on. You can have your revolution. You can have your gatherings. Just leave the rest of us out of it."

I stomped out of the room and slammed the door. I tore you and my mother from the couch and hurried into her room for the night. After you went back to sleep, I poured my heart out. I told Mama about the lies, the red-haired woman, the madness that consumed me, my cousins' involvement, Yakov's surprising response and twisting of the argument, the Bolsheviks, and my father's opinion on the 1905 massacre. She listened to my woes, but her reply was neither what I expected nor wanted to hear.

"Oh, Sinikka, your father was a sweet man with a noble heart." Her smile softened her eyes. "He was also very wise much of the time. However, his opinion on Russian politics did not always chime with my family or our friends. Probably because he was born and raised in Finland, which, although under Russian jurisdiction, is still a foreign nation. So, Arvo had an outsider's perspective."

"You may have your father's Finnish blood, and I know you're proud of that, but you also have my blood. You were born and raised on Russian soil. Yakov is not wrong. You are Russian. And you spend a lot of time in this house, maybe too much. Perhaps it would befit you to attend one of those political meetings. It might open your eyes a bit."

I felt as if she merely fanned the flames inside me. "Shut your mouth, Mama. How dare you suggest such a thing. I'd rather cut off my legs than bend to my lying husband's whim, let alone stray from my father's loyalty to the tsar."

"Sinikka, your father was never loyal to the tsar. He only spoke highly of the Romanovs to tease my family. You heard him say such things without realizing they were humorous to him. It's not your fault. You were young. Arvo never cared for the imperial government or any sovereignty, for that matter. He wouldn't even have left Finland if not for his stubborn ambition to outdo his brothers, wanting to prove he could survive without the Laukkanen bank accounts. However, at his core, and despite all you think you know, your father was fiercely loyal to his family and home country. Does that sound familiar?"

My speechless ire swept me from my mother's room into the kitchen. I poured myself a large glass of Swedish vodka and drank myself to sleep in the rocker.

~

The next day, Yakov gently roused me and asked if I would join him that night for a gathering of concerned citizens. With a throbbing headache and careless of any consequences, I drove him out of the house like a wolf on a lamb. He cranked on the Wolseley and hurried to work. I simmered in discontent all morning long. I snubbed Polina most of the time and grumbled whenever you, Lyov, did not obey me, although I regretted it each time it occurred. I could only imagine how you perceived me at that point, your heavenly guardian fallen to hell, from shining to shambles. I blamed your father for the removal of my wings.

Around noon, my head still swollen with the heat of loathing, I sat in the leather lounge chair with a new glass of vodka. I ignited one of Yakov's cigarettes and looked at you, sitting by the hearth, amusing yourself with one of my wooden puzzles. Watching you play so innocently while I stewed with alcohol and tobacco in hand made me question what I had become. Was it really Yakov or my own head games that fragmented me? I guess it didn't matter anymore, what with the truth now revealed. Either way, any broken thing can be pieced back together using proper skills. It's like a puzzle. I had always been good at puzzles, and Yakov was a sore loser. However, I might have been the worst kind of loser.

To bring me even lower than I felt, while finally closing my husband's case, another mystery lay upon the table, a puzzle I never considered—me. Had I lost my dignity? Had I lost my sense of self or just my mind? I should have been relieved that my husband did not cheat on me, yet the pain in my heart persisted. I felt more bitter and angry than before. But why? And who was going to solve this puzzle?

Yakov came home around three o'clock to a table devoid of lunch. Instead of complaining, he smiled and foraged through the pantry for bread and cheese. He spent much of the late afternoon with you outside, fishing through the ice in the creek. At dinner, he stared at me with sorrowful eyes. He wanted to talk to me but knew I would shut him out. Later, while you were drawing on papers in your room, Yakov found me indulging by the hearth. He casually removed the vodka glass from my hand and placed it on the mantle. I blew smoke in his face, hoping he would choke and cough. He silently responded by igniting his own cigarette, then stared at me for a minute before clearing his throat.

"My friends are dying to meet you, Sinikka." He spoke casually as if all was well. "And I want you to understand who we are and what we stand for. Please, come with me tonight. I know you will appreciate it. I just know it. We can even grab a drink somewhere in the city if you'd like."

I could not find it in my heart to forgive him for causing me such distress, months of uncertainty, and prolific doubt in our relationship. I snatched the glass from the mantle. "Get out of my sight."

He did.

Day after day, Yakov asked me to join him. And night after night, I refused. I often answered his questions in a vicious tone, snarling like a wounded badger. Other times, my silent glares and scowls proved sharp enough to repel him. Yet, no matter how much I shunned him, he persisted. I grew so frustrated that I began sleeping in your room to avoid Yakov in the mornings and evenings. I had already quit making him lunch, but dinner soon followed. He would return from his outdoor playtime with you only to ask me if I was ready to meet his friends and learn about the political issues of Russia. My steadfast retorts did not faze him, even as he cooked himself a low-quality meal while the rest of us ate like upper-class citizens.

To further push your father's buttons, almost hoping that he would now cheat on me just so I could leave, I began to deny him all the goods my cousins had given us, but to no avail. In retaliation, he started buying expensive Russian products from his Bolshevik friends, from vegetables and oil to toothbrushes and aftershave. My mother pitied him and often cooked him meals behind my back, although she too quickly found herself deprived of Nordic goods. You, my son, were the only one who received my complete love, even with your unbroken devotion to your father. While I knew you understood the severity of our arguments, you had yet to learn the cause. I had a feeling that such a day would soon arrive.

On the twenty-fourth of February, Yakov returned home from a significant strike in Petrograd. On his head sat a strange wool cap with a blood-red star on the front. I would soon know it as a *budyonovka*, hat of the Bolsheviks. Yakov rushed into the main room, took Polina's hands, and hoisted her to her toes. They cheered for the people of Russia, who had finally united against the imperial government. Even you, Lyov, joined the merriment and danced around the house as if Christmas had returned. You might recall shouting, "No more famine, no more war, no more tyranny."

"Stop!" I yelled so loudly, I thought my neck veins would burst. "Stop right now! Yakov Ivanovich Brevsky, how dare you bring your radical politics into this house and boast of it in front of Lyov, let alone allow him to chant with you! I ought to break your head for influencing my virtuous son. You as well, Mama. Shame on both of you. We will have no more of this."

"We are for the people's party," Yakov contended sternly but peacefully. "Even the children of this great nation ought to understand that, for they will inherit it."

"No," I snarled with fire in my throat. "My Lyov will take no part."

My thoughts lay besieged by a tempest of rage as alcohol swirled in my stomach. I grabbed your arm and marched you out the front door into the snow. I neither looked back nor slowed my pace, aiming only to get to the Wolseley and drive it straight to Finland. I heard you commanding me to stop, that I was hurting you, that you were cold. But I did not recognize such complaints as valid, not when I believed your future was at risk. I would do anything to ensure your safety and save you from your lying father and his political madness. I needed to get us out of Russia right away.

The startling boom of a gun split the air and I felt pain shoot through my breast. I breathed deeply and fell to my knees. I touched my chest expecting blood. And for a moment, I swear I felt the liquid of life soaking my shirt, cold in the world beyond the walls of my body. When I looked down, however, I realized it was only a clod of snow, snow my numb hands had scooped from the earth after you had finally ripped your fingers from my grip. I coughed and tasted vodka. My breath trembled as tears flowed like wild rivers down my cheeks. I turned to you, Lyov, who stared at me with terror in your eyes. You began to shrink from me, quaking like a sapling in the wind, then started toward the house.

I felt as if I had broken a glass without realizing my own strength, and the shards had cut very deep. I pressed my face into my hands and wept, stumbling over the words that fell from my mouth, "What...have...I...become?"

Yakov approached at a pace that reminded me of what I had just done or at least attempted. I could not tell whether he had dropped his rifle. If he had not, what did that mean? My panting quickened. I felt vodka roiling in my stomach, burning into my chest. I felt ill. Fear coiled about my brain and squeezed. Yakov suddenly clapped a hand on my shoulder, then all went black.

~

I awoke to the usual sounds of the house. You uttered *chuga-chuga* repeatedly, likely leading a toy train around furniture. My mother's rocker squeaked.

I pictured her knitting. A fire crackled in the hearth. I could see that the sun shone beyond the curtains of my window. I wanted to get up and let the light in. Then I remembered yesterday. I had sucked down more vodka than I could handle and tried to take you away from your father.

It felt like a horrible dream, and I prayed it was, but my aching head spared no lies. I had feared sharing a similar fate as Mariya Galkin, beaten down and drowned by alcohol in the wake of her husband's abuse. Yet, it was I who turned out to be the abusive one. I was Boris. I might not have physically harmed Yakov, but I had screamed at him. I had stabbed him with mistrust, hatred, and more threats than I could deliver.

I felt tears beginning to well when a pair of boots stepped to my bedside. I squeezed my eyes shut and heard the clinking of a spoon stirring sugar in a porcelain teacup. A small plate slid across the surface of my nightstand. I felt a soft hand touch my cheek and wipe away my streams of sorrow. I breathed deeply and looked up to see Yakov smiling at me, relief easing the lines on his round face.

"All the factories are closed," he explained as if I had asked him a question. "The city is on strike. We are near the end. I can feel it. If the government does not abide by the people, our numbers will continue to grow. Today is another march, the biggest yet. It will be peaceful but compelling."

"Aren't you angry with me?" I asked.

He nearly laughed. "Sinikka, my sweet. Love *is* never angry. Anger only arises when we give up or don't try to understand each other. Love is understanding. And I love you despite your fears and recklessness. If I hadn't stopped you from going to Finland, Lyov would have. And if he couldn't stop you, it would have been your own heart that turned you around. This I know. I understand you, Sinikka, so love is why all is well."

I couldn't tell whether he was trying to make me feel worse for what I did or was simply relaying his thoughts. Either way, he spoke the truth, and it stung. It hurt more than his lies, more than his months of secrecy, more than any number of days I felt betrayed. Shame gripped me. I knew I did not deserve his love.

Then he laughed. "Plus, you don't know how to drive the Wolseley. You wouldn't have gone far even if you had managed to crank it on. Anyway, today is a day for Russia. I am going to the march. I won't ask you to join. I know you will deny me. Just know that I—"

"I will go," I heard myself mutter.

"What?"

"I will go with you, Yakov. Just let me get ready."

Despite the blatant reluctance and sadness in my voice, your father lit up like a firework and pulled me to my feet, then smothered me with hugs and kisses. I could have spat a hundred hollow words at that moment, yet they would breeze in one ear and out the other. And Yakov would turn his cheek and grin because he viewed my surrender as an opportunity for conformity. And he loved me more than I deserved.

However, I must confess that it was for you, my son, that I agreed to go with your father. I needed you to feel good about yourself and happy to see that your parents stood unified, not a pair of buffoons too blind and antipathetic to comprehend one another. Holding this notion like a charm or crutch, I washed up, dressed, and made breakfast for my family.

Like a sorrowful child, I soon found myself staring out of the Wolseley, bumping southward along the snow-decked road en route to the city. As if watching the pages of a picture book flip beneath the careful thumb of a loving mother, the scenery passed before my eyes.

I looked at the trees garbed in their white coats. Lakes slumbered beneath sheets of ice. A fisherman stood at the edge of a stream, teaching his children how to saw holes in frozen waterways. A pack of dogs pulled men on sleds hauling small loads of timber. A mother and daughter scraped frost from the windows of their cottage. Winter animals peeked from the nooks and crannies of the woods, some scurrying, some flying, some looking back at me, who sat encased in a foreign metal box. This little corner of the world was all I had ever indeed known. It birthed me. It housed me. It nurtured me. And it taught me to do the same for you, Lyov.

I suddenly realized that I knew no other place to call home. Long had I dreamed of Finland, but why, honestly, why? What was Finland to me? Of course, it's not what, but who was Finland? My Papa, Arvo, the father I dearly missed. He lingered like a distant silhouette in my mind. His death had shattered me into pieces that dissipated throughout our house, some taking years to recover, others completely lost. Perhaps that is also why I seldom left the property, although I certainly proved capable of venturing out with Taavi and Elias.

But then, my cousins' presence had always felt like a safe haven, providing me the same Laukkanen warmth and wisdom that Arvo had possessed. Strange as it sounds, I had imagined I could touch my father again or relive old memories if I just stepped across the border as if Finland were some kind of fantasy land. But how could I have ever expected such a thing to come true? How could I ever think that by moving to Finland, I could feel the spirit of my father close to me? And how would that have made me a better mother to you?

Tears trickled down my face as I continued to peer out the Wolseley's open window. Yet those tears streamed not over a frown or trembling lips, but a smile as wide as Russia. I suddenly realized that my father had always been with me and always would, for his strong Finnish blood ran through my veins. The same golden hair that had crowned his head now flowed over my shoulders. I might have been proud of my Finnish heritage, but Finland could never have been my home, for I did not know that country. I did not know anyone besides my cousins who visited me in Russia. This country, this land, this earth was and still is home, the home within me and beneath my feet.

I began to feel whole again.

I turned to Yakov, whose hands confidently grasped the steering wheel while his eyes safeguarded our journey along the snow-covered road. It felt good to drive with my husband again, just he and I out and about. It reminded me of the days before you were born when we would take my father's buggy to the Baltic shore and dance to the songs of wind and breaking waves. I put my hand on Yakov's arm. He grinned at me.

We dove into the sea of chaos called Petrograd. We parked the car outside the Vyborgsky district near the secret meeting place of Yakov's political comrades. Hundreds of people marched through the streets, walking, singing, talking, and shouting to the buildings that oppression and tyranny must end. Men and women in uniforms carried signs that illustrated their woes and the changes they felt necessary.

Your father and I soon walked among them, weaving through a crowd that appeared to be heading in several directions. Some marched toward Kazan Cathedral, while others headed for the port. We followed the third and largest group that sought to protest before the walls of the Winter Palace. I wanted to imagine it as I had when young, a beautiful castle fit for fairytales. But how could I when so many people now threw fists and spat words at it, proclaiming that those who lived within bore hearts as cold and gray as the sky that loomed overhead?

I moved my attention from the dark building to the crowd, where amazement and understanding began to color my thoughts. An older man marched with a spear over his shoulder, its blade stabbed through an empty bread sack. A group of children pulled their brothers and sisters on wagons, announcing, "It's not enough!" Loving couples yelled to the sky. The elderly thrust liver-spotted fists into the frosty air. A group of women with dry, stainless aprons surrounded a city official and beat him for his loyalty to the tsar. I felt my heart pounding, my mind racing. The ends of my lips cracked into my cheeks.

Yakov suddenly pulled a gentleman aside and shook his hand. Festooned on the man's arm was the red-haired woman, Yuliya. I remembered how she had kissed my husband, and for a moment, I thought I would claw her eyes out. Yet, the impulse suffocated in the embrace with which she surprised me. "It's so good to finally meet you," she said with the sincerity of a dear friend. She and her husband, Dimitri, had heard nothing but wonders about me. I cursed myself for playing the belligerent fool living in a wooden box.

Nevertheless, appreciation quickly filled the void, and I felt more alive than ever. These people trusted each other. They were lionhearted Russians uniting for a single, noble cause aimed at saving themselves from calamity and living in the dark.

As we neared the city center, some protesters grew violent toward two dozen police officers who threatened the march with their weapons. Yakov's friends shepherded us to a safer area where a crowd waved freedom banners to the rhythm of their chants. Marching toward the Winter Palace entrance alongside these fine citizens made me feel like a true woman of Russia.

I felt warmth in my breast, butterflies in my stomach, giddy as a child yet nervous as a young bride. But for what? Change. It blew in the wind, grew from seeds in the earth, filled the gaps of hallow things, and ignited the insatiable spirit of humanity, which I was now experiencing. Although I knew it to be the greatest constant in our world, long had I hated it.

Change is giving and taking, ebbing and flowing, birth and death, a puzzle forever in play, performed by nature with perfect remorselessness. But nature does not care how awful I had felt after losing my father, which had spawned a greater terror in my heart, the fear of losing the life I loved. I had cloistered myself to protect that life and those in it.

However, this only worsened as time wore on, fissuring further with the death of Mariya Galkin and striking deepest with my husband's political mischief. I can only assume that things would have turned out differently if I had simply worked with my fears rather than fight or submit to them. If I had communicated with Yakov from the start, my life might be different today. I was a fool, and fools learn the hard way.

Remember this, Lyov. Wholeness comes from love, love comes from understanding, and understanding is created by relaxed hands. The tighter your grip on life, the more pieces you must pick up when it breaks. The more pieces, the harder the puzzle.

I remember the joy that gushed over me as my burdens washed away and the people's cheer filled my head. I wish I could kiss Yakov right now, just as I did that day when I embraced the thrill.

Your father slowly pulled his face from mine and laughed. "You will always have my heart, Sinikka," he proclaimed before turning to the palace to howl for bread and justice in the name of God. As I added my voice to the roar, I noticed that Petrograd's military had come out to meet us. Yakov must have seen the curiosity in my eyes, for he brought his mouth to my ear. "Do not worry, my love. We, the people, hold the advantage."

A commanding officer on horseback shouted from the center of the regiment. The soldiers immediately responded by marching forward, aiming to frighten the crowd and drive us away from the palace square. We, the people, bore no fear and pressed on, our voices louder and emotions stronger.

Suddenly, the blast of a rifle echoed over the crowd. I froze. A row of protesters dropped to the frosty ground for cover. Someone threw a blunt object at the soldiers in retaliation, triggering the front line of the regiment to burst their ranks and start shooting. We dispersed in a roaring torrent of terror. Chaos ensued. The man to my rear shoved me forward. I fell on my face and bit my tongue bloody. My whole life flashed before my eyes. Death hovered above, and I screamed. Luckily, Yakov pulled me up and into his arms, rescuing me from being trampled in the snowy street.

Another round of gunfire ripped through the air. Two bullets passed me. One grazed my shoulder. I shut my eyes and put a hand to the sting, embracing the hot pain for the sake of my husband and, you, our child.

When I opened my eyes, Yakov lay on the ground like a ragdoll, blood oozing from his neck. I cried for help, but no one heard me, consumed by their own fears for safety. Although shock had stricken me with trembles and rapid breathing, I hoisted Yakov by the armpits and used all my strength to drag him from the center of the square. He gurgled nonsense like a sleepy drunkard. I begged him to hold on and keep breathing. By the time I pulled him out of the crowd, he was gone.

I knelt over my husband's body, still shaking, and bawled like autumn rain. Some tried to grab my wounded arm and tow me to safety, but I resisted and wailed. How could I go on without my Yakov? How could I even care about the protest now? I felt a rush of anger in my chest, a hatred for the soldiers who killed my husband. Why did *he* die? It should have been me.

I got up and tried to hoist Yakov over my shoulder, but he proved too heavy for me. So, I laid him to rest beside a building and closed his eyes while whispering a prayer to God. The blood on my hands dripped upon the snow as I overlapped my fingers. I knelt and looked down at his face, remembering all the events that led up to this moment. I recalled my father and my mother's advice. Then, suddenly, I felt Yakov's breath against my ear, lecturing me about the evil doings of the imperial government.

Lifting my eyes from the man who I knew as my loving husband, I saw a poster of the prideful tsar on a brick wall and, in my peripheral view, a troop of soldiers marching my way. I thought of you, Lyov. You needed to live in a country that would allow you to prosper, to grow big and healthy and wise, a country of which you could be proud, a country that would take care of you as I took care of you. You needed Russia, the land of your parents, your home.

I felt a fire rouse in my gut. I knew anger, yes, but I felt immense love. Love for all that I had ever known, for my husband, for you, and I would do anything to ensure the survival of that love. I grabbed your father's wool cap, his *budyonovka*, and placed it on my head, then snatched up a Bolshevik banner that lay on the ground tied to a broken pole. I glanced at your father once more and gritted my teeth with all the love I bore him and the hatred I suddenly felt for the tsar. I bit my lip and rushed into the crowd, where soldiers and civilians fought each other like starved dogs over meat. I waved my banner, turned it about, and rammed the splintered end of the pole into an imperial soldier's face.

~

So ends my story to you, well, at least the portion about your father. I'll try to sum up the rest, though to my reluctance, you may recall it well.

I ran as soon as I had smashed the soldier's face, sprinting with every ounce of strength left in my body to find the Wolseley. Unfortunately, the way was blocked. I fled with others down a long street but turned into an alley after a barrage of bullets pelted the people at my side. By some miracle, at the other end of the alley was a frightened horse, who had also escaped the chaos. I rode him away from the madness through another set of streets and out of the city.

Gratitude filled me when I came home to find you safe. However, fearing that I had put you in great danger, and despite my newfound love for our country, I knew I needed to get you out of Russia immediately. I scribed a letter to my cousins that I would come by rail in the next few days and that they needed to meet me at the first station across the Finnish border. With our bags packed, you, me, and Polina managed to squeeze into a stuffed train out of Beloostrov.

When the train reached Vainikkala, just beyond the border, we exited only to find ourselves blocked by imperial soldiers. They denied us entry into Finland even though it was an imperial state. It made no sense to me. But it seemed the political upheaval in Petrograd had rippled across the land like the bubonic plague.

I saw Taavi and Elias at the gate, calling for me. I went to them, but a soldier barred me. "Please," I begged him. "Let me in. My cousins are right there." I pointed. "I implore you, for my son's safety, let us through."

I saw his eyes soften and heard the sympathy in his voice when he said, "You cannot go." I felt a surge of emotions rising, ready to strike out, but the man added, "Your child can, but not you."

My heart sank deep into my chest. Why couldn't I go? Did they know about the soldier I had maimed in Petrograd? Was this some kind of punishment? Would I soon be arrested? I panicked and thought of your safety. Who would protect you if something happened to me? Certainly not Polina.

Even now, I feel sick remembering that moment. Giving you up hurt more than anything I have ever experienced, more painful even than the deaths of Yakov and Arvo. I had striven so long to prevent just this. Yet, for the love I bore you and the safety you needed, it had to be. I wrapped you in my arms and rubbed my tear-drenched face into your soft hair, muttering blessings and wishes. I kissed you, hesitated, looked you in the eyes one last time, and passed you through the gate to Taavi and Elias.

Returning to our house without you slayed me. I wanted to die but knew such an act would not help us. As time passed, and my heart weighed with sorrow, I still felt that giving you to my cousins was the right choice.

However, I will always wonder why I didn't question the soldier at the border. I also might have asked myself why I felt compelled to get you out of Russia when so many other children stayed. Of course, life is full of possibilities and thoughts about the roads we could have taken. I am a fool, and fools learn the hard way, especially when gipping life too tightly.

As you know, the Bolsheviks became just as tyrannical as the tsars they succeeded. Lenin died, and Stalin took charge with an iron fist. Communism proved to be nothing more than a bandage that tightened year after year over a wound that festers to this day. Now, we are controlled and censored. Everything is monitored. Although many would disagree with me, there is no freedom here. I fight as your father once did, under a new banner, yes, but for the same cause, to change the world in which I live for the health and safety of those I love. For you, Lyov.

I hope to see you again, my darling son, someday, somehow, in our family home on free Russian soil. I pray for your safe return, should you choose it.

With great love from,

Tvoya mama, *Sinikka*

October 19, 1948

MAPLEWOOD

SEVEN

BOURBON COUNTRY

Dread consumed the boy as he walked along the Devil's Spine, a windy dirt road that slithered up the eastern hills above Poor Fork, Kentucky. He balked and shivered when a chilling breeze dragged a mist through the woods to meet him. Many leafless trees creaked their joints, rousing from their late-winter slumber. A raven landed on a branch only to twist its head and caw. The howl of hunting hounds echoed from the east, prompting the youngster to consider turning back.

"No," he murmured, remembering his errand. He forced his feet to continue up the old road, deeper into the timberland. Knowing some of the creepy stories that poured from these hills, he needed to keep his ears open and eyes peeled. When he decided to pick up his pace, he noticed maple stumps lining the road ahead. Suddenly, a gunshot rang from around the bend. The boy held his breath and squeezed the straw sack in his arms. He nervously turned to see if anyone had followed him. He was alone. Silence stole the air.

As the boy sighed in relief, two bloodhounds wandered out of the woods and onto the road, sniffing frantically at the wind. The boy thought to freeze but instinctively took a step backward. The dogs barked and started toward him.

The poor child darted without hesitation, though not in the direction he wished he had gone. As he reached the top of the hill, three men stepped into the middle of the road, each dressed darker than the last, their hats tipped back, guns drawn. The bloodhounds approached from the rear yet stopped dead when one of the men whistled, stepped forward, and growled, "You're in the wrong place, kid."

The young courier slowly realized that this was no man but a barrel-chested woman with a face as rough as tree bark and a voice like sandpaper scratching on metal.

"I said you're in the wrong place, kid. You best turn 'round and get."

"I'm here to deliver this sack to the Buckley house. Top of Devil's Spine, I was told."

"What do you have?"

"Herbs, sir, I mean ma'am. Just... just herbs."

The woman signaled her male peers to approach and escort the boy farther up the road to a large cottage of brick and lumber. White smoke streamed from the chimney. A line of crows huddled on the roof, keeping quiet for a change. A rusty car and two brown trucks rested on one side of the road's end near a smaller, secondary cottage. On the main house's front porch, a man sporting a long, peppered beard sat in a rocking chair with a glass of whiskey and a tobacco pipe. Garbed in quality black pants and a matching vest, a buttoned white shirt, dark leather boots, and offering a smile as sharp as a rose thorn, this man looked like Hell's banker.

The two men brought the boy forward while the burly woman kept the hounds tame and still. "Found him walking to the house, brother," spoke the eldest of the gunslingers. "Heard him tell Big Bertha he's delivering to the Buckley house. Top of Devil's Spine, he said."

The refined gentleman slowly gained his feet, placed his glass on the porch rail, then puffed his pipe and sniffled. "Otis, Dick, you can put your guns away. This little feller's harmless." As they followed his commands, he stepped down from the porch. "What's in the sack, boy?"

"Hemp from Mexico, sir."

"Hemp, for what? I didn't order any hemp. Got

plenty of twine around here."

When the boy didn't respond, Otis nudged him forward with the butt of his rifle and growled, "You answer my brother if you know what's good for you."

"It's just dried hemp, sir," the boy whimpered. "Someone by the name of Buckley ordered it. I... I—I just make deliveries. Please, don't hurt me, sir. Please."

A goofy young man in overalls suddenly burst from the house. "Did somebody say hemp? Praise Jesus; it's finally here!" He snatched the bag from the boy in exchange for a few coins, receiving a nasty glare from the sharp-dressed man. "It's just hemp, Uncle Chester. No need to worry. It ain't no trouble to you."

"Everything's trouble to me, Rufus. You ought to know better. Dammit, you and Burt are brainless enough. You defy God by smoking that stuff, ruining your mind."

"Come on, Uncle, it's just weed. It ain't much different than tobacco or alcohol. And if God didn't want me to enjoy it, He wouldn't have made it so darn good. I believe everyone ought to try this stuff. Makes you feel silky inside."

"I don't know why I let you get away with this every time," Chester grouched. "I don't need mindless workers, let alone nephews who can't shoot a deer standing ten feet in front of them. Take that Mexican shit inside, and don't come out unless I say so. As a matter of fact, scurry back to work in the barn. That means now, Rufus! And as for you, delivery boy, if you ever bring hemp or anything else to my house without the name Chester Buckley associated with it, I'll have Big Bertha lock you up in the shed with the hounds. You hear? Now get."

As the boy darted down the hill, Chester looked at his brother-in-law. "Dick, I want you to take a horse and follow him. Be discreet. I only want to know who sent him. If he heads onto the Wilkins property, make sure your gun is loaded."

"Got it, boss."

"Bertha," Chester commanded, "take the hounds back out on watch. If that boy is from Henry Wilkins's clan, we may have trouble later. Might need some backup."

"Yes, sir, Uncle Chester."

"Otis, come with me." Chester led his brother between the two cottages, into the heart of the property, to the barn near the hillside where Bo, Tobias, Burt, and Rufus sat bottling Chester's latest batch of bourbon. "Another one completed," he announced proudly. "Seven years in the making."

"Another batch and not enough profits to show for it," Otis remarked. "How many bottles this time, Chester?"

"Fifty-four, all to be placed in storage with the rest."

"That mineshaft is going to be filled to the brim soon enough. We got to get rid of this stuff."

"Oh, I know, Otis. But you know what my problem

is? That goddamn Volstead Act. This country was built on liquor. Why would the president sign a document banning such a beautiful thing? What an evil son of a bitch."

Otis chuckled. "Maybe he got too drunk and decided he didn't like it. Wanted to take out his misery on the American people. It's possible, just saying."

Chester spat. "Either way, Poor Fork ain't buying as much as they used to. People fear the consequences, not that the sheriff's doing anything about it."

"Thanks to you, brother."

"Yeah, thanks to me. Teddy Hanes and his deputies may lay off the saloon customers, but that doesn't keep fear out of the people's hearts. They're scared of the statesmen, judges, marshals, and whatnot. Well, I say to Hell with these pompous authority figures. This is Kentucky, bourbon country. We ought to brew our whiskey and drink it without complaints from anyone. Not even Jesus Christ himself ought to care what we do here."

"What do you suppose we do then, Chester?"

"I got a little over six thousand whiskey bottles in the mineshaft ready to be popped and enjoyed. That's a lot of liquor." He paused to think. "Tell you what, Otis. Go into town and start talking to people. Convince them to thirst without fear. Some still make purchases, but many more have stopped since 1920. Take Bo with you. He can talk to folks his age, maybe get a new generation onboard."

"You got it, Chester. I'll head out right away."

"Otis, you don't return unless you have at least ten orders. Twist a few arms if you must. We need to remind the people that they live in a drinking county. Tell them Chester Buckley doesn't sell just any old bourbon. Tell them it's Maplewood Seven."

REED'S
SALOON

The town of Poor Fork never ceased to amaze Bo Buckley. Despite that it rested on the banks of a river, the soil rarely yielded good harvests. Still, the place seemed to thrive. Railroads, constructed two decades prior, ran through the area to speed up the transportation of coal, goods, and laborers willing to work the newer mines. Bo once heard his papa state that Poor Fork would enter an economic boom if the government repealed the prohibition of alcohol.

Yet, right before his eyes, the town appeared to be growing without aid from the local liquor industry. However, being the eldest son of Chester Buckley, Bo felt he needed to prove himself worthy to run his father's business one day. And if that meant working the streets and convincing ten sober people to buy at least one bottle of Maplewood Seven, earning his father's trust would be a piece of cake.

Bo sat alone in Reed's Saloon, the only bar in Poor Fork that continued to serve alcohol. He had learned that the 18th Amendment, passed in January 1920, only forbade the manufacture, sale, and transportation of the devil's juice. Of course, if someone purchased liquor before that date and had a valid receipt, they were free to indulge in the privacy of their home or property, respectfully.

With that in mind, every bar in town had played the game foolishly and ran their shelves dry long ago. They could only now serve water and carbonated drinks like cola and root beer. Before the finalization of the Volstead Act, and unlike his peers, Percy Reed had stocked up on various liquors except for Maplewood Seven, which he did not need to store away, considering he regularly bought the stuff from Chester. Suspecting what would come, Percy had filled his cellar and pantries with non-local products, even hiding bottles and kegs in places no one expected. The credit is due to Chester, without whom Percy would be another loathsome soul slaving away in the mines.

In 1921, Chester created a system undefinable in the new Amendment. If someone in Poor Fork wanted to drink, they needed to buy a special voucher from Howie's Grocery, which looked like a lottery ticket. They could then take the voucher to Percy Reed in exchange for a pint of beer or a glass of liquor. Therefore, Percy did not sell alcohol for cash but gave it to people freely in the privacy of his property. Under the scope of things, Howard Williams, who owned the grocery store, split the revenue from the vouchers with Chester and Percy.

However, an issue recently reared its ugly head. Percy's inventory of imported whiskey looked dry as sunbaked soil. Yet, for some reason, he had not refilled his stock of Maplewood Seven in almost a year. Bo figured the fear of the law finally hit old Percy. Nevertheless, he thought of convincing the graying barkeep to start buying from his father again in secrecy.

"No, no, no," Percy griped. "And don't ask me that question while others are around. You should know better."

"I'm just saying, Mr. Reed, Pa's got a lot of the good stuff. So much that I'm sure he'd lower the price for an old friend like you."

Percy sighed and dragged a palm across his roughly shaved chin. "I admit Maplewood Seven is the best bourbon I've tasted since I first tried Winchester. But accepting bottles from an illegal distillery ain't worth the risk anymore. Bo, you've got to understand that. I really like your father, but if Teddy Hanes got wind of it, I'd—"

"Pa only worries about State Marshal McCrory and the higher federal authorities," Bo cut in, hammering a fist on the counter. "He could give a damn about county bumpkins like Hanes. Far as I know, Pa owns the sheriff and his deputies. You ought to know that, too. No one can touch Chester. And no one can touch you, Mr. Reed. Start buying more bottles from us. I promise no harm will come to you."

Percy shrugged. "Maplewood Seven is already my top-selling liquor. The less I have in stock, the more Howie can charge, which makes us all more money anyway."

"Sorry to tell you, Mr. Reed, but Howard Wilson will do what Chester Buckley says, not what you say. If Pa ever told Howie to steady or lower his prices, your scheme is finished."

"Doggonit, Bo. You got my stones on an anvil. Shit. You truly are your father's son. Fine. Tell Chester I'll take ten bottles a month, but he ain't going to pull that from my cut of the voucher income. I'll swing by the house at the beginning of each month to deliver the payment. That's how it's going to be."

Bo smiled, amazed that he had fashioned such a quick bargain. They shook hands. "Now, Mr. Reed, how about a beer for me?"

"I ain't got much beer left, but for you, Bo, here's one on the house."

Bo sat at the counter and drank his beer, enjoying each sip as if it had been brewed from the sweet nectar of Eden's forbidden fruit. Percy occasionally eyed him from across the bar while serving other locals and cleaning glasses. About twenty minutes later, Otis marched in and laid a piece of paper on the countertop in front of Bo.

"Since when can you write, Uncle Otis?"

"I can't. June Rivers wrote on here. Got her to jot down these orders for me, including one for her husband, Brett. A good man that Brett."

"I didn't know June Rivers knew how to write."

"All them Rivers know how to write, Bo. That's what happens when you run a bank. Got to know stuff like that, even if you're a lady."

"Gosh, speaking of ladies, those Rivers produced a fine daughter if I might say so."

"You're still in love with that Maggy girl, ain't you?"

"She broke my heart before I even tried, Otis. Magnolia Rivers is the prettiest girl in Poor Fork. Or is she?" Bo caught sight of a young woman entering the saloon. Her Victorian cotton dress might have hinted at New England wealth. Still, the worn-out quality of her attire told Bo that she was an ordinary American who had either received it as a hand-me-down or had stolen it from an old lady. Either way, the garb didn't hide her shapely features from his dazzled mind and hungry heart.

"Look at the tits on that ripe thing," Otis chuckled with a slow nod. "Help me, Lord. Jesus would never forgive me for what I'd do to her."

"Shut up, Uncle. That's a rude thing to say about a lovely creature like that. Would you say such things about a beautiful bird?"

"No, because I don't fuck birds. I eat them. If that girl were a pretty bird, I'd savor each bite."

Bo patted his uncle on the shoulder and pushed off the barstool. "You head on back to the house. I'll meet you there. I got a bird to catch."

"Bo, neither of us can go just yet."

"Tell Pa I convinced Percy to buy ten bottles a month. That'll keep his mouth on the pipe."

"Damn boy, you good. all right. I'll head back, but don't do anything I wouldn't do."

"I've strived all my life to do everything you don't do, Uncle Otis."

"Smart-ass."

As Otis exited through the back door, Bo approached the lovely lady. He felt his heart flutter as if every inch closer revealed something new about her. Her sandy blonde hair shimmered in the afternoon sunlight that streamed through the windows. Her forget-me-not eyes turned his way, and her pink lips curved just enough to make him feel nervous.

He told himself that she was the one, the girl of his dreams. Just as he neared, a young man stepped to her side and pulled her to the counter. Garbed in baggy brown overalls and leather boots, this fellow looked to be the working type, perhaps even a miner, except his clothes were unstained. Bo heard Percy greet the man, who replied in a city accent. "Can I please trouble you for some soda pop?"

"We don't sell pop here, boy," Percy answered brusquely. "Got to go to Red Danville's shop for that. We only serve alcohol."

"Hot dog! I thought they banned liquor across the country. May I order a beer?"

Percy laughed. "You must be fresh in town, son. You need a voucher from the grocery store. If you ain't got no voucher, you don't get any beer. That's the rule around here."

"Mr. Reed," Bo called out, joining the newcomers at the counter. "May I please get three beers, another for me and two for my friends here?"

Percy grunted and grimaced, then silently obliged.

"How'd you do that?" inquired the young lady.

"I've known old Percy all my life," Bo answered, smiling sunshine at the girl. "Our families go way back. Isn't that right, Mr. Reed?"

"Suppose it is," grumbled the barkeep, topping off the first of three golden glasses.

"You must be a popular fella here," the young man said.

"Popular? I never thought about that. I suppose I know most of the people in town, so I guess that makes me popular, but I ain't special by any means. Say, what are your names? Where're you from?"

"I'm Daniel Andersen, but you can call me Danny. And this little lady is my sister, Jane. We just got off a long train ride from Norfolk on the Virginia coast."

"Well, that's peachy," Bo laughed. "I've never gone

too far into Virginia, let alone the coast. The name's Bo Buckley, by the way. Say, what're you doing out here in Poor Fork anyhow? There ain't nothing in this part of Kentucky except mountains, rivers, and hunting dogs."

"From what I hear, there's also work to be done," Danny conveyed, his tone sharp as his gaze.

"Danny wants to be a coal miner," Jane giggled.

"No one wants to be a coal miner," her brother argued. "I just need work, good work. Virginia is a troublesome place. Can't find one decent employer. That's why we're here to start over. And I tell you, Bo Buckley, that I'm a damn fine laborer. And if it's any benefit, I know the ways and means of the streets. I know how to drive a car, how to read, and how to talk to people. I got a lot of connections. I like to think I know a bit about everything. And Jane makes a great maid. She can clean a whole house in two hours with the right equipment. No fooling."

Bo couldn't take his eyes off Jane, who responded with a dimpled smile. He felt like a helpless child under the spell of a dreamy song. The moment she looked at her brother, the trance broke, leaving Bo empty as a desert well.

"So," Danny continued, "do you know where we can find work and board in these parts?"

An idea burst into Bo's head. "You know how to bottle stuff, Danny Andersen?"

"No, but I'm a fast learner."

"Good enough. Let's finish our beers, then take a long walk and discuss what you and your sister can do for me."

WARM
WELCOME

"Why in God's name did you bring outsiders to my property?" Chester growled like a bear. "You know the rules, Bo. You know the damned rules. Outsiders only cause trouble, especially Virginians."

Bo rolled his eyes. "Now, Pa, just because you've made some bad deals in Virginia doesn't mean all the folks from there are troublesome. Danny and Jane needed work. I figured we could use a helping hand. Our batches grow bigger every season, and I didn't see the harm since they know nothing about you or anything you do in Poor Fork."

Chester looked at the newcomers sitting at the dinner table in the other room. "Did you bring them here because you like the look of that girl?"

"I think she's beautiful, but he said he could—"

"I don't care, Bo. You think with your pecker, not with your brain. Sure, that girl's a beauty, but how do we know they ain't spying for someone. For all I know, they work for the government or, worse, Henry Wilkins and his pig-stealing family."

"They don't work for Henry, trust me, Pa. Their last name is Andersen, not Wilkins. I already planned out their positions if it makes you feel any better. Jane can work with Mama here and learn to do the house chores. As for Danny, I can show him the ropes. He can bottle in my place while I focus on other important tasks and give you some duty relief. What do you say to that, Pa?"

Chester tugged on his beard. "City folk ain't good workers, Bo. They're spoiled and arrogant. However, considering that you persuaded Percy to buy more Maplewood Seven, I reckon I'll give these Virginians a go. But you need to lay the rules on them hard. Out here in the mountains, we don't tolerate slack regarding our business. Neither do we speak of it beyond this property. We don't even mention our family name unless in the presence of people we know and trust. We don't want "

"I know the rules, Pa. I'll make sure they understand."

"Good. I've worked too hard to make this business run smoothly. all right. Well, you best get started with Danny. Introduce him to the family and let the hounds have a sniff at him. Don't need a chewed-up city boy on my hands. Make sure he understands the meaning of the barn. And tell him not to smoke that Mexican shit that Burt and Rufus love so darn much. I don't need another mindless turd working on my still."

"Got it. What about Jane?"

"I'll introduce Jane to your Ma and sisters. She shouldn't have a problem."

"Thanks, Pa."

"You're welcome, son. When you see Otis and Dick, tell them to treat the new boy like Big Bertha treats her hounds. Keep him on a leash until he's hungry."

Bo began right away by acquainting Danny with the ladies of the house. There was his mother Winifred; his sisters Ginny and Sally May; his aunt Melanie; and her daughter Nancy. Afterward, Bo and Danny went out to the barn, which rested in the shadow of a pine grove at the foot of a steep hill beside a narrow ravine that snaked down from greater heights. While admiring the scenery, Bo explained to Danny that, although the barn looked ugly, unpainted, and dingy as a fish house, an absolute beauty lay within. He opened one of the doors and watched the Virginian's face light up.

"You make whiskey here?" Danny nearly wept with joy.

"Not just any whiskey," Bo radiated with pride. "Extra smooth bourbon with a hint of sweetness."

While walking between the tubs and copper pots,

Bo briefly divulged how they produced their whiskey—the mashing, distilling, fermenting, all the good stuff. He even showed Danny the vats where they kept the grains.

They then went to a line of wooden carts near the back of the barn, granting Bo the chance to introduce Danny to his younger brother Tobias and his cousins Burt and Rufus, who sat around corking glass bottles. After the warm greeting, Bo led the newcomer to the south side of the barn, where an archway opened to a building extension called the rack-house, where they inventoried all the aging barrels. They stepped inside to find Otis inspecting the bungs for leakage.

"We age our bourbon for seven years," Bo happily disclosed, "in barrels coopered and charred by Dick and Pa right here on the property. What makes them special is that they're split-wood barrels. In our case, they're half oak and half sugar maple. We get the oaks from higher in the range, but we grow the maple right here on the property. The original maples came from seeds purchased in Vermont. But that was generations ago when our family decided to make syrup for Poor Fork. Though Ma still makes a mighty fine syrup with the sap, what we produce back here in the barn is far more valuable."

Danny looked at Bo with eyes as wide as his grin. "May I have a taste?"

"From the barrels, no. Only the angels get their share when there's a drip." Bo chuckled. "So, each row that you see is a different batch. The farthest back is the freshest, produced about a month ago. They'll sit in this room for roughly seven years. This row right here, however, ought to be ready in a few weeks. A lot goes into this process. We pride ourselves on a streak of unbroken production, even when times are tough."

"The longest we've ever gone without bottling was four months. Chester, my papa, doesn't tolerate lagging or mistakes. You mess up, and you're out of Kentucky." He hummed. "But if you want to try some finished product, come here" Bo escorted Danny back into the barn and grabbed a bottle from Tobias before he could cork it. "Our bottles are made by the finest glass company in Louisville. Best glass for the best whiskey. Here, you can have this one. It's on me."

Danny tipped the bottle for a swig and swished the stuff around in his mouth as if it were wine. He swallowed it and breathed deeply. "That might be the best whiskey I've ever tasted."

Bo nodded. "Maplewood Seven, finest bourbon in Kentucky."

"Goddamn," Danny proclaimed as if he had struck gold. "This is the cat's meow. I can't wait to help you produce this magnificent giggle water. When do I start?"

"Pull up a stool, grab a handful of corks, and pick a cart. Bottle as much as you can. And make sure they're nice and tight. You'll get paid with housing and food and a weekly allowance."

While Bo watched Danny start on his work in the barn, Chester introduced Jane to the women of the house, instantly impressed by her gentility. She curtsied, spoke well without a flare of arrogance, held eye contact, and maintained a strong posture while sitting or walking. Her beauty didn't matter to Chester as long as she didn't cause trouble with the boys. He briefly wondered if the girl would ever consider giving him grandchildren by marrying Bo. Tossing such thoughts to the back of his mind, he left Jane with the ladies and headed outside.

Winifred feigned a brief smile at Jane. "Since we're already preparing supper, I'll have Ginny teach you how to set the table."

Jane nodded. "Not to sound bold, ma'am, and pardon my saying, but I'm quite familiar with decorating a dining table. Been doing it a long time, ma'am."

"Call me Winnie. And that's fine if you know how, Jane, but as long as you're staying in this house, I need you to be acquainted with *our* family's habits and chores. Ginny, show the girl around before you two get going on the table. Make it quick. Melanie, Nancy, and Sally May can finish peeling and chopping. Still, no time to waste."

As they walked through the house, Ginny explained everything to Jane – expected table manners, essential places to dust, how to polish the wood floors, how to organize Chester's tobacco pipes, almost too much to absorb at once. She further elaborated that supporting the Buckley household took meticulous effort. Winifred had long set a standard for all the girls, which the boys appreciated, and Chester wholeheartedly respected. "Pa's opinion matters above all others. Remember that. Always be honest and avoid causing trouble in Poor Fork. Of course, if you do wrong to Pa and tick him off, the consequences ain't pretty. If you ask Bo, he'll tell you some horror stories."

"Has Mr. Buckley ever killed a man?"

Ginny looked around to ensure no other ears had opened to their conversation. "We don't usually talk about that stuff, especially to guests. But since you'll be here a while and might see things you don't understand, I should tell you that I've seen Papa drag bodies through our property. I was still a child the last time it happened, but I remember. That was before he went to jail, of course, and came back dressed like a city banker. Decided it was time for him to clean up. Made sure us children grew up equally polished too. Said it'd raise the Buckley name and business. However, he didn't demand the same of Otis and Dick and their children. Said that to keep his hands clean, he needed theirs to stay dirty."

"And speaking of dirty," she continued, "I ought to warn you that the scariest person here is my cousin, Patty Ann Harper. She's tall and strong as a bear and the best gunner in our clan. She used to be a bounty hunter, then did something nasty and got locked up for a while. That made her rougher than nails. What's truly frightening about her is her always having those two bloodhounds around."

"Oh, I saw her when Bo brought Danny and me up the hill. I thought she was a man, but as we got closer, I realized she was a mean-looking woman. Could probably snap me in half."

"That's why we call her Big Bertha. She's Pa's guard and keeper of the grounds. Nothing, and I mean nothing, gets by her."

"What about Bo?" Jane tried to keep her cheeks from blushing.

"My older brother? He's all right. He's going to run Pa's business one day, so he tries to act tough and bossy, but he's a real sweetheart by nature. Why do you ask?"

"No reason."

Ginny put her hand to her mouth. "Do you think my brother is handsome? You can tell me if you do. I think that's just the darnedest thing."

"He's got clean teeth for a country boy. I like his bright smile and those big blue eyes."

"You also got big blue eyes, Jane. Maybe you two were made to stare at each other forever. I know I just met you, but wouldn't it be funny if we became sisters?"

The ladies giggled and continued the housekeeping tour.

Danny Means Business

Danny Andersen quickly adapted to life on the Buckley property. He spent most of his time in the barn, observing the inner workings of Chester's business. He learned that Tobias, at fourteen years old, enjoyed mathematics and plucked the banjo better than most city players. Danny considered him to be the most intelligent of the Buckley brood. Burt and Rufus were the polar opposite of their cousin. Although in their early thirties, Otis's goofy fraternal twins seemed to lack awareness of the world, primarily occupied with smoking Mexican hemp and their ability to fashion new slurs. They seemed like harmless creatures, dumb as dirt, easy to shoot if necessary.

Otis Buckley proved sharper than his offspring, always cautious of his words and quick to draw a revolver. He came into the barn three times a day, usually to check on the aging barrels and ensure that the vats got cleaned and bottling done. Surly as Otis appeared with his gray brows permanently furrowed and clothes always black, he usually found a reason to deliver a pleasant comment. He seemed like a step up from Dick Harper.

Dick looked like an aged boxer with greasy dark hair and a thick horseshoe mustache, which faded into a deep scar that sliced from his chin to his ear. He was married to Chester and Otis's homely sister, Melanie. She and Nancy, their younger daughter, looked beefy as autumn cows but spoke softer than fresh snow.

The eldest, Big Bertha, proved to be as hard and mean as a bull, taking after the father. Danny worried that Dick and Bertha were constantly surveying him, even plotting how they might harm him should he ever cause trouble. They often stared at him with fire in their eyes, sometimes cursing or spitting in his direction. Nevertheless, even with the formidable Harpers around, Danny felt safer working for the Buckleys than his old employer in Norfolk.

Bo was the friendliest in the house. He made Danny feel welcome by taking him to Reed's Saloon every other night, where they drank and puffed cigars, laughed at jokes, and exchanged childhood stories. Bo also shared many of his belongings to make his guests feel welcome.

Danny regularly voiced his gratitude but secretly cursed whenever he caught Bo getting sweet with Jane. To ease his growing frustrations, Danny convinced himself that their flirting would never amount to anything. He also felt that it would be hypocritical of him to vilify them since he, too, had found a harp string to pluck.

Ginny Buckley was younger than him, a seventeen-year-old mountain flower. He liked how her honey-brown hair shimmered with a strawberry tint in the sunlight and how her warm laugh always managed to pop a giggle out of him. He thought her sweeter than any pie he'd ever tasted, the most beautiful girl east of the Mississippi. His only problem was that his fondness remained unknown to her.

After a few months of observation, Danny felt he completely understood how things operated at the Maplewood Distillery. However, one day, after bottling the last of a completed batch, Dick Harper brought him and the other boys to the finished goods storage. A gush of confusion poured over Danny's thoughts when they crossed the Buckley property line about a half-mile northwest of the barn, marked on the trees with faded red paint.

He thought it odd that the whiskey depository lay somewhere on the open mountain rather than the well-guarded compound. His curiosity prompted him to inquire about such a decision, but he knew that old

Harper would smack him upside the head if he dared ask. Fearing Dick's menacing attitude, Danny walked behind the horse-drawn cart alongside Tobias and discussed their shared enjoyment of music.

They eventually arrived at what appeared to be an abandoned mineshaft sealed by a pair of rusty iron doors. Without a word, Dick unfastened the padlock and let the sunshine in. When Danny saw the bourbon hoard within, a brilliant idea struck him. He tossed his fears aside and approached Dick. "Why are there so many bottles here? Maplewood Seven is liquid gold. Isn't it selling?"

With a voice as hard and rusted as the iron doors, Dick answered, "The law slowed business years ago, but Chester refuses to do the same with his production. We needed to store the excess product somewhere."

Tobias chimed in. "Hopefully, we'll figure out a way to sell it all soon. There're even a few aging barrels at the back of the mine entry that got put there in 1907. Pa hopes to bring them out one day and bottle them as Maplewood 21, aged three times the normal duration. Three times smoother, too. I bet it's good and strong already."

"Very interesting," Danny remarked under his breath. He had more to say but waited until Dick, Burt, and Rufus vanished into the mineshaft to make room for more bottles. When the moment arrived, Danny took Tobias aside and asked for a favor. "Once we get back to the house, I need you to tell Chester I wish to speak with him privately. I'm a little intimidated by him and don't want to step on any toes."

"I suggest going to Otis or Bo first."

"Fine, I'll talk to Bo."

"Mind if I ask what it's about, Danny?"

"Let's just say I've got an idea that might empty the mine and fill our pockets with cash."

Later, back at the Buckley house, Danny found Bo preoccupied with writing what looked like poetry. "You know how to write?"

Bo leaned back in his chair and cracked a wide grin. "Sure, I do! Pa taught me. He said that all his children ought to know how to write because it makes us smarter and can be helpful in case we get in trouble or something happens to him. He learned from a feller in a Tennessee prison many years ago. Do you know how to write?"

"No, but I do know how to read. I used to read books back in Norfolk. It opened my mind to things I never knew existed. Speaking of that, I got a bold idea that I bet your daddy never thought to attempt."

"What's that, Danny?"

"Expansion."

"Expansion to where? The property's pretty big already."

"Not the property, Bo, the business. The distribution of Maplewood Seven. Remember back in Reed's Saloon when I told you I've got connections?

Well, I wasn't lying. I know a lot of people in Virginia and North Carolina who'd pay good money for your family's bourbon."

"You don't say! Well, why didn't you tell me before?"

"I never knew how much whiskey you had until I saw the mineshaft this morning."

"It's full, I know. Real full."

Danny nodded. "Full of liquid gold. I need to tell Chester about this idea."

"Well, I can help you with that. Let's go."

Chester had spent the day in Poor Fork, comparing Percy and Howie's ledgers to ensure all voucher money and liquor inventory amounted correctly. Knowing that no errors arose, he felt he deserved to recline in his rocker on the front porch and enjoy a glass of Maplewood Seven while puffing his pipe.

However, before he could burn deep into his tobacco or find comfort in the tufted backing, Bo burst out of the house, spinning sugared words about Danny, who stood behind him like a child waiting to play. Chester sighed, annoyed initially but curious about why his son fervently listed Danny's contributions to the family business. He surmised that Bo's passion didn't stem from his friendship with Danny but his secret love for Jane Andersen. And he would do anything to make her happy, even talk her brother up, who it seemed had an idea he wanted to relay.

Once Chester felt his son had buttered him enough, he waved Danny over, ready to endure the impending proposal. With each sip of whiskey, Chester listened to the Virginian talk, his speech evolving from an egg of anxiousness to a feathered bird of confidence. But his self-assuredness soon flickered with an arrogance that finally spurred Chester into a retort.

"You have connections in the city, so what?" He polished off his glass and stood up. "I got connections in towns and cities everywhere: Arkansas, Missouri, Tennessee, the Virginias, the Carolinas, Alabama. But I haven't acted on them. Do you know why? Because this country is drunk on fear. We suffered a war that killed a lot of young men. Sapped the spirit of this great nation. Then, thanks to lobbyists, the government enacted a law unfavored by the majority, banning the manufacturing and sale of alcohol."

"However, because Americans secretly decided to continue their love affair with liquor, a criminal economy was born, run by fancy gangs and foreign thugs in the big cities. Truth is, people, especially those big city dealers, who I'm guessing are your *connections*, are afraid to work with folks like me. Without automatic guns, a fat wallet, shiny cars, and government slack, I appear illegitimate to those outside Kentucky. People don't want to buy from a man without approval from the corrupted lawmen of the states. All I got are docile local sheriffs."

"Now, you probably think I made all that up,"

Chester continued. "Sure, I was born and raised here in the mountains. I like isolation. I enjoy privacy. I love the idea of being out of reach of institutions. But I've experienced things you wouldn't understand in places you probably never heard of. And I read, I read a lot. Yes, I've got my way of getting the news. I know everything that's going on. And let me tell you, Danny; it's too dangerous right now for my high-quality product to be distributed through any non-local connections, mine or yours."

"Well," Danny hesitated. "Uh, what if I knew a way around things?"

"You don't imagine I know my way around things, Danny? Why do you think I run half of Harlan County? I ain't some hillbilly moron with missing teeth and a lack of worldly perception like Burt and Rufus. I know what goes on, and I sure as hell will know when it's time to get the ball rolling again. Now, enough of this talk. I want you to get back to work. We got a lot to do."

"Mr. Buckley, please, let me tell you more about my idea. If you don't like it, I'll zip my mouth and never speak of it again."

"Make it quick, boy, before I change my mind."

"All right, Mr. Buckley. This may sound bold, but hear me out. Give me money to buy a good, sturdy truck. I can register the truck under my name, so it has no tie to yours. It wouldn't trace back to the Buckley name if something were to happen. Then we can build a wooden frame that covers the entire truck bed, leaving just enough space between the wood and the metal to store whiskey bottles. Atop the wood would be a simple cover, a visual deception to the public. We can use anything we want – hay, livestock, corn, pumpkins. You name it, I'll do it. But this way, no one will dare question what we're transporting. I can drive the truck directly to our buyers." He chuckled with an air of pride. "And that's it. Simple. That's how we empty your mine. That's how you become filthy, stinking rich."

After a minute of throaty consideration, Chester eased his head into a nod. "You say you know some folks that'll start you off, huh? People you trust? I hope so because I refuse to contact mine until I see your idea is foolproof."

"I know a few fellas that operate underground clubs and related businesses. Don't worry, Mr. Buckley, I worked this out. It can't fail. I promise."

Chester looked up at the trees and breathed deeply. "I was mistaken before. Sounds like you've got a decent plan. That's a good head on your shoulders, Daniel Andersen. However, I have two stipulations to your proposition. I know you'll want a bigger cut, which I'm willing to accept, but it comes at a steep price."

"Of my total profits, I give ten percent to the local authorities. Keeps them quiet and out of my hair. The rest goes to me, which I typically divide as I see fit among my kin. Since you ain't my kin, I'll have to treat your allowance differently. I can give you five percent of my total earnings, plus a little extra for your travel expenses. But if you do me wrong, Danny-boy, I will castrate you and flay your chest while you still breathe, then fill you with bullets until nothing remains. You hear? One slip, you're a goner."

"That's fair," Danny replied with not so much as a tremble or bead of sweat on his brow, remembering that this was not the first time he had been threatened in the wake of a good idea. "What else you got to say, boss?"

"The second stipulation is about trust. I don't know you that well, so I don't trust you much. Therefore, you ain't going anywhere alone. For all I know, you'll just take my truck and whiskey, and drive off into the sunset, never to return. Therefore, I'm going to have Otis accompany you on your travels."

"Otis?"

"Yes, Otis. You got a problem with my brother?"

"No, sir."

"Good. Otis will sit beside you in the truck until I decide otherwise. Also, you will not sell to anyone within the state of Kentucky. I want Maplewood Seven distributed outside of State Marshal Alias McCrory's jurisdiction. Got that? Oh, and one more thing, your sister, Jane, will marry Bo. That's going to be part of our deal. I don't like arranging marriages, but it seems like a fair price for a great reward."

Danny bit his lip. "Now wait here, Chester. I love

my sister. You can't just treat her like a bullion of silver or an antique clock."

"I just did, Danny-boy. Now, you can either agree to my deal and pick up that truck today or get back to work in the barn. Or you can get the hell off my property, where you might find yourself at the whim of Big Bertha and her hounds. So, what's it going to be?"

In the early afternoon, Danny and Otis rode south on horseback to Kingsport to meet with wealthy folks who Chester knew drove quality cars and trucks. Coursing through mountains and valleys slowed their speed, so they didn't hit town until the following evening. Chester had commanded them to seek out a specific club called Hannah's, where some of his well-off Tennessee friends often lingered and drank.

After Danny and Otis sucked down two glasses of sour mash, they meandered around the room, inquiring about Chester's friends. A few suited gentlemen at a dim-lit corner table greeted Otis with short but welcoming words, paying no mind to Danny. "Go see Earl Colfax," one of them suggested. "He's always willing to help Chester Buckley."

Thanks to his successful export trading company, Earl Colfax owned an estate just outside Kingsport, which Danny and Otis found quickly enough. However, convincing the guards to arrange an immediate appointment took some effort. Once inside, the butler escorted them upstairs to an office resembling a baby library, where they smoked cigars and drank high-end brandy with Earl Colfax.

After listening to the businessman rant about his recent adventure to the French Riviera, Otis handed him a bottle of Maplewood Seven and began negotiating a price for one of the excellent Ford Model TTs on the property. Nearly losing his mind listening to the countryman sputter, Danny cut in with fiery words that made Otis sweat with amazement. Within a few minutes, Mr. Colfax agreed to give them a truck and board for the night in exchange for a second bottle of Maplewood Seven and their horses. Colfax tasted the whiskey to finalize his decision. Danny knew the answer before the man even popped the cork.

Chester hardly had a chance to touch his breakfast when Danny and Otis pulled up to the house in a sleek Ford Model TT. He stepped out onto the porch with a broad smile beneath his whiskers. Otis hastened to his brother's side, eager to divulge all that happened in Kingsport. Satisfied and impressed, Chester met Danny and shook his hand with a firm grip. "You're one of us now, Daniel. I reckon it's safe to say I'm ready to move forward with your plan. After breakfast, I want you to drive to the state office in Harlan and register the truck under your name. Formality will protect our secrecy. Bring the truck back with all the papers, and we'll start building your concealment bed."

"Yes, sir. Right away, Mr. Buckley."

"Call me Chester."

After Danny registered the truck with the state of Kentucky, he and all the boys hauled some fresh pine wood up from a local lumberyard. It only took a few days to construct a false truck bed with a secret compartment, which looked like a skid with two long drawers. Once the boys secured the storage piece to the Ford, they covered it in a layer of loose hay to keep the wood dry. After Chester thoroughly inspected the vehicle, Dick and Tobias went up to the mine to fill a wagon with twenty jugs of Maplewood Seven. When Danny saw them load the storage drawers, he shook his head and turned to the Buckley patriarch.

"Why twenty bottles?" Frustration heated his tone. "I told you we can do fifty, maybe even sixty at a time."

Chester glared at Danny with a frown that slashed through his beard. "If you're going to jump in a hot spring, you best dip a toe in to make sure you don't get boiled alive. I ain't stupid. I need reassurance that this operation will run smoothly. I don't want to lose more whiskey than necessary if something goes awry. If you can successfully transport these bottles across the state line and return with cold hard cash, I'll give you as much whiskey as humanly possible. I'll empty the mine and hasten production. And you, Danny-boy, will get a raise to eight percent."

"Chester Buckley, you got yourself a deal."

They shook hands just as Tobias loaded the last bottle into the truck. Within the hour, Danny and Otis set out on their journey. However, instead of heading to Virginia as planned, they drove back to Kingsport, where Danny negotiated a second deal with Earl Colfax. Not only did the Tennessean wish to push Maplewood Seven through his export business, but he also knew a few gentlemen who owned clubs in a handful of Dixie cities that might be interested.

It seemed all too simple a task for Danny Andersen, laying down the price of six hundred dollars for all twenty bottles. Colfax accepted the outrageous price with a laugh, then offered to write a contract declaring that he would purchase forty containers monthly for a discounted fee of one thousand dollars.

"Two hundred off the top?" Danny tried not to giggle in disbelief. "We are in business, Mr. Colfax."

Otis said nothing the entire time and later told Danny how impressed he felt by the young man's aggressive bargaining talent. Chester, too, seemed quite taken by Danny's skill and speed. When he received the six hundred dollars in cash, he happily divided up the earnings and gave an extra fifty to Danny for his hard work.

To honor the newfound system of business, Chester hosted a small party that evening, inviting a few friends from town along with a handful of easy women for the boys. Burt and Rufus drank and smoked more than necessary, then shut themselves in the tool shed with a woman they planned to share. Three more prostitutes remained, mingling with Otis, Percy,

Howie, and others. One of the dark-haired beauties took a liking to Danny. However, his mind sought pleasures elsewhere.

While Chester and Dick followed Big Bertha to the edge of the property to inspect a few traps, the Buckley women sat on the back porch, mocking the devilish jezebels buzzing around the men by the firepit. Standing in the darkness between the porch and the pit, Ginny gazed upward, adoring the full moon.

Danny had his heart set on Ginny and desperately wished to marry her. However, he figured he needed to make something of himself within the family business to win her over. Undoubtedly, his delivery system proved a step in the right direction. Still, he felt claiming victory over Ginny's heart required much more. He needed Chester to raise him to official family status, becoming a Buckley with fatherly approval. 'One of us' was not enough, not when he could earn the label of *kin*.

From the corner of his eye, Danny noticed Bo and Jane flirting in the moonlit shadow of a tree by the house. He hated himself for selling his sister out. Neither did he appreciate the idea that Bo naturally obtained what he wanted without effort – power, marriage, and kinship. From all their conversations, whether around the property or at Reed's Saloon, Danny found Bo to be half as bright as he acted. Yet, he seemed to make up for his lack of wits with kindness, humor, and pulling his weight as expected.

In the end, however, he showed no signs of ambition.

Besides being the eldest of Chester's children, Danny wondered why Bo deserved to call himself heir to the family business. He felt the position ought to go to someone more suitable, someone oozing with intelligence, someone who knew the ways and means of dealing, a heart of passion who could raise Maplewood Seven to national recognition. The way his sister smiled at Bo made him want to gag. To remedy this anxiety, Danny turned his eyes back to Ginny. She refused to return the gaze or acknowledge his smile. Nevertheless, he told himself he would have her one day.

The rest of the month proved quite busy. Earl Colfax had done Danny a favor by giving some of his upper-class peers a taste of Maplewood Seven. Within a few short weeks, Chester received twenty-two letters through the mail service, each listing an address and an order quantity. At first, Danny and Otis's deliveries only stretched as far as Kingsport, Johnson City, and Abingdon. However, the distances grew as orders began to surge.

Occasionally, they had to sleep in the truck or at a roadside inn. Either way, they raked in plenty of money to keep the wheels turning. Yet, Danny's insatiable appetite to become a member of the Buckley family pushed him beyond any limit. He negotiated his way past a few of his main buyers to reach their sources and sell more directly to those in need. This led him to cities such as Roanoke, Knoxville, and Greensboro, but he didn't stop there.

Before long, Chester decided to pull Otis from the passenger seat, claiming that trust had been earned. Now delivering on his own, Danny felt more driven than ever, although resistance of the heart prevailed. Ginny still refused to lend him a loving glance. In several passing moments, he paid compliments to her beauty and the way she talked. Yet, she hardly acknowledged a single word. This frustrated Danny to the point of ire.

However, on a cloudy day, the Virginian happened to catch her while she waited for her sister to finish pumping water at the well. Confidence bubbled. He struck up a conversation about the weather, and although it felt mildly pleasant, it proved all too brief. At the end of it, he jumped the gun and asked her if she would consider marrying him. "No, Danny," she fired before he could sweet-talk her.

All that summer, Danny found moments that allowed him to ask Ginny for her hand in marriage. While each failed attempt felt like another jab to the heart, he reminded himself not to grow acquainted with constant rejection. Therefore every "no" that Danny received prompted him to conceive a new method of querying. He felt that his persistence would ultimately yield the desired result, whether by a stroke of change in Ginny or by the patriarchal command of Chester. To make matters worse for Danny, his yearning for Ginny only increased with the passing of each month.

Witnessing the blooming love between Bo and his sister further frustrated Danny, fueling his dreams of conquest. A hot stew of mixed emotions began to boil within him, the strongest being envy. Bo and Jane possessed the happiness he craved to share with Ginny. He also loathed that Jane was to marry the man he wished to supplant. Danny's secret hatred for the eldest of Chester's children increased tenfold as time passed, especially when Bo stopped inviting him to drink at Reed's and took Jane instead.

Danny began to mentally denounce Bo's limited work ethic and carefree lifestyle, assuming he now spent most of his time in bed with Jane. Yet, nothing enraged the Virginian more than the fact that brainless Bo would inherit the valuable Buckley business. Danny saw his future brother-in-law as his premier rival. Therefore, he exerted extreme effort to show Chester that he held more value than the eldest son.

In early autumn, Danny achieved a critical goal that he had hoped would render his boss speechless. He set up a handful of connections with the very people who, according to Chester, refused to work with folks like him. They were the big city dealers – mobsters, thugs, gangs, and speakeasy proprietors. Reputably nefarious as they were, these characters enjoyed Danny's sense of humor and aggressive persuasion tactics. He soon found himself delivering Maplewood

Seven to Nashville, Chattanooga, Charlotte, Cincinnati, Charleston, and Richmond, to name a few. He had hit the big time and knew he had paid his dues. Thus, he felt entitled to request a betrothal formally.

"May I have your daughter's hand?" he asked Chester one afternoon on the front porch. "May I marry your sweet, beautiful Ginny Buckley?"

Chester smiled and poured Danny a glass of whiskey. "I like you, Daniel. I like you a lot. You've really grown on me. And I appreciate you as if you were one of my own, which makes it harder for me to tell you that I cannot give you the direct answer you seek. My children are free to *choose* their life partners. They'll not be treated like a bullion of silver or an antique clock, as I recall you once said. Now, if you're asking my permission to court Ginny, I wish you the best of luck. Tell you the truth, I wouldn't mind seeing you two together, make me some handsome grandchildren. But, again, it's entirely up to her in the end. If you can win her, Danny, you can have her. You have my blessing."

Danny ground his teeth and slammed his glass on the wood railing, spilling a few sips of Buckley gold. "Chester, I gave Jane to Bo as a stipulation to our business agreement. We can renegotiate, and you can give Ginny to me. I'll take a smaller cut and work harder. How's that sound?"

"Danny, I just said that none of my children will be treated as commodities. Keep your cut and work

Ginny with the passion of your heart. That's what a real man does. He earns love."

"Bo didn't earn Jane's love. I gave her to him."

Chester laughed. "Boy, you must be blind as a field mole. Bo and Jane have liked each other since the minute you arrived in Poor Fork. With or without your blessing, she would have flocked to him and him to her. There ain't a human, alive or dead, who can stop the nature of the heart, let me tell you. God's plan is unshakeable, be it bliss or pain. Follow the plan or work it to your advantage; things might turn out all right. Fight the plan, and you may end up in a world of pain. For my part in Bo and Jane's love, I merely support hastening the process."

Danny chewed his lip. "You've dealt me a handful of dog shit, Chester, you know that. You refuse to negotiate the future of your kin, yet you made me treat my sister like a piece of property. That's a sin in God's eyes."

"Love is not a sin, Danny. Neither is advocating for love considered a sin. And I didn't force you to do anything. You are endowed with free will. I made an offer that you chose to accept. If you didn't want to use your sister, your answer would have been no. Simple as that."

"Goddammit, Chester! I emptied the mineshaft as promised. You got nothing up there except a few dozen straggling jugs and old aging barrels. You now sell your freshest batches in larger quantities. Why is that?

Because I opened the road for you. Mr. Buckley, I hate to tell you this, but if it weren't for me, you'd still be cramming that mine full of the devil's juice, sitting like a troll on a hoard of gold. Your pockets would be emptying faster than a bottle of gin in a hobo camp. I made your business boom. I am your business now."

"You're right, Danny. You are my business, but it's still *my* business. You work for me. I survived before your arrival and could do it again without you. You seem to believe I fear the 18th Amendment, but you're wrong. I merely detest it, that's all. I've been selling all this time, just like the other distillers and brewers across the country. Still dress the way I do. I own trucks and property and pay my workers their wages. Don't think you're better than anyone else here because you ain't. You're just another employee to me. Now, I really like you. And I just permitted you to court my eldest daughter. If you turn that around on me and try to push me against all I've built, I will castrate you and flay your chest while you still breathe. Then I'll fill you with bullets until nothing remains. I've told you that before, and there it is again. Don't forget it."

He held his glass to Danny's. "But let us not neglect that we're on the brink of a Maplewood revolution. So, here's to you, Danny-boy. I hope you get what you want. I truly do."

A Time
for Two

Bo fell into a dream when he heard his father agree to betroth him to Jane. He didn't care that it came as a stipulation in a deal if their love could be declared official. So, while Danny remained with Chester on the front porch to further discuss business, Bo darted inside and pulled Jane away from her chores. They scurried into his room, where he shut the door and kissed her. It felt true as her name on his lips, warm and kind, her arms wrapped around his neck. After a moment, he let go and sat her down with the good news. "We're to be married, Jane."

"What? How? I thought our meetings had been secret all this time. How are we supposed to get married? Unless, Bo, did you tell Chester about us?"

"He's my pa. I couldn't resist. Since the day you arrived, Jane, he's known how I've felt about you. And you can't expect me to hide our love forever, not when it ought to be shouted from the mountaintops."

Jane sighed. "I suppose it's Danny who I'm worried about then."

"Danny agreed to the marriage. He agreed! I heard it with my own ears."

"Sincerely?"

"Sincere as the sun is bright. So, if you don't mind, I know I don't have a ring yet, but..." Bo slipped off the bed and knelt on one knee. "Jana Lee Andersen, Sweet Jane, moon of my night, will you spend eternity with me?"

With teary eyes and a choking voice, "Yes, Bo, yes. You don't even need to be fancy about it. You could've just told me to meet you in a church, and I'd be there with bells on. Doggonit, Bo Buckley, I love you."

"I love you too, Jane."

"We're going to have three boys and two girls. I hope you know that."

"I love me a big family," he laughed.

A flurry of kisses left them helpless to each other. Their clothes fell to the floor as they tumbled onto Bo's bed, laughter resounding into the hallway. They should have been more careful but couldn't resist the urge. Love held them and wove them together. Nothing in the world could tear them apart, not Chester, not Winifred, not the law, and especially not

Danny. By God's grace, they prayed to one day double the size of the Buckley family, double the size of the Buckley business, and double the size of their generosity toward one another and those they loved. They couldn't have been happier.

Through summer and autumn, Bo and Jane found ways to keep a healthy and playful relationship while appearing dedicated to their everyday duties. Jane managed to charm Winifred to create a new work schedule to free up her afternoons. Since she would play little part in preparing supper and evening chores, she gained charge of cooking breakfast, dusting, sweeping, and tending to the outhouse. It seemed a bit much to take on in such a short time, but Jane felt it worthwhile to spend uninterrupted quality time with her beau.

Similarly, Bo rigged a schedule approved by Otis. Tobias, Burt, and Rufus didn't seem troubled, considering Bo's extra morning work allowed them to sleep a little longer. He typically rose before the sun and marched straight to the barn, tending to the tubs, pots, vats, barrels, and bottles. He even sifted through the grain containers for insects and spiders.

Once done, he would return to the house and eat a special breakfast prepared by Jane. After a cup of coffee and a kiss, Bo would head back to the barn to make labels for the outbound jugs and bottles. On certain days, he drove into town to meet with Percy's brother, Derek Reed, who knew some people in the cork business. Since cutting out Chester's cork connection a year earlier, a German fellow in Virginia, Bo managed to save his pa hundreds of dollars.

Bo usually wrapped up around two o'clock, when Jane completed her chores. On some days, he would finish extra early and steal her from her tasks, upsetting his mother. They cherished their quality time, too often forgetting about the world or giving the family attention outside their working schedule. And Danny was always on the road, so they figured he didn't mind. Plus, the regulars at Reed's Saloon seemed to brighten whenever they saw Jane at Bo's side. "Keep her coming," they said. Bo didn't think twice and decided to bring her with him from then on.

On warm days, Bo and Jane went to a meadow by a creek just west of the property to lay about and talk like a pair of lazy bears. They spent many hours walking through the forest and listening to birds sing. Sometimes, they rode horses into the heights of Appalachia, looking for breaks in the trees through which they could view the beauty of Kentucky. They occasionally strolled into the valley to climb magnolia trees and pluck any lingering pink flowers.

The couple often ended up by the Cumberland River, either to swim or simply saunter along the banks. Even when the weather turned cold, they continued to frolic in the woods, though rainy days had them spooning in bed for hours. By the end of November, Chester and Winifred complained that they hardly ever saw their son and future daughter. The lovebirds didn't care when their hearts thumped louder than the parents' words.

There came a week in early December when Jane felt a little ill. Her nose dripped, and she coughed like Chester after smoking too much tobacco. Bo demonstrated his partner skills by tending to her as best he could, checking her temperature every hour, and wiping her nose every few minutes with his hankie. He warmed her daily with clean blankets that he personally washed and dried. He fed her hot potato and chicken soup while recounting wild tales of his pa and grandpappy. Bo would have stuck by her side until death if she hadn't reminded him of his duties to the family business. Loyal as Bertha's hounds, he listened to his fiancé. He returned to his work routine while Ginny and Sally May filled in and nursed Jane back to health.

A few days before Christmas, Bo took Jane into town to look for a ring at Thomas Black's finery shop. After a glance about the place, they found themselves hovering over a gold band studded with bulbous diamonds. Thomas ensured they knew of its mighty expense since the jewels had been mined and transported from Africa to Antwerp and then to New York. While Jane had heard of Africa and Belgium, Bo's ignorance of these foreign places rendered the ring more precious to him. "I'll take it," he proclaimed.

The jeweler shook his head. "Mr. Buckley, this

pretty little gem costs five hundred dollars."

"Mr. Black, if you could please lower it to four hundred, I'll pay with cash."

"Got the money on you?"

"Oh, I came prepared."

"Gee, Bo, where'd you get so much allowance? Are Chester's earnings on the rise again?"

"Not these days," Bo lied. "But mine sure are."

"Fair enough. Here's the ring. For you, Bo, I'll tag on a personal guarantee. If you lose it, I can't replace it. But if it scratches or breaks for any reason, bring it back, and I'll do what I can to remedy the situation."

"Thank you, Mr. Black."

"No, thank you, son. And congratulations to you two. Tell Chester and Winifred I'm proud of you. Let me know when you've set a date for the wedding."

Bo and Jane left the store and stopped by Reed's Saloon for a drink. They laughed and sang and cheered. Their excitement knew no bounds. After a beer and a few shots of Old Forester to top off their bar visit, the couple headed back home.

However, Bo guided Jane down a long detour that cut around to the east before bending north. He walked her along the main road, which closely followed the Cumberland River. They stepped off the road at a broad curve, passing through some trees and bushes and onto the riverbank. Bo picked up a flat pebble and skipped it across the water's surface. She had never seen anyone do that before, so he taught her how. After skipping over a dozen pebbles, he cupped some water and splashed her.

"That's freezing!" She giggled and flung water back at him, which only started a wet fight. The next thing they knew, they looked as if they had endured a downpour, their clothes and hair completely soaked. "We can't go back looking like this," she complained with a smile that roused Bo's urges.

"Not to worry," he chuckled. "It may be winter, but today's looking quite bright. Let's just take off our clothes and lay them out in the sun. Meantime, we can go for a cold swim. Don't worry, I'll keep you warm." The river proved a little shallower than expected and chilly as imagined, but the pair submerged quickly enough. They swam about and splashed like fish, laughing, talking, and joking. However, they eventually slowed their play and held each other tight, warming with nose rubs and kisses.

"Aren't you scared someone might see us?" Jane whispered.

"No. People swim naked all the time. That's the way it should be, anyway. People in the Bible are always naked, ain't they?"

"You're so silly, Bo. In the Bible, they usually wear fancy robes or rags or something. Maybe not Adam and Eve, though."

"Well, as of right now, I feel like Adam and Eve in Paradise. Ain't no better place to be, in my opinion."

"It's nice here," she remarked while admiring the

sun-reflected ripples surrounding them. "I never thought I'd fall in love with Kentucky, let alone fall in love *in* Kentucky."

"How is it where you're from, Jane?"

"Norfolk? It's just a city. Lots of people. Lots of smoke and horses, cars, boats. There are rivers, big rivers. The one we're in looks like a stream compared to the ones I'm used to seeing. Norfolk's also got libraries, government buildings, shops, parlors, eateries, bakeries, too much to name if you ask me. There's also the ocean."

Bo's eyes widened with curiosity. "I've never seen the ocean. Is it pretty?"

"It's beautiful. I didn't appreciate it that much when I lived there, but ever since Danny and I left, I've come to miss it terribly. Tell you the truth, I think it's something everyone ought to see at least once in their life."

Bo grinned. "One day, Jane, we'll go to the ocean. We'll get on a boat and go fishing. We can even take some of the family with us, starting with our future children, of course. But also Mama, Papa, Tobias, Ginny, Sally May, Melanie, Nancy, even Otis, though maybe not Burt and Rufus."

"What about Dick and Bertha?"

"Nah," he laughed. "They can stay behind and watch the property. But, uh, Jane, can I ask you something else? Why did you and Danny leave Norfolk in the first place?"

"It's a long story, and I don't think you want to hear it, at least not from me."

"Why? Did Danny do something wrong? You know you can tell me anything. I won't chatter."

"All right. Let's just say that Danny worked for powerful people who did horrible things. To earn his wages, which were mighty handsome, he needed to obey their rules and always finish the jobs given to him. That usually involved holding a gun to someone, even hurting them. In his defense, he didn't always work for those people. They just happened to offer him employment one day. Sure, the money was nice, but he only did it to support my mother and me after our father disappeared. That man was a brute to all of us."

"Anyway, everything seemed peachy for a while. Danny started working his way up the ladder. His ambitions grew. Then, out of nowhere, our mother died. That was hard on both of us, but I think it broke something in Danny. He continued to work and support us, keeping us off the streets, but sometimes came home in a dark mood and had blood on his shoes. A few months later, the state accused him of raping a woman he claimed to be his lover, though I still don't know if that's true. He won't admit it. To make matters worse, while on a job, he got in a fight with a man who was supposed to be his friend, but the fella turned out to be an informant for the government." She paused and pulled away. "I... I shouldn't tell you anymore. I'm sorry, Bo."

He gently reeled her back and smiled. "Just tell me why you left, and I won't ask any more questions. I promise."

"Okay. Well, Danny made a hard deal with a judge named Harold Phillips, a tough authority with a soft spot for young working men. My brother had thirty days to give up his earnings to the judge and leave Norfolk for good or go to prison. Danny figured it best for us to just get out of Virginia. So, we hopped on a train to coal country. Next thing I knew, I was looking at you in Reed's Saloon."

"At least it's got a happy ending."

She kissed him. "Yes, it does."

Bo carried Jane to a dry spot along the bank and made love to her under the afternoon sun. Afterward, they put on their damp clothes and returned home. Winifred's eyes lit up when she saw the ring on Jane's finger. She scorned Bo for spending too much money and that Chester shouldn't see it until their wedding day. The young man replied, "Nothing in the world is too much for my sweet Jane. Even Pa ought to understand that."

Christmas and New Year's Day whisked by with the wind and snow. Production of Maplewood Seven nearly doubled as business boomed during the holidays. All ran smoothly as silk throughout winter until, in late February, Jane became ill again. However, her symptoms appeared troublesome to Bo. She passed through various stages of discomfort, often feeling imbalanced. She seemed happy and energetic one moment, then nauseated and drowsy, vomiting at times. And her nose neither dripped nor stuffed. She hardly ever coughed or displayed any signs of fever or flu. And no ointment, soothing song, or hot soup seemed to remedy her condition.

Even with his mother and the other ladies of the house tending to Jane, Bo became sick with fear, occasionally sharing her symptoms. Although winter had peaked and appeared ready to put away its frost for spring, Bo dreaded that the worst had yet to come.

TROUBLE IN PARADISE

"Chester!" Winifred stepped onto the front porch. "When're you going to get Otis's boys to stop smoking that Mexican hemp? This ain't Satan's den; it's a good Christian household. And I'm tired of smelling it all day, always having to open the windows even when it's cold."

Chester rocked back in his chair and puffed his long wooden pipe. He peered deep into the forest surrounding his house and sniffed the winter air, taking in the soothing scent of pine. There might have been a hint of hickory, but those trees grew near the ravine by the barn. A frosty wind suddenly ruffled the overhead canopy, tickling the myriads of pine needles into a harmonious dance that mimed the roar of a churning river. Sunshine pierced the spaces separating each dancer, spraying various hues of light that wistfully oscillated in unison over the snow-coated earth.

A chill rolled through Chester's shoulders. He nearly laughed, realizing he was experiencing a rare instance of tranquility, a sense of oneness with God. He felt so close to peace of mind that he hoped his wife would quit her nagging and return inside before the feeling vanished altogether. He supposed that's why it was known as a fleeting glimpse.

"Are you listening to me, Chester Buckley?"

His concentration finally broke. "Doggonit, Winnie, I heard you the first time! Jesus, Lord, have mercy on me for trying to enjoy a few minutes of peace. God knows how rare it is these days."

"Well, you need to tell those boys to stop smoking that green shit in the house."

"Don't worry, sweetheart. I'll have a talk with Burt and Rufus. Not like I haven't already. Told them that stuff would scramble their brains like eggs. Of course, no matter how often I tell them, they don't listen. Otis has smacked them upside their heads more times than I wish to count. Still, they pretend everything's peachy. Maybe their minds are already fried like bacon."

"Can't you threaten them or something, Chester?"

"Come on, Winnie, you know me. Real threats and abuse are only good for business, not for kin. It just ain't right. Take it from me. My fuse is short because my pappy used to beat me at least once a day. That's why I try my best to teach our children the opposite, that all kin need to be treated with respect regardless of their stupidity. Though, I reckon a spanking is in order every now and again."

"Burt and Rufus have no respect for you, me, or their father since everything they hear goes in one ear and out the other."

"I hear you," Chester mumbled as his eye suddenly caught three horses trotting up the hill. Big Bertha marched like a soldier behind them with the hounds at her side but didn't bother introducing the trespassers as she was wont to do. Chester reluctantly broke from his rocker and signaled Winifred to head inside, unsure what might happen in the coming minutes. He put down the pipe and placed his black Stetson hat over his crop of graying hair. Growling under his breath, he rose to his feet and stepped off the porch to meet the riders just as they curbed their horses near the trucks.

"Good morning, Teddy."

"How're you doing today, Chester?" Teddy said with a flare of glee. He slid out of his saddle and passed the reins to one of his men. "Hope you had a merry Christmas and a happy New Year."

"Sure did. Nineteen-twenty-four will do us better than last year, I hope. Wife good? Children?"

"They're good, Chester."

"Care to come in for a hot breakfast? It's mighty

cold out here."

"No, thank you. Your Winnie's a fine cook, but I already ate."

"So, what can I do for you, Sheriff?"

Teddy placed his hands on his hips and stepped closer. "Do you mind discussing this over a glass of your delicious Maplewood Seven? If there's one thing that'll warm me up in this weather, it's your prestigious elixir." Chester escorted Teddy to the porch and poured. The sheriff took a sip and breathed deeply as if the bourbon brought new life to him. "You make a darn good whiskey, Chester. Sure as hell showed your daddy who the real distiller is. Yup, really proved you're the better man. Speaking of Maplewood Seven, how goes the business, what with the law these days?"

"Cut the shit, Teddy. You and I have been at this for years. We both know the law."

"I know the law quite well. And I'm sure you do, too, but what about Bo and Otis?"

"They know the law. I made sure of that."

"Got any new workers that don't know the law, Chester?"

"Quit pissing around and give it to me straight, Teddy. Why are you coming to me with interrogating words? You clearly have more on your mind than a thirst for fine whiskey."

"That's fair, Chester. Well, as you know, I've got several deputies, officers I trust. I send these good men off to parts of the county to collect information for me. Keep me informed and whatnot. Most of the time, it's just hogwash, nothing that matters. Lately, however, I noticed a nice new Ford Model TT driving through town occasionally. At first, I shrugged it off, given that motorized vehicles are becoming more popular these days."

"Then one of my boys told me that he saw the TT bumping down the Devil's Spine. I know you and your favorite downhill neighbor, Henry Wilkins, own some trucks. So again, I thought nothing of it. Before long, another deputy witnessed this same slick Ford crossing the Virginia state line. Returned about a week later. Two days after that, it crossed into Tennessee. Came back once more, then went out again to God knows where. Seems like a constant stream."

"You already know where I'm getting at, don't you, Chester? Obviously, you got a new feller onboard, and you're using him to do the dirty work. Your bourbon ain't selling in Poor Fork like it used to, so you figured out a way to make more money."

"Now, before you argue, know that I didn't come here to arrest you and drag you back into town. I know how much people love you around here. I would look like a villain. And you and me, we've known each other since boyhood. We're old friends, ain't we? And what do friends do? They help each other. So, here's what's going to happen next, Chester. I'm going to help you by keeping quiet about your business expansion. Your earnings have gone up, I suspect, which brings about trouble. Stirs the pot with higher authorities. Money, the law, illegal distribution—you know what I'm talking about."

"What do you want, Sheriff? More than the ten percent you already receive?"

"Oh, I know I ain't getting ten percent these days. You're earning more than usual like I said. However, my cut hasn't bumped. In the wake of your rising income, I'm sure my portion has reduced to five or six percent. Now, I don't think that's right, and that's not how it works."

"Get to the point, Hanes."

Teddy leaned in a bit closer. "I want fifteen percent."

"Fifteen? I ought to shoot you dead right now, you son of a bitch."

"No, you don't want to kill a lawman, old friend. That's bad business. Make it easy on yourself. Just shake my hand and tell me we got a deal. Fifteen percent of your increased rate. No bullshit."

Chester looked at the deputies perched on their horses with grins stretched across their stupid faces. Biting his lip, he agreed to the terms and shook the hand of Sheriff Teddy Hanes. "I expect complete loyalty," Chester demanded. "No Marshal McCrory under any circumstance, you hear? Complete and utter loyalty."

"Oh, Chester, you know I can't keep the Marshal

from snooping around, but you can trust that my mouth will remain one hundred percent shut if he does. Personally, I'd be more worried about your old pal, Henry Wilkins. Your good neighbor may have poor eyesight these days, but he's never been shrewder."

When Teddy and his whipping boys rode out of sight with Big Bertha behind them, Chester hurried to the barn wearing a scowl as cold and deep as the snow beneath his boots. "Where the hell is Danny Andersen? Otis, Tobias, I need an answer now!"

"He's on delivery to Nashville," Otis answered. "Probably spent the night there, so he ought to be back today. Why?"

"If you see him before I do, tell him I need to speak with him."

"You got it, brother."

"And where in God's name is Bo? Feel like I haven't seen that boy in weeks."

"He's off with Jane," Tobias replied from the bottling carts. "He starts working early in the morning so he can spend the rest of the day with her. Been doing it for months."

"Hells bells, Tobias, it is early morning. Damn child! Bo thinks being in love gives him the right to quit working."

"Chester, brother," Otis stepped in. "Bo's a good worker and still puts in quite the effort. In fact, I've never seen him work so much in his life. He gets it done fast and accurately. He tends to the barrels and bottles, checks the fermenter, and mashes the corn and grains. He does it all. Gets most of it done before the rest of us are even out of bed. Normally, I ain't the defending type for love, given that my wife was a filthy whore, but the boy's got the bug. He's doing right by it while trying to make his pappy proud. You ought to respect that and give him a break. Remember, he's your son. He's got your determination."

Chester took a deep breath. "You're right, Otis. I appreciate you letting me know, though I don't understand why Bo couldn't tell me that himself. Nevertheless, it's Danny that's got me riled up."

"What'd he do?"

"Let's just say I had a hard talk with Teddy Hanes."

Otis growled in his throat. "Goat-sucking nitwit. What the hell did Hanes want?"

"I'll tell you later, brother. Tobias, come now. Let's go sit with the family and eat breakfast. I need to chew on something before my teeth grind into powder."

~

Danny returned around noon, reflecting that Nashville had proven to be a thirsty beast in its post-yuletide season. His buyers had stepped up their game, hounding for larger deliveries, probably because underground clubs were more popular than ever. He chuckled as he slid out of the truck and grabbed the briefcase on the passenger seat. He felt proud of himself, feeling that he had come a long way and surely deserved this success. He opened the door to the house, eager for a hearty meal, only to find Chester standing in front of him like a bull ready to charge—nostrils flared, teeth gritted, eyes ablaze.

Danny recognized the emotion and quickly turned to flee out the door, yet Chester snatched him by the collar and shoved him against the frame. The briefcase dropped to the floor and burst open. Stacks of hundred-dollar notes scattered like autumn leaves. Holding Danny off the ground with nothing but his right forearm, Chester pressed his weight into the Virginian's throat, choking him. "You lack discrepancy, Daniel, you know that. I ought to break your goddamn neck right now. Stupid boy."

Ginny, Sally May, Melanie, and Nancy rushed out of the kitchen and into the family room. Winifred, who came in last, shouted, "No violence in the house! Put him down right now!"

Danny's face swelled with a red hue that rapidly deepened into purple. Winifred panicked, realizing that her husband's ire had consumed him. She raced to his side and tried to push him away from the door, but he thwarted her with his left arm, knocking her to the floor.

While Ginny went to help her mother up, Sally May darted out the back door and shouted for help. Otis, Tobias, Rufus, Burt, and Dick rushed in and pried Chester off the young man. Chester's face glowed with the fury of a winter furnace while Danny sunk to the ground, gripping his neck and coughing until he rediscovered his breath.

"I'm going to kill you, Danny-boy," Chester snarled, unable to charge with Dick and Otis gripping his arms. "I told you, if you ruin me, I'll destroy you."

Danny couldn't speak. He wanted to, but his throat felt pinched.

"What the hell did he do?" Winifred hissed at her husband.

"Teddy Hanes's men caught sight of him delivering Maplewood Seven."

"I... I did... I did exactly as you ordered," Danny managed to speak finally, still struggling to get his words out. "I... I took the stuff out of state. I didn't sell to... to anyone in... in Kentucky. I... I swear."

"He knows," Chester began, as he balled his hands into fists and ripped his limbs free from the hold on him. "He knows we've upped our earnings, you idiot. His deputies saw you driving back and forth. And because of that, he threatened me with the law. And do you know what I'm forced to do with the law?"

Danny looked up and bobbed his head, breathing heavily. "You buy it."

"That's right, Daniel. Unfortunately, the price steepened due to your lack of prudence."

"I can't change myself, boss. I can't change the truck or the routes out of Poor Fork. You know that sort of stuff is out of my hands. I never imagined the sheriff would have scouts on the road."

"Well, he does, Danny. He does. He and I are counterparts. I'm the happy devil on the shoulder, and he's the filthy angel. If I were a lawman, I'd be him. And if he made whiskey, he'd be me. You see where I'm getting at. He ain't a simpleton. The man's clever. He wants to know I'm doing better because when I'm making good money, so is he. Now, because of you, I have to give him fifteen percent of our increased earnings."

The others in the room gasped and groaned.

"Now, now." Winifred wagged a finger at her husband. "It ain't Danny's fault. The boy's just doing what you told him. He didn't know about the sheriff. It's your mistake, Chester. You knew that Teddy had scouts, and you didn't say a darn thing. Don't go blaming others for your problems. That's how you start trouble in paradise."

Chester stepped away from the line of his kin only to stare Danny deeper into the corner of the entryway. Without a word, he spat at the Virginian's feet, stomped outside onto the front porch, and slammed the door behind him. The noise rattled Danny's ears, igniting a headache. As he pushed toward his feet, Winifred extended a hand, which he waved away. "Thank you, but I'm fine," he muttered before hurrying into the room he reluctantly shared with Burt and Rufus.

Sitting on his bed in the corner of the room, Danny pulled a bottle of whiskey from under the frame and rubbed the cork with his thumb. With the other hand, he briefly touched his neck, feeling that his pride had been throttled more than anything. Upon taking his first swig, someone knocked on the door. Before he could answer, Ginny stepped in.

"You all right, Danny?"

"Goddamn that Chester Buckley."

Ginny folded her hands and took a step closer. "Sorry about Pa's temper. When it comes to family, he's a softy. But with business, he can be the devil, as he sometimes says. Is there anything I can do to help you?"

Danny looked up at her and saw a twinkle in her sweet hazel eyes that roused a smile on his reddened face. He again felt the burn on his skin beneath the throat apple and recalled Chester's rage. Despite all that Danny had done for the family business, Chester neither gave him his daughter nor defended him when things looked sour. Instead, the old man simply tried to kill him. Yet Ginny, standing before him now with a half-grin between those freckled cheeks, made Danny feel like he had done something correctly. "Care to take a stroll with me?" he said, twisting his frustration into cheer.

~

Danny looked at Ginny with curious eyes as they walked toward the barn. "You know, I figured I was a ghost to you." He laughed under his breath. "You hardly ever give me the time of day. So, I got to ask, why do you suddenly care for my well-being?"

"I don't know." She shrugged. "I feel bad, I guess. But that doesn't mean I want to marry you, Danny Andersen. It just means that you're a part of the family. And I love my family. Since your sister's going to marry my brother, we'll be related. Not by blood, of course, unless they have children. I'm sure they will. Bo's always wanted a big family, and I've heard Jane say the same thing."

"Can we not talk about Bo and Jane?"

"Why? Do they bother you?"

"N-no. I just... I just want to talk about something else or do something fun. Do you want to go do something with me, Ginny?"

"I suppose. I can't be away for too long. I've got chores to do before supper."

"Oh, come on, Ginny. Live a little. Let's go somewhere that no one goes. Know anywhere like that around here?"

"Well, there's a barn my grandpappy built about thirty-five years ago. He wanted to raise pigs since the soil here ain't fitting for crops. And as I've been told, over and over, Henry Wilkins sabotaged the whole thing by stealing the pigs, which is why Grandpap decided to make whiskey instead of raising livestock."

"Pa said that Grandpap got so angry, he wanted to distance our property line from the Wilkins's, so he sold that chunk of land to a Jellico mining company. For whatever reason, the miners never showed up to claim the land. Nowadays, Pa likes to say it's still our property even though we already got paid for it. Uncle Otis calls it no-man's-land because no Buckley or Wilkins goes there. The barn ain't in good shape anyway. Been abandoned since the day the pigs were kidnapped. Still has some of Grandpappy's old tables and tools, all left where they were last used."

"Fascinating story, Ginny. Mind if I ask where this old barn is?"

"It's over yonder, a little way to the south. As I said, it's past the property line. Big Bertha and Dick don't go there during their rounds. Honestly, I don't know why anyone would want to go there. It's a scary place. Last time I went, Bo tricked Sally May and me into thinking we would see a deer give birth. When he got us inside the barn, he shut us in and barred the door. He laughed and laughed, and we screamed, yet no one heard us since we were so far from the house. We thought Bo had left us there 'cause he got quiet. So, we found some rocks and smashed the windows. That's when Bo burst into the barn, all frightened."

Danny snickered. "Why'd he do that?"

"Turned out, our screaming attracted a bear. That's why Bo quit laughing."

"What happened in the end?"

"We waited hours in the barn before the bear finally got bored and ran away. When we got back to the house, Pa whipped my brother's butt with a leather belt as if he was ten years old again. There wasn't blood or anything, just bruises."

Danny smirked. "Very interesting. Sounds like a chunk of your family's history I'd like to see for myself. Would you care to walk me to the barn?"

"I reckon so, but I don't want to linger. Like I said, it's a scary place. Kind of haunted."

"We won't be there long, I promise. We'll be in and out. I just want to see it. Kentucky is a lovely place, much more beautiful than where I'm from."

"All right, Danny. It's over this way. Follow me."

The Devil Within

On a brisk morning in early March, Jane lay in bed with Winifred seated beside her on a chair. Having just been informed what had ailed her the past few weeks, Jane exclaimed, "I need to tell Bo right away."

"Not yet," Winifred commanded, and was about to explain why when Melanie popped her head into the room, asking for help in the kitchen. "We'll finish this talk later, Jane. I know it's a big deal, but keep it a secret for now. We'll tell everyone soon enough. This is something the whole family will want to hear."

Jane folded her arms and thrust herself back to the pillow as Winifred paced out of the room. She wanted to tell Bo the news immediately, but if she tried to sneak through the back door in the family room,

Winifred would likely catch her and order her back to bed. She sulked for a few minutes, brooding over the idea. Then, a little bird landed on the windowsill, chirped a few times, and took off. A thought struck Jane and filled her with joy. She burst from her bed and dressed for a winter stroll.

Bo stood in the rackhouse, inspecting the oldest batch of Maplewood Seven, which required bottling within the week. As he prepared to tag the barrels that needed tapping, Jane stepped into the room. "Wha " He dropped his pencil and clipboard on the closest barrel, then rushed to sweep her into his arms. "What are you doing here? Mama said you couldn't get out of bed until she knew what was wrong with you."

"I snuck out the window. I had to see you."

"What for? Is there trouble? Are you okay?"

She could hardly contain herself. "Can we please take a walk?"

Bo chuckled. "If that's what you want, sweet sunshine. Please, lead the way."

Jane quickly towed Bo out and around the barn close to the ravine, where no one could hear or see them. "Do you think it'll snow some more?"

He bobbed his head and sang, "When the sky is gray an' winter winds are a-blowing, you may think of rain, but then it's starts a-snowing."

"You're so silly, Bo." Jane's giggle quickly melted into sobriety. "That's why I love you. Just another reason why I had to sneak out of the window. I have to tell you something and it's pretty darn serious." She gestured for him to sit on a rock by a hickory tree.

He complied. "What is it?"

"Now, I know we ain't married yet, Bo. And Jesus, why, he knows we're good people at heart. He knows we mean well. I'm sure he doesn't mind our love or the fact we've made love without swearing oaths before a preacher. At least, that's what I believe."

"Jane, we're young and alive. We have fun, and we love each other. In the name of God, Jesus, and every other feller in the Bible, I'd make love to you forever, even if we never got married. I just love you so darn much. That's my oath."

"Good, that's great," she laughed nervously. "I love you too. Sorry, I'm just trying to butter you up. My sweet, handsome Bo, you're going to be a father."

He stared at her in awe. "A father? Me?"

"Your Mama figured it out. I'm pregnant. We're going to have a baby."

Bo stood up, goosebumps running across his skin. "Oh, Jane, I'm so happy. I don't even have the words, but... but we can't have a baby out of wedlock. Pa would shoot me with his shotgun. He's a good Christian and expects the same of me."

"Bo, that's what I was saying before. Jesus doesn't mind. He forgives all."

"I thought you were just playing smart or something. I didn't know *this* was coming."

"Are you angry with me, Bo?"

"No, Jane. Absolutely not. I love you, and I love this child already. I'm so thrilled. I'm just-I'm confused and scared. I... I need some time to think about how to handle this with Pa. It's a lot to take in all at once."

"Okay." She breathed in deeply. "As long as you're all right with everything. Otherwise, if you don't want the child, I'll pack up and leave."

"Jane, you and I will never part. I swear it. And our child will grow up strong. If it's a boy, we'll name him Chester like Pa. If it's a girl, we'll name her Abigail. I've always liked that name."

"I like it, too. I'm so glad you're not angry."

"My love, I could never be angry with such a beautiful thing. Though now I feel shaky as a fish on dry land."

"Why don't you take a walk in the forest? Maybe that'll ease your soul."

"A wonderful idea from a wonderful woman."

As Bo stood up, he and Jane heard shouting from the house, but they were too far away to decipher the words. They laughed and shrugged it off, assuming Burt and Rufus were getting reprimanded for smoking hemp in the house again. The pair let the noises slip from their minds as they held each other for a while beneath the shelter of the hickory tree. Eventually, they decided to head to the back porch, where Bo kissed Jane and opened the door for her.

He turned his head momentarily and saw Danny on the far side of the yard, disappearing into the shadow of the woods with Ginny. Bo thought it a little strange, considering Ginny never cared for Danny much, or so he had heard her say. He wondered why she would go off with him and to the south of all places. She knew the property line was cut short in that area. He suddenly remembered all that Jane had told him about Danny, the horrible things he did that caused them to vacate Virginia. Withholding his apprehension, he smiled at Jane, gently shut the door, and hastened after Danny and his sister.

As Bo gained on them, his boots heavy on the untouched layer of snow, he wondered what worried him so much. Regardless of past actions, he considered Danny to be his friend. They used to work together, drink, smoke, talk, play cards, and laugh at silly things. Of course, that changed when Bo got engaged and started devoting all his free time to Jane. Nevertheless, Danny had always been a hard-working young man with a good head on his shoulders, soon to be his brother-in-law and uncle of his child. Then again, Jane had hinted that her brother had a history of dealing trouble, having been employed by powerful people who did awful things to stay in business.

"That's why he knows so much," Bo whispered to himself. "He's been around. He's experienced all the nasty things to understand what to do and what not to do. That's where his connections come from. That's how he sells Maplewood Seven so darn easily. Mercy, Jesus, Lord, give me the strength to confront this. I pray his troublemaking days are over. I pray I'm wrong about this awful feeling in my gut."

Bo followed Danny and Ginny with the caution of a fox, slipping between shadows in the forest. He remained distant but wanted to get close enough to hear their conversation. Ginny walked with her hands cupped together as she was wont to do, while Danny seemed to swagger as if he had business on his mind. Occasionally, he tried to brush a hand across her thigh or rump. Bo scrunched his nose at the sight of it, and his growing concern drove him nearer.

Finally, they arrived at the old barn. It hadn't changed since the last time Bo visited the place about a year prior when he tricked Ginny and Sally May into going inside. He remembered how he had locked them in with a rusty padlock and laughed until they started screaming and breaking the windows with rocks, which drew the attention of a grumpy male bear. The moment the beast had decided to charge, Bo broke the lock with a solid boot-kick and barred himself within. He and his sisters huddled closely in a dark corner until the bear lost interest, and its grunts of disappointment vanished into the woods. What a day that had proven to be. He wished that bear would return right now and scare Danny and Ginny back to the house.

Danny fondled the broken padlock while opening the barn door. He muttered something cheeky and laughed, then stepped inside and drew in Ginny. Bo darted from tree to tree before easing his back to the rotting exterior wall of the barn. As he tip-toed toward one of the broken windows, he heard Ginny burst, "No, Danny. For the last time, I will not marry you!" Bo peered through a jagged piece of glass stuck to the frame, watching how Danny leaned against a dusty tool table, tapping his fingers in frustration. Ginny stood in front of him with her arms folded.

"You're pretty when you're mad," he teased.

"Will you stop, Danny? I'm not angry. I just thought we were going to talk and stroll about the trees. Instead, you made me come to this unforgiving place. And you keep bringing up things that make me feel uncomfortable."

"Ginny, I love you."

"No, you don't, Danny. Don't say things you don't mean."

"Oh, but it's true. I love you like Bo loves Jane."

"Is that what this is about? Bo and Jane?"

Danny shook his head and bit his lip. "Goddammit, Ginny. I told you not to talk about them. I don't want to hear about it."

"You're the one who brought them up, not me. You know what I think, Danny. I think you're jealous of your sister. You are, ain't you? Yeah, that's it. You envy her, Danny. You just want what she has. She found love with someone who happens to be your friend, my brother. And now you hound me with words of love and marriage just because you wish to feel the same."

"Bo is not my friend. He's a worthless, lazy, undeserving maggot."

"Okay, Danny, I'm going back to the house. You're getting riled up, and I don't like it."

"No, Ginny." He grabbed her wrist.

"Let go of me."

"Marry me."

"Like hell, I will. Let go!"

Danny moved closer and tried to kiss her, but she stepped back and slapped him. He bit his lip, grappled her arm with two hands, and swung her onto the tool table. He pressed her face to the dingy wood with one hand as the other lifted her dress. While she struggled to break free, Danny yanked her hair back, loosened his belt, and forced himself upon her. "Stupid bitch," he growled. She screamed for help and tried to reach for the rusted shear on the table, but Danny steered her hand away. "No one's coming for you. You hear me? You should've just said yes. You should've just said yes!"

Bo hooked an arm around the villain's neck and squeezed with every ounce of strength he could muster. He tore Danny away from Ginny and hammered his free fist into the man's gut, driving the wind out of him. Yet, such a blow seemed to hardly weaken Danny, whose sweaty hands clawed at the arm that choked him. Danny gritted his teeth and snarled in agony as Bo jerked him sideways, battered his chest and ribs, then reeled hard in the other direction. "You got the devil in you, Andersen. The devil don't belong in my house or with my sister. You've gone too far!"

Danny suddenly shifted forward, loosening the grip on him, and whipped his head back. Bo stumbled and groaned as he placed a hand over his bloody nose, which had likely broken. The Virginian took the opportunity to button his trousers before turning around to tackle Bo to the ground.

He managed to get a few punches in before a teary-eyed Ginny shoved him off with a shriek. While Bo struggled to his feet, Ginny darted to the barn door to shout for help, but Danny proved too quick, caught her by the hair, and kicked her legs out from under her. Just as she hit the dirt, Bo charged like a bull and bashed the devil in the back of the head with his elbow.

Danny lost his balance but effectively recovered and revolved a fist meant to crack a jaw or break a tooth. However, Bo anticipated the move, ducked, and shoved Danny against the tool table. He should have kept at it and finished Danny off, yet he froze as if lightning had struck him.

He remembered Jane at that moment, the woman he loved, wondering how she might feel if he killed her brother. And so, they just stood there, breathing in the cold dust that their boots had stirred. Then Danny pivoted a foot and tried to bolt, but lost his breath when Bo slammed a fist into his gut and bloodied his face with a knuckle as wide and weighted as a stone.

Just as Bo was about to lay his final blow, Ginny

cried joyfully as if Danny had already been cut down. "Kill that devil!"

Bo instinctively turned his eyes on her. In a flash, Danny reached back, grabbed the rusty shear, sprung forward, and drove the blade deep into Bo's chest. Bo staggered back and choked, fanning air toward his mouth. Danny lurched from the tool table and yanked the shear out only to thrust it back in and twist.

Ginny screamed and darted out the barn door. Danny sprinted after her. Blinded by tears, she shouted for help and ran into the forest. Her dress might have dragged and ripped on shrubs that protruded from the blanket of snow, but she didn't stop. Yet, she proved too slow against the light-footed legs of Danny Andersen, who caught her by an oak tree and rammed her head into the trunk, knocking her unconscious. Silence seized the winter air.

Danny palmed his thighs and bent over to slow his breath. He used a torn sleeve to wipe the sweat and blood from his brow. Then he noticed that deep red streaks marked Ginny's dress. "Shit," he hissed, realizing the gravity of his hot-headed actions. He looked down at the blood that stained his clothes, then to the tracks that trailed up the hill from the barn where Bo lay on the cold earth with a shear in his rips. "Shit."

He contemplated what to do next, yet indecision suddenly plagued his mind. He first considered fleeing Kentucky for good, ditching everything, including his sister, and saving himself. However, he couldn't help but wonder if it lay in his best interest to dispose of Bo's body first.

Would blatant evidence prompt Chester to immediately seek him out? And what would become of Jane? Ginny still breathed, though Danny knew her voice would bring the flaying knife upon him. He paused the drumming in his head to quietly study the barn and debate burning it down. "Shit," he muttered again, figuring it would behoove him to bury Bo rather than burn him before taking further action. But where to hide a dead Buckley?

Danny lugged Bo out into the forest. He veered east of the barn and away from the red-lined trees on the north side of the hill, which marked the Buckley property line. Danny felt certain that when Big Bertha next patrolled the perimeter, her dogs would catch his scent and lead the monster woman beyond the boundary. Therefore, Danny decided to circle back past the barn and up a lazy slope to the south, where he settled on a spot between two hillocks.

He dug a shallow grave in the muddy ice with an aged shovel he had found lying under the tool table, then pushed Bo into the hole alongside the bloody shear. After piling on some dirt and snow, he returned to the north side of the barn to cover his blood trail with fresh wintry powder, dried leaves, and urine. As for the blood in the abandoned building, he scraped the cold dirt around and raked it over until the deep red appeared indistinguishable from the dark earth.

Once he felt confident in his concealment efforts, he returned to Ginny. He shook his head at her, disappointed by her refusal to marry him. He hoisted her over his shoulder and went to a half-frozen stream nearby. As he began to wash the blood off his face, an idea sprung to mind. He stopped cleaning and roused Ginny with a splash of frigid water. "Wake up, wake up!" He used the tone of a playful lover. "Ginny, my sweet, wake up."

She jolted awake, opened her eyes, and screamed at the sight of Danny. "Murderer!"

He plowed a hand into her face and shoved her into the snow. "You keep your mouth shut. Nothing happened. It was only a bad dream."

She pushed his hand away. "No, Danny, you sick devil. I saw what you did. You killed my poor brother. I saw it with my own eyes. You evil bastard, you raped me, and you killed him, raped me, and you killed him!"

"Shut up! Nothing happened here. Not to you and certainly not to Bo. In fact, as we walked along this stream, I tripped and fell on a rock, which is why my mouth was bleeding and how I got this gash on my forehead. You fainted at the sight of it, and while I attempted to rouse you, my blood stained your clothes. I tried really hard to wash it out, but I was worried about you, which is why you're here now."

"That's not what happened," she snarled. Hot tears raced over his cheeks as she tried to push herself up and away from Danny. However, he caught her and forced her back down.

"It is what happened," he spat. "When we get back to the house, that's what you'll tell everyone. Then you're going to clean up and help your mother with supper like you always do. All this will have been a bad dream."

"I'm going to tell them the truth, Danny, and you can't stop me."

"Ginny, if you don't tell them exactly what I just said, I will slaughter your entire family like a herd of dumb cows, take you away from here, and make sure every night of your life is filled with agony. I swear by the Almighty that I will not fail in this if you dare speak a word. Got it?"

Trembling and panting, Ginny nodded, her face wet as the earth beneath her feet. As the sky darkened, Danny pulled her up and walked her back to the house. Looking wan as the winter moon, Ginny told the Virginian's story to Chester and Winifred. Their scrunched brows and flared nostrils revealed their skepticism, but how could they argue with their innocent daughter. In the meantime, Danny cleaned himself up nicely and returned to work, although the thought of fleeing quickly consumed his mind.

Hellhounds on the Trail

Chester woke up and went out to the barn, puffing his pipe all the while. The moment he stepped inside, he examined the pots and fermenters and realized that they had not yet received their daily check, which seemed strange considering Bo performed the task every day around dawn. He then noticed that the oldest batch of Maplewood Seven had not been prepared for bottling as scheduled for that morning. He walked over to Tobias, Burt, and Rufus, who seemed a bit frantic, struggling to complete several jobs evidentially beyond their skillset. "Where's Bo?" Chester asked them. "He hasn't done his daily maintenance or brought out the barrels. And it seems like you boys are now doing him a favor and finishing up his grain inspection."

"He hasn't worked at all, Pa," Tobias remarked, his eyes glossed with worry. "I haven't seen him at all. I asked Jane. She said she saw him head out on a walk two days ago. Never came back, which is why things ain't checked. Otis usually does it if Bo ain't around, but he went on a delivery run to Virginia with Danny. They got us a new client, and Danny needed extra help."

Chester crossed his arms. "Where do you think Bo went?"

Tobias shrugged. "Maybe into town. Might have stayed the night somewhere as he's done in the past, though I don't know why he would now with Jane being here and all."

Chester shook his head. "I've been in and out of Poor Fork the past two day dealing with Howie and Percy, and I sure as hell would have spotted my eldest son if he were about. Did Jane say why he went for a walk in the first place or what direction?"

"No. Maybe you should ask her."

Chester hurried inside and found Jane hard at work, preparing breakfast with the Buckley girls. Her cheeks looked wet and glowed like sun-lit roses, and a troubled heart clearly hid behind her busy eyes. He pulled her aside. "Do you know where Bo went?" Jane shook her head and pouted, unable to voice an answer. Chester turned to Ginny, who also seemed quite disturbed by something, her face vacant as a snowfield. "Ginny, do you know where your brother went?"

Hesitation held her breath until she finally sputtered, "L-L-Last time I saw Bo was out by the b-barn. He was walking around. P-Probably went into the forest or... or something."

Her fumbling words stirred another concern in Chester's mind, yet he couldn't hamper his determination to find Bo. He panned back to Jane. "Is there a chance he went into town without your knowledge?"

"I don't think so. I don't think he did."

"Something wrong, Jane? Your lips tell me one thing, but your eyes tell me otherwise. You too, Ginny. What in God's name are you two hiding from me?"

"Oh, leave them alone," Winifred barked, who suddenly entered the room with a handful of fresh rags.

"No, it's fine," Jane decided with a long breath. "Bo went off after I told him I was carrying his child. O Lord, he seemed so darn happy, even said so, but now I'm just worried that he might've been scared inside and ran away."

"Wait, wait, I'm going to be a grandpappy?" A grin crept through Chester's peppered whiskers.

"Yes, Chester, you will." Jane's lips wiggled like a caterpillar. "But Bo mentioned that you and God might not like it. He got all worried. Like I said, he told me he was happy about it, even though we ain't married. He said he felt a bit shaky, so I told him he ought to take a walk, and, well, he did. And I came inside the house to get on with my day."

Chester belted a sigh of relief. "Bo is one for the woods. He probably just went for a long walk in the forest. He's been known to sleep under the stars when his head is full. But Jane, you need not worry about this child. You're going to make a fine mother. You and Bo are going to get married come springtime, and that baby will be born into the Buckley home on a warm sunny day."

Jane threw her arms around Chester and pressed her cheek to his collar. "Thank you, Chester. Thank you so, so much."

"You can call me Pa. You're a Buckley now, Jane. You got Buckley blood running through you. Still, I do need to find Bo. It's not like him to miss this much work, and I got a strange feeling in my bones. Don't know what it is, but I got to follow it. I'm going to send Dick Harper into town. Ginny, take your sister and go look for him by the mineshaft. You know he likes that area. Might be camping out that way." Ginny grabbed her sister's hand without a word and hurried out the back door.

"Something's wrong with that girl," Winifred whispered to her husband. "There's no light in her eyes anymore, and she refuses to talk to me about it. And she's got a nasty bruise on her shoulder. Don't know if you saw it, Chester. I don't think it's from fainting."

"Maybe not, but at least Ginny's here and safe. I'll talk with her once my eldest son is back in this house." Chester hurried to the dog shed to speak with Dick and Big Bertha.

~

Danny and Otis returned from a significant deal in Richmond the next day. When Chester saw the truck pull up, he approached them and inquired about Bo, hoping they had seen him before they left for Virginia. Otis apologized for having no answer and handed his brother a heavy suitcase filled with banded cash. "How long's Bo been gone, brother?" he asked.

"Three days now. I'm beyond concerned. I think he might be hurt or lost. Poor Jane thinks she scared Bo off and that he might have fled Kentucky."

Danny stepped in, not a hint of fear on his breath. "Why does she think she scared him off?"

"Didn't she tell you before you left? She's pregnant."

Danny swallowed his spit as a cool wave of guilt rolled up his spine.

"Otis," Chester commanded, "put your stuff in your room and round up a search party. Call in our cousins from across the river if you can. We're going to scour the entire valley, no, the entire region. Might even have to cross into Virginia. Grab all the guns you can carry. Get started as soon as possible. I've already got Bertha on the prowl. Danny, you're coming with me."

Danny felt the first spike of nervousness. "Why?"

"What do you mean 'why?' You're on my team. Come on. Take the suitcase inside, grab a gun, and we'll get going. Hop to it, boy. My son's missing."

While the Buckleys prepared to comb the region, Danny hurried into the house and placed the suitcase on Chester's favorite upholstered chair. As he did so, he heard a young woman lamenting in the other room, the echo of a grieving heart. Jane. He felt a sting in his chest and churning in his stomach, the gnaw of regret.

He had murdered the father of his sister's unborn child. "What have I done?" he whispered to himself. Danny suddenly felt encumbered, stricken with stomach-digging dread. The time to run had arrived. He schemed quickly, figuring he could steal the TT, head out west, and change his name. No Buckley would ever find him, no matter how hard they searched or how many resources they could reel into their net.

Danny hustled into the kitchen to find himself a drink. He needed to calm the storm in his head to plot a failsafe escape from the Buckley property. Yet Ginny sat by the ice chest, staring into the abyss, blocking his path. When Danny stepped near, she cowered and burst into tears, quickly turning her face to the wall. Sally May, who stood on the other side of the kitchen, brightened with surprise at Ginny's reaction to Danny. Alarmed and terrified, Danny darted into the room he shared with Burt and Rufus, where he started collecting his belongings into a potato sack. Amidst his scramble, he heard the roar of engines igniting. Chester, Otis, and Dick had fired up the trucks.

"Shit," he hissed. He knew the rugged Appalachian mountains offered no speedy escape route, and he had never planned a decent alternative route to the Devil's Spine. He could neither walk nor ride a horse. The Buckleys would catch him like wolves on a fawn. He sat on his cot and took a deep breath, hoping it might calm him and allow his mind to conceive other possibilities. After a few minutes, he decided to play along and dutifully search for Bo as if he knew nothing. If asked again, he would repeat that he was as clueless as everyone else.

~

Chester and Danny drove into town in the Ford Model TT. They visited Reed's Saloon first, but Percy confessed that he had not seen Bo in roughly two weeks. Chester then dragged Danny around town, asking if anyone could guess his son's whereabouts.

While the worried old man talked to Howard Williams in front of the grocery store, Danny noticed the hawk eyes of Sheriff Teddy Hanes, who stood near the post office alongside a grim-faced lawman wearing the badge of a high rank. Danny panicked as if they knew of his misdeeds, then turned back to Chester. "Maybe Bo's up at the mine," he rashly urged. "I... I don't know if anyone's checked there."

Chester shook his head, grievous thoughts dancing behind his weary eyes. "Ginny and Sally May already searched the place yesterday."

"Maybe he's there now. He might be on the move for all we know."

"I guess it couldn't hurt to investigate a second time. All right, Danny. Let's go."

By the time they returned to the house, Otis, Dick, and the other boys had returned from their hunt on the roads. They informed Chester that their cousins across the river neither saw nor heard from Bo and didn't have the resources to comb the woods in such frigid weather. Chester cursed and snarled that he was the head honcho of the Buckley family and that the lesser cousins had no right to deny him their aid.

Working a hard-cut frown and furrowed brows, he demanded that Otis and Dick lead the boys to the storage mine for a second check, as Danny had suggested. "I already checked the mineshaft twice this morning," Dick rebutted, grumpy as an old cat. "He ain't there, boss."

"Where the hell can he be? Goddammit, my stomach's roiling with dread." Chester paused to think. "All right, so here's what we're going to do. I need to get Ginny out of the house, so I'm going to take her, along with Danny and Big Bertha, to search the southern rim of the property. Even go as far as to check out Pa's old pig barn. Otis, you take your boys to the west end beyond the ravine and look for signs of activity, anything. Dick, you wait on the back porch and protect the women in case something happens to the rest of us. Let's move out."

Ginny protested to remain indoors, but Chester felt adamant about her accompaniment. He pulled her from the house by the arm and made her walk beside Danny while following Big Bertha and the bloodhounds. Ginny trembled like a cold fledgling and held her eyes to the ground, especially once the dogs picked up Bo's scent in the woods near the southern property line.

Chester noticed Ginny's condition worsened as they neared the old pig barn. The weight of her breath became ever more obvious, and she winced whenever she lifted her head. He caught her shooting a fretting eye at Danny before turning away to fold her arms and shiver with a weak sob.

"Chester," Danny blurted, realizing that if they found the body, Ginny would likely call him out, and he'd be quick to fail to denounce her. "I got to go back to the house right now. I-I need to use the outhouse."

"We're in the woods, boy. If you need to piss, pick a dang tree. If you need to shit, get it over with and wipe yourself with a wet leaf."

"I'd feel more comfortable in the outhouse. Plus, the snow... "

Before Chester could retort, Danny took off running. Chester thought it queer and felt the urge to chase him down, but his suspicion disappeared when the hounds began to yelp from the hillocks on the other side of the barn. Chester and Bertha hurried over to find them shoveling their noses into a snow mound beside the roots of a gnarled oak tree. Ginny fell to her knees near the barn and pressed her elbows into the snow, covering the hot tears that streamed from her eyes.

In the meantime, Chester watched Bertha's dogs dig deep into the mound until they came across a decaying metal surface. Bertha got down on her knees and scooped the snow around the agitated pups. Chester could only watch, his mind racing, hands restless. Bertha suddenly paused to glance at him. "What is it?" he muttered.

Bertha removed a rusty shear from the mound, its tip stained with old blood. Chester snatched the tool and whacked at the side of the snowdrift, frightening the bloodhounds. Eventually, he grew frustrated and tossed it aside, only to deepen the hole with his bare hands.

His eyes began to well, but the truth didn't strike until he unearthed a frozen face. Bo's eyelids appeared shut with little decomposition, but his mouth appeared stuffed with mud, and his chest an ugly clutter of browned blood, torn cotton, and particles of nature.

Chester took off his hat and set it over Bo's face. Bertha stood behind him, glowering as she stared at the makeshift grave. The woods seemed to darken, and snow began to fall. Forest murmurs echoed through Chester's head like a cacophony of excited crows, dampening the distraught moans of his daughter while heightening the bitter silence of Big Bertha. The bloodhounds might have howled, but Chester didn't hear them. He looked upon his beloved eldest son, the one he trusted most, heir to the Buckley property and Maplewood Distillery.

"He was to be a father," Chester mumbled to no one, his breath trembling. "He was my son, and he was to be a father! Jesus, my Lord, give me justice. Show me who did this, and I swear I will make things right. I swear, I will. Please guide my vengeance and let it be swift."

The rage surged within. He knew that blood and fire shadowed his future, yet as for the one to suffer his revenge, he could not begin to guess. However, as he touched Bo's wound with a shaky finger, a reel of memories poured through his mind like a river of snowmelt in spring. The signs had been right in front of him all along. The bridge of trust burned to ash. He felt like a blind old buffoon.

He stood and turned to Ginny, who knelt in the snow by the barn, weeping upon the earth. He stomped to her side and yanked her to her feet by the arm. "Ginny, I need you to tell me who did this, and I need you to tell me right now."

Terrified, she covered her mouth with both hands and tried to hold back another bout of sobs.

Chester's eyes widened. "You were there, weren't you? Don't hide it from me, daughter. I can see right through you. Just speak, and I promise my justice will be swift as the Lord smites."

"He threatened to kill me, Pa." She whimpered. "He threatened to kill you, Mama, everyone in our family if I dared talk. I wouldn't marry him, so he hit me and forced himself upon me in the barn against the tool table. Bo came out of nowhere and pulled Danny off. They fought. They fought hard. I tried to run, but Danny caught me and hurt me again. Then Bo beat him good. Bloodied him. But Danny, he managed to grab the shear."

"Ginny, that's enough. Bertha, take the hounds to the house. I want you to catch that city-slicking son of a bitch. I'm going to tear him limb from limb." Bertha hurried off, the bloodhounds at her side. With a fire roaring in his eyes, Chester picked up his daughter and carried her back to the house as fast as his legs could move in the late-winter snow.

~

Knowing that Dick guarded the back door, Danny snuck in through the front, avoiding the ladies in the kitchen. He tore his bed apart, looking for his secret stash of money. His curses and growls troubled Jane in the next room. She hurried to the door and shook her head at him. "Why are you in a panic, brother?"

"I'm leaving," he spat.

"You can't leave, Danny."

"I need to get out of here before Chester returns."

"Why, what'd you do this time?"

250

"I'm so sorry, Jane. I'm sorry that I won't be here to see your child. I'm proud of you for that, but I need to hurry. I went too far. I did something... I did something really terrible."

"What... what in God's name did you do now?"

Danny gave up on the stash of money and finished packing his potato sack. Jane pushed his chest with a soft hand as he tried to exit the room. "Dammit, Danny, what'd you do?"

He looked into her blue eyes, full of worry. "Get out of my way."

"Not until you tell me, Danny."

"Get out of my way!"

He shoved her to the ground and flew out the front door just as Dick Harper burst through the back. Winifred, Melonie, and Sally May hurried out of the kitchen to gripe about the clamor. "Danny ran off," cried Jane. "He took some stuff and bolted."

Otis, Burt, and Rufus suddenly entered the house with Big Bertha. "Dick," Otis commanded. "Load up your shotgun, and let's get."

"What's happening?" Jane demanded.

Chester stepped into the house and put Ginny on her feet, who ran into her mother's arms and wept. Chester panned over the eyes of his family, who stared at him for the final word. "Danny Andersen raped Ginny and murdered our beloved Bo. Stabbed him in Pa's old barn with a rusty shear."

Jane fainted. Melanie gasped and knelt to help her.

Winifred and Sally May shrieked and panted until tears reddened their eyes and cheeks. Tobias cried and cursed. "The time to mourn will come soon enough," Chester affirmed. "But right now, we need to catch that goat-sucking, son of a bitch."

Without further delay, Chester, Otis, Dick, Big Bertha, Burt, Rufus, and Tobias rushed out the front door armed with dogs, guns, knives, and torches. Chester thought to use the trucks, but Danny fled on foot, so they did likewise to better track him.

They hastened down the Devil's Spine toward Poor Fork, the bloodhounds sniffing and snorting. Danny's footprints appeared clearly in the snow and veered into the woods at the bottom of the steep hill toward the west end of Henry Wilkins's property.

Danny heard the hounds in the distance behind him and knew they would close in fast if he didn't pick up his pace. His heart thumped twice the speed of his feet, trudging through the snow. The afternoon sky seemed so dark and gray that Danny felt like the cape of nightfall would soon envelop the world. He made a sharp turn and slid into a small ravine, then wiped his tracks with a broken branch and hid with his back against the roots of a tree. At first, he heard only his breath and the tiny crunch of snow beneath his hot feet. But the air soon filled with the grunting of dogs and the cursing of men. Otis whistled several times to scare Danny into thinking they knew his whereabouts.

Danny remained still. The bloodhounds

approached the tree above the ravine yet diverged when they heard something to the east. The clamor of the search party soon faded, so Danny took off in the opposite direction, keeping low in the ravine, which he quickly learned was a frozen creek.

The ice beneath his feet occasionally cracked, but not loud enough to give him away. He sensed freedom on the horizon, so close he could taste it. He thought of heading west, hitching a ride to Missouri, Colorado, or Arizona. Perhaps, one day, he'd reach the California coast and see the Pacific Ocean.

With happy thoughts to warm him, he climbed out of the wash only to find himself on the Devil's Spine. His head must have been in the clouds since he didn't notice the vehicle tearing up the hillside. He turned his head and braced as the driver pumped the brakes and laid on the horn. The car came to a grinding halt.

Danny breathed relief and thought to ask for assistance, but the driver's grim face pulled a recent memory to mind, and the red in the lawman's eyes beamed through the window. A jolt of fear forced Danny to retreat into the ravine once again. When he heard one of the car doors shut, he scurried back the way he came.

The ravine wove through the hills like an elaborate seam in a white blanket. Danny followed carefully, his confidence returning with each step toward the deeper woods. He figured he could reach the Virginia state border by dawn if he didn't stop.

Suddenly, his right foot broke through the ice of a deep pond in the wash. He instinctively swore aloud and tried to pull free, but his boot quickly filled with the weight of frigid water. He struggled to escape, enduring the freezing burn, thinking he had jinxed himself with his hopeful thoughts of freedom.

Danny finally managed to yank his foot free, but it felt heavy, then numb. He sat down on the ice and rubbed his pant leg to regain the feeling, but to no avail. He lifted his head to curse at the sky, only to see Big Bertha standing on the high bank of the ravine.

Danny scrambled to his feet just as the hounds stormed down the embankment. He tried to limp into a sprint, but his frozen foot dragged like an anchor. One of the dogs pounced upon his back while the other snapped at his bad leg. Danny fell face-first onto the ice and slipped into a cold, black world.

~

Danny awoke with a chill, finding himself posted upright, two feet off the ground, his arms and legs spread to their greatest extent, fastened to two pines with tightly wound hemp rope. The frost and wind of a late winter afternoon stabbed at his naked body like a swarm of wasps, consuming him, forcing his limbs to rattle and his eyes to water. The agony proved so intense he could neither force a scream nor begin to attempt an escape.

"What'd I tell you, Daniel Andersen? What'd I tell you? If you do me wrong, I will castrate you, flay your

chest, and fill you with bullets until nothing remains."
Danny slowly lifted his bloodshot eyes to Chester, who
stood before him, holding a sawed-off shotgun over his
shoulder. Lined up behind him with torches speared
into the snow—Otis, Dick, Burt, Rufus, Tobias, Big
Bertha, and the bloodhounds seated abreast.

Danny suddenly lost control of his nerves, so his
bowel and bladder released their contents. The
Buckleys exploded into laughter while Chester
remained stern as he stepped around the piss-stained
snow and pressed his shotgun barrel into Danny's
stomach. The rough metal scraped his soft skin,
drawing first blood.

"He was to be a father, Danny. A father to your
sister's child. How could you do such an abominable
thing? Are you incapable of love or friendship? Don't
you have any sense, any heart? Are you so goddamn
stupid and cold that you'd stab an innocent man to
death? And then you had to go and rape my daughter
all because you were too much of a coward to win her
with honor. You're a filthy demon, you know that; a
goat-sucking demon! Now, tell me why you killed my
beautiful boy?"

Danny choked on his retort. Chester pulled a pistol
from his belt and scowled as he pulled the trigger,
blowing out one of Danny's kneecaps. After the
Virginian let out a bloodcurdling scream, Chester
proclaimed, "What do you know, you found your voice.
Glad to hear it, Danny-boy. Now you best answer my

question, or I'll take your other knee. Why'd you kill my Bo?"

"I-I w-w-wanted... "

"You wanted what?"

Danny shook his head. Chester thumbed the pistol hammer.

"I wanted what he had!"

"Speak louder, boy."

"Bo... h-he was holding you back. He was holding the d-distillery back, your life's work. He just wanted my s-sister, that's all. He was... he was hungry for love, not for b-business. He was too k-kind and soft-hearted to have ever filled your shoes. But I c-could, and I can. I have the strength, am-ambition, and will to b-build Maplewood Seven into... into an empire. And I was... I was just hoping th-that by m-marrying Ginny, I could g-gain a future, even... even earn your r-respect and have a foothold in the family. I... I could be a Bu-Buckley and... and put Maplewood Seven on the map like you always dreamed. Like you always dreamed, Ch-Chester."

"Did you honestly think you could gain such things by raping my daughter and murdering my eldest son? Do you think that's how the world works?"

Danny began to sob.

"You thought you could silence my sweet Ginny and bury the truth with Bo? You thought you could just cut him out and assume I'd never find out? Well, Daniel Andersen, let's see how you like being cut out." Chester returned his pistol to its holster and stepped back only to signal Big Bertha to his side. She approached without an ounce of emotion on her stone-white face. She pulled a hunting knife from her belt and went to work.

Chester stood still with one hand on his hip, the other holding the shotgun over his shoulder while his eyes rested on Danny. He watched the boy cringe, whine, and scream as Bertha slowly neutered him. To further Chester's retribution, she also removed Danny's manhood and, when finished, tossed the organs to the hounds. "No," Danny wailed, slipping in and out of consciousness.

"Is that what my daughter shouted when you forced yourself upon her?"

"Brother," Otis called out. "We best hurry. We're on the Wilkins property."

"Well," Chester chuckled. "Lucky for old Henry, he'll be the center of attention when the authorities find dead Virginian scum on his land." Danny tried to speak again but choked as Bertha began to flay his chest with cold precision. Chester never once looked away from the torture, for every flail and moan brought the ends of his grin higher.

At last, Bertha completed her remorseless work on Danny's chest and tossed the skin to the wind. She then returned to her place in line amongst her kin. Chester followed, though his satisfied grin quickly inverted into a frown that cut deep into his peppered beard.

No words seeded the air as the seven members of the Buckley family hoisted their guns and fired round after round, unrelenting as a troop of passionate soldiers. Thunder filled the forest as a torrent of bullets pumped into Danny until nothing but a minced corpse hung in the winter woods of East Kentucky.

When the gunfire finally ceased, Chester heard someone shout, "The Maplewood Seven." He turned to the ravine, where white-haired Henry Wilkins, Marshal Elias McCrory, and Teddy Hanes, with his deputies, stood aglow in triumph. Chester spat at the frosty earth and laughed.

A BEAUTIFUL DAY IN BUDAPEST

THE BLUE

DANUBE

"O Budapest. It is a dark city, no less drab than the supine gray clouds that mope across its sky. It stands as the pride of Hungary, jewel of the Magyar, yet it is not unlike any other great city of Europe. With its magnificent palaces, bedizened opera halls, and chromatic visage, it attempts to paint a picture of harmony and affluence. However, the reality of this is appreciably contrasting."

"Although it is formally of imperial status, it still yearns to belittle outside communities, like a school bully whose parents never spanked him as a punishment. It might well portray the role of an endowed, sophisticated metropolis, yet what art is here? It is not Paris. What spirit is here? It is not

Rome. What music is here? It is not Vienna. What literature is here? It is not London. What might have once been a lovely countryside has been raked over with tar roads, crippled bridges, graceless buildings, grotesque manors, tacky apartments, tasteless restaurants, and the bleary boot-heels of scurrilous citizens."

"The Great War whittled Budapest into scraps. But to everyone's dull surprise, it has rebuilt itself as a mechanic does a worn and beaten car, a car with impressive features, yet can barely drive a mile in the snow. Budapest may seem clean to its long-time inhabitants, however, to a frequent traveler who has experienced the best of Western civilization, it is a puddle of stagnant water. It is a cesspool, one that births mosquitos who relish nothing less than aimless buzzing until they can suck the gold blood from human pockets and fill their bellies with the wine of life. O Budapest, tomorrow shall undoubtedly be one of unrivaled misery in your company." So wrote Leonard Sterling about his reluctant arrival to the Hungarian capital.

I feel, and still often do, that Leonard was born a cynic. For though his train arrived a quarter after five, he felt he might have reached Budapest sooner had the engineer not stopped in Bratislava for an extended personal break. I remember him later complaining, "Who prevents a train full of unquiet passengers from reaching their destination on time? Who decides that a cup of hot liquid and a tiny plate of toast is more important than punctuality?" He went on about the subject for another minute, adding that most people are foolish and malleable, easily claimed as prey for the wolves of the world. He certainly fancied himself a predator among the higher mouths of the food chain, considering his ruthless pursuit as a salesman.

This perception persisted maliciously as he exited the train station and hastened to the street curb, where he pushed his way through a small line of taxi-callers. He needed not holler or raise an arm. Instead, when the gentleman beside him opened the door to a cab that had just pulled up, Leonard thrust himself in, snidely thanked the poor fellow, and slammed the door in his face.

"*Hova?*" inquired the cab driver in his native tongue.

"The Blue Danube Hotel," Leonard answered in his most proper American tone.

"*A Kék Duna?*"

Leonard lit up a cigarette and venomously reiterated, "THE... BLUE... DANUBE. You know, like the musical piece by Johann Strauss."

In the minutes following, as the cab wove through the busy streets, the nervous driver might have noticed that Leonard was one to mumble to himself, whispering insults toward those who did service for him regardless of reasonable quality. The unfortunate cabby, knowing little English, but serving enough customers in his time, may have also grasped that this foreigner's character assumed hostility rather naturally. At the very least, the chauffeur must have surmised that there would be no tip in his near future.

Leonard smoked three cigarettes in the time it took to drive from the Budapest Railway Terminal to the hotel selected by his employer. All the while, he could not abstain from convincing himself that luck had stiffed him once again. "How wretched to be here," he muttered, or so I imagine him recalling the ceaseless traveling he had endured the past few months. Marching from hotel to hotel, rarely granted a peaceful moment or the slightest possibility of enjoying any one destination.

Each day plagued Leonard with a similar routine. It usually began with a saltless breakfast in his room or the nearest café, followed by the day's business appointment, often resulting in a luncheon with a humdrum client who liked to talk. Later, after desperately returning to his hotel for sanctuary, he would spend several hours needling a pen over documents and noting upcoming engagements. He typically took dinner in his room while continuing his work, then washed his dreary day down with a glass of brandy before allowing his swollen head to crash upon a pillow. Leonard fancied himself a soldier of modern industry.

The Blue Danube was a pleasant hotel on the upper east bank of the eponymous river, constructed in neo-renaissance fashion at the height of the Austro-Hungarian Empire when astounding wealth flowed lavishly through the city banks and businesses. Still, whoever commissioned the hotel must have greatly admired Johann Strauss II, the Waltz King of Vienna. Personally, I have always been very fond of the composer. As for Leonard Sterling, well, I would soon come to learn his opinion on such matters.

As Leonard's taxi pulled into the porte-cochère, he gathered his belongings and capped his head with a London derby he had purchased at the start of his summer travels. Exiting the cab, he tossed three English Pounds on the seat and shut the door without sparing a single breath of gratitude. I would guess that the driver then reached back and grabbed the partially crumpled bills, yet before he could complain that they were of the wrong currency, his apathetic customer had already stepped out of sight and into the lobby.

I first noticed Leonard Sterling in the hotel's popular cocktail lounge. It was the last Thursday of August 1930, and although the room held a quarter of its weekend capacity, tobacco fog filled the room as if a contributor occupied every seat. Many in attendance were habitués, some stewing in their loneliness, others nodding to their scratch-throated compatriots. Still, many more were yoked by the heavy red-light music that wove through the smoke like some wild wanton serpent.

I was performing that night, my voice bouncing

generously into the well-cupped ears of my audience. With Abeo tooting the brass horn, Imre fingering the piano, Sandor scratching the snare, and Dezso dragging on the bass, we delivered two hearty handfuls of fleshy jazz numbers.

I had just commenced another set of flirtatious lyrics when I noticed Leonard take a seat at a central table, neither too far nor too near. He removed his hat and briefly combed his hair, then ordered a brandy before lighting a cigarette with the suavity of an English baron.

It proved a bit difficult to make out his features in the dusky room, yet his haughty presence evoked my presumption of his handsomeness – robust, broad-shouldered, a strong chin, greased hair finely toothed in New York fashion.

He was all black and white, suit and tie, gold cufflinks striving to shine in the perverse ambiance that haunted the room. Normally, I would have drooled over such a man, but by that point in my life, experience had taught me to live like an early spring day, vibrant and cheerful with a lingering nip of winter frost.

The finale of my performance passed quicker than expected. My bandmates packed up and took to their rooms as soon as the applause ebbed back into the natural gravelly hum of the lounge. I recall thanking the audience and stepping off stage with a glint in my smile. A kind gentleman with a red fedora scrambled from the other side of the bar to offer me a glass of Brolio chianti. I politely refused and told him I would reconsider his offer if he attended my show on Saturday.

The Blue Danube had hired me for the summer of 1930. After my residency, I was to return home for a few months before considering a contract with a new jazz club on the other side of town. I remember thinking about this as I casually stepped behind the bar for a quick shot of Irish devil juice. It felt smooth going down, a gentle burn on my tongue, not in my throat. I lit a gasper, thinking nothing of the evening, yet I knew he was watching me. I felt his eyes yearning to climb over my shoulder and look upon my face.

From the counter, partially hidden by Jon, the only Flemish barkeep in Budapest, I half-observed Leonard Sterling. He seemed disappointed, judging from the way he hastily scratched his chin twice before polishing off his glass of brandy. He stabbed the table's ashtray with his small cigar and capped his head with the derby, tossed some coins on the wood, and stepped out into the lobby.

Jon noticed my wandering eyes. "Is someone pestering you this evening?" His Hungarian didn't sound quite broken, as usual.

"Not physically," I casually replied, my words swimming in the smoke. "Merely a curiosity among the strange faces in the audience."

Jon shrugged as if he didn't understand and

handed me a bottle of Tullamore D.E.W. "A little nightcap, madame?"

I nodded and kissed his cheek. "You're one of the good ones," I told him before exiting the lounge with the bottle in hand.

The lobby of the Blue Danube emanated an ambiance both old-fashioned and sumptuous. Not as elegant as the Grand Budapest Hotel, but still of regal quality, certainly worthy of business moguls and foreign ambassadors. Similarly, Leonard styled himself as a member of the American gentry to prevent clients and strangers from judging him as a commoner of the West. His mannerisms complimented his posture and skyward chin to better display a refined citizen with predatory instincts, repressing the truth of his low-born origins, which, to his disappointment, often flared.

Even before I had learned this about Leonard, I sensed it in his presence as I passed him near the service counter. I refused to lend him a glance. However, I could not refrain from lingering upon hearing his voice for the first time. Warm and rich, it caressed my ears, smooth as the whiskey I had so lustfully indulged in only a few minutes prior, a voice seldom appreciated beyond public radio.

"Yes, I have a reservation," he explained to the hotel clerk. "One night prepaid for Leonard J. Sterling. If identification is required, I can provide you with credentials."

"No need, sir," answered the clerk in a nervous, highly defective English accent. "Leonard J. Sterling, British-American Cigarette Company?"

"That is me."

The young man handed over the room key and a piece of paper. "Need anything, please call for service."

Leonard eyed the young man with a flat expression and leaned into the counter. "Might I ask you, sir, why they call this place the Blue Danube?"

The clerk's immediate confusion shone like a dying star through his vacant gaze.

"I mean," Leonard continued, "the river is blatantly polluted, anything but blue. And Johann Strauss II, composer of the eponymic orchestrated piece, was Austrian, not Hungarian. Shouldn't this hotel stand in Vienna?"

The clerk shrugged to which the American lightly scoffed.

"Pray tell, who names a sophisticated hotel after a Viennese waltz? That's like saying there's a hotel in St. Petersburg called The Nutcracker or a restaurant in Prague called The Moldau. Next thing you know, there will be an ice cream parlor in Manhattan called Rhapsody in Blue."

I snickered. Leonard suddenly turned his sight on me like a policeman recognizing a bank robber in his presence. Our eyes met. Lightning flashed in my mind. Music rippled through my soul like an evil spirit pressing to remind me of something I had long wished to forget. Luckily, our contact was as brief as a breath. I hurried up the stairs at that moment, never glancing back to see if he had done the same or even turned away at all.

AN ENGLISH

BREAKFAST

Lunacy saturated the Friday morning papers, beginning with a man who allegedly committed suicide by hanging himself from the bow of a ferry on the Danube. I thought it quite odd until I dove deeper into the column, where it noted that a police detective suspected this to be a gang-related incident. He proposed that although the murder was certainly achieved, the culprits were of amateur skill, clearly failing to waterboard the victim while leaving a solid trail of clues in their sloppy escape.

One page over, I read that a residential building in Szeged had caught fire, where many innocents burned to death. However, a woman and her three children were miraculously saved by a black cat, a scenario upon which the article's author decided to elaborate, touching on the notion of sweet irony. The papers divulged other events throughout Hungary – political rallies, rising unemployment, financial challenges, increasing animosity among ethnic groups, interviews hinting at a rise in socialism and fascism in parliament and the aristocracy.

Pushing beyond local borders, a few columns harped on the economic crises in America and Germany, not to mention a bit of trouble with Mussolini in Italy. Wishing to start my day without fearing that the world was plunging into chaos, I flipped to another page.

Boredom quickly found me, and my mind began to drift. I nibbled on my jam-smeared toast and sipped some coffee before indulging another drag of my stogie. It had been a slow and quiet morning in the hotel's streetside café. Fridays typically drew in a crowd of introverted renaissance men and boisterous elderly couples, but this particular morning seemed to deviate from the norm.

The newspaper suddenly lured me back with an article whose author had interviewed a man who claimed he could walk across Lake Balaton like Jesus, but only if completely stripped of his clothing. He had allegedly performed this feat several times and knew of witnesses to prove it. I dove into this wild story, happy that my day would begin with a good laugh. Yet, as my eyes panned over the first sentence, *he* set foot in the café. My brain gasped.

Leonard Sterling again cloaked himself in black and white, yet he neither sported his derby nor his cufflinks. He had combed back and smoothed his sable brown hair, still wet with Brilliantine, revealing a broad forehead and slightly receding hairline. Even without the partial darkness of the music lounge, his chin remained prominent, albeit his face seemed more oblong than I remembered. He wore a hard expression like a soldier highly skilled in the art of war, yet bore no scars to prove his experience. He struck me as a man who regularly shaved, fearing that his skin would hastily bristle out like a bear.

If I did not prepossess the recognition of his American origin, I might have presumed him Dutch or German or even Finnish. I additionally perceived that he had donned a cape of pride before entering the café, ever prepared to impose unnecessary knowledge on others, believing himself to be all the wiser.

I further studied him from behind my smoke and newspaper, analyzing his profile with only three tables between us. Upon finding comfort in his chair, he ordered a coffee and fired up a cigarette. Already we had two things in common. Just as the server approached Leonard to take his order, a familiar rowdy gentleman of Newark blood entered the café, George Samson.

I had known George for half a year. He was what some might call the charming, dark-haired American dreamboat. He could easily lure a woman into his net with those sparkling brown eyes and that infectious smile. He even combed his hair like John Barrymore, all Hollywood suave, figuring it would deliver him a world of luck.

He strolled toward Leonard with a musical swagger, one hand tugging on the lapel of his blue-pinstriped jazz suit, the other loosely wheeling an unlit gasper that he tucked into the feather band of his fedora as he rounded the table. He rolled up his right sleeve just a tad, enough to flash his silver watch before patting Leonard on the shoulder. "Mr. Sterling, Leonard, Leonard, Leonard, good old Richmond Leo!"

"Good morning, George. It's been some time."

"Come on," George exclaimed merrily, taking a seat while flattening his thin mustache with the side of his thumb. "It's only been about a year since Atlantic City, right?"

"You have a terrible sense of time for a wristwatch enthusiast." Leonard snuffed his cigarette as if it offended him, then reached into his coat for another. "Three arduous years have passed since Atlantic City."

"That long?" George held his gleeful smile despite his comrade's sober tone. "Gosh, it seems like yesterday we were putting on our best suits and draining our pockets together. We were crazy, like musketeers or cowboys or something. Ah, those were such good days, not that these days are bad or anything."

274

"On the contrary, George, these days are quite dreary. It's just that your white smile simply refuses to yellow."

"What are you talking about, Leo? Don't be all fog and rain. I hear you've been working out of London. You know, spending too much time with the Red Coats will turn you into a sad sack of scones or, at the very least, a bumbling drunk. You know why the Scots and Irish produce so much whiskey? To help the Brits with their sorrows. You know why the Scots and Irish consume so much whiskey? To forget that they helped the Brits in the first place."

Leonard chuckled. "You're a chipper fellow, George. Nothing gets you down."

George yanked a matchbook from his pocket and ignited his Camel Joe. "Well, I mean, why should I feel low? I've no reason. Life is a beautiful thing. There's so much to do, so many places to see, women to dance with, fellows to laugh with. As a matter of fact, I got some pals to introduce you to. I invited them here. I hope you don't mind."

"I suppose I have no choice."

"Leo, Leo, don't you worry, buddy. These guys are the bees-knees. They may not be American, but they know how to party. They'll show you the ways and means. They smoke the finest gaspers in Central Europe. They drive jazzy machines, nothing like them hayburners farting up the streets in Modern Gomorrah. These guys know food, and they got class, but most importantly, they know where to find a choice bit of calico, if you catch my drift. Wait, wait, wait, here they come now. Just you wait, Leo, you'll love these guys."

Two debonaire gentlemen strolled into the café at that moment. Indeed, it was through them I had met George, who suddenly stood up to shake hands and kiss cheeks. Leonard rose like a cantankerous bear emerging from hibernation, following in his friend's footsteps, carrying out the universal actions in greeting newcomers.

George introduced them with a boisterous cordiality that oozed with pretension. "This is Aron Jakab," he announced. "He's one of the cleverest bankers I know, meticulous as a Medici. Drinks like an Irish meatpacker. Handles my finances at the Hungarian National Bank. And this other cavalier, a man of extraordinary talent, is Laszlo Kozma. Might just be the wittiest rooster this side of the Atlantic. He's a technician down at the national radio studio. Best in the biz."

"Enchanted," Leonard remarked flatly as he reseated and put out his cigarette. Clearly annoyed, he turned his sight to the street-side windows and sipped his coffee, then grimaced as if he had forgotten something vital to his daily routine. Perhaps he realized that the server for whom he had been waiting, had hastily retreated upon George's clamorous arrival. Leonard fired a peevish glare at his friend before

276

desperately waving the waiter over to request an English breakfast.

"English breakfast?" The server echoed, sincerely perplexed.

"Leo," George butted in with an airy chuckle. "They don't serve English food here, but I tell you what, the Hungarian cuisine is to die for. The breakfast, especially, will keep you stuffed until dinner."

Leonard glared at the waiter. "Garçon, an English breakfast, please! Eggs, beans, sausage, and a biscuit. I'm sure you can conjure up such a meal with what supplies you have in your hotel kitchen."

The poor fellow, barely knowing a fleck of English, nodded nervously, though he seemed relieved when the other gentlemen ordered local cuisine in his native tongue. While the server fetched their cups of coffee and tea, I overheard a few of George's jokes but lost interest when his words trailed into one of his nonsensical prattles.

Not to say George wasn't an exciting person, quite the contrary. Leonard, on the other hand, wore a loathsome frown while staring abysmally at the café entrance as if each second with these people included a fresh nail in his skull. Similarly, I grew bored observing that table. Why devote attention to something uninteresting when our world holds so many wonders?

One of the astounding beauties of life is discovering things we did not know existed. I always felt that my singing career had delivered me that luxury. For the most part, I performed for a different audience each night, fresh eyes to meet, clean hands to shake, new opportunities. Each venue with whom I signed a contract granted me a unique perspective on the changing world. Truly, every place I visited felt unlike its predecessor.

The dozen times I performed in greater Europe, I fell in love with unusual foods, exclusive wines, au courant clothing styles, intriguing languages, the list goes on. Every person I have ever known has kept my interest in some manner of respect, all except one. And now, at the café, I added a second person to that list, Leonard J. Sterling.

When Leonard had entered the music lounge the night before, he wore an air of mystery and intrigue like Jay Gatsby, acting as if he knew the secret behind Houdini's most mesmerizing magic trick. Now it became evident that he was bitter as an artichoke and annoying as a fly on a cow's ass.

I shook my head and returned to the newspaper article about the silly Jesus imposter. However, before I could immerse myself, the server approached and offered me more coffee. I caught him staring down my blouse as he poured me a fresh cup. Of course, the instant he figured out I wasn't blind, he startled himself and spilled the hot liquid all over the floor, some splashing against my Mary Jane strap shoes. He sputtered a series of apologies and attempted to clean, but before he could drop to his knees with a rag and peer up my skirt, I flicked my cigarette ash toward him and hotly advised that he scurry back to the kitchen before I called the manager.

The fool lingered and beseeched me like a feudal serf to forgive him for his clumsiness and inappropriate gaze. Frustration and embarrassment encumbered me as his pleading resounded into the lobby, drawing the attention of people who needn't learn of his folly. "Leave the dame alone!" George suddenly cried out, hurrying to my rescue. "Beat it! *Verni, Verni!*"

The server finally shut his mouth and scampered into the kitchen. George took a napkin from the table and knelt to kindly wipe the tips of my shoes, never once glancing up the length of my legs. "Ah, Tülay, what would you do without a little George Samson in your life?"

"Well, I would raise my voice to Orbán, the hotel manager, and replace that perverted server. Perhaps with one of integrity who would silently pour my coffee and clean the mess on the floor without so much as a glimpse toward my chest or legs. Nevertheless, I thank you, George, for your alacrity."

"You wow me, Tutu. What a spitfire! Must be that ferocious Ottoman blood, *ha-ha*. You know, the dogs in this city are always barking up your tree. But then, who wouldn't jump at the chance to ruffle your leaves or run their hands over those long olive branches?"

"You make a fine jester, George. Befitting of kings."

"Ah, come on, honey. You know I'm just tugging those golden strings. A man's got to try when it comes to gorgeous dames like yourself."

"You're far too kind."

"By the way, what are you doing this morning?"

"Enjoying solitude."

"Witty as a rabbi! Why don't you join the gents and me? We ain't fishermen looking for a daily catch like mister smooth-tonic over there."

I could not help but laugh. "You never cease to charm, do you?"

"Not in a thousand years, darling."

~

I sat between George and Laszlo, my coffee close, my cigarette closer. George was telling us a wild story about his ex-girlfriend in New Jersey when I felt the phantom pressure of heavy eyes. It was Leonard. He stared at me covetously as if I were the English breakfast he had so brusquely ordered and now awaited. I ignored him and purposely flirted with the other boys, a natural defense of mine. And with such delightful company, how could I resist?

Aron began as a friend of a friend some years ago, but had long become a comrade over the unnecessary middle party. Laszlo and I go back even further. Our friendship blossomed in Los Angeles when, as a student of the young radio industry in 1923, he interned at KNX, where I began my singing career. A few years later, I bumped into him at a party in some mansion outside Budapest. We've been the best of friends ever since.

And George Samson, well, Aron and Laszlo introduced us. He proved to be the most transparent human I had ever known. His only goals in life were to win the trust of wealthy men and the hearts of beautiful women. Leonard, on the other hand, was a hard-shelled crustacean with no good reason to gawk. The man knew nothing of me, my history with his tablemates, my pains, or my pleasures. Worse, I could tell that if he remained in my presence for much longer, my irritation with him would evolve into loathing.

When I had initially joined the table, Laszlo and Aron greeted me with their usual happy smiles and kisses. George then politely extended a hand toward his American confrere. "And this handsome gent, my dear lady, is Leonard Sterling. Leo, this is Tülay Varga, the hottest jazz singer in Hungary."

"I can certainly believe that," Leonard commented excitedly. He cracked a jagged half-smile as if my acknowledging him was the code to unlock his safe. "I saw you perform last night in the lounge. I admit that you were quite exquisite."

"Thank you," I replied while finding my seat. "It was nothing out of the ordinary."

"As you say, but I must also compliment your American accent. It sounds quite authentic."

"As it should. I was raised in Pasadena, California."

"Really?" Leonard seemed thrilled by that notion. "A woman of your exotic beauty, surely you must have some Mediterranean or Persian heritage?"

"I am Turkish, born in Istanbul, though my parents hail from Çanakkale."

"Very interesting. I've never heard of Turks living on the Pacific coast of America."

"Have you ever been to Los Angeles, Mr. Sterling?"

"Several times, yes."

"Then you ought to know that the world is deeply attracted to it. Not only is California a warm and beautiful place, but Hollywood has become a melting pot of inventive minds. Like New York, people from all over the globe flock there to strike it rich in show business, even a few Turks."

"I lived in Burbank for a few years," Laszlo remarked in his well-practiced English. "I knew it would be the best place to learn about the radio industry."

"And that worked out just swell now, didn't it?" George applauded with a grin. "Listen, Tutu, darling, what are you doing tonight?"

"Are you about to invite me to one of your soirees?"

George joyously displayed his pearly whites. "Am I that readable?"

"You're about as readable as this morning's column on Lake Balaton's Jesus imposter," snickered Aron in Hungarian.

All of us laughed except Leonard. He did not speak a word of Hungarian. Ergo, he couldn't possibly have found pleasure in the morning headlines. "What do you say?" George persisted. "Party tonight? It's on a rooftop, and I suppose it's more of a gala, what with a handful of bigwigs attending, but it's a shindig nonetheless. Laszlo knows where it is."

"Why not," I yielded with a sigh, shooting a glance of irritation at Laszlo. "I suppose I do have the night off anyway."

By some miracle, I soon found a sense of comfort, drank my coffee, smoked, and chatted like a morning sparrow. It was amidst this merriment that George inquired of his American friend's opinion on Budapest. Leonard hastily recounted his dark thoughts while arriving at the main railroad terminal and his taxi ride to the Blue Danube Hotel. The venom behind each word proved strong enough to blacken the beautiful metropolis we all loved, lowering our smiles and spirits. Upon completing his tale, Leonard leaned back and loosed a crooked smile as if broadcasting his experience had hoisted a burden from his soul.

Silence befell us until George feigned a laugh and swung the mood back into an awkward jubilance through a joke about the pope. I again noticed Leonard's penetrating gaze. He half-blinded my thoughts like a beam of sunlight reflecting off polished chrome. I could hardly focus on the conversations, preferring to coddle a nasty desire to gouge his skull free of those blue looky-loos. I thanked God when the server arrived with the food, drawing Leonard's attention away. Unfortunately, the big-headed American barked before the server could escape. "What is this?"

The waiter looked at the plate with a blatantly reluctant grin.

"What is this?" Leonard reiterated more harshly.

The young man muttered something in Hungarian that George quickly translated. "It's an English breakfast, Leo. It's what you ordered."

Leonard slowly twisted his head toward the server as if it were the devil himself who bamboozled him. "This is not an English breakfast! Where are the beans, where is the sausage, and what is wrong with these eggs? They are infested with spices. Honestly, do you expect me to tolerate color-spotted eggs on a soggy loaf of black bread? And what is this sauce? What is this meat?"

"That's cow tongue, Leo."

"Cow tongue? Where am I, China?" Leonard pounded the table with a heavy fist. I laughed. I had witnessed surly customer complaints before, but never had I seen someone erupt like Vesuvius over a mistaken breakfast. Laszlo and Aron joined in my amusement. George soon followed with his ever-sunny giggle. Leonard panned over us with blazing eyes and a stone-cut frown. "How dare you mock me. As a paying customer and a roomer at this confounded hotel, not to mention an American traveler, I am entitled to superior quality service."

"Calm down, Leo," George advised, hardly trying to reduce his mirth.

"I will not calm down! I am a United States businessman, a guest of this dismal country. I deserve respect!" Leonard rose from his seat and turned to George. "How can you suffer this atrocious city? These people know nothing about decent hospitality. I've barely been here twelve hours and already the food is terrible, the hotel service ghastly, even the music sounds like feral cats fighting in an alleyway." He tilted his head in my direction with nostrils flaring. I swear his next thought called to unsheathe a hidden pocket gun and shoot me dead.

Leonard's booming ire shocked me to the point that I did not realize he had deeply insulted me. I gawked in awe and disgust as he pushed past the server and exited the café with his chin held high. Laszlo and Aron quickly began to discuss their repugnance of Mr. Sterling, mostly his xenophobic statements and antithetic pageantry. And to be frank, his nationalistic remarks seemed overly exorbitant considering America had just plunged into a severe economic depression. "What an ugly man," I heard Aron say. Rightfully, I should have contributed to their discourse, but the burn of Leonard's poisonous words regarding my talent had finally seeped into my blood.

George softly patted my hand. "Don't listen to him,

Tülay. Your music is superb. It's lovely. It's fun. You can dance to it. It moves people. Leo's just a rusty crank. Give him a break. He'll come to his senses. He's just stressed about work or something. I mean, that's all the guy does these days."

I sipped my coffee and sparked a fresh cigarette. "You're probably right. It surprised me, that's all. And it hurt."

"The guy said one thing, and it's not true by any means. For God's sake, he genuinely complimented your appearance and voice barely ten minutes ago. Plus, it's not like he tore you limb from limb or anything. Just one negative slip of the tongue."

"I guess so. Just one meager slur." Whether or not my dismissiveness was valid, I had endured enough drama in my life to hold onto Leonard's slight. I momentarily caressed one of George's hands. "You're a good friend."

He offered a radiant smile.

Music was my life, my livelihood, my escape from the madness of this ever-infringing world. Therefore, one might sympathize that any spurn toward my creativity felt like a punch in the face. And that's what Leonard had accomplished with his vulgar statement. Although I would later realize that it was not the words that burned me most, but rather the capricious conduct of the dragon. One minute, he charmed me with a yearning gaze. The next, he posed as Satan, pointing at my soul as if to declare it suitable to drown in his lake of fire. I looked at George Samson with this last thought in my head. The New Jersey sleaze might have owned a bloated heart that needed popping, but that heart still thumped with kindness. "It was only a sentence," I said to him. "One stupid comment."

~

When feeling frustrated, sad, or livid, nothing soothes like a hot, bubbly bath, especially when accompanied by first-rate Irish whiskey and cigarettes. It's best to be alone, but I was not. Laszlo kept me company, though he did not partake in the soaking. He remained fully clothed, seated in an upholstered chair beside my tub. He loved Irish whiskey as much as I did. Our daily habit of consuming emerald juice began during our club-hopping days in Los Angeles. I had yet to visit Ireland but always told myself that if their culture was as smooth as their alcohol, I would immigrate there in a heartbeat.

"To the Irish," I announced, tapping my glass to Laszlo's.

"To the Irish, for their pioneering of fantastic liquor."

We both enjoyed a long draught before Laszlo leaned forward in his chair as if to stretch his back. He glanced at my chest, partially clothed in oily suds, then swiftly lifted his eyes to mine, restraining a compliment he too often relayed. He acted quite virile around our friends, but I knew his deepest secrets, the ones that separated him from other men. We talked like siblings, after all. Still, I wondered how no one could see beyond his happy flamboyancy.

Then again, if I didn't know him to such an exceptional degree, I would have thought him the Hungarian version of George. And if that were the case, Laszlo and I would have been lovers long ago, not to say I wished to sleep with George Samson. Laszlo was different, appreciably caring, cautious, lovable without restraint, not to mention handsome. I could just squeeze him. I often wished that he did fancy women. I would have dragged him into my bath and ridden him down like the Orient Express.

"What do you make of this Leonard Sterling character?" Laszlo asked me in the tongue of his country.

"He's an ass."

"Before that savage outburst of his, I'd say he showed some interest in you, Tülay."

"George Samson is interested in me. The man makes that quite clear, always has. Leonard Sterling was merely fishing."

"Fishing, exactly, he was fishing. That means interested. I'm not stupid, honey. I saw it a mile away." He giggled. "You know, although he carried himself with high esteem, I thought he was rather fetching."

"I never denied that he's attractive, just an ass. One can very easily be both."

Laszlo hinted at more whiskey.

288

"I know he's here on business, but why speak of Budapest so maliciously?" I complained while refilling his glass. "This is a wonderful place, a beautiful old city. Well, it's two cities really, if he only understood its rich history. The man spat insults that clearly sprang from deeper sources than his breath. I saw the disgust perspiring on his face. I just don't understand how anyone can badger something of which they know nothing?"

Laszlo chuckled in his throat. "Judging a book by its cover, they call it."

"Precisely. And he dared to bring his Americanism into the matter. I might have spent the first years of my life in old Constantinople, but it was in California that I grew up. I'm an American citizen, yet you don't hear me using it as an excuse to belittle others."

"Tülay, Tülay... " Laszlo had this goofy smile that always made me want to laugh. "You need to stop thinking about this man. You might never see him again."

"Not if he's going to that soiree that George wants me to attend."

"So, you'll see him one more time. Big deal. Then he's gone, and you will never have to see him or hear his voice ever again. His stout opinions will return to America where they belong."

I snorted. "And I'm sure Mr. Sterling will find himself a proper English breakfast there."

We both snickered, after which Laszlo briefly

studied my nakedness. "Look at you, Tülay. Olive skin, green eyes, dark wild hair, the body of a goddess. You are truly breathtaking. I hope you know that."

I rolled my eyes at him and shook my head. "For God's sake, I don't need an ego boost, Laszlo. You know I can't stand poetic flattery."

"You love poetic everything, my dearest. You are a musician. And you ought to be accustomed to such compliments by now since men seem to drool over you like starved lions in the Serengeti. It is quite unfortunate that you have—"

"Neither do I need a preacher, Laszlo."

He shook his head and puffed his cigarette. A moment of peace blessed the air, just the two of us sipping our glasses of whiskey, the steam from my bath weaving about the thin plumes of tobacco fog. "Leonard Sterling... what an ass."

"George Samson... what a gent." Laszlo went on to feign examination of the contents in his glass. "Why do these Americans have such, such—"

"Boring American names?"

He smiled. "I suppose. They just strike me as stereotypical Americans lost in the roar of the last decade. I won't deny that George is a good man. If I had to flirt with a snake charmer, it would be him. He's sharp. And regardless of sincerity, he knows how to make everyone in the room feel appreciated. If you were to lay with anyone new these days, George ought to be your first choice."

"How many Hungarian women has he slept with?" I inquired humorously.

"He has bragged to me on occasion."

"How many?"

"Twelve as of this summer, and those are just the ones of which he spoke highly."

"Twelve, huh? My, he has been busy. Must really have a few tricks up his sleeve."

Laszlo giggled. "A few? More like two hands-full and then some."

I sipped my whiskey and shifted in the tub. "I'm curious, how do you suppose a suave devil such as George is friends with a gray slab like Leonard Sterling?"

"People from all tiers of society share mutual interests. Other than our personal limitations, you and I have little in common, yet we have been close friends for countless years."

I extinguished my gasper in the water, then smashed the wet butt into the ashtray on the tub's rim. "We have quite a lot in common, Laszlo. Don't ever deny that. We love cigarettes, good music, wine, whiskey, men. You name it, we share the pleasure. And to cap that cup, our *limitations*, as you call them, are half of what keeps us close."

"Yes, I do suppose harboring secrets allows intimate moments like these."

I grew silent at that notion, as I despised talking about things I yearned to forget, even if discussed indirectly. "Leonard Sterling. Leo," I groaned, regressing our conversation. "Hardly a lion, so his name indicates. He strikes me as a man of little appetite."

"Why do you continue to talk about Leonard Sterling? Are you interested in him after all?"

"No, that's disgusting," I rebutted. "That would be like falling in love with a pig."

Laszlo laughed. "I'd say that succumbing to an emotional attachment to George Samson is more like falling in love with a pig. An interest in Leonard would be like mopping up a bathroom floor and enjoying it. The man is surely a mess, though at the hand of what trauma? Maybe Pandora is acquainted with him as she is with you and me."

"Perhaps, but we don't scream at servers over minute mishaps. Why would anyone order an English breakfast in a Hungarian café anyway? I've known Englishmen to order the local cuisine with grins twisting up to their ears."

Laszlo shrugged. "Leonard is obviously queer as a kangaroo. And he most certainly attempts to walk in boots larger than his feet. The fool hides in the shadow of his egocentric American attitude. He's like an old apple, shiny of rind but rotten of pulp. Or maybe I'm wrong and he's actually a tasty, fresh apple with an unpolished rind. Or—"

"Please stop talking about apples. I'm famished as it is. It's past noon anyway. What do you say to a hot meal on this cloudy summer day?"

"I would be delighted."

"What are you in the mood for?" I readied my glass for the final sip of the Irish.

"I'm feeling a bit French. Le Bon Bistro de Louie?"

"Laszlo, my friend, pass me my towel. I hope you're craving escargots."

ESCARGOTS &

CIGARETTES

Louie Géroux owned the most exquisite French bistro in Budapest. He stood a mountain of a man, tall and cumbersome as they come, although his size could neither hide his genuine compassion nor his exceptionally vast knowledge of wines. Better yet, he happened to be a dear friend of Laszlo and an adoring fan of my music.

I had entertained at his bistro many times over the years, each performance drawing in a bigger crowd than his restaurant's capacity. That never mattered to Louie. The longer they waited outside, the hungrier they became. The hungrier they felt, the more food they ordered once seated. The more food they ordered... well, let us conclude that Louie's appreciation could hardly be contained.

So, as one might expect, the moment Laszlo and I set foot on his patio that late August day, Louie greeted us with a rosy-cheeked smile and a bottle of his finest Sauvignon already uncorked.

After salutations, kisses, and a few saucy comments, the middle-aged Norman escorted us to his most exclusive table at the back of the restaurant. Behind shimmering curtains of gold-embroidered scarlet satin was a romantic den composed of luxurious, tufted crescent-shaped booths that half-rounded a circular table festooned with Parisienne blanche napery and three tapered candles in sparking crystal stems.

Louie mirthfully shared in our first sample of the wine, which, doubtless, proved one of the most delectable reds I had ever indulged. I remember how Laszlo and I tittered gaily while Louie ranted about the popular mispairing of Syrah with cheeses of mild flavor. "It must always be served with potent cheeses like gouda or fromage bleu."

He then offered us a few slices of fresh Tome de Couserans to pair with the red Sauvignon just to demonstrate that his opinions on such matters were fact. Eventually, however, Louie acknowledged that we wished for an appetizer and rushed to the kitchen. In the meantime, Laszlo and I thought we'd step outside for a cigarette and secretly poke fun at Louie's pretentious lectures on how best to serve wine and cheese. Amidst preparing my lips for the final puff, a cab pulled up to the curb not more than six meters away. Out stepped George Samson with his cocky smile tilted directly at me.

"Tülay, Laszlo, what are you two doing here?"

I flicked my cig to the ground and snuffed it with a quick twist of my shoe. "Just paying a visit to Big Louie."

"Well, what are the odds we bump into each other twice in one day?"

"You know very well I work at the Blue Danube, so my being *there* was no coincidence."

"Come on, Tutu. Never deny the surprises life has to offer. I know I don't!" He winked at me. I could almost smell the perfumes of twelve different adventures emitting from his pin-striped suit.

"What brings you here?" Laszlo inquired, twisting the left end of his thick mustache.

"Well, ever since you guys showed me this place, I've come here almost every weekend. Usually, I bring my dates, but today I'm meeting up with Leo."

"Ugh," I grunted under my breath. "Why?"

George threw up his hands. "I don't know. I talked to him earlier and he seemed a bit frustrated after his business meeting, so I figured I'd offer to buy him a nice lunch. What better grub than Louie's, eh? You know, Leo told me how much he means to apologize to everyone for his behavior in the café this morning. He feels pretty sore about it."

"He certainly ought to," I snapped. "He was unnecessarily rude."

"I know, I know. Leo can be a bit of a grizzly. But can you really blame him? The man's routine is monotonous. You should see it from his point of view. The poor bastard's got a tough gig. That's why I'm never stiff with him. I just let his moods roll and roundabout."

"You're a caring man," Laszlo remarked, in a tone more surprised than appreciative.

"Thanks, Lazzy. Hey, what do you say I join you guys, is that all right?"

I gestured to the restaurant. "We were hoping—"

"Tutu, sweetheart, it'll be fun. Come on. We've already had breakfast, and we'll certainly be having dinner tonight at the rooftop party. Might as well spend the day together, right?"

I could only bluff a smile as we all strolled into the bistro. Back at the table, we began to talk and drink. Before long, the troubles of the morning faded from my mind. I eased into a familiar comfort, losing myself in playful conversation while innocently flirting with George and laughing at Louie's passing jokes.

About an hour into our fun, as George pretended to read my palm, Louie delivered a silver platter of hot escargots. The dish looked exquisite, well-oiled, coated with diced garlic, spices, and crumbled parmesan. George insisted I go first, but I let Laszlo luxuriate in the first morsel. He chewed for a good minute before relaying his delight in the exploding flavor. Louie stood table-side as he was wont to do, to ensure his customers felt satisfied with their initial tastes.

"Parfaitement merveilleux," Laszlo commented in his roughest French. "As always, my kudos to Chef Ervin."

"The greatest kitchen master in all of Budapest," Louie sang. "They say we French have the best taste in food. Well, I feel I must alter that notion and say that we have the best taste in chefs."

We all laughed before lighting up cigarettes. Louie quickly scuttled back into the kitchen, letting us revel in our escargots. After chomping away one of the smaller snails, I washed it down with the wine and enjoyed another drag.

If only all life's moments felt so delectable, to indulge in flavorful spirits and choice cuisine beside a few comrades with a cigarette betwixt the forefingers. I relish such times. Alas, all good things must end, for every rise into light shares space with a plunge into darkness. I heard his voice calling from the entrance, "George? Is George Samson here?"

George flashed a finger and left the booth only to return with Leonard Sterling, who seemed taller than I remembered. "Good afternoon," he saluted awkwardly, extending a limb to politely shake our hands. While posting himself directly across from me and, before he could glance about the table, Leonard's eyes laid slowly upon the escargots. I sensed his repugnance. Yet, to my astonishment, he miraculously dismissed the negative comment on the tip of his tongue and swiftly replaced it with an overly zealous grin.

"Tülay, Laszlo," Leonard began in an apologetic tone. "I'd like to take this opportunity to outwardly reflect and render a better impression of me. I beg you to forgive my obscene remarks and vulgar attitude this morning. I had a critical meeting today with an elderly client, and I was aware, before leaving my hotel room, that this gentleman would prove a tough sell. The promise of this event becoming severely onerous stymied my cheerful mood and, as you witnessed, eventually usurped it with foolish indignance, which I mistakenly unleashed upon the wrong people."

"Additionally, I felt a little out of my element. I... I still do. I must admit that I am not a socialite of any sort and find it difficult to adjust to new people. Also, I've never been to Hungary until now. As I divulged this morning, my first thoughts on Budapest were dreadful, to say the least. I don't think you'd appreciate hearing my perception on the subject again. Nevertheless, I desire to rectify the situation and pay for this meal."

"You are forgiven," Laszlo cordially replied. "And have no fear about the bill. This lunch is free. Louie is a dear old friend and never hesitates to please those closest to his heart."

Leonard's meager attempt at an ardent smile had me grinning in secret. I looked at George, who appeared relieved by his friend's thoughtful atonement. "Leo, Leo, you never cease to amaze me. It's just like Atlantic City. From stiff to charming. Man, I could never compare myself to—"

"George, that's enough. Please. Here, take this." He pulled a bulky cigarette pack from his coat pocket and handed it over. "Pass this around, please. Inside are the smokes I'm currently attempting to market throughout Europe. They're called Full Moons, 'So smooth, you'll float to the stars and back.'"

"That's the slogan?" George chuckled.

"Unfortunately."

"Kind of stupid, don't you think?"

"I think it's cute." I surprised myself with that comment. "An irrelevant catch, but I can see it drawing attention to the hopeless romantics of the world."

"It's drawn very little thus far," Leonard somberly retorted.

George slowly shook his head. "Leo, old pal, I think you work a little too hard to have nothing come of this business."

Leonard sighed. "Perhaps you're right. I do work all day and night. My routine is as dull as this cigarette's motto. For two long months, I have been traveling like a medieval barber. From hotel to hotel, I go without a moment of peace. Not that I ask for peace, considering

300

sales work has consumed my life. Although I admit, I would welcome a few hours of pleasure."

"Each day has certainly become a reflection of the last, today being the first exception on my international tour. It's like this: I wake up and eat a saltless breakfast, either in my room or at the nearest café. Then, I attend the day's business appointment, which often results in a luncheon with a humdrum client who prefers to gab and gossip. Later, after returning in desperation to my hotel for sanctuary, I usually end up spending one to three hours needling a pen over documents and noting upcoming engagements. I typically take dinner in my room while laboring over those meddling papers. Of course, it all ends when I wash my dreary day down with a glass of brandy before permitting my swollen head to crash upon a pillow."

George pursed his lips. "Ouch. I got to say, Leo, that doesn't sound like a fulfilling lifestyle."

Leonard nodded with a feigned tickle of the lips. "I'm a soldier of modern industry. Naturally, I accept my duties and wage war as a salesman. I must be a wolf amongst sheep."

"I'll tell you something, Leo. Today is a change for you. You're with George Samson right now. You've already broken a couple of rules to your routine, and I intend to help you break the rest. I bet, in your two months of traveling, you haven't gone to a single shindig."

"No. I cannot recall one as my schedule does not allow it."

I peered into my wine glass then and considered, how jejune is this man? My God, he is a dispiriting dolt. Where is the life in him? Where is the fun? Where are the vim and the verve? At least George and Laszlo knew how to suckle from the teats of life. With these thoughts in mind, I turned to George, who then passed along two cigarettes, one for me and one for Laszlo. I stroked the little thing and laid it on the table.

Dare I indulge in this product? My friends had already ignited theirs and were quick to comment on its robust flavor, claiming it to be smooth as midnight jazz. Leonard sounded relieved to receive such praise, though the rigid lines on his face yielded only dissatisfaction. He looked at me and saw that I had not yet tried mine. I ignored his gaze and ate a snail before taking the cigarette and adding it to the tin tobacco case I kept in my handbag. "I will try it later," I told him.

Leonard's upper teeth ground over his lower lip and pulled the flesh back, obviously displeased at my refusal to try his cigarette and critique it in front of him. He turned to George. "This is quite the gloomy city. It reminds me of Scotland. Is it always like this?"

"Only when you're here," I commented, immediately irritated by his rash twist of tone.

Leonard stabbed me with his eyes as Laszlo pressed a hand against my sleeve. "What she means is that it just happens to be gloomy today. It's a coincidence. It's been a lovely summer season."

George lifted my hand at that moment and kissed it. "She's a doll, ain't she? A tiger amongst us bears. Ain't that so, Tutu?"

"Rawr," I whispered loudly to him, jokingly, of course.

George raked his teeth over his lower lip in a subtle manner, quite unlike his compatriot, and lit up with an irresistible grin. "Stunning!"

"As are you, George."

"George," Leonard broke in. "What kind of food does this bistro serve?"

George seemed reluctant to pull away from me. "It's a French bistro. They got French food, a little Italian too. I always get the roast beef, so I never need to look at the menu."

"And where is the server?"

Louie happened to appear at that moment with more wine. As Leonard spoke to the Norman in his best French, which proved discordant as the music of Schoenberg, George turned to me again. Sweet words oozed like honey from his lips. I felt like a moth being drawn to the flame. No matter how much I wished to resist, it seemed a vain effort, as if some natural, primitive weakness had overthrown my sense of reason.

My father used to read me stories as a child, mostly from the Qur"an or *A Thousand and One Nights*, the latter of which contained a tale about a barber whose brothers were lured toward women who managed to trick them and embarrass them. I felt like one of the barber's brothers to George's mystical tricks. I used to think that only women were capable of seduction, yet George invalidated that notion with his very existence. It felt strange to think that I had never fancied him before and given into what I imagined him capable of.

Since the day George and I met, he had labored ceaselessly to win me over. I was the doe who always managed to outrun him. Although I now felt the sinking of his razor-like claws. Perhaps it was Leonard's awkward, idiosyncratic presence that raised George's status in my mind. When two characters sit side by side, the more vulgar one usually causes its counterpart to shine. Still, despite this temptation with George, something about Leonard Sterling continued to hold me on edge. He certainly repulsed me, yet he oddly baited my curiosity.

"You like dancing?" George asked me. "What am I saying? Of course, you do! You're a singer. Singers love to dance."

"I can't disagree, but then I am not fond of every dance style."

"Prickly pear, huh? What's your favorite: foxtrot, tango, swing, quickstep, paso doble?"

"The waltz."

"The waltz? Really?" He snickered. "A boring dance for a vibrant woman. For Pete's sake, my grandmother loved waltzes."

"What's wrong with the waltz?"

George slurped another puff of his Full Moon. "I'm a man of action. I love the fast paced, soulful stuff that makes you sweat. I like fat horns and thumping drums. Waltz music is all soothing strings and mostly slow."

"Waltzes can be fast too. They are elegant, intimate, and romantic."

"Anything can be intimate and romantic if you like it enough."

"I'm just saying, George. Johann Strauss II, whose music I'm sure you've heard, is my favorite composer. He is the king of the waltz. If you have ever doubted the awesomeness of waltz music, I promise that that would change if you took the time to listen to the work of Herr Strauss. No doubt, you would quickly find yourself tumescent with elation."

"I'll take your word for it, toots."

"Take her word for what?" Leonard inquired, ending his conversation with Louie.

"Nothing, Leo. We were just talking about dancing."

"Dancing, huh? I have not danced since—"

"Atlantic City?"

"I'm afraid so."

"Three years since you last danced, Leo? I would say I'm shocked, but with everything you've told me today, how could I be? Your poor soul."

"My soul?"

"Have you ever met a gypsy, Leo?"

"I can't say I have."

"Living in Hungary, you meet a lot of gypsy folk. You know, the Roma type. I met one who told me that we, as humans, need to feed our souls. An example, I suppose, would be like dreams, the aspiration type. Most people go their whole lives without fulfilling their dreams, which explains why so many are incredibly miserable and drink until their livers drown, and they keel over the barstool. Not to say your dream is to dance, but dancing can make you feel better, avoid such sadness. It sure makes me happy. And if it ain't the dance itself, it's the dancer. You just need the right partner, Leo. Either way, it's all about making you feel whole, feeding your soul like I said, as the gypsy said."

"Wise words for a playboy," I commented.

"They ain't my words. It was the gypsy woman. Though, well, maybe it was a Jew? Yeah, yeah. Sorry. It was a Jew leaving a synagogue, and I had made a remark about her generosity toward some bum. We started talking, one thing led to another, and she began to explain the beauty of generosity and how it helps feed the soul. Something like that."

Leonard put down his cigarette. "George, how the hell do you mistake a Roma for a Jew? They are completely different."

"No, no, I really met a gypsy once. I'm not lying. Plus, the Roma people ain't much different than Jews.

Sure, they have contrasting religions, but they're both, you know, wandering peoples, nomads. Same thing with Muslims, not much different."

"My parents are Islamic," I interjected with a chuckle. "Trust me when I say that Muslims and Jews are not like Roma. They are quite different."

George threw his arms in the air. "Gypsies, Jews, Muslims, it doesn't matter. The point is that feeding the soul is important, and I think everyone ought to make it a goal to do so."

"Can you define *soul*, George?" Leonard asked.

"Most religions incorporate the concept," Laszlo added excitedly.

"Can we stop this?" George griped, annoyed and a bit nervous. The first time I had seen his confidence falter. "I-I don't like where this conversation is going. The point is, Leo, you need to dance. I will make sure you do so tonight at the party. End of discussion."

"We will see," Leonard retorted, doubt hanging on the tip of his tongue.

"But I know who I'll be dancing with." George turned to me. "Tutu, I've always wanted to share a few kicks with you."

"As long as it's a waltz."

George cringed but took up my hand nonetheless and kissed it. Amidst the gesture, I made eye contact with Leonard, a chilling flash of intimacy that subsided sooner than comprehension allowed. Before I could attempt to imagine what thoughts colored his mind, Louie returned to the table and took a seat, firing up a cigarette before flinging a little snail into his big mouth. George laughed and began a story I knew would end with a punch or joke.

As he held Louie's attention, mine slipped back at the realization that George was anything but serious. He had touched on the relationship between the human soul and dancing, the basis of a tasteful, intellectual discourse.

Yet he didn't wish to support or deepen the conversation. It frustrated him. Subjects requiring critical consideration proved too heavy for his airy brain. A man of such surface continuity could never understand greater human wisdom, always choosing the easiest way or shortest route, ever eager to forgo the responsibilities of adulthood and remain adolescent of nature.

I believe Leonard Sterling recognized this as well and, thus, grew irritated with his friend. I saw the displeasure weighing down his shoulders, the same feeling that might prompt an animal to fight or flee. Laszlo also seemed quiet, giggling only when Louie burped or made a wisecrack about George's fancy blue suit.

While Louis now spun an entrancing yarn detailing an experience in his youth in Le Havre, I felt a hand creep over my leg. I looked at George, whose grin stretched with the exhilaration of a child in a candy shop. I swiftly shoved him away and scooted toward

Laszlo, who momentarily rose to release me from the booth. "Excuse me," I quietly announced, before casually walking to the water closet. After washing my hands, I popped through the kitchen side door, snuck out the back, ignited a cigarette, and rounded the building to the street.

The city air felt ripe and refreshing, a welcome relief to the claustrophobic symptoms I was beginning to experience at the table, what with George closing in like a hunter, Laszlo hypnotized by the rhapsodic tales of his infrequent French lover, and Leonard...just... *ugh*! I had no desire to return to the bistro; a strange moment for me. Even in extraordinary and awkward situations, I rarely felt such acute discomfort.

Was this all because of Leonard Sterling? The man was nothing to me. Why did he haunt my thoughts? Was Laszlo right in his thinking? He knew the minds of men better than most women. Did there exist a sinister, twisted form of allurement between Leonard and me despite the thick wall of animosity? And George, oh George. My physical attraction to him, which I had long denied, finally and painfully surfaced. Yet his playboy attitude never failed to disgust me. Always had and always will. I could never forgive myself should I have succumbed to his devilish enchantment.

I took in the city to calm myself. The streets bustled with business and tourism. The sky remained gray, yet no variance in weather could ever hamper the peoples' love for Budapest. Whether it rained, hailed, or snowed, wine bottles would still uncork, cabs would patter in haste toward their rendezvouses, shops would roll out umbrellas or canopies to shelter their lively patio tables and stations. Budapest persisted unwaveringly through every season and weather condition, neither sleeping at night nor napping during a holiday.

I loved this city. In fact, I sometimes wished I could be Budapest or at least take its pulse to feel the thumping of its heart. I always thought it odd that I was considered a foreigner in Los Angeles, given that I spent most of my youth there. I suppose that would make me twice a foreigner now, yet I had never felt so at home here. Withholding my next thought, I walked across the street, paid the toll for a ferry, and crossed the Danube.

~

One of my favorite books was *The Picture of Dorian Gray* by Oscar Wilde. I had read that story at least two dozen times and, once more, found myself doing so while lying in bed with a broken cigarette dangling from my fingers. Although I had drained my glass of Tullamore D.E.W, the road to inebriation stretched at least another kilometer. Nevertheless, I read and hoped Mr. Wilde would unveil the answer to a question that troubled me.

Alas, about four chapters in, I realized the futility of my search. I had little ties to the specifics of Dorian,

Henry, and Basil, and I prayed my life would never turn out like that of Sibyl Vane. Truly, it was Oscar himself and his noble study of the human experience that I revered and connected with most.

Suddenly, and I don't know how I failed to recognize it sooner, I found that George Samson lived in the story, playing the lead role of Dorian, ever seeking to remain young and beautiful. In fact, the more I brooded, the easier it became to compare the two.

They shared sinful tastes, indulged in their devilish egos, and loved to hear themselves talk. But, most of all, they were devoted hedonists. Plunging deeper into comparing the real world with Oscar Wilde's tale, I thought then that, should I have permitted myself to roll with George, would that not make me Sibyl, the subsequent sufferer of Dorian's attitude, the true victim of the tale? And in that case, who might Leonard Sterling be?

I poured another glass of Irish juice and downed a mouthful. "O Oscar," I whispered to the faded book cover. "You and your fellow countrymen understand me. You know how to speak through your literature, and your whiskey helps to conjure the hermetic meaning of things." I reached into the nightstand drawer for another cigarette but found only disappointment. Annoyed that I would have to fetch another pack of gaspers, I pulled my nakedness from under the sheets and slipped on comfortable clothes.

Then came a knock on the apartment door. As I should have expected, I could never enjoy more than a few hours of solitude. Laszlo swooped into the room as if a fire roared downstairs. He was about to open his mouth when I demanded a cigarette. He tossed me one, and I lit it just as his lips parted. "Where did you go?"

"Where am I now, Laszlo?"

"That's not what I mean, Tülay. Why did you leave me alone with George and Leonard?"

I shrugged. "You enjoy the company of men as much as I do. I suppose I felt the need to squeeze in some personal time away from people before, later, being swarmed by them."

"Swarmed?"

"The party tonight. I am still going, but only because I never go back on my word."

"Well, the next time you're going to abandon me with two American hounds and half a plate of cold escargots, please give me a clue so that I, too, ought to exit abruptly and unannounced like Sherlock Holmes."

"I'm terribly sorry, Laz."

"Eh, it's all right. What made you leave anyway? Was it Leonard?"

"He certainly contributed, but, surprisingly, it was mostly George."

"Intriguing. What did he do?"

"He put his hand on my thigh."

Laszlo burst into laughter, a witchy cackle more precisely. "Oh, my sweet Tülay. You left because a handsome fellow put his hand on your leg? I've seen a man grope your breasts in public, yet you did not run away then. I think there's more to this. You must have a secret fondness for George; otherwise, you would not have fled from his touch after indulging in flirtatious banter together. If I were a woman, I'd let him crawl up my skirt in a heartbeat. God knows he probably has a hotdog the size of a baseball bat."

"You're so foul, Laszlo. If you hunger for his hotdog, why don't you put some mustard on it and take a big bite."

"You are so naughty."

I giggled. "You really know how to cheer me up. Thank you."

"It's one of my many jobs as your best friend. It's too bad you have no female companions."

"Yeah, well, women are fickle and begrudging. Not that men aren't perfectly capable of such qualities, they're just a bit more controllable."

Laszlo shook his head. "If you met some of the men I know, you'd say the exact opposite."

I snorted. "That's because all the men you know are women in disguise."

"Touché," Laszlo playfully pointed at me with a look of surprise. "Anyway, my dear, what have you been doing the past few hours?"

"Have you ever read *The Picture of Dorian Gray?*"

"I can't say I've ever even heard of it."

"That's funny and a clear lie considering our enduring friendship and my enthrallment with the little novel. Nevertheless, you have something in common with the author."

"What's that?"

"You harbor the same secret lives."

"Interesting. But why do you ask if I've read it?"

"No reason," I retreated, figuring there was no point in blowing up a few runaway thoughts. "Say, what time does that soiree begin?"

"At ten o'clock."

"What time is it now?"

"Nearly nine."

"Nearly nine? Good grief, why didn't you say something when you first arrived?"

"I was going to but—"

"Never mind, I have to get dressed."

"Are you going to use the toilet?" he hastily inquired.

"No, why?"

"Because in my body's abrupt and weary opinion, escargots and cigarettes are better off as enemies than companions."

THE WALTZ

An unexpected breeze of Mediterranean warmth blew in from the south to kiss the Carpathian night and stroke away the gloom that had plagued the day. Yet, it proved too passive to fully liberate the moon and stars from their shrouded veil. Budapest raved and reveled nonetheless, its nightlife exploding with extraordinary events. People flooded the bars and streets. Restaurants swelled with weekend tourists and salacious businessmen. Local lovers flocked to the riverside parks and boardwalks to break from the hot scenes brewing in the city's underbelly. Smoke billowed from chimneys and cigarettes and trains.

I'm sure a wine glass or two spilled somewhere and offended someone, while elsewhere, two naked humans shouted amidst the throes of passion. Contrariwise, there likely existed another couple in the throes of violent tempers, lashing at each other's faults like lions over a gazelle.

On the city floor, an unkempt chauffeur drove wildly after achieving inebriation with his last bit of coin and would die that night in the wake of his alcoholism. Somewhere else, a homely pianist performed Chopin before a banquet of elegant admirers, hoping the woman closest to the stage would follow him to his bed that evening. A second musician in the city would feel a similar emotion.

Alas, on this strangest of days, her slate of integrity had been cracked at the base and would fissure further if she failed to act and help herself. But was that indeed her issue? Would it not have been easier to forgo this charade, evade the tumultuous storm that threatened her heart by casting her die into the Danube, and venture home, never to return to Budapest? "I am not a coward," I told myself. "It's only a party, and they are mere men. They are not famous. They are not important. They are not Moses, Jesus, Muhammad, or Allah. They are ordinary men."

I loosened my hair and pinned it with style. I lavished my lips and cheeks lightly to demonstrate sophistication while remaining my natural self. I plucked my brows and scented my neck, then threw on an emerald Moorish dress I picked up two years ago on an excursion to Cádiz, over which I draped a shoulder scarf of delicate black lace. Laszlo showered me with compliments, mostly pointing out that I resembled a modern Turkish princess with a splash of

Hollywood glitz. In my mind, I felt a little underdressed for a fancy gala, but I figured it couldn't hurt to look a little saucy on a day that had me swimming in strange, often opposing emotions.

I swore to stride ardently this night, playing the perfect lively me. I had spent most of my waking years on stage, giving the public my very best. Like Gloria Swanson and Josephine Baker, I lived and breathed the life of a performer. 'Why should that change now?' I considered, smiling internally. 'Why should I let my guard down even for a moment?' I refused to be any man's fool and would stand courageous like my friend Oscar Wilde. I knew my story would surely thicken this night, but I could not allow the characters to become too real. They needed to remain fictional.

With one arm looped through Laszlo's, I stepped off the lift and climbed a small flight of stairs onto the terrace rooftop of a newly constructed building a few kilometers south of the Blue Danube Hotel. I had attended numerous soirees in many countries and cities, yet none appealed so fervently as this one tonight in Budapest.

It might have lacked celebrities and politicians, but the revelries within made up for the lost talents. In my heartfelt opinion, most of the credit for such ambiance belonged to the stage crowded by tuxedoed musicians armed with a peculiar but vivacious blend of classical and modern instruments. It was an orchestra bred to play everything from Mozart and Franz Liszt to Duke

Ellington and George Gershwin. What an ensemble! I certainly melted to the flames that slithered out of each melodic note.

Laszlo and I pushed past the coat-check and strutted to the center of the terrace. On the fringes of the dancefloor ran two trains of tables topped with fine wines, gourmet cheeses, appetizers, cigars, French chocolates, and a grand buffet of diverse fare. I saw buttered basil duck, filet mignon, veal goulash, cabbage paprikash, rosemary turkey, spinach-crammed peppers, buttered oysters, pasta, pies, salads, grilled carp with lemon and capers, assorted spices, caviar, the list goes on. I did not expect to find an ice sculpture of a swam resting upon the main table and, although the thawing process had already begun, I felt nothing short of enchantment. I lit up a cigarette and soaked in more sights and sounds.

After fully rounding the terrace with Laszlo, receiving nods and smiles, we meandered between clusters of mingling businessmen. To our disappointment, nothing of intrigue leaked from the mouths of these fat cats. It was all shoptalk and card exchanges stewing in the musky fog of big cigars.

I then spotted the familiar face of Leonard Sterling, who stood close enough to the ring of penguins to appear associated, yet distant enough to take no part in the discussions and, instead, settled his gaze on the orchestra. Given his vigilance throughout the day, I half-expected him to notice me, but to my surprise, his head never turned an inch.

At some point, I saw a gaggle of flappers converging by one of the larger tables. I paid no mind to them at first, until I recognized George gleaming among them. He immediately noticed me and burst from the swarming birds like a leaping dolphin. "Tutu, Lazzy, glad you guys could come. Isn't this party stupendous? Look around. We got fancy food. We got fine cigars. We got handsome men and gorgeous women. We got sweet music. We got everything here. You simply can't get much better than this. Hey, Laszlo, you see those ladies over there with them pearl strings? They're Parisian. I know how much you like the French. Why don't you go mingle with them for a while, maybe take one home tonight?" He laughed.

"I suppose," Laszlo remarked, doing his best to act accordingly. He shot a look of exhaust at me before releasing my arm, leaving me alone with the playboy of Newark.

George grinned. "So, how do you like the party, really?"

"I've only just arrived."

"Well, then the party's just begun." He gifted me a grin as bright as diamonds. "Say, can I ask you something? How come we never got together before?"

I thought that was bold of him. "Got together?"

"Yeah, yeah. I mean to say, how come you and I have never gone out drinking together or gotten a bite? If you're not alone or with your band, you're usually with Laszlo, and I know you ain't blowing his whistle."

"Don't be a hypocrite, George. Aren't you always hanging off Aron's shoulder, eager as a pirate to snatch up any unsuspecting ring-fingered woman you can find?"

"Ouch, darling. You got me, okay. But hey, you know what, I'm still new to town. What can I say? I need an escort."

"I'm sure you do."

"That's not what I meant, Tutu." He paused to glance at his wristwatch. "Hey, hey, what do you say we snag some grub, eh? You hungry yet?"

"I suppose."

George quickly looped his arm through mine and towed me across the terrace to one of the buffet tables. With a hint of reluctance in his eyes, he released me and began to fill a dish. As he shifted down the line, the tall gentleman to my right offered to fix me a plate. George shot a glare at me but said nothing. In fact, he removed himself from my presence to tong some bread rolls from the adjacent table. I shook my head and laughed inside. The milksop claimed to fancy me, yet dared not fight for me when swooped by another hawk.

I turned to the gentleman who generously organized my plate with buttered shrimp, two muscles drenched in sweet crème, peppered vegetables, a thick slice of Italian garlic loaf, and a mini quiche. The culinary combination seemed tasteless, but I felt such a thoughtful gesture should not be refused, especially if it saved me from a lip-smacking American hound. I looked up and thanked him for his assistance, hoping he would hand me my plate and allow me to walk away.

Instead, he smiled and asked if I would sit with him. I felt guilty considering his kindness, so I nodded innocently and followed. As we approached his table, I looked over my shoulder. George stared at me from the buffet, his face oddly riddled with worry. In the same view, I caught Leonard gawking from beside the stage. The hunters roamed this night, and it appeared I was the only available quarry.

Friedrich Wagner might have failed in assuming my taste in certain gourmet foods, but he proved charming as a table companion. For a man who could have been mistaken for a Neanderthal, he had his wits about him and spoke Hungarian with a heavy Bavarian flow. While we ate together, he inquired of my upbringing, my purpose in Budapest, and why a woman of such exotic caliber, as he put it, attended the party alone. Of course, I answered these questions with care as I had never been one to divulge my personal history to absolute strangers. Inversely, Friedrich opened his life book with the zeal of a Grimm fairytale.

"I grew up in the lovely town of Nuremberg along with a brood of siblings, and parents who labored endlessly as shoemakers," he explained cheerfully. "I spent much time in the woods during my youth, but I now live and work in Berlin. I am a union administrator assistant. I like to think I am of immense help to the workforce of Deutschland who, right now, are very much suffering beneath the iron heel of the injudicious Weimar Republic."

"Helping people maintain careers is a positive thing," I kindly remarked. "Might I ask what a German union administrator assistant is doing in Budapest?"

"I am seeking support for my political party beyond my native borders, hoping to acquire friends and allies in neighboring regions."

"You are a fascinating man."

"And you are a ravishing woman. You mentioned that you are from America, but you do not resemble the women of American cinema."

"That's because I'm Turkish."

He cleared his throat and shifted his attention for a moment before talking again. "If you do not mind my asking, how did you come by this event?"

"George Samson."

"The American investor?"

I nodded.

Fredrich hummed. "I thought of conversing with him, possibly gaining his support, but he strikes me as a man who knows very little about politics and much less about investments."

I didn't know what to make of his presumption, so I defaulted to asking him the same question. "How did you come by this rooftop shindig?"

"I was invited by the host, a highly regarded investor whose dear friends are patrons of my political party. If you have not noticed by now, my dear lady, this gala is a recruiting event for me and several of my more affluent associates. Might I ask what you know about German economics or the new nationalist movement?"

A sense of discomfort began to take hold as I felt unsure where this conversation would lead. He started to repeat his question, but a growing fist in my gut prompted me to avert his politics and cut him off. "You have a very intriguing name. Friedrich Wagner, like Friedrich Handel and Richard Wagner."

He seemed pleased by the comparisons. "Actually, my father once told me that we are distant cousins to the great Wagner family. I do not know if he lied, but I cherish the notion of feeling connected to such an astonishing figure of my homeland. Richard Wagner also happened to share many of my personal views. If you do not mind, I would like to ask you something private. How do you feel about the Jewish and Roma communities in Europe?"

"Excuse me?"

"Jews and Roma. How do you feel about them? What is your opinion on their communities and contributions to humanity?"

"I have a handful of Jewish friends and two Roma acquaintances if that is sufficient enough of an answer for you, though I do not know why you inquire of such a strange thing."

"Are you a Jew?"

"No, I told you, I'm a Turk."

"Are you Christian or Muslim?"

I spotted George once again, the hungry hound, and beckoned him with relief in my voice and reluctance in my heart. "George, George Samson, will you join me for a moment?"

George sniped a grin at Friedrich and motioned me to take his hand. "Please, George," I insisted. "I'm craving a dance more than this food. Friedrich, will you kindly excuse me? It was a pleasure talking with you." I nervously escaped my seat, abandoning my meal, and clung to George, who quickly hauled me away. "Thank God you were close. He seemed so charming at first, but the conversation veered down a dark, unexpected path."

George winged his arm over my shoulder. "Herr Wagner ain't someone you want to tango with, darling. Someone as stunning and cultured as you, Tutu, no way. That man is scum. I'm probably the only investor here uninterested in what he has to say."

"Why is that?"

George pointed to a balding man in a solid black suit. "As you know, I invest in commercial properties. But I'm also a collector of watches, and that man, Mr. Fejes, is the one who sells them to me. He happens to be the most prominent dealer of antiques and jewelry in all of Hungary. Coincidentally, he is also one of the biggest investors in Austrian land development. He's awfully close with some of the folks at the Hungarian National Bank, which is how I met him. Friedrich Wagner is his compatriot. They come off as nice guys, but I wouldn't mess with them. They're all Nazis."

"Nazis? What's a Nazi?"

"It's a stupid political thing. You'll never have to worry about them since you don't live in Germany." George's glimmering teeth suddenly returned, along with his confidence. "Goddamn, you are a fox. You ought to be in the pictures, you know that? Come on, what do you say we dance?"

I patted his shoulder and pushed away from him, thankful for his intervention yet disappointed that he never strayed from a playboy attitude. "I think I need a moment to myself. Do you mind, George?"

"Not at all, sweetheart. Just don't forget about me." He flashed those pearly whites to which I responded with a feigned grin before scurrying to the barkeep for a glass of whiskey. I sipped the stuff but immediately realized it was a robust and peaty scotch. Amidst cringing at the earthy taste, a bejeweled woman hissed at me to move away from the counter to get her gin fix. Exacerbation gripped me. First George, then a Nazi, back to George, and now this vexatious harlot? I felt cramped. I felt warped. Not one hour had passed, and I was already sick of the greed and frivolity that plagued this rooftop. I quickly sought a lonely corner of the terrace for a breath and a cigarette.

~

My mother once told me that a few moments of solitude a day can bring peace to one's mind. It helps to maintain a stable relationship with Allah. I cherished this notion despite my level of secularity and managed to find a handful of these moments that day in late August, but none felt so accurate as when I stood alone in the corner of that rooftop terrace. I had forgotten about my cigarette, whose ember spitefully charged to the butt and burned me out of my mental hole, at least for a moment. I flicked the pinched paper over the side of the building and ignited a new one. Doing so, I gazed out at the city.

The stage stood behind me, facing the center of the roof, where the music poured forth only to blend into the soundscape of Budapest. Thus, I tuned into the world above and below. Cars tooted and honked at one another in the traffic by the riverfront. A siren blared somewhere down the thoroughfare, probably an ambulance or police car. I could never tell the difference.

I heard a weary old sot bark obscenities at the passersby from a well-lit street corner. Across the intersection, a moon-touched yet pious carouser boldly contended his compatriot's vulgarity with the true nature of the Jesus imposter of Lake Balaton. From where I stood, five stories high, the rest of Budapest cried out with a passionate thrust into the heat of the night.

"Wait," I heard myself say. A new wave of music suddenly caressed my ears, countering the works of the jazzy orchestra behind me. On the fourth floor of a taller building across the street, I saw an ample room with open windows wherein some kind of celebration roared, like the one in which I attended, though not without a sense of sentiment. I believe it was a birthday bash. Either way, they also had a music ensemble whose players avidly resurrected the most playful melody from one of my favorite pieces, 'Tales from the Vienna Woods Waltz' by Johann Strauss II.

I moved closer to the roof's edge, hoping my little ears could better grasp the beautiful music. I listened intently for a solid minute until a humorous thought broke my focus. If I had lived seven decades earlier, I would have married Johann and, later, adopted Oscar Wilde as my dearest friend.

Music and books had always been a part of my life, guiding me when needed, often the prime topics of my conversations, the underlying support beams of my social and professional lives. Oscar had rescued my afternoon as was expected of a friend. Now Johann slipped beneath the night covers to play my violin with his bow. I closed my eyes and let the music envelop me. I wanted to melt away or hope to be whisked off by the wind. If I had died that instant, my final breath would have been one of gratitude. For when better to be vanquished than amidst a blissful moment.

"Tülay," muttered a deep voice all too suddenly.

Were my words about to ring true? Was Johann here, returned to life? I opened my eyes and turned to find Leonard Sterling standing with a cigarette in hand. "Care for a Full Moon?"

I feigned a half-smile and showed him my cigarette.

"Ah. I should have guessed." He quieted for a moment, bending his sight toward the city. "Do you want to know what I truly thought of Budapest when I first arrived?"

"I believe you already revealed the unpleasant details this morning at breakfast."

"I spun quite a yarn, yes, but I did not divulge the *emotions* of my initial impression."

"You painted a nasty portrait, I recall. Such gruesome art requires emotions, does it not?"

"Fair enough, but please, allow me to share something I composed last night. Rather than brush up hateful art, it shall be poetically grotesque."

"Pessimistic, perhaps?"

"You be the judge, my lady."

"I'm listening." I puffed my ciggy.

Leonard withdrew a small piece of paper from his pocket, unfolded it, and inhaled. "O Budapest. It is a dark city, no less drab than the supine gray clouds that mope across its sky. It stands as the pride of Hungary, jewel of the Magyar, yet it is not unlike any other great city of Europe. With its magnificent palaces, bedizened opera halls, and chromatic visage, it attempts to paint a picture of harmony and affluence. However, the reality of this is appreciably contrasting."

"Although it is formally of imperial status, it still yearns to belittle outside communities like a school bully whose parents never spanked him as a punishment. It might well portray the role of an endowed, sophisticated metropolis, yet what art is here? It is not Paris. What spirit is here? It is not Rome. What music is here? It is not Vienna. What literature is here? It is not London. What might have once been a lovely countryside has been raked over with tar roads, crippled bridges, graceless buildings, grotesque manors, tacky apartments, tasteless restaurants, and the bleary boot-heels of scurrilous citizens."

"The Great War whittled Budapest into scraps. But to everyone's dull surprise, it has rebuilt itself as a mechanic does a worn and beaten car, a car with impressive features yet can barely drive a mile in the snow. Budapest may seem clean to its long-time inhabitants, however, to a frequent traveler who has experienced the best of Western civilization, it is a puddle of stagnant water. It is a cesspool, one that births mosquitos who relish nothing less than aimless buzzing until they can suck the gold blood from human pockets and fill their bellies with the wine of life. O Budapest, tomorrow shall undoubtedly be one of unrivaled misery in your company."

I wanted to laugh. "Intensely morose as I predicted but poetic in a dark, romantic sense."

"I write on rare occasions."

"You really wrote those words? I never took you for a writer."

"Again, on rare occasions."

"Leonard Sterling, I thought you were a soldier of industry?"

He almost laughed. "Even the factories close for holidays. Here, you can have this." He folded up the paper and handed it to me, which I amusingly accepted and tucked into my brazier.

As silence stepped between us, I half smiled and studied his profile just as I had in the café that morning. I considered him handsome, rustic in ways, not a fleck of that glamorous city-boy air that George commanded. Then again, and I had been struggling to admit this to myself all day, I didn't know why I found him attractive when, clearly, he was an ordinary Joe with a receding hairline.

Remembering the music across the way, I turned my back to Leonard. Everyone in the city seemed to be enjoying a night of festivities and excess, especially the birthday party across the way. I peeked into their world again, watching the people dance, kiss, drink, smoke, talk, indulge and discover. On the terrace behind me roared something similar, though what began as stupendous had quickly plunged into... well, whatever it was now, it didn't feel like my kind of party.

330

How I yearned to soar to the building across the alley if only I possessed a pair of wings!

"Are you jealous of them?" Leonard asked with a touch of humor on his tongue.

"What?" I looked over my shoulder.

He scratched his chin. "Are you jealous of them?"

"Them, who?"

"The people in that building, the ones on the fourth story."

"Jealous, me? No."

"I think you are."

"How would you know?"

"I suppose I'm jealous myself. Not to mention, I'm a people person."

I exploded into laughter.

"What's so funny?" He stepped to my side.

"You are not a people person. Although I have only known you for part of a day, it has proven enough to understand that you ought to be exiled and isolated to St. Helena like Napoleon."

"That's rude."

"You're rude."

"I certainly can be."

I looked him straight in the eyes. "Tell me everything you've experienced since coming to Budapest, all the details in pure honesty. I guarantee you will discover that this day strongly invalidates your claim of being a *people person*."

Leonard divulged all that had happened to him

since arriving at the Budapest Railroad Terminal, including things I already knew. He spoke of his taxi ride, his hotel experience, and his lack of preferred breakfast. His business meeting did not fare well. The client was an elderly chap who drifted in and out of sleep. Poor Leonard was forced to occasionally rouse the man, fearing that the next time the geezer rolled his head would be the end to more than just their fruitless appointment.

Next, Mr. Sterling endured an array of miscommunications with a few local transportation operators while trying to make his rendezvous with George at Louie's Bistro. Not long after I had escaped the restaurant, Leonard consumed a bowl of beef bourguignon. Unfortunately, the moment he returned to his hotel room, the bourguignon spewed out his back end. After taking some Pepto-Bismol to settle his stomach, he lay in bed and read a Robert Burns pocketbook until the pain subsided. "Next thing I knew," he concluded, "George was howling at my doorstep."

I enjoyed another drag of my Camel. "Judging by how you explained yourself, I'd say I have a pretty good idea of what makes you tick."

"Am I a people person?"

"Not even close."

"Why, no?"

I blew smoke at him. "Must you pry?"

"Yes."

I nodded and considered my day. "Perhaps today was just a one-off mind shaker, where storm clouds momentarily blotted your sky. Or maybe each event you endured was God's revenge on you for your constant cynicism. Albeit, if you were, in fact, born a cynic, then I suppose God needing revenge would be pointless considering your every waking moment would feel miserable, bearing in mind that you must interact with people each day."

"Who do you take me for, Dorian Gray?"

I chuckled at that. "You might have a few similarities."

He shook his head. "No, no, I must protest. Vanity requires personal upkeep, too much gusto for my taste. Truly, I can care less about myself. I'm too outwardly productive. If anything, I'm less of a cynic and more of a malcontent. And if there is a character relatable to myself in Wilde's story, I feel it's Basil Hallward. He's a character of sorts, but without the negligence of reality that Dorian increasingly cultivates. I might even consider him sincere."

"Would you say that George is like Dorian?"

"Minus the misanthropic aspect, without a doubt. Although, I think if George owned a portrait of himself in the same manner as Dorian, he'd have hung himself one-hundred times over. I mean, it's no pleasantry staring into the smutty, piggish eyes of the devil."

I could not help but laugh, and neither could Leonard. After a minute or so, our voices faded, allowing the soundscape to rise again. A moment without words graced us, tranquil as a mountain lake. Leonard soon finished his cigarette and sipped twice from the glass in his hand. He must have noticed my ear drift toward the party across the way.

"You like Johann Strauss the Younger?"

"He's my favorite," I replied.

"Plainly! I see the way you move to his art. And why not? Surely, the waltz is a sophisticated, often romantic dance. Speaking of Strauss, I believe you heard my remark to the clerk in the lobby last night about the name of the hotel."

I allowed my lips to rise. "I admit it was a little funny. You must know a thing or two about music."

"A thing or two, perhaps," he confessed, hardly withholding his pride. "I played piano as a child and well into adolescence. My parents regularly placed me in competitions, although I never won a single award. Nevertheless, I was always a top contender, a finalist, if you will. I typically performed Mozart, Beethoven, and Chopin, given that their pieces were commonly used as competitive material."

"Personally, I preferred to play what I truly enjoyed hearing—the elaborate works of Liszt, Tchaikovsky, Saint-Saens, and Grieg, to name a few. A lugubrious notion, I feel as though people these days don't fully appreciate classical music. The power of symphonious orchestration has taken the backseat to the modern era's love affair with the thumping rhythm of jazz, not that there's anything wrong with jazz. Jazz is riveting. I like your jazz."

"Stop saying jazz."

"Sorry." Leonard scratched his chin again. "I mean to admit that I thoroughly appreciated your performance last night at the club. Again, my apologies for the needless, vulgar comments I spat this morning. You have a wonderful voice. Good vibrato. It's just... It's just that classical is, well, classic." He paused for a moment, watching me soak in the city. I caught him and smiled again.

"Sorry," I said, feeling a bit warm. "I often get caught up in the sights and sounds. And with everything you just said, I—"

"Don't apologize," he sliced in while lighting another cigarette.

I studied his smoking face as he puffed thrice and expelled a thick cloud. "I'm curious, Leonard, and forgive me for the inquiry, but George mentioned Atlantic City a few times throughout the day. Is that a place of significance to you?"

"To put it kindly, I hate that he continues to mention it. It was a happy time for him, like always, but miserable for me."

"What happened?"

"I suppose I can tell you." He took a sip of his drink. "Believe it or not, George and I were once inseparable, hardly straying from each other's side like brothers of war. Despite my inclination toward the arts and his toward... well, talking, I suppose, he and I appeared compatible in those days. We were the best of friends, a couple of city lads enamored by the modern era and compelled to live a wanton lifestyle, not to mention we had both served our country during the Great War."

"I was known as Richmond Leo then, given that I was born and raised in Richmond, Virginia. I knew a few New Yorkers who considered most Virginian folk uncouth. Thus, they labeled me to ensure that no one in Manhattan forgot my birthplace. Silly, I know. Anyway, together, George and I typically spent our weekends flirting abroad on the East Coast, mostly in Connecticut and Massachusetts."

"There was this group of Irish girls we befriended up in Boston. George and I quickly fell under their spell, prompting us to visit them as often as possible, especially on the weekends. Quickest by train, of course. These girls... these girls were like beautiful witches, always drawing us into their lair. We drank with them, raved at parties and music clubs, danced in the streets, even, dare I say, shared intimacy as a group. Looking back, we were like wine-spun Greeks of the Dionysus cult."

He took a drag of his cig. "As time pattered on, the male-to-female ratio, coupled with building emotions, turned the group of girls into a pit of hyenas. In the end, George discreetly jumped between three of the dames while the fourth, Mary Lee Carr, became my sweetheart. We were a couple, although I will admit I wasn't always faithful in those days, mostly due to my old philandering habits. After two rough years, I detached myself from George and quit the lifestyle, fully committing myself to Mary Lee. Against her parent's wishes, she moved into my Manhattan apartment. That was the summer of 1927."

"Mary Lee and I got married that summer by Niagara Falls. It was lovely. I remember I wanted to spend our honeymoon in Los Angeles or Mexico, somewhere warm and far away from the craze of New York. Mary Lee, on the other hand, had this strange desire to go to Atlantic City. She was now my wife, and I wished to please her, so we traveled there instead. While enjoying the beachy pizazz of the city, George happened to appear. Unaware to Mary Lee, I ran into him while waiting for her in one of the hotel hallways."

"He hadn't changed at all, still a terrible influence. Told me to sneak out of the room that night after Mary Lee fell asleep. As you might suspect, I fell prey to George's charm. I was still vulnerable then, too weak of will. I broke the moral code I had created to sustain my relationship with Mary Lee. I acted like a goddamn fool. So, George took me to a local juice joint where they sold forbidden pleasures such as alcohol and cocaine. He persuaded me to indulge with him every night, and I regrettably conformed. I drank. I smoked. I fondled the women who circled the card tables, even coupled with a few under the boardwalk. It was shameful, really it was."

"On the morning of our second to last day in Atlantic City, Mary Lee heard me slink back into our room, though she did not speak and feigned slumber. Suspecting acrimony, she followed George and me that night. Mary Lee found herself unable to enter the club, so she hid in an alleyway where she eventually saw us leave with three flappers at a later hour. She trailed us down to the beach. George took two of the girls while I took another. We crept into what our wasted brains believed to be a secluded area. We all got naked and, well, Mary Lee caught us red-handed."

"I felt like a villain. Henceforth, I was banned from socializing with George Samson, at least if I wished to keep my marriage. And I did. Still, George occasionally wrote me letters, which is how I learned of his immigration to Hungary. Anyway, a few months after Atlantic City, my employer, the British-American Tobacco Company, decided to promote me to a position called international spokesperson, otherwise known as a traveling salesman. I've tried to live a modest life ever since, but I find I have only become aloof."

"Wow," I quietly remarked, utterly surprised by the depth of the story and the genuine, sorrowful air by which it was told. "So, George was the rot in your apple."

"You could say that, but I chose to follow him. It's not his fault that he's more persuasive than a Rockefeller. He's always been that way. He is George

Hubert Samson, the Bacchus of New Jersey, the Newark tomcat, a goddamn popinjay. The man is so charming, he could seduce Medusa." He knocked back the last of his drink.

"Just so," I agreed while flicking newly formed ash from my cigarette. "Nevertheless, against the so-called modest life you now strive to lead, you persist as a purveyor of indulgences. Cigarettes and alcohol are certainly counted among pleasures, you know."

He caught my jest and smiled. "Indeed, they are."

"At least your Atlantic City experience taught you one of life's most pure and simple truths."

"My dear Tülay, the truth is rarely pure and never simple." He tossed his cigarette and returned to the party. I knew those words, a famous line from The Importance of *Being Earnest*. "O Oscar," I whispered to the city air, "perhaps you knew me better than I thought. Unless that was just Leonard Sterling."

I meandered back into the party, feeling less nervous. I had forgotten about the Nazi advocate and began to reflect on which life experiences best contributed to the creation of my current self, just as Leonard had explained about himself. Everyone I had ever known had experienced something that they perceived to be dramatic or traumatic, which consequently impelled them to alter their daily cerebration. In other words, everyone harbors the memory of a significant personal event that stands as a catalyst for change, for better or worse. Everyone has their own Atlantic City. Yet, it is through the recognition and usage of such post-event changes that might earn one a token of true wisdom.

I never imagined that the purpose of that strange day in late August was gifted to me as a means of learning a universal lesson from Leonard Sterling, of all the people in the world. I've known a few wise elders, a handful of petty criminals, a dozen corrupt businessmen, and more fools than I can count, but surely Leonard had jumped from the base of that ladder to the highest dowel. Then again, our verbal exchanges throughout the day were scant and coarse, forcing me to take pleasure in the one real conversation we had shared, and it felt incomplete to me. I sensed that there lingered unspoken emotions, facts unattended. Regardless, and odd to admit, I believe I understood Leonard above and below the surface. Is it possible to find absolute trust in someone after a five-minute discussion and two cigarettes? I think so.

~

I found my way back to the bar and convinced the tender to open a bottle of Bushmills he had stashed in the well. No one hides Irish whiskey from me. Laszlo sought me out from the other side of the party and introduced me to some of Aron's newer banking friends. They acted respectable and casually complimented my dress. One of them even asked me out on a date, to which I politely declined. An outsider stood among the Hungarian bankers, a Russian socialite named Borya, who tried to convince me to return to the Soviet Union with him, claiming he could make me a hit music sensation in Moscow and Leningrad. I commended his generosity to ease his impending disappointment.

Aron then directed my attention to his lady of the evening, a comely Rumanian with sharp amber eyes and a voice as soothing as ocean waves. I felt I could not compete with her beauty, shining like a brilliant star strapped in a hot red dress. Aron's friends gathered around her like vultures on a carcass. He was proud of her, I could tell. Little did I know then that he would marry her in the coming year and immigrate to the United States.

Laszlo and I danced together as the night dwindled down. Many guests began to leave while the rest smoked by the exit or crowded around the dance floor. The ice swan had melted down into a bowl rimmed by silver nubs. Most of the food, like the swan, had been devoured by the night's energy. Nearly every server had begun to wipe down tables and chairs.

While listening to one of Laszlo's comical stories about Big Louie, I lit up the last cigarette of my new pack and watched the band play. It was a French jazz tune I often performed myself, a steamy little number. Everyone knew that the best ensembles played their hottest stuff at the end of the night. What better way to go out than with a bang. I clapped my hands and laughed as they finished the song, which had sped up and crashed with a blaring trumpet solo. Frankly put, it proved as jazzy as jazz could be. As I slowed my applause, I made eye contact with Leonard Sterling. A fog of yearning loomed between us.

The leader of the band and head percussionist stepped to center stage and announced in Hungarian that they would perform one more jazz piece. "It will be very much like the previous song, but we want to speed it up a bit. We're going to start off with a solid and smoky beat. By the end, Zoltan over there on the trumpet will roar like fire. Hold on to those hats, ladies and gents. Here we go!"

The drums sprang into a jungle beat, thumping like the rhythmic chug of a steam train. The clarinet and violin chimed in while the lead trumpet descended upon a loose arpeggio. A second trumpeter started up a lower rhythm with the violin, while the main horn broke from his scale to weave a new line alongside the clarinet. Laszlo took my hand and pulled me into a hot-footed dance. I dropped my gasper the moment my hips began to sway. I suddenly forgot the world, forgot my troubles, forgot the time and how I might get back to the hotel. I felt a surge of joy rise in my chest like an impending fit of laughter before the end of a good joke.

Leonard then approached and asked kindly, "Laszlo, may I dance with the lady?"

Laszlo laughed at me with eyes that screamed 'I

knew it' and shuffled toward the stage. I smiled at Leonard as we moved our feet to the saucy rhythm. At the beginning of the day, I saw him as a stiff and stubborn, arrogant American. By the end, I knew him as an intelligent, shoe-loose lover of the arts who had simply forgotten how to adequately express himself.

I realized that he and I were more alike than I wished, which was why I resented him so much yet could not remove him from my mind. Then again, none of it mattered when we felt free as the wind. Our legs twisted side to side. Our shoulders bobbed back and forth. He laughed, and I couldn't help but join him. It was wild. Yet just as the music began to pick up more speed, George Samson burst from a circle of suits and bounced over, hastily slipping between Leonard and me.

"You look like your absent treatment, Tutu, no offense to you, Leo. An airtight doll like this ought to swing with a sweet hopper. What do you say, darling, we tangle our feet like a couple of crazy fire-walkers?"

Leonard straightened his back and lifted his chin. "George, I asked the lady first. Can't you see we're enjoying ourselves?"

"Oh, come on, Leo. Shove over and let me dance with her. Share the lady, like old times."

Without another word, George bent a hip and yanked me into his arms. I shot a bewildered glance at Leonard, who clenched his fists and chewed his lip. George dipped me back and reeled me in as if to start a tango. I felt no desire to dance with him, yet his grip proved too strong for me to escape, so I went along with it.

George certainly knew how to shuffle. I'll not deny that. His enchanting smile glistened each time our eyes met. My legs gyrated side to side. He drew me close, face to face. I could smell the vodka on his breath. He spun me twice, wheeled me back, and heeled around before twirling me a third time. He licked his lips and jerked me toward him again, cupping my ass with one hand while the other crept up my neck.

"George, stop it," Leonard demanded, noticing my discomfort. I tried to pull away from George, yet he only muscled me closer and laughed. I pressed my hands against his chest to push him off. He held firm. I shouted for him to let go, even hit him, but he groped harder. "Get the hell away from her," Leonard barked, finally prying me from George's grip.

George shook his head and shoved Leonard from my touch. "Why don't you do the world a favor, Leo, you sopping sack, and jump off the goddamn building!"

Leonard threw a glance of forgiveness in my direction, then balled a fist white, cocked his arm, and shot his knuckles into George's left cheek, launching the man into a dizzy stumble. He tripped over his shoe and crashed like a mighty tree to the floor. The music ceased, and the onlookers gasped in shock. George managed to gain his feet and hawked a wad of thick blood. "You've always been a scoundrel, Leo," he nagged before attempting a few swings. "Even when we partied back in the States, all those years, you were always cramping my style. I tried helping you. I really tried. But your stupid wife—" Leonard threw another fist at George's face, nearly blasting him out of his shoes, yet the man refused to quit his provocation. "Even your wife, your cuckoo Irish wife... "

"Shut your mouth, George, before this gets uglier."

"Go to hell, Leo, you mangy Scottish rat!" George suddenly realized everyone was staring at him, judging him, whispering about the blood on his shirt. He looked blotto as a deranged hobo. "What are you all looking at? What are you looking at? I'm still the top dog. I'm the New Jersey love hound, the Newark tomcat, the playboy of Hungary." I shook my head at him when our eyes met. "Get lost, Tülay," he snarled. "And go hang yourself, Leo." He looked at the crowd. "Ah, choke on it, Budapest, I'm out of here. You can all rot in hell." He turned toward the exit and tripped over his own shoe again. No one helped as he picked himself up, spitting the same curses, then departed with his tail between his legs.

Once George had gone, the crowd seethed with comments of discomfort and concern toward Leonard, then awkwardly gathered their things before filing out. The band packed up their instruments hastily and trailed after the guests. Even the host shook his bald head and asked the servers to speed up their cleaning. The mood lay dead on the floor. Leonard sauntered to the corner of the roof behind the stage, where he became a shadow. Laszlo tugged at my arm and handed me my coat. "Let's get out of here, Tülay."

"You go home, Laszlo," I told him. "I'm going to linger a bit longer."

"With Leonard?"

I didn't give him an answer and kissed his cheek before strolling across the rooftop. He thought to call after me but shrugged and linked himself to the rear of the exit line instead. It felt like all of Budapest was ready to turn in for the night. Well, almost all of Budapest. The orchestra in the neighboring building found my ears, finishing up a pleasant piece from Tchaikovsky's Eugene Onegin. I nodded to the sound and walked to the corner where Leonard stood, facing the city.

"You know," he said as I approached, tobacco smoke rising above his figure, "Pyotr Tchaikovsky endured a rough life. He speared through phases and relationships like a crazed warrior. Some believe that he battled immoral desires that haunted him for years. Although, in my opinion, naming them as such is a byproduct of bigotry. Nevertheless, we cannot necessarily override our most natural tendencies. Very few in history have surmounted what feels organic, even great thinkers, conquerors, and genius composers. But is it such a crime to embrace what feels right? Sometimes I wonder, is it a blessing or curse that we possess the ability to remember the past?"

I shook my head as I came to his side. "No one has the right to deny you the opportunity to be yourself, Leonard. Especially not the laborious sales jobs and George Samsons of the world." I paused to feel a change in the direction of the wind. "Tchaikovsky surely struggled with his past, every twisted memory and emotion scuttling back into his daily life like diseased rats. Yet I believe that, despite it all, he found in himself the ability to recognize such conflicts and repurpose them for the greater good by transforming them into art, into music that moves people, that changes people. Perhaps we can all take a page from his book."

I took off my coat and laid it on the roof ledge in a fashion that did not allow the pockets to protrude, then patted it down to ensure nothing fell out. Leonard noted my precaution but said nothing. "Forget about George," I advised in an amiable tone. "Forget about Atlantic City. They are part of your past, not your present. You say you're a soldier of industry. Well, what do soldiers do after a great battle? They muster their strength and march on to the next one, using what they've learned to help them survive."

"I suppose I can't disagree with you." He laughed a little and casually offered me a Full Moon. "I know they're not the best, but they get the job done."

"To the stars and back." I lit up my cigarette and

leaned against the roof ledge, listening to the tiring voice of Budapest. The Tchaikovsky piece had ended, allowing a minute or two of peace. Then came a familiar melody slowly flooding the air like a new moon tide, the first wave enveloping my heart. A cliché thought suddenly coursed through my mind, prompting me to gaze upon the tall gentleman beside me, Leonard Sterling.

"The Blue Danube," I remarked.

"The Blue Danube," he softly repeated before removing his coat.

Without any words, he lifted my left hand and gently drew me into a world of fantasy. The piece drifted toward its central theme as we lightly circled away from the ledge. With cigarettes still in our right hands, we put our palms together. He gracefully wrapped his arm around my waist, gently pressed the small of my back, and led me into a waltz. I remember twirling about the rooftop, our feet gliding on water. He arched me back, drew me close, and eased me into a spin.

We hardly paused for a quick drag before flinging our gaspers away to fully appreciate the work of Johann Strauss II. The song soon climaxed, the melody robust with strings and horns and woodwinds, a snare drumming up the backbone. Tingling waves of mirth rolled up my spine as we floated to the center of the rooftop, away from the music. Although the melody had faded into the greater hum of the city, its phantom notes continued to pour through my ears and all over my heart. Without the eyes of jealous onlookers and hot-headed partygoers, all felt on high. I felt free again and loose and full of life. I thought it absurd that I had loathed him all this time when, in the end, we were undoubtedly perfect for each other, Leonard and me.

Suddenly, the song ended. Our bodies pressed together, our skins steaming, vestures loosened, lips so close I could have kissed him without anyone to stop me. "Let's get out of here," he whispered. I let go of him, embracing the flame that burned through every limb and follicle of my body. I didn't care about the sweat beading on my forehead or that my chest felt moist as a summer dew.

We grabbed our coats and silently rode the lift, only to laugh carelessly upon exiting the lobby. Once on the street, Leonard called for a cab. The ride felt like an eternity. Impatience and elation held us on edge. Neither of us found a voice. We could only smoke Full Moons, hold hands, and grin like children on Christmas morning.

Stepping into the lobby of the Blue Danube Hotel, I looked at Leonard and remembered the first time I saw him in the lounge, a cavalier halved by shadow. I thought him so enigmatic then, yet a mere twenty-four hours later, I felt I knew him as I knew myself, a soul long deprived of earnest nutrition, now on the brink of satiation.

We soon arrived at the top of the stairs, where two hallways ran in opposing directions. "My room is this way," he said to me with a gesture and smile, sincere as a Basil Hallward. I felt my ardor suddenly ebb the moment I heard those words. I remembered Atlantic City and knew it would be wrong for Leonard to relive it in any sense, let alone mirror it myself. Undoubtedly, one night of ecstasy did not amount to a lifetime of guilt, no matter how divinely right it seemed. I felt my fingers reach into my coat pocket and fish out a ring. Leonard's smile widened into a mild, absolved chuckle.

"I'm sorry," I uttered meekly.

He placed his hand over mine and gently nudged it toward my chest. "It's quite all right, Tülay. I suppose it's probably best that the past does not repeat for either of us." A pause struck the air like a swift sunrise and dispersed the storm of yearning between us.

"I suppose this is farewell then," I decided with great reluctance, relieved of mind yet pinched of heart. "I'm sure you'll be on another train tomorrow."

"Back to London, yes."

"Well, it's been quite a day, hasn't it?"

"It certainly has, Tülay."

"Goodnight, Leonard."

As I turned to walk away, his warm, rich voice once again caressed my ears. "You know, as I told you before, my first impression of this city was rather dark, surely warranting a day of gloom. Now, I can't help but believe it was a beautiful day in Budapest."

THE

SHAPE

OF

GRACE

Smoke inked the blue sky over the distant bastion of Sevastopol. Mortars boomed. Machine guns spat. Homesick soldiers wailed. Destruction marched with fervor. The roar of battle echoed through the air as if a hundred clouds huddled over Crimea to rattle off thunder. Yet, in a flash, it all drowned in the sloshing waves of the Black Sea. The voice of a world enraged suddenly found quiet.

The only lingering sounds were that of mewing gulls and deep churning waters. A sea lion or two might have swum near, but they went unnoticed. The buzz of an engine zipped overhead like a bee in haste to its hive. It might have been a bomber or a simple biplane en route to view the carnage in Sevastopol. Nevertheless, it vanished before being spotted, and with it, the din of civilization abated completely.

Gerhard swore, not because he barely averted capture, but because some insolent Soviet had shot his leg. The saltwater stung his bullet wound with every hill and trough over which the currents nudged him. The fist-sized gash above his left ear had induced a headache with such flare that he could not recall how he even acquired the wound. Although the sea chilled Gerhard to the bone, his wounds pierced his senses as if podded by the devil's pitchfork. Moving his leg in any direction proved an agonizing test of strength. Undoubtedly, the shivering did not help. And if not for the driftwood under his arms, he might have slipped beneath the ocean surface the moment he began his seaward escape.

"How could I let this happen?" he whispered to himself as if the Black Sea might betray him. "I'm the best soldier in my contingent, stronger than anyone else, the sharpest gunner, the swiftest runner. Even my salute to the flag and Führer is more poised and disciplined, my *sieg heil* louder and more passionate than anyone. Yet how did I, the finest Germany has to offer, fail to make the escape ships? Damned Soviets."

The day passed into night. Gerhard found no sleep, and each elapsing minute felt like another hour, perpetuating the nightmare. At some point, he raised his eyes to the moon and stars, their beauty explosive as fireworks frozen in time. Yet how could he enjoy the art of nature when he felt such pain, such unrelenting cold?

'No wonder they call it the Black Sea,' he thought. 'Black as the reaper.' He wished that the springtime weather would warm the night, yet even if such a thing transpired, he remained three-quarters submerged in an icy grave. His teeth chattered into his brain. Snot flooded from his nostrils. His arm muscles throbbed, and his head drummed. In time, the darkness of the world fell away. He heard himself breathing steadily, although that eventually slipped into nothingness. All thoughts froze like the stars above, allowing his awareness to drift into eternity.

~

Air and warmth filled Gerhard's chest, drawing him

up from the darkest depths of the void. He immediately snapped into a coughing spell, hammering at the layer of mucus that barricaded much of his throat. A soft hand quickly caressed the back of his head, lifted, pressed a cup to his lips, gently tilted, and poured. The liquid felt hot and slightly salty, a broth brewed to clear away the blockage like some master healing elixir. His eyelids fluttered open to the face of a young woman, who stared back with owlish eyes, brown as chocolate, beneath a mane of black hair strapped under a green headscarf.

Gerhard felt a sense of security in the woman's hands, a motherly touch that soon eased his head back to the pillow. The moment he felt himself sink into the down-stuffed sack, he noticed three people standing behind his caretaker – a girl, probably half the age of the one beside his cot, a middle-aged woman offering no more than an icy glare, and a graying man whose eyes sank into deep purple crescents.

The young woman uttered foreign words to her companions, *"Toy a boudin."* The older folks, presumably the parents, began to whisper to each other. Gerhard might have stiffened in terror had they been soldiers of the Red Army. Nevertheless, he found no immediate relief and prayed that they lived beyond Soviet control. Their language sounded Slavic but not Russian. He deciphered that rather quickly, having lingered around enough prisoners to know the difference. He mustered up the strength to pose a question in his tongue. "Where am I?"

The younger ladies retreated from the bed in fright while the older woman pointed at Gerhard and hissed *"Nemski,"* which sounded like *Nemetskiy*, meaning *German* in Russian. 'Damn,' he thought, feeling like he had doomed himself by speaking. He imagined that citizens of the Allied Forces had been trained to recognize, report, and even kill German soldiers. If this family had failed to determine his origins before, they certainly made up for it now. He closed his eyes and braced for defeat, ready to die for his country and Führer.

Likely recognizing Gerhard's internal struggle, the old man knelt beside the bed and whistled a shush. The young soldier opened his eyes to find the man expressing ease, relaxing the family behind him. "Krasimir," he said, placing a hand over his chest before leaning close to dab Gerhard's head wound with a damp cloth. Gerhard suddenly realized that he could not feel his legs. With worry snaking into his mind, he licked his lips, which felt rough and stung under the weight of his tongue.

Krasimir drew back a portion of the blanket covering Gerhard's legs to reveal their condition. Although the bullet wound had been cleaned and dressed, the infection had stained his thigh the plush colors of a hyacinth garden, like the ones his mother used to grow. He thought that the Black Sea would have flushed out the contamination. Unfortunately, while the freezing water had slowed the spreading poison, it also fed on his skin, leaving trails of white and pink blotches up and down his legs.

He lifted one of his hands to find his flesh shriveled, his bones pining to burst through. Feeling like a skeleton in tight rubber reminded him of stories he often heard back at the card tables in Sevastopol. Stories about the labor camps in Poland, where the Führer's top militant organization, the Schutzstaffel, housed all the Jews he had captured over the years.

Word had it that these camps operated under such intense conditions that most prisoners died, but those who managed to linger looked like frail sacks of skin and bone. Gerhard hated the idea that a German as proud and strong as him could be reduced to the same weakness as a Jewish prisoner.

Krasimir spoke to Gerhard in a voice as gentle as a sea breeze and patted his chest with a fat hand before standing up to leave the room. The young lady with the headscarf reached for another cup of broth and pressed it to Gerhard's lips. A few sips thawed his chest and soothed him to sleep. His dreams varied in color and texture, yet remained grounded, revealing glimpses of days past and passing days. He drifted between a warm bed and a freezing sea, two weeks with his eyes in his head, staring at the ceiling, stationary as the household objects surrounding him.

To Gerhard's surprise, the family tended to his every need, though mostly the young woman with the

green-as-spring headscarf, whose name he learned
was Denika. Although the ends of her lips never
cracked into a smile, she nursed him with unrelenting
care, supplied him with food and water, and even
cleaned the bedpan whenever he urinated or
defecated. She occasionally read him stories at night
to aid his sleep and mend his dreams. He might not
have understood her words, but her voice pleased his
ears as field flowers delighted the eyes.

Keeping Gerhard clean seemed to be Denika's most
challenging job. Rubbing him down with a wet cloth
not only frustrated her, since she had to change the
linens after each wash, but it hardly removed the sour
odors that wafted from the soldier's corner of the
kitchen.

One day, Denika and her mother, Irena, helped
Gerhard out of bed to an old cattle trough outside that
appeared to have been dragged through mud and
sand. Although he did not like the look of the metal
tub, the thyme and lemon-scented water it contained
alleviated his skin irritations and cleared the mucus
that had remained in his throat since the Black Sea
spat him ashore.

Gerhard pulled his hands from the water to find
that flesh and fat had begun returning to his bones.
Although his lips and wounded leg still required time
to heal, he felt like a new man, refreshed as an oak in
spring. While soaking in such thoughts, Gerhard
observed the sisters as they scrubbed his limbs with

bars of soap.

Lala, the younger girl, with ash brown curls and bright eyes, wore a smile like a happy rabbit. She was cute, but too new to puberty for his liking. Denika looked about his age, he thought; strangely more exotic and beautiful than any of the girls back in his hometown of Rosenheim. Yet, she ceaselessly bore an expression as cool as a winter sky, her eyes too often shaded by what he believed to be a cloud of melancholy. He stared at her and wondered, does she not know her beauty? How can someone so lovely and caring not radiate joy? Does the sun not know its own brilliance?

She met his gaze with a glare as hollow and haunting as a witch's cave. He pushed for a smile, but the darkness in her eyes forced him to look away. He tried not to think about her face, but the image had burrowed into his mind. He needed to consider something else, so he lifted his sight to the family's house and realized its petite size and condition.

Had it stood in a city, a government official might have considered it condemnable with its roof crumbling in places, wood panels cracking and rotting along the base, windows half boarded. Even the planked veranda looked like it could hardly support the rocking chair by the door. Gerhard wondered why they lived in such a miserable shack.

While the house boasted of impoverishment, the land beneath it hinted at wealth. The building resided at the eastern rim of a field of ryegrass that stretched about a quarter mile north to south, rushing to the edges of a forest whose trees and meadows burst with vibrant flowers. Gerhard turned his head to the west, where he could faintly make out the shape of a huge farmhouse painted shell white. From this direction flowed a breeze as cool as wet sand, carrying the scent of salt and the distant hum of beach breakers. "Where am I?" he muttered to himself.

~

While watching the family bustle about the house like birds of spring, Gerhard lay in bed, contemplating the distance between him and Sevastopol. How long had he drifted at sea? Did anyone ever go looking for him? In what country did he land? In the few weeks he had spent with the family, he picked up a fair number of words and phrases in their language, enough to understand basic conversations and pose a few essential questions to Denika.

"I don't know how long you floated at sea," she told him slowly and softly, cautious thoughts working behind her brown eyes. "Maybe a few days. And I don't know if anyone ever looked for you. No one has come asking for you."

"And what country is this?" Gerhard said, trying to offer his nurse a hint of a smile.

She swerved her eyes away. "Bulgaria."

Gerhard nodded in relief, remembering Bulgaria had pledged allegiance to the German Empire. And

362

just his luck, for all allies of the Führer allowed contingents of special German forces to comb their lands and weed out enemies of the Reich. 'Hopefully,' he thought, 'they will find me and return me home, and this kind family will be graciously thanked for supporting Deutschland.' While waiting for the day he might be found, he decided to make the best of his situation and get to know his caretakers.

Though usually garbed in warmly hued dresses that accentuated her hazel eyes, Irena always looked upon Gerhard with the coldness of an alpine glacier. She rarely spoke or acted without carefully chewing on her options over a cigarette. Krasimir lived much of his life in overalls and seldom offered an expression of joy from behind his graying whiskers. Unlike his wife, he conversed more often, though his daily work in the field and interest in the birds that lingered by the road were hardly entertaining to Gerhard. Lala, the youngest in the household, lived the life of a wild child. She hated wearing shoes and spent much of her time dancing in the wind with the ryegrass, seeming either clueless or disinterested in the burdens of her parents.

Denika, on the other hand, clearly understood, if not shared in, the unspoken sorrows of Krasimir and Irena, wearing the knowledge over her shoulders like an iron shawl. She neither smiled nor laughed, yet even the most sullen and stormy of skies could be considered beautiful, as Gerhard perceived. He could not pinpoint why, but he found himself thinking about her more frequently. Perhaps it stemmed from the motherly manner with which she nursed him or that her quiet presence reminded him of the mountains near Rosenheim, a peaceful place he often explored as a child. Either way, whenever he gazed upon her face, he felt a yearning to help her, a desire to lift the veil of darkness and draw her lips into a smile. Even her deepest frowns began to tickle his heart.

It did not take long for Gerhard to memorize the family's routine. The mornings began at the table with food and hot tea freshly prepared by Irena. Talk of housework and weather patterns typically broke up the bouts of silence and sipping sounds. Afterward, Krasimir and Denika would leave the house to labor in the fields with someone by the name of Nayden. Meanwhile, Irena would educate Lala with leather-bound books, fold-out maps, and an old scroll they never opened in front of Gerhard.

Krasimir and Denika usually returned in the early afternoon with sweat on their brows and a sack full of food. They ate lunch, then took turns bathing. The family spent most of the afternoon tackling household chores, which included taking care of Gerhard, talking in the salon, playing games, reading, and passing the time with activities as if they were waiting for something to happen. Although nothing ever happened in their house on a farm by the sea. Everything seemed normal to Gerhard. All but one thing.

Every night after supper, the family would leave Gerhard with a book or paper and pencil, something to occupy his mind, while they quietly shifted into a room around the corner from the kitchen like a clowder of cats. Gerhard had seen the door to the room in passing, always shut, never revealing what lay within. He wondered what went on in there, listening intently from his cot, which rested in a recess of the kitchen. Unfortunately, the walls muffled the family's voices like a stone barrier.

On Fridays, the family did not eat at the table but took their meals in that *other* room. And on Saturdays, they seemed to possess an air of passivity, avoiding any form of strenuous labor until after sunset. All the meals for that day, excluding dinner, had been prepared throughout the prior afternoon.

Since Gerhard knew little about Balkan culture, he perceived the family's routine as harmless, assuming they followed odd Bulgarian customs. Nevertheless, something about the secluded room disturbed him, perhaps because he was the only one that never entered. He wanted to ask Denika about the room, but every time he looked upon her face with intention, his thoughts melted to the flame of yearning.

~

There came a day when Krasimir lengthened his bill of kindness toward Gerhard by giving him a pair of crutches crafted from beech branches and twine. Gerhard tried them out, eager for mobility and excited to test his strength. At first, he moved quite slowly and often needed assistance, but he took pleasure in the fact that he could now sit at the dinner table and wander outside whenever he pleased.

Gerhard's renewed mobility forced the family to create new ground rules, specifically a curfew about when he needed to return to bed. Although they did not mention it, Gerhard felt that these changes had everything to do with the secret room, the one they visited each night, as if it were a beautiful mistress. He wanted to rip the door down. And why not? He lived here too. Shouldn't he have at least been shown what lay inside?

As a soldier of the unified German forces, the *Wehrmacht*, he had been trained to ensure that he always knew every aspect of his environment. A matter of safety and security, much like a cat new to a home. Every door must be opened, otherwise there will be scratching and yowling.

Gerhard had noted that the family locked the door to the forbidden room and hid the key. As to where, he had yet to learn. He felt it was a clear act of distrust and, worse, a bother that he could not simply shrug away. A quandary soon set upon his brain and grew like an anxiety-induced tumor, that while he had come to respect and depend on the family, even adore one of them, the notion of harboring secrets during wartime was a common sign of danger.

'But how could I ever accuse these people,' he

contemplated one night after everyone had gone to sleep. 'They may be blue most of the time, but they are compassionate. For this, I am very grateful. More so, I am amazed. The world is at war. And who, during such tumultuous times, would dare to house and care for a stranger, let alone a competent soldier? Certainly, this family is of the highest quality. And such quality, such benevolence, ought to be repaid. But how can I give back? I have no money, no cooking skills. I can refurbish a rifle better than most, but not a sink or a wagon.'

He rolled to the other side of his small bed and continued his train of thought. 'I'm about as useless as my left leg. Well, perhaps once I'm fully healed, I can learn craftsmanship from Krasimir and help him fix up the house. Maybe refurbish the paneling, and rebuild the damaged sections of the roof? If I could just give them something before I go home, something they can remember me by and prove that this fine German soldier was not just another ungrateful stranger they decided to help. That would be the just and honorable thing to do. And on that distant day when death finds me, I can leave this world knowing I gave back to those who gave to me.

~

Krasimir had long removed the bullet from Gerhard's thigh, and Denika gave him a lemony salve to rub into the wound every morning and afternoon. To his discontent, his leg remained stiff as a metal pipe, hardly bendable. And his nerves, no longer plagued by numbness, returned to the forefront of his attention with bolts of pain that struck from the depths of the injury. Gerhard nearly laughed each time he felt the teeth-gritting throb, telling himself that Germans love a good fight and never give up, even if it kills them. "I'll be walking just fine within a fortnight," he told Denika, his confidence resurfacing.

By the first Friday of July, Gerhard felt much stronger. He still needed the crutches, and the pain certainly persisted, but his leg better withstood the pressure of his body weight. He ventured outside after breakfast and found comfort in the old man's rocker on the porch. As he drew in a deep breath, reveling in the crisp aromas of dewy earth and sea salt, an unfamiliar sense of joy crept upon his mind. 'I think I'm beginning to love this coastal haven of a farm,' he thought. His grin reached for his ears, and his eyes began to well in awe.

Krasimir and Denika stepped onto the porch, ready for another day of work. Gerhard rubbed the emotions out of his eyes to postpone their headway and inquired in his best Bulgarian, "What do you do at the farm?"

"We tend to the fields and the cattle who graze across the road," the old man replied with such weight in his words that they seemed to drag from his throat.

Gerhard puffed out his chest. "Can I help?"

Denika looked at her father, so surprised by the offer that Gerhard thought he saw her lips crack into the faintest of smiles. Krasimir shook his head without a moment of consideration. "Sorry, but you still need to heal. If you wish to return to your best, I suggest you hop back inside and relax."

"I am..." Gerhard began but struggled to find the Bulgarian word for *restless*. Without digging too deeply into the matter, he decided to use a similar word that he felt would convey his condition, one that Lala used all too frequently. "I am *bored*. Yes, I'm very bored. It is difficult to sit around, day after day."

Krasimir lent a nod of understanding. "It is the difficult things in life that help us appreciate moments of ease. Besides, if you do not rest and heal, you will neither have the strength to return home nor be useful to us here. Sorry, Gerhard. Come, Denika."

As father and daughter walked down the rye-fringed path and out of sight, Gerhard sulked and stewed over that last response. After a long sigh and good itching of the chin, which he had shaved that morning, he decided to smoke out his bother with a cigarette that Krasimir had rolled the day before. Neither paper nor tobacco tasted of quality. Then again, these people lived like medieval peasants, or so he judged. Still, despite their blatant hardships, they never once complained, not aloud at least. They seemed to enjoy their simple life on the farm by the sea.

Gerhard soaked in the scenery for another hour before retiring. He slowly meandered into the family room and reclined in Krasimir's upholstered chair. Irena stood in the kitchen with Lala, teaching the girl about spousal responsibility, apparently paying no mind to the house guest. Gerhard momentarily scanned the room and took in another lungful of distasteful tobacco.

His wandering eye soon panned over the door of the forbidden room. 'My bane,' he thought, feeling warm, the first sign of a fever, or maybe just his curiosity sparking up. He bit the butt of the cigarette and hoisted his weight onto the crutches again, then glanced toward the kitchen to ensure that Irena and Lala remained occupied. Satisfied, he hobbled to the door, trying to ignore the hammering pain in his leg and keep his footfalls soft as a cat's.

He twisted the knob. It hardly flinched. He tried to peer through the tiny space between the door and frame, but the room lacked illumination. "Goddammit," he whispered in his native tongue. Frustration bent what little patience he kept. "What in God's name is in there?" In his youth, curiosity had fueled his ambitions. As a soldier, however, he had learned to mold such inquisitiveness and environmental awareness into instinct to ensure survival. "Lack of knowledge is lack of trust," he exhaled. "What you don't know can kill you." He pressed his shoulder into the door. Nothing.

"Gerhard?" Irena called from the kitchen.

"*Ich komme*," he answered, too quick to think that

he should have said he was coming in Bulgarian, not German.

As he found a seat at the kitchen table, Irena gently commanded Lala to run along and play outside. She then poured Gerhard a cup of tea and lit up a cigarette. He extinguished his smoke in the glass ashtray on the table and sipped the hot liquid. Silence tightened the air. He sensed she wanted to ask him something important, so he drummed up his growing Bulgarian vocabulary to prepare his mind.

"You like it here?" she finally inquired.

"*Da*," he replied with a smile. "Bulgaria is a lovely country."

"You like my family?"

"Yes, you are good people, honest, generous. I am grateful for your kindness to me, sharing your house, caring for me. I want to return the favor. Is there anything I can do to help here?"

After a moment of silence and a long draw of her cigarette, Irena blew smoke across the table, fogging the space between them. "You wish to do something for us to show your gratitude."

Gerhard nodded at the statement.

"When you are healed, you will leave. That is how you can repay us."

"Leave?"

"You leave this house, this farmstead."

He understood her words but not her meaning. Why would she wish him to depart when he offered

371

her assistance? He thought of Denika and her enticing brown eyes, cold but wondrous as a midnight moon, surely cloistering a desire for affection. He nearly floated into a daydream, but Irena's stern glare speared him to his seat, forcing him to muster a response.

"Where exactly would I go?" he asked.

"Back to Germany or Switzerland or Austria. From wherever you came."

Gerhard raised his posture like a soldier prepared to salute. "I want to stay here."

"No, you cannot. Krasimir and I forbid it."

"But Denika—"

"What about Denika?"

Gerhard choked on his tongue. He was neither in the safety of his birth nation nor surrounded by fellow countryfolk, yet it seemed that his itch to depart had unexpectedly vanished. He felt comfortable in this little house abaft a verdant glen somewhere on the Bulgarian coast.

"We do not wish to be troubled by the war," Irena further imparted, her words harsh as a fist in the chest. "That is why you must leave when you are fully healed; when you no longer require those crutches."

"You say this because I am a soldier, don't you?"

She nodded after a moment of deliberation. "Soldiers bring war."

Gerhard slowly sipped his tea and considered that at the current healing rate of his bullet wound, he would see a complete recovery in less than a month. This was great news. He would be capable of his former duties and skills, enjoying the body he had on the day the Russians laid siege to Sevastopol.

However, the thought of leaving now felt like a distant desire. His mind cried, 'How can I leave this beautiful farm on the coast, this house, this family? How can I leave Denika? I want to be with them, be with her. I want to fill Denika's empty eyes with joy, break the ice from her lips, and raise them into a smile.'

An idea sparked in his head. 'My leg. If I remain active, my recuperation will slow and prolong my stay. The pain persists anyway, and I need more time to work Denika's heart to my advantage. She must already sense my attraction to her. I need to tell her how I feel, and soon.' He imagined Denika's face aglow with affection and the shape of her body she so well concealed in her layered dresses. He felt his blood rush to his loins like the Inn River in the wake of a young summer storm. Yet the emotions ceased against the dam of a bother he could not easily ignore—the room.

Whatever lay in that space now teased his curiosity more than ever, somehow trumping all visions of peace while threatening his love for Denika. 'It must contain something of immense value,' he surmised inwardly. Moreover, why would Irena inform him of his imminent exodus unexpectedly, rather than once he felt better or back when he first woke? Did she catch him staring at the door or witness his attempt to open it? Did she mean to thwart his interest with firm words of departure? Were these people harboring something illegal? What kind of dark secret could a lonesome peasant family possess?

"As you wish, Irena," Gerhard finally concurred, placing his teacup on the table. "I will leave when I am well."

Irena acknowledged his acceptance with yet another nod before pushing her lips into an expression that reminded Gerhard of a sachet whose drawstrings had been tugged too tight. She offered him a cookie, no longer vocalizing the tone of a sober authority but that of a pleasant housewife.

He nibbled at the sweet treat, finding it hard as dirt, then glanced at Irena, who sat painstakingly upright in her chair, sucking down her cigarette like the last glass of a good wine. Silence filled the gap between them again, though Gerhard felt the air had grown intolerably stale, much like the cookie. Irena must have sensed it too. She drilled her cigarette into the ashtray, poured him another cup of tea, and stepped out onto the front porch.

Meanwhile, Gerhard leaned forward in the chair and looked to the right of his cot, where his shredded, sea-beaten military uniform lay. As an ordinary citizen, he might never have guessed it once belonged to a soldier of the German Reich. Feeling like a lone wayfarer, he examined the thick cotton shirt he now wore, one of Krasimir's brown night tops. Remembering his former glory, Gerhard abandoned his tea and cookie at the table and climbed upon his crutches.

Wandering back into the salon, he realized that the family had left him alone in the house. He felt safe to assume that Irena had gone outside to watch over Lala, who enjoyed playing along the edges of the rye and wood. But then he could not hear the girl, who loved to laugh and shout while rolling wildly in the grass. Perhaps she had run off as she was wont to, so the mother instinctively followed to rein her in and return her to safety. Thanks to prior observation, Gerhard knew that such a task consumed considerable time. They would not reappear for at least twenty minutes if this was true.

Audacity propelled Gerhard to the locked door of the secret room. He jiggled the handle. Nothing. He pressed his nose to the small space below the upper hinge and sniffed like a gopher hound. He hoped to catch a whiff of something unordinary, scents to feed his mind clues about what lay within. Alas, only thyme and lemon tingled his nostrils, the same balmy aromas that haunted the air of the house. Gerhard returned to his cot, scored by the vexatious whip of defeat.

~

Krasimir and Denika returned in the early afternoon with freshly washed clothes for their guest: blue denim trousers, a summer-striped collared shirt, white briefs, crew socks, and a pair of beaten leather boots. After voicing his gratitude for their continued generosity, Gerhard shared a wonderful meal with them, spent an hour in the rocker on the porch, then conked out for a long nap.

When he awoke, he found a plate of cold food resting on the floor beside the cot. He sat up and glanced around, finding the house lifeless as a crypt. He meant to pick up his plate when he suddenly heard muffled voices seeping through the kitchen wall. "What in God's name are they doing in that room?" he hissed.

Gerhard eased out of his squeaky bed and crept into the living room, softly pressing his back to the wall near the kitchen entrance. He felt like a soldier again, apprehensive, vigilant, eager to confront the Soviets as they stormed the fortress of Sevastopol. He held up his crutches like rifles and placed the bulk of his body weight on his right leg, hoping to prevent the floors from creaking and giving away his position. Yet, upon his first step, a sharp bolt of pain, searing as a hot iron on flesh, shot through his leg from thigh to foot. Both body and breath trembled, muscles tightening. The agony quickly drew heat to the surface of his skin.

Gerhard ground his teeth to push through the terrible throbbing, lifting his bad leg with a long breath and placing it down a few inches further before sliding his right foot inward. Beads of sweat formed like morning dew on his forehead and trickled over his brows. He put a single crutch to the floor, hoping to hasten his pace. With one step, his heart thumped louder than the voices behind the wall, clouding his judgment.

However, another step granted just enough clarity for a melody to tickle his ears. Gerhard felt the truth closing in, the family's wicked secret. Long had it frustrated him, haunted him, nipped at his daily thoughts and nightly dreams. He merely needed to shift nearer and widen his ears.

Out of nowhere, his supporting crutch stuck through a hole in the timber floor. He tried to yank it without creating a raucous, but the wood gripped stubbornly. Fear of fully reinjuring his leg forced him to work harder. He pulled and pulled, but the damned thing refused to budge.

"Twist it out instead," he advised himself, clenching his jaw. He wrenched it with all his strength. The crutch snapped. Gerhard fell backward, crashing to the floor like a tree upon a bed of glass. Krasimir burst from the forbidden chamber and quickly closed the door behind him with the shivering hands of one caught in a winter squall.

"Gerhard," he uttered in a tone of surprise, but with enough suspicion behind the word that his following sentence, whatever it might have been, never fell from his mouth. Krasimir briefly froze, his face plain as fresh snow, almost as if he had forgotten something. Gerhard thought the man had suffered a heart attack.

Yet a flurry of blinks and a chest-filling inhalation returned Krasimir to the room. "S-sorry, Ger-Gerhard, I-I'll help you," he stuttered, shaking off whatever thought had plagued him. He guided the soldier to his feet and back to the kitchen. As they neared the cot, the rest of the family exited the secret room and locked the door behind them.

While eating a cold dinner in his bed, Gerhard contemplated the mystery of the room. 'This is ridiculous,' he grumbled internally. 'Why can't I picture the interior of that place? I'm better than this. I should know. Did I hit my head too hard? Did the Black Sea curse my brain or strip me of imagination and memory? And this family—they're kind, Denika— my desire, yet why do they keep me out of that confounded room? Why do they not tell me about it?

They must know that I wish to learn, especially Krasimir. I would ask, but then they might give me the boot without an answer before I fully heal. Worse, what if, by asking them, they decide to harm me? And fate opposes me every time I try to open that damned door. Oh, what could make it so forbidden, as if it housed the Ark of the Covenant? I want... no, I must know what's in it.'

Gerhard hardly slept that night, his mind torn between the hospitality and secrecy of the family. Deeper still, he wrestled between his growing affection for Denika and his hunger to smash into the verboten chamber. When slumber finally arrived, it ferried him into a dream that swiftly encaged him in a cube of walls, white as polished porcelain. There appeared only one way out, the old wooden door to the room of rooms. Gerhard grasped the handle and rattled it. Even here in the core of his mind, it remained locked.

~

Krasimir spent the morning on the front porch whittling a small branch into a new base for the broken crutch. In the meantime, Irena took Lala to an old lemon tree that hunched over a small hump of earth south of the house by the edge of the wood. Gerhard sat at the table in the kitchen, enjoying a jelly-filled pastry with some black tea, when Denika entered the room and sat in the adjacent chair.

"I'm the one who found you," she admitted in a voice as soft as an ocean breeze, perhaps to hide a truth the others hoped to conceal.

Gerhard nearly choked, hurrying to gulp the warm tea and wash down the dry, floury flakes in his mouth. He finally cleared his throat and gawked at her, unsure whether he ought to smile or let his jaw drop in awe. "You found me?"

She searched the air as if the words needed to convey the story lingered in the distance. Then she drew in a long breath and looked him in the eyes. "I was collecting seashells to make a necklace for Lala when I came across your body entangled in seaweed and driftwood. I thought you were dead. I did not know whether to feel scared or sick or, well, it doesn't matter anyway. When I realized that you were still breathing, I became even more anxious. I thought to leave you for the gulls, who were already pecking at your leg, but I didn't. I couldn't."

"I hurried to Nayden's barn and called for help. Before long, you were placed on a makeshift stretcher and carried to the farm. Nayden and the others said you were likely to die. They could tell you were a soldier of sorts but couldn't determine for whom you fought. If you had awoken then, they might have killed you, afraid you would harm them. When they decided to do nothing to help you, I offered to take you in. They all thought I was mad. And, certainly, Father objected. When he asked why, I answered, 'Because you taught me the importance of compassion, and I feel God brought him here for a reason.' Father conceded, of course, until he... we... found out you were German. But, as he got to know you, his bitterness subsided, and now I think he likes you."

Gerhard withheld the laughter in his heart, revealing an awkward smile that might have hinted at his internal struggles. "And you, Denika, do you like me?"

"You are kind to us and show appreciation for our hospitality. So... yes, I... I like you."

Spying a flicker of joy in her eyes and what he believed to be a rudimentary smile, he felt his moment had come. "Denika, I think you are so beau—"

"Gerhard," Krasimir hollered, stepping into the

house. "I fixed your crutch." He leaned the wooden supports against the wall by the cot.

Gerhard felt his heart thumping so loudly that he imagined it might burst from his chest. "Thank you very much," he replied slowly, trying to conceal that he suddenly felt out of breath.

Denika allowed the ends of her lips to gently curl. "What were you going to say?"

Gerhard gazed into her eyes of chocolate, those dimples like tiny finger bowls, cheeks smooth as stone softened by centuries of water flow. He wished to voice his emotions, but how could he do so with her father in the same room? Would uttering the words fracture the harmony of the house and any fragment of trust the family had placed in him?

"Nothing," he muttered, whipping his feelings back just as Krasimir sat across the table. "Nothing you probably don't know."

Despite withholding the words that he longed to say, Gerhard felt as if he had broken a record or accomplished a daring feat, for to earn even the most fleeting of smiles from Denika meant that he had breached her well-guarded walls. 'I must have touched her heart somehow,' he thought. 'Perhaps she understands my heart too, my yearning. If not, why on earth does she, far more than her kin, tend to me so caringly and sit beside me in such a loving manner?'

He hungered for her kiss, to feel her lips, stroke her hands, and coil her hair about his fingers. And now that he knew it was she who rescued him, his adoration further ripened. However, while his heart swelled twice its size, his mind continued to shrink beneath the weight of the secret room. Gerhard feared that he could not possess both Denika and the knowledge of that forbidden place. Naturally, one would inevitably overwhelm the other, the outcome entirely dependent on his reaction to his increasingly volatile emotions.

"I wonder," he muttered that night as he lay alone in his cot. "Perhaps I could have both. What if I simply ask Denika what's in that room?" The idea felt like a failure the moment it tumbled from his tongue. After all, would not such a question pare her trust in him? Then again, considering her admittance to saving him from certain doom, was there a chance she might indulge him? "No, no," he breathed into the cool air. "If the family keeps the door locked, she might be sworn to never acknowledge such an inquiry. Blasted! I can't ask any questions or expose how I feel without... " The words slipped into the night. He clenched a fist.

Gerhard could hardly begin to contemplate why, but in the following days, he found himself spending more time with Denika. Perhaps he had broken her shell, for she opened her mind to him. She began to exclude herself from her routine activities in the salon to take Gerhard outside, where they would sit on the grass and talk. He unraveled stories of his life in Rosenheim, memories he had not recalled in years. He spoke of fights and contests won, mountains conquered, accomplishments in the national youth organization, badges and uniforms earned, even the number of women he had persuaded to kiss him. He puffed out his chest and folded his arms. 'Victory has always been mine,' he concluded on Wednesday afternoon as they sat together near the edge of the field.

Denika giggled and tapped his forearm with her fingers.

He shook his head. "What's so funny? I hardly think my achievements are a laughable matter."

Denika extended her legs and patted her dress to ensure the wind wouldn't push it back, then placed her hands on the earth behind her hips and reclined. She waved her bare feet to the rhythm of the swaying heads of rye. "You might have succeeded all your life, which is commendable, I suppose, but victory has not always been yours. The sea defeated you. It crushed you, dragged you, chewed on your flesh, and spat you out on the shore with just enough skin to keep your bones in place. And I'm glad for it."

"You're glad I was defeated and nearly died?"

"Yes."

"Why?"

"You're no longer the man you boast about."

"I disagree. I am exactly who I have always been, a strong, purebred German warrior who supports his country and Führer with the fierce loyalty of a sheepdog." He recognized the disbelief on her face, so he lifted his head high and said, "*Heil Hitler*."

Her eyes dimmed and swerved to the grass.

Regret prodded his stomach. "I'm so sorry. I didn't mean to upset you."

She returned her owlish gaze upon him. "I hate Hitler. He is evil, a wretched devil. But you, Gerhard, you might have grown up worshiping him in your youth, taught to hate, parade, mock, conquer, and light the world on fire. Yet here, now, you sit by this lonesome field, soft as a fledgling, your eyes full of joy and love."

Gerhard did not know what to say. Part of him wished to spit on her for insulting his Führer, but what she expressed wielded a truth that melted the steel of his will. He wanted to kiss her and leaned in, but she spoke again.

"If you could go home, what would you do?"

"I think I would reenlist as a soldier," he answered with more doubt than intended.

"I don't think you would. The sea defeated you for a reason."

"You really believe I've changed?"

Denika wrapped her arms around her knees. "I grew up in Varna, not too far north of here. I was a happy child. Spent a lot of time on the beach and in the fields, always around family and friends, glowing like a star in a constellation. But when we came here to live on Nayden's farm, I became a lonely star, quiet, distant, faint. Part of me still feels like that. However, it is only a part, not the whole. The rest of me now feels bright again, a bit of sunshine. And it's all thanks to you. Taking care of you has taught me many things; about you, of course, but also about myself and the possibilities of this life, and that what we call truth is not valid unless we experience it."

She laughed under her breath but continued before Gerhard could ask about her last sentiment. "And then there's the way you looked at me in all my dimness, the way you still look at me. I know you have changed because I have changed. The Gerhard in your stories is far from the kind of man whose company I should keep, let alone enjoy. Now, do you understand?"

Gerhard's heart hammered in his chest as the urge to kiss her gushed throughout his body once more. Yet, a thought curbed the impulse: a picture of home. He closed his eyes and wondered, 'But what is home? Is it not where the heart lives?' He wanted to laugh over the whirlwind he had created within himself. 'Is my heart in Germany with my family and friends, with the flag and Führer, or here in Bulgaria with Denika?' He sniffed the salted air and opened his eyes to find Denika's hand on the grass beside his.

~

The following day, Denika led Gerhard to the lemon tree on the hump of earth by the forest. Its branches elbowed and corkscrewed into a mane of green leaves festooned with what looked like yellow-saturated lightbulbs. When Gerhard finally stepped beneath the

385

shelter of the tree, the citric aroma reminded him of the cheese and lemon blintzes his mother made when he was a child. He reached for one of the plump fruits.

"Wait, they're not quite ready, but very soon," Denika said with raised brows before shifting her gaze to the west.

Gerhard acknowledged the request and turned to mimic her, discovering that the little hill granted a view he did not expect. Nayden's farm looked like the outline of a fat number eight, whose rye field shimmered like the skin of a green and gold turtle, stretching from Denika's house to the main stead.

There, it flanked the big house and barns but abruptly ended at the shoulder of a wide dirt road that punched out of the northern forest, cut directly south across the property, and vanished into the sticks on the other side. Gerhard could make out a few clusters of cows in the pasture across the road. A house nearly as dilapidated as Denika's stood at the farthest reach of the property, ahead of a thin line of what looked like oak trees. Beyond that, the land must have dropped to the beach, for the blue waters of the Black Sea spread across the eastern horizon like an enormous bed upon which rested the almighty sky.

For a moment, Gerhard stared at the salted water with disdain, the source of his wounds, the vast pool from which birthed his now most painful memories. He wished to curse it. Yet, after swerving his eyes toward Denika, he could not help but forgive the sea, even thank it for delivering him from the hell-fires of Greater Europe to this little slice of paradise, where dwelt the most angelic creature in the world. With a delicate touch, he took her hand in his own. She tightened her grip and offered him a grin. Without voicing it, he decided he would remain here forever.

~

On Friday morning, Denika helped Gerhard to his feet. He stood upright without crutches for the first time since his watery escape from Sevastopol. Pain still jabbed his nerves behind the healing wound, and he might have limped like a horse with a broken shoe, but it was a prideful limp. Krasimir fetched an old bottle of wine to celebrate. After a toast and a few shallow draughts, he and Denika left to labor on the farm. Once they vanished into the rye, Irena told Gerhard she needed to attend to some business in the nearest village and asked if he could look after Lala.

"Happy to do it, madam," he replied with a laugh in his throat. Irena departed within the hour.

Lala possessed a spontaneous mind, a spirit so free that it conjured up a touch of envy in Gerhard, reminding him of his brazen youth. Whether inside or out, Lala danced like a woodland nymph, singing and laughing ever frivolously. Gerhard thought to watch her from the porch, but she insisted he join her on the grass. Barely halfway there, she incited him to chase her, knowing he would never catch her, although she eventually slowed, showing pity for the crippled houseguest.

Lala led Gerhard to the forest's edge, where wildflowers and weeds flourished like a city of the Renaissance. He watched her pick a handful of petal-studded beauties, disregarding the possibility of getting poked or stabbed by thorns. He felt that if he could muster such audacity, surely he would already have won a kiss from Denika and the knowledge of that stupid, barred-up room in the salon. Sadly, all he could do now was watch Lala decide which flowers she most preferred. After finalizing her choices, she crudely bundled them with a thin green vine and handed the bouquet to Gerhard.

"These are for you," she said with a grin as bright as summer.

"For me?" he chuckled. "How sweet of you."

"Give them to my sister."

"Why don't you give them to her?"

"Because..." She fingered her dark curls. "Because I think you two should make babies."

"Make babies? I don't... " He paused to analyze the notion. Marrying Denika sounded like a dream come true, well worth the rest of his life. He imagined growing old with her, sitting on the veranda while watching their children play upon this smiling parcel of land in rural Bulgaria. Gerhard accepted the flowers with a brief bow of the head. When he and Lala returned to the house, he placed the bouquet on his bed, ready to give it to Denika the instant she arrived.

"Are you hungry?" he asked the sprightful youth.

"I want to nap first," Lala answered. "We can eat after." She strolled into the other room and hummed aloud for a few minutes, though the house soon fell silent. In the meantime, Gerhard moseyed into the salon and sat in Krasimir's chair, quickly reclining into a series of daydreams about Denika. He thought of her wholesome heart and beauty, flawless as a diamond, picturing what she might look like naked, only to catch himself feeling bashful.

"A cigarette ought to calm my excitement," he told himself.

Next to the chair resided a conventional end table with a single drawer and a cubby stuffed with old books. Gerhard leaned over to withdraw a few leather-bounders, which he placed on his lap. He skimmed over their covers, thinking he might attempt one, but laughed after realizing that he could not read Bulgarian, let alone any language that used the Cyrillic alphabet.

After shoving the books back in place, he remembered the cigarette he had craved. He opened the drawer of the table, where he found four pre-rolled cigarettes, a matchbook, a box of cards, and four rings.

He lit up a smoke and began to fumble with the rings. Three shined of sterling silver, no less immaculate than an August sky. The fourth ring looked like unpolished gold, hardly reflecting any light. However, embedded into grooves along its exterior were tiny, faceted emeralds. Gerhard perceived each ring as unique, although the gold one seemed particularly interesting. Curious, he slipped it on. "Too loose," he laughed under his breath. "Probably belongs to Krasimir's fat fingers." Feeling bored as a child in an empty room, he tumbled the rings into one palm, pretending to toss dice, which reminded him how much he enjoyed gambling games, especially those partaken by his comrades back in Sevastopol. Fortune favored him in those days. Of course, his winning streak died with the soldiers who cheered on and contended him.

Gerhard shook his head, waving away the mournful memories, and placed the rings back in the drawer in exchange for the wooden card box, which resembled a hand-sized treasure chest. He opened it and saw an ace resting atop the deck, conjuring a smile. As he removed the deck of cards, he heard something clink. At the bottom of the little box, sheltered by a slightly bent joker, lay a small copper key.

Gerhard lifted the key and placed the cards back in the box. At first, he thought nothing of it. He lazily drove it between two fingers and drew it up into the air like an infant sword. Suddenly, his brain illuminated. Gerhard pushed to his feet and limped in haste to the door of the forbidden room. He grabbed the knob and jiggled it, then fondled the key with a moist palm and stuck it in the lock hole. Before turning it, he peered over his shoulder and listened for voices or footsteps.

Nothing.

He twisted the key with slow precision, his nerves inflamed by wonder and apprehension. He scratched his chin and thought twice about his actions and once about Denika. "Is this right?" he whispered to the door. Breathing heavily and beginning to sweat, he recalled Lala's fearlessness, a similar bombast and boldness that he once had. "Am I still that man?" He gently pushed the door inward. Darkness engulfed the room, but the light streaming inward revealed a large candle on a pedestal next to the doorway. Without delay, he swung back to the end table, grabbed the matchbook, and lit the candlewick whose bright flame shed light on the family secret.

A seven-branched candelabrum of unpolished brass stood proudly at the center of a round table, accompanied by four gold-rimmed ceramic plates beside which rested pocketbooks stamped with Hebrew text. Faded tapestries clung to the walls, each displaying a famous scene from the Old Testament.

Relics and heirlooms ornately stocked the nearby shelves next to a cabinet whose well-dusted surface accommodated an old, tapered candlestick embossed with a six-pointed star. A medieval illustration of men and women performing miracles beneath a cloud of ancient words rested upright on an easel like an idolatrous picture of a family ancestor. Beneath it, an assortment of gold and silver lockets shimmered in the firelight, each finely bejeweled, enriched with symbols and words that Gerhard surmised to be names of people. Lastly, hanging from a small, blunted hook on the side of the cabinet was a worn, black skullcap.

A bolt of pain struck Gerhard's stomach. "How did I miss this?" he hissed to the air, feeling as though he might vomit. "It all makes sense now. The terror upon my waking, the underlying sorrow, the fear that plagues the air around the family, the poor conditions of the house, the secrecy of their emotions, their past, their beliefs, their reasons for living here, the secrecy of this abominable room.

These people are hiding. They are Jews in hiding, and Nayden is sheltering them. Where did my suspicions fail? Did the Black Sea wipe my ability to discern? The answer now seems plain as the sky is blue. All this time, I've been living in a house with Jews. I, a loyalist and soldier of the Great Reich, accepted hospitality from Jews. I ate their food, drank with them, smoked with them, laughed with them, even began to fall in love with them."

He recalled what he had learned about Jews through the Hitler Youth leaders, the works of Joseph Goebbels, and the speeches of the Führer. That these nationless people caused wars, economic deficits, and widespread disease. That they meant to steal German jobs, overpopulate German towns, and stain German culture with their own. Whether any fleck of truth existed in such claims, Gerhard did not know. Nevertheless, as an adolescent, he had been convinced to follow his Führer and wrestle the Jewish world enemy to the ground, then get rid of them by any means necessary.

He remembered the Jews of Rosenheim. Everyone condemned them, shunned their businesses, forced them to wear badges on their clothes, even burned their books and smashed their windows. Like a film replaying in his head, he recounted the day the Gestapo finally marched them away.

Anyone who resisted, anyone who hid, and anyone who dared to shelter a Jew were exposed and purged. Gerhard once pointed at a man he saw sneaking from one house to another, so he shouted, "*Jude, Jude,*" after which a pair of officers appeared like ghosts from an alley and wrenched the suspect from the town. Gerhard felt nothing less than joy that day, thrilled that he had contributed to the wishes of the Führer.

All his life, he gloried himself as a modern warrior, fearless, loyal, the perfect showcase of German ideology. He had always been one to drink, gargle, and piss national pride. And why not? Even in the most troubled times throughout history, his people used their strengths to guard and fight for their beliefs. Yet, since Gerhard's arrival in Bulgaria, what had become of his strengths and beliefs? Did the German warrior drown in the Black Sea?

'The sea defeated you for a reason.' Denika's words broke into his head and rang like a church bell as memories of recent months marched through his mind. He remembered how Krasimir had welcomed him with open arms despite his reluctance and the potential danger accompanying the generous act. The old man had sacrificed his family's safety to shelter a wounded German soldier. No less than her husband, and despite her obvious disdain, Irena cooked for Gerhard almost daily, fattening the flesh on his bones, renewing his strength. Lala contributed to his healing in her own way, sharing in games and laughter, even reminding him that life can be joyous through simple acts like picking wildflowers.

And Denika, sweet and lovely Denika, who had long dwelt in a shrouded mind of sadness and loss, had chosen to rescue Gerhard from death and nurse him back to health. She taught him how to speak Bulgarian and revealed to him the hidden beauty of the countryside, drawing out his inner dreamer. She fed him with her hands, prepared salves for his wounds, washed his body, clothed him, and told him stories.

Despite the knowledge that his nation wished to purge the world of hers, she treated him like a husband fresh from the battlefield. She proved to him that life extended far beyond honor, war, and patriotism. That there were more similarities than differences between people, and that love wielded greater strength than fear. Why this Jewish family decided to shelter a staunch supporter and solider of the Reich baffled him completely.

Deeper in thought, he remembered a neighbor boy

named Heinrich, who he learned was a Jew only because he had watched the Gestapo evict them. Gerhard had spent much of his childhood playing with Heinrich and his sister, a generous family, from what he recalled, much like Denika's. Yet, on the day the officers took Heinrich away, Gerhard smiled through the window, the same smile he shared with Denika when he held her hand in the shade of the lemon tree. He suddenly felt ill again and wanted to vomit, uncertain whether he hated or loved these people.

Gerhard limped out of the room, locked the door, placed the key in its home beneath the joker, and shoved the box of cards into the drawer. He threw himself into Krasimir's chair, raking his fingers over his face. "They're Jews," he wheezed. "They're goddamn Jews." He felt a profound urge to flee the house and seek the closest German camp or supporting contingent and report the family. "Stop this," he muttered, feeling like the walls were leaning inwardly. He squeezed his lids shut. "God, I wish this were a dream, just a terrible dream, one from which I can escape and reawaken to normalcy."

"Gerhard?"

His eyes snapped open to a quiet room. Lala stood before him with a grin so full her cheeks puffed out like baby parachutes. He glared at her as if her dainty little figure had mutated into that of some devilish beast.

"I'm ready to eat now," she sang, utterly impartial to his silent revulsion. "Come on. Let's fry up some eggs."

"If that is what you want," he grumbled before breaking from the chair.

From his position at the dinner table, Gerhard watched Lala cook eggs, a tempest of an endeavor. She wasted butter, salt, and spices and burned over half of the batch. All the while, she laughed and chirped as if Gerhard genuinely cared to listen. He forced his mind to focus on random objects, hoping to bar the encroaching madness. Yet, the iron words of the Führer marched over each thought, proudly parading the posters and films of Herr Goebbels.

Gerhard thought he heard one of his old bunkmates gabbing about the labor camps constructed in Poland, how they housed Jews, Poles, Roma, and homosexuals, many of whom were being cleansed indefinitely. Whistles screamed. Blasts echoed. A high-ranking officer shouted at Gerhard to remain at his post while his fellow soldiers evacuated the Crimean fortress to a Rumanian naval ship.

His brain verged on exploding when Lala placed a plate of scrambled eggs in front of him, half charred like the leftover wood of a campfire. The war dissolved, and all he could hear were the footsteps of Irena entering the house. Gerhard took a deep breath and tried the eggs.

That night, the family dined in their Jewish chamber. They seemed quieter than usual, but that did not matter to Gerhard now that he knew what lay within. As if the walls had collapsed, he could hear them praying, singing, and reading from their books. Meanwhile, he sat up in his cot with a glass of wine and a cigarette, cursing his situation.

He perched until about eight o'clock when the family dispersed from the room. Krasimir quietly ventured outside for a breath of fresh air. Irena returned to a laborious sewing project she had started a few days prior. Lala commissioned her little brain and hands to create a penciled masterpiece of anthropomorphic creatures sauntering happily across a blank sheet of paper. Denika floated into the kitchen on a cloud of felicity and pulled up a chair beside the soldier. Uncertain about what he ought to do or feel, his head drooped like a bluebell, though his sight lingered on the bouquet of wildflowers lying between his legs.

"Are you all right, Gerhard?"

As if his head were filled with sand, he slowly hoisted it and turned to Denika, whose face radiated such warmth that he nearly burst into tears. She might have appeared plain as a potato – brown eyes, brown dress, brown shoes, light olive skin, a green headscarf penning her tangle of black hair. Yet, to Gerhard, she glowed like a sun aiming to dissolve the world of shadows into which he had fallen. Feeling weak beneath the boot of his own disarray and speechless as a mime, he picked up the flowers and passed them to Denika.

"Here," he muttered.

With her mouth open in awe yet no words to fill the gap, Denika accepted the bouquet and blushed. She pressed her nose into the flowers and admired their pleasant fragrances and lush textures. "They are beautiful, Gerhard." She kissed his cheek. "I don't know what to say other than thank you. You are more noble than I could have imagined. I must admit, and I mean this sincerely, I treasure our friendship."

Gerhard sat up straight as an arrow, feeling as if he had taken another bullet, one that sent shockwaves through his mind and shattered the glass through which he had been quarreling with himself. Between the kiss, which wielded a potency comparable to the touch of Midas, and the words, scented and nourishing as fresh honey, Gerhard felt he had been cleansed of darkness, allowing the ends of his lips to crack into his cheeks and salted water to fill his eyes.

With the silence of a hallowed angel, Denika floated from the chair to her knees on the edge of the cot, draped her arms about Gerhard, and pressed her cheek to his cold ear. Unsure whether he had died and gone to heaven or had entered a fever dream, he slowly winged his arms over her back and secured her body within a soft grasp. Tears trickled down his nose and cheek as he leaned his head deeper into the love that embraced him. He felt accepted, that home had found him and nothing could ever rob him of it.

Krasimir entered the kitchen at that moment only

to lay eyes on his daughter wrapped in arms with a member of the German Empire. He spat icy words in Bulgarian that cued Denika into a speedy retreat, first from Gerhard's arms, then into the other room. After all this time, the old man still didn't trust him, and for good reason. Gerhard might have relinquished activity as a soldier, but he still possessed the ability to commit atrocities.

In fact, on any given day prior to his escaping Sevastopol, he would have dragged these people from their shack and tossed them to the Gestapo like a bundle of twigs ready to be burned. Therefore, he posed a grave threat. And Krasimir's glare, which aimed to stab Gerhard from across the kitchen, simply proved it. He was in over his head. He had fallen in love with a Jew. A Jew in hiding. A Jew whose family feared him.

Gerhard knew that he could not escape history. For though his heart had finally claimed victory in the name of Denika and under a banner of understanding, the past still clutched to him like an angry child on a parent's leg, heedless of being dragged around the house. Was it even possible to rid himself of the teachings and duties of the country that had shaped his life for the sake of the love that had saved him from death? Even if he managed to bury the past, history had a way of resurfacing. The Germans still roamed the streets and fields of conquered and supporting nations. What if they found Denika? Would they send her to one of the terrible labor camps in the north?

Nightmares plagued Gerhard's mind that night. As if strapped to a chair in a cinema house, he watched reels of Jews marching in chains, hammering, assembling, working under the screaming whip of German abhorrence. Yet, in every face along the benches and chain gangs, he saw Denika, a heart of compassion, undeserving of such hateful torture. In every pair of eyes that stared mournfully at the firing squads, Gerhard saw the woman he loved, the woman who had nursed him from death despite the evils of his past.

He repeatedly broke from sleep, his gut churning intensely, his mind stricken with fear. He heard things that made his skin crawl—the creaking of wood, the scuttling of a rodent, the wind hissing through the space under the front door. Any one of them could have been a German officer eager to ship Denika off to her doom. He prayed for an end to this hellacious struggle between then and now. He even imagined shadows leaning in with long arms, hoping to syringe him with more nightmares. And they must have succeeded, for each time he managed to resume slumber, the films of suffrage replayed from the beginning.

With dawn came further misery and a headache jammed between his eyebrows. It was now Saturday, the day of rest for all but him. Irena generously passed out premade pastries with butter, lemon marmalade, and hardboiled eggs. Gerhard hardly consumed his ration, feeling unworthy of the sugary breakfast, averting eye contact with Krasimir and any answers to questions that might prod his fears. No one considered asking what pestered him, reinforcing the truth that he remained an outsider. Of course, the family knew nothing of his discovering their secret and the accompanying traumas. They only recognized his affection for Denika, which they fiercely rejected. Nevertheless, to honor the Sabbath, they pretended all was well and went about their day, grinning, laughing, and praising God.

About mid-morning, Denika approached Gerhard with a small basket and asked if he wished to join her for a walk. While his mouth eagerly agreed, his eyes bent toward Krasimir, who sat in his chair reading what looked like an unmarked bible.

Then Gerhard's sight fell upon the door to the Jewish room. He wished he could travel back in time and stop himself from entering or at least forget what he had seen. The angry child gripping his leg, the Gerhard of old, beckoned him to condemn the one he loved. "Medicine," he demanded in thought, looking up at the ceiling as if to ignore the evil or at least avert its vile suggestion. "Another dose of Denika ought to do me good and quell the spread of such poison."

He followed Denika outside, but just beyond the porch, a misstep fired pain through his healing leg, up a river of nerves, and into the pulse of his headache.

He tried to ignore it, yet he felt surprisingly heavy, and the world around him spiraled. Sweat formed and beaded over his brows like the first drops of a rainstorm. His lids weighed down and blurred his sight. Then, a gale of exhaustion swept him off his feet.

Gerhard opened his eyes a moment later to find that Denika had caught him mid-fall. She laughed and mocked his sense of direction, aiding him to an erect stance. As if something divine had touched him through her, a fountain of relief filled and cooled him, although the ache between his brows persisted and the sting in his leg deepened.

"Can you make it to the lemon tree?" Denika asked him.

Gerhard knew his face expressed agony, but he forced a half smile to show his determination. "Seems my leg wound has turned on me. Nevertheless, with you here, Denika, I know I can make it."

"Do you want me to get your crutches?"

"No." He ground his teeth and shifted into a deep limp. "I can do this."

They slowly walked up the slope at the southern edge of the field. The lemon tree crooked over the mound with its woody arms reaching forth to offer the world its ripened fruits, yellow as sunflower petals. Denika plucked a plump lemon from a drooping branch and offered it to Gerhard. "If we pick a dozen more like this one, we can make enough lemonade for the whole family," she suggested.

402

Every word that spilled from her tongue drenched Gerhard in elation. He felt light as a bird, his heart pumping with such gusto that he filled her basket with ripe fruits to the brim. She giggled and grabbed his free hand to guide him to the edge of the hillock's crest, yielding a familiar view of the stead. As a salty breeze danced about them, they smelled the lemons together and admired the quiet world in which they lived.

With Denika by his side, Gerhard felt he could conquer the past and seal it in a tomb beneath his mind. Yet, with such relief filling him, why did the spot between his brows continue to throb with pain? Denika suddenly gripped the collar of his shirt. He half-expected her to kiss his lips, but she only meant to turn his sight to a specific point in their view.

"What's happening over there on the road?"

A cloud of dust stormed in the wake of two vehicles that burst from the forest, but slowed as they approached Nayden's farm. Gerhard recognized the leading car, a gray Peugeot 402 Estate, common among German officers on business. However, judging by the trailing Peugeot DMA truck with its paneled and tarped bed, that business lay not with the farmer but with whom he had been sheltering. The basket fell from Gerhard's hand, and all the juicy lemons rolled down the face of the hill.

"Go back to the house, Denika."

"Why?"

"Because you and your family are in grave danger."

403

"What do you mean? How so?"

"Those vehicles belong to the German government, and they've come to take you away."

Her mouth dropped. "How do you know?"

"Unfortunately, I've seen them many times before. They're Jew hunters."

"How did—"

"There's no time to explain, Denika. And it doesn't matter what I know or think. Those men down there will sniff you out faster than a hellhound. They will capture you. They will throw you in that truck and put you on a train to a work camp in Poland, where you will die slowly and in agony. Denika, they will murder your entire family. And I refuse to let that happen, so please, go right now. Hurry!"

"I'm not leaving you, Gerhard."

He could not believe she spoke such words. He might have asked her to marry him in that moment were it not for the imminent danger. "No, I won't reach the house in time. My leg is still too weak and nagging more than it has in a long time. But you, Denika, you are strong and must survive. Please go."

"Not without you," she affirmed, threading her hand through his armpit and around his back, lending support and speed to his gait as they started down the slope. He repeated his words, imploring her to leave him, but she gave no answer this time and trudged on. Gerhard listened for any sign of the Germans approaching, but it seemed they had yet to restart their engines.

Bursting through the front door, Denika implored her family, "We need to gather what we can carry and get out of here."

"Why should we leave?" Krasimir barked, rising from the comfort of his armchair.

"There are Germans at Nayden's house."

Krasimir shot Gerhard with blazing eyes. "This was you, wasn't it? You brought them here. This is your fault, Nazi scum."

"*Aba*, it wasn't him," Denika contended.

Gerhard shook his head and waved a hand. "No, Krasimir, I didn't call anyone to my aid. I swear to God. And how could I anyway? I don't have the means. Trust me when I say that I only wish to help you."

Krasimir roared in mockery. "You help me? You, a solider of Hitler, help a Jew? I cannot begin to believe--"

"Believe it!" Gerhard shouted, then softened his tone. "Please, I beg of you. Go. Take your family and flee into the forest right now. Do not look back. Do not stop."

Krasimir must have recognized Gerhard's sincerity, for he quickly turned to his family and told them to hurry. In no time, they gathered what they could into bags and rucksacks, then filed through the house's rear door. Gerhard limped after them onto the grassy lot between the house and the fern-carpeted forest. He stopped dead in his tracks as the family hastened toward the timberline. His headache clanged like a bell and his bullet wound stung as if someone were driving a cauterizer into it. He tugged his pant leg up to find tiny streams of lucent yellow liquid trickling over his knee.

Denika rushed back and hooked his arm, working to pull him into a run, but he anchored to the grass like a stubborn horse. Although he yearned with all his heart that he could go with them, he knew that to do so would bait death along and continue to endanger the family. He breathed deeply and looked at Denika, a face once vacant with every glance that now shone as bright as the sun. Her wide eyes, wet like melting chocolate, searched his expression for an answer to her silent question.

"Sweet angel, I cannot follow you." He felt as if each word weighed more than his wounded leg. "You must go without me."

"Gerhard, please. Do not do this. Not now."

He gave her a smile riddled with grief. "Although it breaks my heart, I must linger here alone. My leg will only slow you down. I have to stay and distract whoever comes to the house. I do not fear my death, only yours, Denika. I have always boasted that I am strong, proud, and loyal as a hound."

"And you truly are, Gerhard," she confirmed, "but that will not save you."

"No, but it will save you. I will not be responsible for your death. I once told your mother that I would do anything to repay your family for reviving me. Well, this is it. Please, find it in your heart to forgive me. Now go."

She stroked a strand of his blond hair and kissed him with such fierce pull that he began to cry. He longed to taste her lips and draw her into his arms again. He wished he could marry her and have children who could play on this verdant parcel of land, where they could grow old like the lemon tree. But such a dream was not his fate. He would prefer her to escape and love another than see her snatched by the dreaded Schutzstaffel, those Jew-scavenging vultures. When she released him from her embrace, he caressed her face with one hand and wiped the tears from her eyes. "Go," he whispered.

Denika slowly backed away, holding her gaze upon him, lips trembling, breath staggering. Irena touched her shoulder, prompting Denika to turn and hasten. Before they could get too far, Gerhard called for Krasimir. The old man urged the others on and looked to the young soldier, probably wondering why he dared delay him further.

"I'm sorry, Krasimir, but before you go, there is something I must know. Why did you take me in? Surely it could not have been out of love for Denika. You could have killed me the moment you learned I was German. Yet, despite the unforgivable cruelties my people have committed against yours, not to mention that the world is at war, you allowed me to live and live well. Why?"

With his feet slowly shifting toward the timberline and his grip tightening on the neck of the rucksack slung over his shoulder, Krasimir cracked a smile. "The Torah commands us to greet each person cheerfully, wash their feet upon entering our house, and feed them as if they are family. Although we must always take caution, God encourages us to treat strangers with compassion, with grace, regardless of their background. And why not? In the end, we are *all* children of God."

Gerhard watched the family vanish into the forest. He grinned for a minute and chuckled under his breath, enduring the searing pain between his eyes. He thought himself crazy and felt that if any radicals back home, or even his old friends from the Hitler Youth ever received word of his clement actions, they would rescind all ties and pretend they never knew him.

But then, he no longer cared about his reputation as a modern warrior of Germany, one who would fight for the cause of the Führer. "It was all an illusion." He laughed as if his whole life up until now had been a joke. "A terrible, greedy dogma handwritten by Hitler and his cohorts to rid the world of those they hated simply to hate and gain power and shift the weight of their guilt and problems upon the innocent. I was guilty, too. Still am. Though I hope I might be forgiven someday."

Relieved of heart, Gerhard limped into the house

and found renewed comfort in Krasimir's armchair. He reached for the end-table drawer and pulled out a lonesome pre-rolled cigarette. Before igniting it with the lighter left behind, he glanced at the door that once shielded secrets from him. It now rested agape with the room beyond nearly devoid of Jewry. All that remained were the faded tapestries.

He lit the cigarette just as three officers of the Schutzstaffel burst through the front door. With scowls sharpening the features of their faces, they took immediate notice of Gerhard sitting snugly in the salon with a gratified expression and smoke billowing lazily from his mouth. His brain drummed upon the spot between his brows, and the pain in his leg felt worse than ever, probably reeking of infection. Yet, his liberated soul numbed any thoughts of sorrow or regret.

"Where are the Jews who live here?" hissed one of the officers, stepping into the room without a fleck of caution.

"There are no Jews in this house," Gerhard idly replied in his native tongue.

"You are German?"

"Born and bred, Sir. I'm also a soldier like you. At least I was. Fought in the Ukraine and defended at Sevastopol. Missed the rescue ships, but I escaped. I served my purpose and have since resigned."

Indifferent to Gerhard's statement, the lead officer signaled his compatriots to search the house. At the same time, he marched about the salon, head twisting and eyes shifting like a serpent on the prowl. Noticing the room with the open door, he strutted in and shined a small flashlight on the walls, momentarily studying the tapestries. With a frown as deep as his cleft chin, the officer stepped before Krasimir's chair and placed the short barrel of a black revolver to the pulse between Gerhard's eyebrows. "I will ask you again. Where are the Jews?"

"And I will tell you again, Sir, there are no Jews here. Never were. It's just me on this big, beautiful farm. My haven. Wonderful life here."

Hearing the click of the hammer, Gerhard took a drag of his cigarette and allowed the world to fade from his mind. With the headache finally vanquished, a grin emerged and brightened his face. He felt strong, proud, and loyal as a hound, the finest Germany had to offer. But more than anything, he felt at peace with leaving this world, knowing he gave back to those who gave to him.

Thank you for reading *Twisted Tales of the Twentieth Century*.

I hope you enjoyed spending time with the Twisted Tales cast. Stay tuned because there's still the second half of the century to go!

The sequel, *Twisted Tales of the Twentieth Century: 1950 – 1999 Collection*.

Do you fancy staying updated with news about my books?

• Join my mailing list at: www.jabierman.com

• Like me on Facebook: www.facebook.com/jabiermanauthor

• Follow me on Instagram: www.instagram.com/j.a.bierman/

Also, if you have a moment, I would greatly appreciate if you could review Twisted Tales of the Twentieth Century at the store where you purchased it. I would love to know what you thought of the book.

Thank you for your support!
J.A. Bierman

Twisted Tales

of the

Twentieth

Century

<hr/>

J.A. Bierman